# Magic

## White & Black

# MAGIC, WHITE AND BLACK

### The Science of Finite and Infinite Life

#### CONTAINING

## PRACTICAL HINTS FOR STUDENTS OF OCCULTISM

BY

## FRANZ HARTMANN, M. D.

"For in our searchings are fulfilled all our desires, and we obtain the victory over all worlds."—*Khand, Upanishad.*

**EIGHTH AMERICAN EDITION REVISED**

Merchant Books
1911

# DESCRIPTION OF THE FRONTISPIECE.

At the foot of the picture is a sleeping *Sphinx*, whose upper part (representing the higher principles) is human ; while the lower parts (symbolizing the lower principles) are of an animal nature. She is dreaming of the solution of the great problem of the construction of the Universe and of the nature and destiny of Man, and her dream takes the shape of the figure above her, representing the Macrocosm and the Microcosm and their mutual interaction.

Above, around, and within all, without beginning and without an end, penetrating and pervading all, from the endless and unimaginable periphery to the invisible and incomprehensible centre, the " Father " of All, the supreme source of every power that ever manifested or may in the future manifest itself, and by whose activity the world was thrown into existence, being projected by the power of *His* own will and assuming form in *His* imagination.

The *Omega* (and the *Alpha* in the centre) represent the " *Son*," the Absolute having become manifest as the *Universal Logos* or *The Christ*, the cause of the beginning and the end of every created thing. It is *One* with the " *Father*," being manifested as a *Trinity in a Unity*, the cause of what we call *Space*, *Motion*, and *Substance*. The " regenerated " spiritual man, whose *matrix* is his own physical body, draws his nutriment from this universal spiritual principle as the physical foetus is nourished by means of the womb of the mother, his *soul* being formed from the *astral* influences or the *soul of the world*.

Out of the *Universal Logos* proceeds the " *invisible Light* " of the Spirit, the *Truth*, the *Law*, and the *Life*, embracing and penetrating the *Cosmos*, while the visible light of Nature is only its most material aspect or mode of manifestation, in the same sense as the visible sun is the reflex of its divine prototype, the invisible centre of power or the great *spiritual Sun*.

The circle with the twelve signs of the Zodiac, enclosing the space in which the planets belonging to our solar system are represented, symbolizes the Cosmos, filled with the planetary influences pervading the *Astral Light.* Here is the store-house of Life, the *Iliaster* of Paracelsus, in which the *Mysterium magnum* (the Spirit) is active.

The activity in the Cosmos is represented by the interlaced triangle. The two outer ones represent the great powers of creation, preservation, and destruction, or *Brahama, Vishnu,* and *Siva,* acting upon the elements of Fire, Water, and Earth—that is to say, upon the original principles out of which ethereal, fluid and solid material substances and forms are produced.

The two inner interlaced triangles refer more especially to the development of Man. *B, C,* and *D* represent *Knowledge,* the *Knower,* and the *Known,* which trinity constitutes *Mind* or *Consciousness.* E, F, and G represent the *Physical Man* (Stoola-Sharira), the Ethereal or *Inner Man* (Sukshma-Sharira), sidereal body of Paracelsus, astral body, Kama rupa, etc., and the *Spiritual Man* (Karana-Sharira, the divine Archæus, the spiritual Soul). The centre represents the divine *Atma,* the personal *Christ,* being identical with the *Universal Logos.* It is, like the latter, a Trinity in a Unity, receiving its light from the *Param-Atma* and radiating it again from the centre. It is the spiritual seed implanted in the soul of man, through whose growth immortal life is attained. Its light is the *Rose of the Cross* that is formed by *Wisdom* and *Power,* being joined together into one and sending its influence through the world. But below all is the realm of *Illusion,* of the most gross and heavy materialized thoughts, sinking into Darkness and Death (*the Eighth Sphere or Chaos*), where they decompose and putrefy, and are resolved again into the elements out of which the Universe came into existence.

It will be noticed that the three A's form a five-pointed star in the centre of the double interlaced triangle representing the six-pointed star. The five is continually seeking to expand and to come in perfect harmony with the six, while the latter is forever striving to enter the five and to become manifest therein. In other words, the dark and corporified centre seeks for eternal freedom and light; while the unlimited light seeks for corporification and form. One has a centripetal and the other a centrifugal action, and as neither can conquer the other, there results perpetual motion; the pulsation of the eternal heart of Divinity; the law of evolution and involution. If the five-pointed star were to become a six-pointed one—if the Rosicrucian Rose had six leaves instead of five—this turning of the wheel would have an end; there would be *Nirvana,*—eternal rest.

# PREFACE TO THE THIRD EDITION.

THE favor with which "Magic" has been received by those who are interested in the study of the hidden mysteries of Nature, made it expedient to publish a third edition of this book. From an insignificant pamphlet, written originally for the purpose of demonstrating to a few inexperienced inquirers, that the study of the occult side of nature was not identical with the vile practices of sorcery, "Magic" grew into a book of respectable dimensions, and now this new edition is to be still more enlarged, and I hope will also become still more useful.

The most serious objection which has been made against this book has been on account of its title; but the causes which induced me to select such a title were suggested by the purpose for which the book was intended; nor would I at present be able to find one more appropriate for it, for "Magic" means that divine art of exercise of spiritual power by which the awakened spirit in man may control the living elements.

But if we desire to master any forces whatever, either within or beyond our own sphere, it is above all necessary to know what these forces are, and we have no better means to study the qualities of any internal forces than by observing those which are active within ourselves, the perception of the processes. The art Magic is the exercise of spiritual power, which may be obtained by practising self-control, and this power cannot be acquired in any other way. The constitutions of all men are fundamentally the same, and in each human being are magical powers germinally or in a latent condition; but they cannot be said to exist before they become active and manifest themselves, first interiorly, and afterwards in an outward direction.

It was not my object, in composing this book, to write merely a *code of ethics*, and thereby to increase the already existing enormous mountain of unread moral precepts, but to assist the student of Occultism in studying the elements of which his own soul is composed, and to learn to know his own psychical organism.   I want to give an impulse to the study of a science, which may be called the "*anatomy and physiology of the soul,*" which investigates the elements of which the soul is composed, and the source from which man's desires and emotions spring.

To arrive at this end the merely intellectual reading of books on Occultism is entirely insufficient.   The divine mysteries of nature are above and beyond the power of conception of the semi-animal intellect.   They must be intuitively grasped by the power of the spirit, which enters into the substance of which the world is formed.   If we cannot perceive a spiritual truth with the eyes of the spirit, intellectual reasoning and book learning will not enable us to perceive it clearly.   Books, dealing with such subjects, should not be masters to us to whom we must blindly follow ; they should merely be our assistants.   They are merely useful to describe the details of things which we already—although perhaps indistinctly — see with our spiritual perception ; they are merely servants to hold up before our eyes magnifying mirrors, wherein we see the truths, whose presence we feel in our own soul.

*Jacob Boehme,* the great theosophist, says in regard to the study of Occultism : " If you desire to investigate the divine mysteries of nature, investigate first your own mind, and ask yourself about the purity of your purpose.   Do you desire to put the good teachings which you may receive into practice for the benefit of humanity?   Are you ready to renounce all selfish desires, which cloud your mind and hinder you to see the clear light of eternal truth ? Are you willing to become an instrument for the manifestation of Divine Wisdom ?   Do you know what it means to become united with your own higher Self, to get rid of your lower Self, to become one with the living universal power of Good, and to die to your own insignificant terrestrial personality ?   Or do you merely desire to obtain great knowledge, so that your curiosity may be gratified, and that you may be proud of your science, and believe yourself to be superior to the rest of mankind ?   Consider, that the depths of Divinity can only be searched by the divine spirit itself, which is active within you.   *Real knowledge* must come from our own interior, not merely from externals ; and they who seek for the essence of things merely in externals, may find the artificial color of a thing. but not the true thing itself."

Let therefore those who wish to acquire "Magic," *i.e.*, spiritual or divine power, follow this advice ; let them rise mentally into the highest regions of thought and remain therein as its permanent residents. Let them cultivate their physical bodies and their mental constitutions in such a manner that the matter of which they are composed will become less gross and more movable and penetrable to the divine light of the spirit. Then will the veils that separate them from the invisible world become thinner.

The following pages are an attempt to show the way how Man may become a co-operator of the Divine Power whose product is Nature ; they constitute a book which may properly bear the title of "Magic," for if the readers succeed in practically following its teachings, they will be able to perform the greatest of all magical feats, the spi-ritual regeneration of Man.

# PREFACE.

Our age is the age of opinions. The majority of our *educated* people live, so to say, in their heads, and the claims of the heart are neglected. Scepticism is king, and wisdom is only permitted to speak when it does not come into conflict with selfish considerations. The guardians of science attempt to bring the infinite truth within the grasp of their finite understanding, and whatever they fail to comprehend is supposed by them to have no existence. Our speculative philosophers refuse to recognize the incomprehensible power of universal love whose light is reflected in the human soul; they wish to examine eternal truths by the flickering candle-light of their minds' reasoning from the basis of sensual observations; they forget that Humanity is a *Unity*, and that one individual cannot encompass the All. They ask for scientific reasons why man should be faithful and true, and why he should not consider his own personal interests above those of the rest of mankind.

It is universally admitted that man's final destiny cannot depend on the theories which he may have formed in his mind regarding Cosmology, Pneumatology, plans of salvation, etc., and as long as he possesses no real knowledge, one set of beliefs or opinions may perhaps be as good as another; but it cannot be denied, that the sooner man frees himself of erroneous opinions and recognizes the real truth, the less will he be impeded by the obstacles which are in the way of his higher evolution, and the sooner will he reach the summit of his final perfection.

The most important questions seem, therefore, to be: " Is it possible that a man should actually know anything transcending his sensual perception, unless it is told to him by some supposed authority? Can the power of intuition be developed to such an extent as to become actual knowledge without any possibility of error, or shall we always be doomed to depend on hearsay and opinions? Can any individual man possess powers transcending those which are admitted to exist by modern science, and how can such transcendental powers be acquired?"

The following pages were written for the purpose of attempting to answer such questions, by calling the attention of those who desire to know the truth to a consideration of the true nature of Man and of his position in the Universe. Those who believe that they already know it of course will not need the instructions which these pages contain, but to those who desire to know they may be of some use, and to the latter we recommend the advice given by Gautama Buddha to his disciples: "Believe nothing which is unreasonable, and reject nothing as unreasonable without proper examination."

This book was not written for the purpose of convincing sceptics of the fact that phenomena of an occult character have taken place in the past and are occurring at present; though an attempt has been made to prove the possibility of mystic occurrences, by offering some explanation in regard to the laws by which they may be produced. No space has been devoted to lengthy illustrative examples of phenomena. Those who require them will find such evidence in the books whose titles have been given at the foot of the pages.

# PREFACE TO THE SIXTH EDITION.

IT is the usual fate of books that are written to suit the spirit of the times, that even if they create a sensation at their first appearance, the interest for them soon dies out; either because they are superseded by others, giving expression to more advanced thought, or because their contents were suited only to a limited circle of readers. This has not been the case with "*Magic, White and Black*," which was born in India in the year 1884, and the number of whose readers has increased year by year, so that now after sixteen years a new edition is again called for. Moreover, the book has been translated into different European languages, all of which goes to show that it is considered by many as a standard work on theosophy, metaphysics and occult science, and there is no doubt that it will hold its position as such; because the truths which it contains are eternal and will never grow old, and the form in which they are represented is generally regarded to be comprehensible and clear.

Magic is that knowledge of the spiritual powers hidden within the constitution of man, which enables him to employ them consciously and intelligently. If he employs them for the purpose of attaining perfection through the realization within himself of the highest ideal, common to all mankind, it is called "white magic"; and he may use these powers for beneficent purposes and in harmony with the universal law of love and justice; if he employs them for low or selfish purposes, or in opposition to divine law, he makes the high subservient to the low, he degrades the spirit, and with it himself. This misuse of divine powers is called "black magic," and it was not my object to teach this art, but to warn the readers against it.

Within the last twenty years the desire to know more about that which belongs to the higher or spiritual life of man has grown and spread all over the world; but the methods of investigation differ. Among the scientific circles of the West there is observable a general striving for materializing the spirit ; that is to say, to drag down spiritual truth to the lower material level and make it comprehensible to the semi-animal intellect, without taking the trouble to try to raise oneself spiritually to those heights, where alone the light of truth can be perceived in its own purity. This kind of research will never produce anything higher than opinions and theories, based upon external observations and inferences; because the speculative intellect cannot rise above itself and spiritual truth can be grasped only spiritually. This is what St. Paul teaches when he says (I. Corinth., II., 6): "We speak wisdom among them that are perfect; yet not the wisdom of this world, nor of the great ones of this world, that comes to naught, but we speak the wisdom of God in a mystery, even the hidden wisdom, which God ordained before the world to our glory.

The other way of investigation, which is the only true one and more generally followed in the East, is to spiritualize the body; to render ourselves more spiritual, so as to be able to receive, feel and grasp spiritual truth. The power to do this is within ourselves, as is taught not only by the sages of the East, but also by the Christian bible, for it is written : "Know ye not that ye are the temple of God and that the Spirit of God dwelleth in you?" (I. Corinth., III., 16.) In this Spirit of God in man rest all of man's divine and magical powers. To call the attention of the readers to the divine powers existing within themselves, thus to lead them to a knowledge of their own higher nature, to aid them in entering a higher life and finally to state what the greatest mystics of the East and West have taught in regard to the nature and the development of these powers, has been the aim of          *The Author.*

Florence (Italy), May 9, 1900.

# PREFACE TO THE SEVENTH EDITION.

THE constantly increasing demand for this well known work, during the past years, is the cause for the appearance of the present edition.

"Magic, White and Black" has done much to awaken interest in the mysterious powers latent in man. It has stimulated many to attempt the developing of the moral, mental, and spiritual sides of their nature.

The success of the book was assured from the beginning, not only from its elevating teachings, but from the easy and popular style in which these teachings were presented.

Previous editions have been circulated in all parts of the world. Each reader has acknowledged the helpfulness of the book and has created in others the desire to possess it.

THE PUBLISHERS.

# MAGIC.

---

## INTRODUCTION.

" There is no religion higher than the recognition of the truth."

WHATEVER misinterpretation ancient or modern ignorance may have given to the word *Magic*, its only true significance is *The Highest Science, or Wisdom based upon knowledge and practical experience.*

If you doubt whether there is any such thing as Magic, and if you desire any practical illustration about it, open your eyes and look around you. See the world, the animals, and the trees, and ask yourself whether they could have come into existence by any other power than by the *magic power of nature.* Magical power is not a supernatural power, if by the term " supernatural" you mean a power which is outside, beyond, or external to nature. To suppose the existence of such a power is an absurdity and a superstition, opposed to all our experience ; for we see that all organisms, vegetable and animal ones, grow by the action of internal forces acting outwardly, and not by having something added to their substance from the outside. A seed does not become a tree, nor a child a man, by having substance added to its organism by some outside workman, or like a house which is built by putting stones on the top of each other; but living things grow by the action of an internal force, acting from a centre within the form. To this centre flow the influences coming from the universal storehouse of matter and motion, and from there they radiate again towards the periphery, and perform that labor which builds up the living organism.

But what else can such a power be, except *spiritual power*, and *as such it is supernatural*, although acting in nature; for nature is neither Spirit nor God, but a product of the Divine Spirit, an image formed in the universal Mind by the power of the Divine Will. God is All; but All is not God, and the magical powers of Justice, Wisdom and Love, etc., are not products of nature, but attributes of the spirit. As such they are higher than nature, although not outside of it. It penetrates to the very centre of material things. It cannot be a mere mechanical force; for we know that a mechanical force ceases as soon as the impulse which originated it ceases to act. It cannot be a chemical force, for chemical action ceases when the chemical combination of the substances which were to combine has taken place. It must therefore be a living power, and as life cannot be a product of a dead form, it can be nothing else but the power of Life, acting within the life-centres of the forms.

This Life or *Will* in nature is a magician, and every plant, animal, and man is a magician, who uses this power unconsciously and instinctively to build up his own organism; or, in other words, every living being is an organism in which the magic power of life acts; and if a man should attain the knowledge how to control this power of life, and to employ it consciously, instead of merely submitting unconsciously to its influence, then he would be a magician, and could control the processes of life in his own organism.

Now the question is: Can any man obtain such a power as to control the processes of life? The answer to this question depends on what you mean by the term "man." If you mean by "*man*" an intellectual animal, such as we meet every day in the streets, then the answer is: No! for the majority of the men and women of our present generation, including our greatest scientific *lumens*, know absolutely nothing about that universal thing or no-thing, which produces what we call "Life," and which we may call the "Will;" because we know that no action ever takes place without an effort of what we call "Will," exercised with or without relative consciousness. Some of them have not even made up their minds whether or not they will believe in its existence. They can neither see it nor feel it, and therefore they do not know what to make of it.

But if you mean by "man" that intelligent principle,

which is active within the organism of man, and which constitutes him a human being, and by whose action he becomes a being very distinct from and above the animals in human or animal form, then the answer is: *Yes !* for the divine power which acts within the organism of animal man is the same and identical power which acts within the centre of nature. It is an internal power of man, and belongs to man, and if man once knows all the powers which belong to his essential constitution, and knows how to use them, then he may enter from the passive into the active state, and employ these powers himself.

Absurd as it may seem, it is nevertheless a logical consequence drawn from the fundamental truths about the constitution of man, that if a man could control the universal power of life acting within himself, he might prolong the life of his organism as long as it pleased to him; if he could control it, and knew all the laws of matter, he might render it dense or vaporous, concentrate it to a small point, or expand it, so as to occupy a great deal of space. Verily, truth is stranger than fiction, and we might see it, if we could only rise above the narrow conceptions and prejudices which we have inherited and acquired by education and sensual observation.

The most strange things happen continually in nature, and hardly attract our attention. They do not seem strange to us, although we do not understand them; merely because we are accustomed to see them every day. Who would be so "foolish" as to believe that a tree could grow out of a seed—as there is evidently no tree in the seed—if his experience had not told him that trees grow out of seeds in spite of all arguments to the contrary? Who would believe that a flower would grow out of a plant, if he had not seen it, for observation and reason show that there is no flower in the stalk? Nevertheless, flowers grow, and cannot be disputed away.

Everywhere in nature the action of an universal law is manifest, but we cannot see the law itself. Everywhere we see the manifestations of a will; but those who seek for the origin of Will within their own brains will seek for it in vain.

The art of magic is the art of employing invisible or so-called spiritual agencies to obtain certain visible results. Such agencies are not flitting about in space, ready to come at the command of anyone who has learned certain incantations and ceremonies; but they consist principally in the unseen but nevertheless powerful influences of the Emotions and the Will, of desires and passions, thought and imagination, love and hate, fear and hope, faith and doubt, etc., etc. They are the powers of what is called the soul; they are employed everywhere and by everybody every day, consciously or unconsciously, willingly or unwillingly, and while those that cannot control or resist such influences, but are controlled by them, are passive instruments, "*Mediums*" through which such unseen powers act, and often their unwilling slaves; those who are able to guide and control such influences by gaining control over themselves, are, in proportion to their controlling capacity, active, and powerful, and true Magicians. We see, therefore, that with the exception of irresponsible persons, every one who has any will power is, in so far as he exercises that power, an active Magician; a *white* magician if he employs them for good, a *black* magician if he uses them for the purposes of evil.

We all cannot honestly say "*we have life;*" for life does not belong to us, and we cannot control or monopolize it. All we can say without arrogance and presumption is that we are instruments through which an universal principle that produces what we call "*Life*" manifests itself in the form of a human being. We are all *Mediums*, through which an universal *Will* which causes Life acts. He who thinks that he has any power whatever of his own, thinks foolish; for all the powers he has are lent him by nature, or—more correctly speaking—by that eternal spiritual power, which acts in and from the centre of nature, and which men have called "God," because they have found it to be the source of all good.

No one will deny that Man, besides having physical powers, is also temporally endowed with mental and spiritual energies. We love, respect or obey a person, not on account of his superior bodily strength, but on account of his intellectual and moral worth, or while we are under the spell of some real or imaginary authority that we may believe him to possess. A king or a bishop has, as a person, not necessarily any more power than his lackey or butler, and must make himself known before he will be obeyed; a captain may be the weakest man in his company and still his soldiers obey him. We love beauty, harmony, and sublimity, not on account of their usefulness for material purposes, but because they satisfy an inner sense, which does not belong to the physical plane.

What would be a world without the magic power of love of beauty and harmony? How would a world look if made after a pattern furnished by the modern " rationalistic philosopher "? A world in which beauty and the power of good were not recognized could be nothing else but a world of maniacs. In such a world art and poetry could not exist, justice would become a convenience, honesty be equivalent with imbecility, to be truthful would be to be foolish, and Self-interest the only god worthy of any consideration.

Magic is that science which deals with the mental powers of man, and shows what control he may exercise over himself and others. In order to study the powers of man it is necessary to investigate what Man is, and what relation he bears to the universe, and such an investigation, if properly conducted, will show that the elements which compose the essential man are identical with those we find in the universe ; that is to say, that the universe is the *Macrocosm,* and man—its true copy—the *Microcosm.*

Microcosmic man and the Macrocosm of nature are one. How could it be possible that the Macrocosm should contain anything not contained within the Microcosm, or that Man should have something within his organism which cannot be found within the grand organism of nature? Is not man the child of nature, and can there be anything within his constitution which does not come from his eternal father and mother? If man's organization contained something unnatural, he would be a monster, and nature would spew him out. Everything contained in nature can be found within the organism of man, and exists therein either in a germinal or developed state ; either latent or active, and may be perceived by him who possesses the power of self-knowledge.

We are born into a world in which we find ourselves surrounded by physical objects. There seems to be still another—a subjective—world within us, capable of receiving and retaining impressions from the outside world. Each one is a world of its own, with a relation to space different from that of the other. Each has its days of sun-

shine and its nights of darkness, which are not regulated
by the days and nights of the other ; each has its clouds
and its storms, and shapes and forms of its own.

If we ask of science to teach us the true nature of these
worlds and the laws that govern them—but physical science
deals only with external forms—she gives only a partial
solution of the problems of the objective world, and leaves
us in regard to the subjective world entirely in the dark.
Modern science classifies phenomena and describes events,
but to describe how an event takes place is not sufficient
to explain why it takes place. To discover causes, which
are in themselves the effects of unknown primal causes,
is only to evade one difficulty by substituting another.
Science describes some of the attributes of things, but the
first causes which brought these attributes into existence
are unknown to her, and will remain so, until her powers
of perception will penetrate in the unseen.

Besides scientific observation there claims to be still
another way to obtain knowledge of the mysterious side of
nature. The religious teachers of the world claim to have
sounded the depths which the scientists cannot reach.
Their doctrines are supposed by many to have been
received through certain divine or angelic revelations, proceeding from a supreme, infinite, omnipresent, and yet
personal—and therefore limited—*Being*—the existence of
which has never been proved. Where is the proof that
such revelations are either true or divine ? Surely, a
blind belief in the contents of a book cannot be real knowledge; nor can it be reasonably supposed that the theologians themselves have any actual knowledge of what
they teach. We dare say that there are but few clergymen
who are personally acquainted with God. Nevertheless
thousands are engaged in teaching others that which they
themselves do not know, and in spite of a very great
number of religious systems there is comparatively little
religion at present upon the Earth.

The term *Religion* is derived from the Latin word *re-
ligere*, which may be properly translated " to bind back,"
or to " relate." Religion, in the true sense of the term,
implies that science which examines the link which exists
between man and the cause from which he originated, or
in other words, which deals with the relation which exists
between man and the world of causes. True religion is

therefore a science far higher than a science based upon mere sensual perception, but it cannot be in conflict with what is true in science. Only what is false in science must necessarily be in conflict with what is true in religion, and what is false in religion is in conflict with what is true in science. True religion and true science are ultimately one and the same thing; a religion that clings to illusions, and an illusory science, are equally false, and the greater the obstinacy with which they cling to their illusions the more pernicious is their effect.

There should a distinction be made between "*religion*" and "*religionism*;" between "*science*" and "*scientism*;" between "*mystic*" and "*mysticism.*"

The *highest* aspect of *Religion* is practically the union of man with the Supreme First Cause, from which his essence emanated in the beginning.

Its *second* aspect teaches tne relations existing between that Great First Cause and Man; in other words, the relations existing between the Macrocosm and Microcosm.

In its *lowest* aspect religionism consists of the adulation of dead forms, of the worshipping of fetiches, of fruitless attempts to wheedle oneself into the favor of some imaginary deity, to persuade "God" to change his mind, and to try to obtain some favors which are not in accordance with justice.

*Science* in her *highest* aspect is the self-knowledge of the fundamental laws of Nature, and is therefore a spiiitual science, based upon the knowledge of the spirit within our own selves.

In her *lower* aspect it is a knowledge of external phenomena, and the secondary or superficial causes which produce the latter, and which our scientism mistakes for the final cause.

In its *lowest* aspect scientism is a system of observation and classification of external phenomena, of the causes of which we know nothing.

Religionism and Scientism are continually subject to changes. They have been created by illusions, and die when the illusions are over. True Science and true Religion are one, and if joined to Practice, they form the three-lateral pyramid, whose foundations are upon the earth, and whose point reaches to heaven.

*Mystic* in its true meaning is spiritual knowledge;

that is to say, the knowledge of spiritual and "super-sensual" things, perceived by the spiritual powers of perception. These powers are germinally contained in every human organization, but only few have developed them sufficiently to be of any practical use.

*Mysticism* is a hankering after illusions, a desire to pry into mysteries which we cannot comprehend, a craving to satisfy our curiosity in regard to what we ought not to know, as long as we have not the power to understand it. It is the realm of fancies, of dreams, the paradise of ghost-seers, and of spiritistic tomfooleries of all kinds.

But which is the true religion and the true science? There is no doubt that a definite relationship exists between Man and the cause that called humanity into existence, and a true religion and a true science must be the one which teaches the true terms of that relation. If we take a superficial view of the various religious systems of the world, we find them all apparently contradicting each other. We find a great mass of apparent superstitions and absurdities heaped upon a grain of something that may be true. We admire the ethics and moral doctrines of our favorite religious system, and we take its theological rubbish in our bargain, forgetting that the ethics of nearly all religions are essentially the same, and that the rubbish which surrounds them is not real religion. It is evidently an absurdity to believe that any system could be true, unless it contained the truth. But it is equally evident that a thing cannot be true and false at the same time. The truth can only be *one.* The truth never changes ; but we ourselves change, and as we change so changes our aspect of the truth. The various religious systems of the world cannot be unnatural or supernatural products. They are all the natural outgrowth of man's evolution upon this globe, and they differ only in so far as the conditions under which they came into existence differed at the time when they began to exist ; but true religion is supernatural ; for it is that clinging of the soul of man to that which is higher than his semi-animal and impermanent nature. Each intellectual human being, except one blinded by prejudice, recognizes the fact that each of the great religious systems of the world contains certain truths, which we intuitively know to be true ; and as there can be only one fundamental truth, so all these religions are branches of the same tree, even if the forms in which the truth manifests itself are not alike. The sunshine is everywhere the same, only its intensity differs in different localities. In one place it induces the growth of palms, in another of mushrooms; but there is only one Sun in our system. The processes going on on the physical plane have their analogies in the spiritual realm, for there is only one Nature, one Law.

If one person quarrels with another about religion, he cannot have the true religion, nor can he have any true knowledge. The only true religion is the religion of Love, and love does not quarrel. Love is an element of Wisdom, and there can be no wisdom without love. Each species of birds in the woods sings a different tune; but the principle which causes them to sing is the same in each. They do not quarrel with each other, because one can sing better than the rest. Moreover, religious disputations, with their resulting animosities, are the most useless things in the world; for no one can combat the darkness by fighting it with a stick; the only way to remove darkness is to kindle a light, the only way to dispel spiritual ignorance is to let the light of knowledge that comes from the centre of love shine into the heart.

All religions are based upon internal truth, all have an outside ornamentation which varies in character in the different systems, but all have the same foundation of truth, and if we compare the various systems with one another, looking below the surface of exterior forms, we find that this truth is in all religious systems one and the same. In all this truth has been hidden beneath a more or less allegorical language, impersonal and invisible powers have been personified and represented in images carved in stones or wood, and the formless and real has been pictured in illusive forms. These forms in letters, and pictures, and images are the means by which truths may be brought to the attention of the unripe Mind. They are to the grown-up children of all nations what picture-books are to small children who are not yet able to read, and it would be as unreasonable to deprive grown-up children of their images before they are able to read in their own hearts, as it would be to take away the picture-books from little children and to ask them to read printed books, which they cannot yet understand.

Very stupid indeed and insignificant would be the stories

contained in the *Bible*, and in other religious books, if the
personal events described therein were referring merely to
certain occurrences having happened in the lives of certain
individuals who lived some thousands of years ago, and
whose biography can seriously interest no one to-day.
What do we care now about the family affairs of a man
called Adam or Abraham? Why should we want to be
interested in knowing how many legitimate or illegitimate
children the Patriarchs had, and what became of them?
What is it to us whether or not a man by the name of
Jonah was thrown into the water and swallowed by a
whale? What happens to-day in the various countries of
Europe is more interesting and important for us to know
than what happened at the court of Zerubabel or Nabu-
chodonoser.

But fortunately for the Bible and—if we only knew
how to read it—fortunately for us, the stories contained
therein are by no means merely histories of persons who
lived in ancient times, but they are allegories and myths
having very often a very deep meaning, of which our ex-
pounders of the Bible, as well as its critics, usually know
very little. Fictions are necessary to represent truths ;
but they should not be mistaken for the truth itself. The
truth is eternal, and cannot be grasped by that which is
neither eternal nor true. We need fictions to bring it
within our grasp as long as we have ourselves merely a
fictitious existence.

The men and the women of the old and new " testament" are much more than mere persons supposed to
have existed at that time. They are personifications of
eternally active spiritual forces, of which physical science
does not even know that they exist ; and their histories
give an account of their action, their interrelations within
the Macrocosm and its counterpart the Microcosm ; they
teach the history of the evolution of mankind in its
spiritual aspect.

If our natural philosophers would study the Bible in its
esoteric and spiritual aspects, they might learn a great
many things which they desire to know. They might
learn to find out what are the true powers of the " living
faith," and which are required to produce occult phenomena at will; they might find instruction how to trans-
mute lead or iron into pure gold, and to transform
animals into gods.

But it is a truth, based upon natural laws, that man can see nothing except that which exists in his mind. If his mind is filled with illusions, he will see nothing but illusions, and the deepest of symbols will be pictures without meaning to him.

If our children—the big ones as well as the little ones—are only looking at the pictures without learning the text, they are apt to grow to believe the pictorial representations to be the very things they are intended to represent; they become accustomed to forget that forms are only illusions, and that formless realities cannot be seen. It is so much easier to believe than to think. Children should not linger over their picture-books so long as to neglect their higher education. Humanity has outgrown the infancy of its present cycle, and asks for more intellectual food; the age of superstition is passing away, and the demand is not for opinions but for knowledge, and knowledge cannot be obtained without an effort. The expressed opinion of one person can only give rise to knowledge in another, if corroborated by the same or a similar experience of the latter. A person can only truly believe that which he knows, and he can only actually know that which he has perceived.

There is a difference between perceiving and understanding the truth. We may perceive the truth with our heart, and we understand it with our brain. In other words: We may feel the truth intuitively, and examine it intellectually. If our present generation would cultivate the faculty of feeling the truth with their hearts, and afterwards examine that which they feel by means of their intellect, we would soon have a far better and happier state of society everywhere. But the great curse of our age is that the intellectual faculties are strained to their utmost power of resistance, to examine the external form of things intellectually without perceiving their spiritual character by the power of intuition.

Men, instead of living in the sanctuary of the temples which they inhabit, are continually absent from there, and reside in the garret under the roof, looking out through the windows of the garret after the illusions of life. Day and night they stand there and watch, careful that none of the passing illusions may escape their observation, and while their attention is absorbed by these idle shows, the

thieves enter the house and the sanctuary without being
seen, and steal away the treasures.   Then at the time
when the house is destroyed, and death appears, the soul
returns to the heart and finds it empty and desolate, and
all the illusions that occupied the brain during life fly away,
and man is left poor indeed, because he has not perceived
the truth in his heart.

The real object of a religious system should therefore be
to teach a way by which a person may develop the power
to perceive the truth.   To ask a man to believe in the
opinion expressed by another, and to remain satisfied with
such a belief, is to ask him to remain ignorant, and to
trust to another person more than to himself.   A person
without knowledge can have no conviction—no faith, and
his adoption of one particular system depends on the circumstances under which he is born, or brought up, or surrounded.   He is most liable to adopt that system which
his parents or neighbors have inherited or adopted, and if
he changes from one system to another, he, generally
speaking, does so from mere sentimentality, or on account
of some selfish consideration, expecting to obtain some
benefit to himself by that change.   From a spiritual standpoint he will gain nothing under such circumstances ;
because, to approach the truth, he must love the truth for
its own sake, and not on account of the personal advantage
that it may bring ; from an intellectual standpoint he will
gain little or nothing by exchanging one superstition for
another.   The only way by which Man can hope to arrive
at the truth is to love the truth on account of its being the
truth, and to free his mind from all prejudices and predilections, so that its light may penetrate into the mind.

What is the religionism of to-day, but a religion of fear ?
Men do not wish to avoid vice, but they wish to avoid the
punishment for having indulged in vice.   Their experience
teaches them that the laws of nature are unchangeable, but
nevertheless they continue to act against the universal
law.   They claim to believe in a God who is unchangeable,
and yet they implore His assistance if they desire to break
His own law.   When will they rise up to the true conception that the only possible God is that universal power
which acts through the law, which is itself the Law, and
cannot be changed?   To break the law is identical with
breaking the God within ourselves, and the only way to

obtain forgiveness after He is broken is to restore the law, and to create a new God within ourselves.

It may be well to study the opinions of others, and to store them up in the book of our memory, but we should not accept them on any merely external evidence, nor reject them without investigation, but weigh them in the scales of reason and justice. Even the teachings of the world's greatest Adepts, unimpeachable as they may be, can only instruct us, but give us no real knowledge. They can show the way, but we must take ourselves the steps on the ladder. Were we to recognise their *dictum* as the final aim, to be accepted without any further investigation, we should again fall back into a system of belief for the sake of authority. Knowledge gives strength, doubt paralyzes the will. A man who does not believe that he is able to walk will not be able to walk as long as he does not believe; a man who *knows* by experience that he can command himself will be able to do so. He who can command himself can command that which is below him, because the low is controlled by the high, and there is nothing higher than Man having obtained a perfect knowledge of Self.

The knowledge of Self is identical with Self-knowledge, because the true self of Man is God; it is unlimited, and knowing its own self it knows everything by its own power. It is knowledge independent of any opinions, dogmas or doctrines, no matter from what authority they may proceed. If we study the teachings of any supposed authority external to our own selves, we at best know what the opinion of such an authority is in regard to the truth, but we do not necessarily arrive thereby at a self-knowledge of the truth. If we, for instance, learn what Christ taught about God, we are only informed of what he knew or believed to know, but we cannot know God for all that, unless we awaken to a realization of his presence within our own heart. The knowledge of even the wisest of all men, if communicated to us, will be to us nothing more than an opinion, as long as it is not experienced within our own selves. As long as we cannot penetrate within the soul of Man, we can know little more about him but his corporeal form; but how could we penetrate within the soul of another as long as we have not the capacity to enter our own? Therefore the beginning of all real knowledge is the knowledge of Self.

Does "rationalistic" speculation confer any true knowledge of Man? The range of her power of observation is limited by the perceptive power of her physical senses, assisted by physical instruments; she has no means to investigate that which transcends physical sense, she cannot enter the temple of the unseen, she only knows the external form in which the reality dwells. She only knows the illusive form of man, she knows nothing whatever of the essential and real man. In vain shall we look to her for the solution of the problem, which thousands of years ago the Egyptian Sphinx propounded.

Do the popular religious systems confer any true knowledge of Man? The conception which the average theologian has of the mysterious being called man is as little as that of the professor of modern science. He looks upon man as a personal being, isolated from other personal beings around whose infinite little personality centres the interests of the infinitely great. He forgets that the founders upon the principal religious systems taught that the original and essential man (Adam) was an impersonal power, that the real man (the Christ) is a whole and cannot be divided, and that the personal man is only the temporary temple in which the universal spirit resides.*

The misconceptions arising from ignorance of the true nature of Man are the cause that the popular religious opinions held by the average theologians in Christian and Pagan countries are based upon selfishness, contrary to the spirit of that which true religion teaches. Christians and "Heathens" clamor for some personal benefit to be conferred by some imaginary person upon their insignificant personal self, either here or in the problematical hereafter. Each one of such short-sighted persons wants to be saved *himself* above all, the salvation of the rest is a matter of second consideration. They expect to obtain some benefit which they do not deserve, to wheedle themselves into the favor of some personal deity, to cheat the "devil" of his just dues, and to smuggle their imperfections into the kingdom of Heaven.

The only reasonable object which any external religious system can possibly have, is to elevate man from a lower

---

* Bible: Corinth. iii. 16.

state to a higher one, in which he can form a better conception of his true dignity as a member of the human
family. If there is any possibility of imparting to a man a
knowledge of self, the churches are the places where such
a knowledge should be imparted; but to accomplish this
the claims of the spirit should predominate over those of
the form, the interests of religion and the interests of the
"Church" would have to cease to be amalgamated, and
the Church should again be founded upon the rock of the
living faith instead of the craving to obtain some selfish
personal benefit in this world or in the hereafter.

He who is led by selfish considerations cannot enter a
heaven where personal considerations do not exist. He
who does not care for Heaven but is contented where he
is, is already in Heaven, while the discontented will in
vain clamor for it. To be without personal desires is to
be free and happy, and "Heaven" can mean nothing else
but a state in which freedom and happiness exist. The
man who performs beneficial acts induced by a hope of
reward is not happy unless the reward is obtained.

A man who performs a good act with the hope of reward
is not free. He is the servant of Self, and works for the
benefit of Self and not for absolute Good. It is, therefore,
not the power of Good which will reward him, he can only
expect that reward from his own personal Self.

The man who performs evil acts, induced by a selfish
motive, is not free. He who desires evil and is restrained
by fear is not his own master. He who recognizes the
supreme power of the universe in his own heart has become
free. He whose will is swayed by his lower personal self
is the slave of his person, but he who has conquered that
lower self enters the higher life.

The science of Life consists in subduing the low and
elevating the high. Its first lesson is how to free oneself
from the love of self, the first angel of evil.

This "Self" is composed of a great many selves or *I*'s,
of which each one has his peculiar claims, and whose
demands grow in proportion as we attempt to satisfy them.
They are the semi-intellectual forces of the soul that would
rend the soul to pieces if they were allowed to grow, and
which must be subdued by the power of the real Master,
the superior "I"—the Spirit.

These "*I*'s" are the *Elementals*, of which has been said

2

so much in occult literature. They are not imaginary
things, but living forces, and they may be perceived by him
who has acquired the power to look within his own soul.
Each of these forces corresponds to some desire, and if it
is permitted to grow is symbolized by the form of the animal which corresponds to its nature. At first they are
thin and shadowy, but as the desire which corresponds to
them is indulged in, they become more and more dense,
and gain great strength as our desires grow into a passion.
The lesser Elementals are swallowed by the bigger ones,
the little desires are absorbed by the stronger ones,
until perhaps at last one Master Passion, one powerful
Elemental remains. They are described as having the
form of snakes and tigers, hogs, insatiable wolves, etc., but
as they are often the result of a mixture of human and
animal elements, they do not merely exhibit purely animal
forms ; but frequently they look like animals with human
heads, or like men with animal members ; they appear
under endless varieties of shapes, because there is an endless variety of correlations and mixtures of lust, avarice,
greed, sensual love, ambition, cowardice, fear, terror, hate,
pride, vanity, self-conceit, stupidity, voluptuousness, selfishness, jealousy, envy, arrogance, hypocrisy, cunning,
sophistry, imbecility, superstition, etc., etc.

They constitute the false " I's " or " Egos " in man ; for
even if man in his self-conceit may imagine that he knows
his true self, and that this self is only one, a deeper thought
will convince him that he is not self-existent, but an ever,
changing product of nature. He will then see that, as long
as God has not awakened in his soul, he is not truly self-
conscious ; but that it is Nature, having become self-conscious in his organism ; creating therein these various
states of self-consciousness, each of which he mistakes for
his own true self.

These Elementals live in the soul-realm of man as long
as he lives, and grow strong and fat, for they live on his
life-principle, and are fed by the substance of his thoughts.
They may even become objective to him, if during a
paroxysm of fear or in consequence of some disease they
are enabled to step out of their sphere. They cannot be
killed by pious ceremonies, nor be driven away by the exhortations of a clergyman ; they are only destroyed by the
power of the *spiritual* Will of man, which annihilates

them as the light annihilates darkness, or as a stroke of lightning rends the clouds.

Only those who have awakened to spiritual consciousness can have that spiritual will, of which the non-regenerated know nothing. But those who are not yet so far advanced may cause those elementals to die slowly, by withdrawing from them the food which they require, that is to say, by avoiding all desires and thoughts which correspond to their character. They will then begin to wane, to get sick, die and putrefy like a member of the body which has become mortified. *A line of demarkation* will be formed in the soul-body of man, there may be " inflammation " and suffering. A process, similar to that which takes place if a gangrenous part of the physical body is thrown off, takes place; and at last the putrid carcass of the Elemental drops off and dissolves.

These descriptions are neither fancies nor allegories. *Theophrastus Paracelsus, Jacob Boehme*, and many other writers on Occultism write about them, and a due appreciation of their doctrines will go far to explain many occurrences mentioned in the history of witchcraft, and in the legends of the lives of the saints.

But there are not merely animal germs within the realm of the soul of man. In each human constitution there are also the germs which go to make up a Shakespeare, a Washington, Goethe, Voltaire, a Buddha, or Christ. There are likewise the germs which may grow to make a Nero, Messalina or Torquemada; and each germ may develop and take a form, and ultimately find its expression and reflection in the outward form, as much as the density of the material atoms, which are slow to transform, will permit; for each character corresponds to a form, and each form to a character.

Man's microcosm is a garden in which all kinds of living plants grow. Some are poisonous, some are wholesome plants. It rests with man to decide which germs he wants to develop into a living tree, and that tree will be himself. There are within him the germs of matter and soul and of spiritual activity; in him are the seeds from which spring intellectual and emotional functions, and the deepest of all is the hidden will at the centre; the spirit, which is to become the immortal man; the true Self.

To accomplish this task it is not necessary to become a

misanthrope and retire into a jungle to feed on the pro ducts of one's own morbid imagination; the struggle caused by the petty annoyances of everyday life is the best school to exercise the will power for those that have not yet gained the mastery over Self. "To renounce the vanities of the world" does not mean to look with contempt upon the progress of the world, to remain ignorant of mathematics and logic, to take no interest in the welfare of humanity, to avoid the duties of life or neglect one's family. Such a proceeding would accomplish the very reverse of what is intended; it would increase the love of self, it would concentrate the soul to a small focus instead of expanding it over the world. "To renounce one's self" means to conquer the sense of personality and to free one's self of the love of things which that personality desires. It means "to live in the world, but not cling to the world," to substitute universal love for personal love, and to consider the interests of the whole of superior importance than personal claims. The renunciation of self is necessarily followed by spiritual growth. As we forget our personal self, we attach less importance to personalities, personal things, and personal feelings. We begin to look upon ourselves not as being permanent, unchanging and unchangeable entities, standing isolated among other isolated entities, and being separated from them by impenetrable shells, but as parts of an infinite power, which embraces the universe, and whose powers are concentrated and brought to a focus in the bodies which we temporarily inhabit, into which bodies continually flow and from which are incessantly radiating the rays of an infinite sphere of light, whose circumference is endless and whose centre is everywhere.

Upon the recognition and realization of this truth rests the only true religion, the *Religion of the Universal Love of all Beings.* As long as man takes only his own little self into consideration in his thoughts and acts, the sphere of his mind becomes necessarily narrow. All our popular religious sects are based upon selfish considerations. Each of our religious sectarians speculates to obtain some spiritual, if not material, benefit for *himself.* Each one wants to be saved by somebody; first he, and then perhaps the others; but, above all, he himself. The true religion of universal Love knows of no "self."

Even the desire to go to heaven or enter the state of *Nirvana*, is, after all, but a selfish desire, and as long as man has any selfish desires whatever, his mind perceives only his own self. Only when he ceases to have a limited illusive " self " will his real self become unlimited and be omnipresent. He who desires unlimited knowledge must rise above limitation.

Looked at from that height, the personality appears exceedingly small and insignificant, and of little importance. Man appears as the centralization of an idea, persons and peoples like living grains of sand on the shore of an infinite ocean. Fortune, fame, love, luxury, etc., assume in his conception the importance of soap-bubbles, and he has no hesitation in relinquishing them as the idle playthings of children. Neither can such a renunciation be called a sacrifice, for grown-up boys and girls do not " sacrifice " their popguns and dolls, they simply do not want them any longer. In proportion as their minds expand, do they reach out for something more useful, and as a man's spirit expands, his surroundings, and even the planet on which he lives, appear to him small as a landscape seen from a great distance, or from a high mountain, while at the same time his conception of the infinite grows larger and assumes a gigantic form. This expansion of our existence " robs us of a country and a home " * by making us citizens of the grand universe; it separates us from our mortal parents and friends to unite us with them for ever as our immortal brothers and sisters; it lifts us up from the narrow confines of the illusory form to the unlimited realm of the Ideal, and releasing man from the prison-house of insignificant clay, it leads him to the sublime splendor of Eternal and Universal Life.

Every form of life, the human form not excepted, is nothing more than a focus in which the energies of the universal principle of life are concentrated, and the more they are concentrated and cling to that centre, the less are they able to manifest their activity, to grow and expand. Self-satisfied man, who employs his capacities only for his own selfish purpose, contracts them into himself, and as he contracts he becomes more and more insignificant, and as he loses sight of the whole, the whole loses sight of him.

---

* Bulwer-Lytton: " Zanoni."

If, on the other hand, a person who is not in possession of sufficient energy attempts to send his forces into the region of the unknown, scattering them through space, without having strengthened them by the development of the intellect, they will wander like shadows through the realm of the infinite and become lost. Harmonious growth requires expansion along with a corresponding accumulation of energy.

Some persons are possessed of great intellectual power, but of little spirituality; some have spiritual power, but a weak intellect; those in which the spiritual energies are well supported by a strong intellect are the elect. To become practical, we must first learn to understand the thing we want to practise, by observation and receiving instruction. Understanding is a result of assimilation and growth, not a result of cramming. It is an awakening to a state of consciousness of the nature of the thing that comes within the range of our cognition. A person coming to a strange country in the evening will, when after a night's rest he wakes in the morning, hardly realize where he is. He has, perhaps, been dreaming of his home and those that are left there, and only after he opens his eyes and awakens to a full sense of consciousness of his new and strange surroundings, will the old impressions fade away, and he will begin to realize where he is. In the same manner old errors must disappear before new truths can be realized. Man only begins to exist as a spiritual being when his spirit comes to life.

To become perfect, physical health, intellectual growth, and spiritual perception and activity should go hand in hand. Intuition should be supported by an unselfish intellect, a pure mind by a healthy form. How to accomplish this can neither be taught by a science which deals only with illusory effects, nor by a religious belief based upon illusions; but it is taught by the *Wisdom Religion,* the knowledge of self, whose foundation is truth, and whose practical application is the highest object of human existence.

This Wisdom Religion has been, and is even to-day, the inheritance of the saints, prophets, and seers and of every one who is wise, no matter to what external system of religion they may have given their adherence. It was known to the ancient Brahmins, Egyptians, and Jews, Gautama

Buddha advised his people to strive for it. It formed the basis of the Eleusinian and Bachic mysteries of the Greeks, and the true religion of Christ is resting upon it. It is the true religion of Humanity, that has nothing to do with confessions and forms. Now, as in times of old, its truths are misunderstood and misrepresented by men who profess to be teachers of men. The *Pharisees* and *Sadducees* of the New Testament were the prototypes of modern churchmen and scientists existing to-day. Now, as then, the truth is daily crucified between superstition and selfishness and laid in the tomb of ignorance, from whence it will rise again. Now, as then, the spirit has fled from the form, being driven away by those that worship the form and hate the spirit. Wisdom will for ever remain a *secret science* to the idolators adoring the form, even if it were proclaimed from the housetops and preached at a market-place. The dealer in pounds and pennies, absorbed by his material interests, may be surrounded by the greatest beauties of nature and not comprehend them, the intellectual reasoner will ask for a sign and not see the signs by which he is continually surrounded. The tomb from which the Saviour will arise is the heart of men and women ; if the good in them awakens to self-consciousness, then will it appear to them as a sun, shedding its light upon a better and happier generation.

The existence of the magic power of good will probably be denied by few ; but if the existence of good, or *White Magic*, is admitted, that of evil, or *Black Magic*, is not any more improbable.

It is not *man* who exercises good or evil magic powers, but it is the God in him who works good or evil through the organism of man. God is good or evil according to the conditions under which he acts; for if God did not include evil as well as good, he would not be universal. God performs good or evil deeds according to the mode in which he must act ; in the same way as the sun is good in spring-time when he melts the snow and assists the grass and flowers to crawl out of the dark earth, and evil, if he parches the skin of the wanderer in tropical Africa and kills persons by sun-stroke. God causes the healthy growth of a limb and the unhealthy growth of a cancer by the magic power of his unconscious will, which acts according to law and not according to whims. Only when the Divinity in Man has awakened to consciousness and knowledge, will man be able to control his own magic (spiritual) power and employ it for Good or for Evil.

A person having created (or called into consciousness) in himself an impersonal power may employ it for good or for evil, but if he employs it for his own personal gain, he loses that power, because in such a case the sense of his personality becomes more permanent and his personal Self has no power. Every day we may read of persons who have used high intellectual powers for vile purposes. We see persons making use of the vanity, greediness, selfishness, or ambition of others to render them subservient to their own purpose. We see them commit murder and instigate wars for the benefit of their own purposes or to attain some object of their ambition. But such events belong more or less to the struggle for existence. They do not necessarily belong to the sphere of black magic, because they are usually not caused by a love for evil, but by a desire of a personal benefit of some kind. The real black magicians are those that are doing evil for the sake of doing evil, who injure others without expecting or receiving any benefit for themselves. To that class belong the backbiter and the slanderer, the traducer and seducer, those who create enmity in the bosom of families, who oppose progress and encourage ignorance, and they have been rightly called the *Powers of Darkness*, while those who do good for the sole purpose of doing good are the *Children of Light.*

The struggle between Light and Darkness is as old as the world; there can be no light become manifest without darkness, and no evil without good. Good and evil are the light and shadow of the one eternal principle of life, and each is necessary if the other is to become manifest. Absolute good must exist, but we cannot know it without knowing the presence of evil. Absolute evil cannot exist, because it is held together by a spark of good. A soul in which there were no good whatever would rage against itself, the forces constituting such a soul would combat each other and rend it to pieces. Man's Redeemer is his power for good. This power attracts him to that which is good, and at the end, when the supreme source of all power, from which life emanated in the beginning, withdraws that activity into itself, the powers of darkness will suffer, but the Children of Light will be united with the source of all Good.

# CHAPTER I.

## THE IDEAL.

"God is a Spirit, and they that worship him must worship him in spirit and in truth."—John iv. 24.

THE highest desire any reasonable man can cherish, and the highest right he may possibly claim, is to become perfect. To know everything, to love all and be known and beloved by all, to possess and command everything that exists, such is a condition of being that, to a certain extent, may be felt intuitively, but whose possibility cannot be grasped by the intellect of mortal man. A foretaste of such a blissful condition may be experienced by a person who—even for a short period of time—is perfectly happy. He who is not oppressed by sorrow, not excited by selfish desires, and who is conscious of his own strength and liberty, feels as if he were the master of worlds and the king of creation; and, in fact, during such moments he is their ruler, as far as he himself is concerned, although his subjects may not seem to be aware of his existence.

But when he awakes from his dream and looks through the windows of his senses into the exterior world, and begins to reason about his surroundings, his vision fades away; he beholds himself a child of the Earth, a mortal form, bound with many chains to a speck of dust in the Universe, on a ball of matter called a planet that floats in the infinity of space. The ideal world, that perhaps a moment before appeared to him as a glorious reality, may now seem to him the baseless fabric of a dream, in which there is nothing real, and physical existence, with all its imperfections, is now to him the only unquestionable reality, and its most perfect illusions the only things worthy of his attention. He sees himself surrounded by

material forms, and he seeks to discover among these forms
that which corresponds to his highest ideal.

The highest desire of any mortal is to attain that which
exists in himself as his highest ideal. A person without
an ideal is unthinkable. To be conscious is to realize the
existence of some ideal, to relinquish the ideal world would
be death. A person without any desire would be useless
in the economy of nature, a person having all his desires
satisfied needs to live no longer, for life can be of no further
use to him. Each one is bound to his own ideal; he
whose ideal is mortal must die when his ideal dies, he
whose ideal is immortal must become immortal himself to
attain it.

Each man's true ideal should be his own higher spiritual
self. His Christ, or God. Man's semi-animal self is not
the whole of man. Man may be regarded as an invisible
power or ray extending in a line from the (spiritual) Sun to
the Earth. Only the lower end of that line is visible,
because it has evolved an organized material body; by
means of which the invisible ray draws strength from the
earth below. If all the life and thought-force evolved by
the contact of the lower end of that line with matter are
spent within the material plane, the higher spiritual self
will gain nothing by it, and when death breaks the communication between the higher and lower self, the lower
self will perish, and the higher one will remain what it was,
before it evolved a mortal inhabitant of the material world.

Man lives in two worlds, in his interior and in the
exterior world. Each of these worlds exists under conditions peculiar to itself, and that world in which he lives
is for the time being the most real to him. When he fully
enters his interior world during deep sleep or in moments
of perfect abstraction, the forms perceived in the exterior
world fade away; but when he awakes into the exterior
world the forms seen in his interior state are forgotten, or
leave only their uncertain shadows on the sky. To live
simultaneously in both worlds is only possible to him
who succeeds in harmoniously blending his internal and
external worlds into one.

The so-called Real seldom corresponds with the Ideal,
and often it happens that man, after many unsuccessful
attempts to realize his ideals in the exterior world, returns
to his interior world with disappointment, and resolves to

give up his search ; but if he succeeds in the realization of his ideal, then arises for him a moment of happiness, during which time, as we know it, exists for him no more, the exterior world is then blended with his interior world, his consciousness is absorbed in the enjoyment of both, and yet he remains a man.

Artists and poets may be familiar with such states. An inventor who sees his invention accepted, a soldier coming victorious out of the struggle for victory, a lover united with the object of his desire, forgets his own personality and is lost in the contemplation of his ideal. The extatic worshipper, seeing the Redeemer before him, floats in an ocean of rapture, and his consciousness is centred in the ideal that he himself has created out of his own mind, but which is as real to him as if it were a living form of flesh. Shakespeare's Juliet finds her mortal ideal realized in Romeo's youthful form. United with him, she forgets the rush of time, night disappears, and she is not conscious of it ; the lark heralds the dawn, and she mistakes its song for the singing of the nightingale. Happiness measures no time and knows no danger. But Juliet's ideal is mortal and dies, and having lost her ideal Juliet must die, and the immortal ideals of both become again united as they enter the immortal realm through the door of physical death.

But as the sun rose too early for Juliet, so in all engagements of evanescent ideals that have been realized in the external world, happiness vanishes soon. An ideal that has been realized ceases to be an ideal ; the ethereal forms of the interior world, if grasped by the rude hand of mortals and embodied in matter, must die. To grasp an immortal ideal, man's mortal nature must die before he can grasp it.

Low ideals may be killed, but their death calls similar ones into existence. From the blood of a vampire that has been slain a swarm of vampires arises. A selfish desire fulfilled makes room for similar desires, a gratified passion is chased away by other similar passions, a sensual craving that has been stilled gives rise to new cravings. Earthly happiness is short-lived and often dies in disgust ; the love of the immortal alone is immortal. Material acquisitions perish, because forms are evanescent and die. Intellectual accomplishments vanish, for the intellectual forces are subject to change. Desires and opinions change and

memories fade away. He who clings to old memories,
clings to that which is dead. A child becomes a man, a
man an old man, an old man a child ; the playthings of
childhood give way to intellectual playthings, but when the
latter have served their purpose, they appear as useless as
did the former, only spiritual realities are everlasting and
true. In the ever-revolving kaleidoscope of nature the
aspect of illusions continually changes its form. What is
laughed at as a superstition by one century is often
accepted as the basis of science for the next, and what
appears as wisdom to-day may be looked upon as an
absurdity in the great to-morrow. Nothing is permanent
but the real ideal, the truth.

But where can man find the truth? If he seeks deep
enough in himself he will find it revealed, each man may
know his own heart. He may send a ray of his intelligence into the depths of his soul and search its bottom,
he may find it to be as infinitely deep as the sky above his
head. He may find corals and pearls, or watch the monsters of the deep. If his thought is steady and unwavering,
he may enter the innermost sanctuary of his own temple
and see the goddess unveiled. Not everyone can penetrate
into such depths, because the thought is easily led astray ;
but the strong and persistent searcher will penetrate veil
after veil, until at the innermost centre he discovers the
germ of truth, which, awakened to consciousness, will grow
into a sun that illuminates the whole of the interior world,
wherein everything is contained.

Such an interior meditation and concentration of thought
upon the germ of divinity, which rests in the innermost
centre of the soul, is the only true *prayer*. The adulation
of an external form, whether living or dead, whether existing objectively or merely subjectively in the imagination, is useless, and serves only to deceive ourselves. It
is very easy to attend to external forms of external "so-
called worship," but the true worship of the living God
within requires a great effort of will and a power of will,
which few people are able to exercise, but which can be
acquired by practice. It consists in continually guarding
of the door of the sacred lodge, so that no illegitimate
thoughts may enter the mind to disturb the holy assembly
whose deliberations are presided over by the spirit of
wisdom.

How shall we know tne truth? Truth, having awakened to consciousness, knows that it is; it is the god-principle in man, which is infallible and cannot be misled by illusions. If the surface of the soul is not lashed by the storms of passions, if no selfish desires exist to disturb its tranquillity, if its waters are not darkened by reflections of the past, we will see the image of eternal truth mirrored in the deep. To know the truth in its fulness is to become alive and immortal, to lose the power of recognizing the truth is to perish in death. The voice of truth in a person that has not yet awakened to spiritual life, is the " still small voice " that may be felt in the heart, listened to by the imperfect, as a half-conscious dreamer may listen to the ringing of bells in the distance ; but in those that have become conscious of life, that have passed through the first resurrection of the spirit in their own heart, and received the baptism of the first initiation administered by themselves, the voice of the new-born *ego* has no uncertain sound, but becomes the powerful *Word* of the Master. The awakened principle of truth is self-conscious and self-sufficient, it is the great spiritual sun that knows that it exists. It stands higher than the intellect and higher than science, it does not need to be corroborated by " recognized authorities," it cares not for the opinion of others, and its decisions suffer no appeal. It knows neither doubt nor fear, but reposes in the tranquillity of its own supreme majesty. It can neither be altered nor changed, it always was and ever remains the same, whether mortal man may perceive it or not. It may be compared to the light of the earthly sun, that cannot be excluded from the world, but from which man may exclude himself. We may blind ourselves to the perception of the truth, but the truth itself is not thereby changed. It illuminates the minds of those who have awakened to immortal life. A small room requires a little flame, a large room a great light for its illumination, but in either room the light shines equally clear in each ; in the same manner the light of truth shines into the hearts of the illuminated with equal clearness, but with a power differing according to their individual capacity.

It will always be perfectly useless to attempt to describe self-knowledge to another man. Only that which exists relatively to ourselves has a real existence *for us,* that of which we know nothing does not exist for us. No proof of the existence of light can be furnished to the blind, no proof of transcendental knowledge can be given to those whose capacity to know does not transcend the realm of external phenomena.

There is nothing higher than truth, and the acquisition of truth is therefore man's highest ideal. The highest ideal in the Universe must be a universal ideal. The constitution of all men is built according to one universal law, and the highest ideal must be the same ideal to all and attainable to all, and in its attainment all individuals become reunited into one. As long as a man does not recognize the highest ideal in the Universe, the highest one which he is able to recognize will be the highest to him; but as long as there still exists a higher one than the one he perceives, the higher will unconsciously attract him, unless he persistingly repulses its attraction. Only the attainment of the highest ideal in the Universe can give permanent happiness, for having attained the highest there is nothing left that could be possibly desired. As long as there is still a higher ideal for man, he will have aspirations to reach it, but having reached the highest its attraction ceases, he becomes one with it and can desire nothing more. There must be a state of perfection which all may reach, and beyond which none can advance, until the Universe as a whole advances beyond it. All men have the same right to reach the highest, but not all have the same power developed, some may reach it soon, others may lag on the road, and perhaps the majority may fall and have to begin again at the foot of the ladder. Each ripe acorn that falls from an oak has the inherent capacity to develop into an oak; but not each finds the same conditions for development. Some may grow, a few may develop into trees, but the majority will enter into decomposition to furnish new material out of which new forms may be developed.

The highest truth in its fulness is not known to a man in the mortal form. Those that have attained to a state of perfect consciousness of absolute truth require no form to hold it, they belong to a formless tribe; they could not be one with an universal principle if they were tied by the chains of personality; a mind expanded, so that the prison-house of flesh can hold it no more, will require that prison-

house no longer. Form is only required to shelter the
spirit in the infancy of his development, as long as he has
not attained full power. Having attained the knowledge
of evil and the power to control it, and having by the realization of the truth "eaten from the tree of life and
attained immortality," * he can protect himself by his own
power, and requires his clothes of flesh no longer.

Imperfectly developed man, unless he has become very
much degraded, feels intuitively that which is true. The
scientist who reasons from the plane of sensual perceptions
is farthest from a recognition of the truth, because he mistakes the illusions produced by his senses for the reality,
and repulses the revelations of his own intuition. The
philosopher, unable to see the truth, attempts to grasp it
with his intellect, and may approach it to a certain extent ;
but he, in whom the truth has attained the state of self-
consciousness, knows the truth by direct perception, he is
one with it, and cannot err. Such a state is incomprehensible to the majority of men, to scientists and philosophers as well as to the ignorant, and yet men have existed,
and exist to-day, who have attained that state. They are
the *true Theosophists*, but not every one *is* a Theosophist
who goes by that name, nor is everyone a *Christ* who is
called a Christian. But a true Theosophist and a true
Christian or *Mahatma* are one and the same, because both
are human forms in which the universal *spiritual soul* has
attained a state of self-consciousness.

The terms "Christian" or "Theosophist," like so many
other terms of a similar kind, have almost entirely lost
their true meaning. A "Christian" now-a-days means a
person whose name is inscribed in the register of some so-
called Christian Church, and performs the ceremonies
prescribed by that social organization.

But a real *Christian* is something entirely different from
a merely external one. The first Christians were a secret
organization, a school of Occultists, who adopted certain
symbols and signs, in which to represent the truths they
knew, and thus to communicate them to each other, while
hiding them from the eyes of the ignorant.

A real *Theosophist* is not a dreamer, but a most practical
person. By purity of life he receives the power to perceive higher truths than average man is able to see.

---

* Bible : Genesis iii. 22.

As the truth is only one, men in all countries, in whom the truth has become self-conscious, have the same perception. This explains why the revelations of all prophets are identical with each other, provided they have attained the same power. The truths revealed by a Jackob Boehme, or Paracelsus in Germany, are essentially the same as those revealed by the Thibetan Mahatmas, they only differ in extent and in mode of expression. An ecstatic Christian saint in England or France would tell the same tale as an ecstatic Brahmin in India or an ecstatic red Indian in America; because all three, being in the same state, would exactly see the same thing. The truth is there, visible to all who are able to perceive it, but each will describe what he sees according to his mode of thinking and in his own fashion. If—as the ignorant believe—all the visions of saints and lamas, sanyâssi, and dervishes, were only the result of hallucinations and fancies, not two of them, having never heard of each other, would have the same vision. A tree will be a tree to all who are able to see it, and if their sight is clear no preconceived opinions will change it into something else; a truth will be seen as a truth by all who are able to see it, and no preconceived opinions will alter it or change it into a lie. To know the whole truth is to know everything that exists; to love the truth above all is to become united with the consciousness of all; to be able to express the truth in its fulness is to possess universal power; but to be one with immortal truth is to be for ever immortal.

The perception of the truth rests in the equilibrium of the intellect and the emotions. As long as the mind has not awakened to a state of direct recognition of the truth, it will only see the shadow of its presence and hear the indistinct whispering of its voice. The sound of that voice may be drowned in the turmoil of the intellectual workshop, its light may be obscured by the storms of the emotions. To understand that voice and to behold that light distinctly and without any foreign admixture, heart and head should act harmoniously together. To perceive the truth, purity of heart and strength of mind should go hand in hand, and it is therefore taught that men must become like children before they can enter the sphere of truth. Head and heart, if supported by reason, are as *One* but if they act against each other they form the absurd *Two* that produces illusions. The emotional maniac is only guided by his heart, the intellectual fool only listens to the dictates of his head, he lives—so to say—in his head and neglects the heart. But neither the revelry of the emotions nor intellectual fanaticism discloses the truth ; only in the " stillness that follows the storm," * when the harmony of both is restored, will the truth be discovered. A man who only follows the dictates of his emotions, resembles one who in ascending a mountain peak becomes dizzy, and losing nis power to control himself, falls over a precipice ; a man who is only guided by his sensual perceptions influencing his intellect is easily lost in the whirlpool of multifarious illusions. He is like a person on an island in the ocean examining a drop of water taken from the ocean, and being blind to the existence of the ocean from which that drop has been taken. But if heart and head are attuned to the divine harmonies of the invisible realm of nature, then will the truth reveal itself to man, and in him will the highest ideal see its own image reflected.

We sometimes hear some people boast that they are controlled by their intellect ; but no one boasts that he is controlled by his emotions. The former are as much in error as the latter ; for a *free* man is not controlled by either of the two ; he is his own master. By the power of his will and reason he controls the intellectual workings of his brain no less than the emotions of his heart, and only such a person is wise. Heart and brain are not ourselves. They are instruments which have been lent to us by nature. They should not govern us ; but we should govern them, and use them according to the dictates of the universal law, whose words we can only hear, when we are free from the bonds of the animal self.

Material man, entombed in his chrysalis of clay, can only feel, but not see, the rays that radiate from the sphere of infinite truth ; but if he bids his emotions be still l and commands his intellect be not deluded ! he may stretch his feelers into the realm of the spirit and perceive the light of truth. His heart should be used as a touchstone to examine the conclusions arrived at by the brain, and the brain should be employed like scales to weigh the decisions of the

---

＊ " Light on the Path," by M. C.

heart; but when his self-knowledge has been awakened, there will be no more difference of opinion between the head and the heart, the perceptions of the one will be in harmony with the aspirations of the latter, the one will see and the other will feel the truth.   Then will the lower ideals vanish before the light of truth, for truth is a jealous goddess and suffers no other gods beside her.

Man is usually guided only by his intellect, woman is often guided only by her emotions.   To reason from external appearances has become a necessity to men in consequence of their material organization, which like a shell surrounds the soul of men or women, in which alone rests the power of sensation and perception; but if the innermost man, the true spirit, sleeping in every mortal, awakens to life, he emits a light that penetrates through the veil of matter and illuminates the soul.   If the germ of divinity, hidden in the centre of the soul, is permitted to awaken, it emits a spiritual light, which reaches from man to the stars and to the utmost limits of space, and by the help of that divine light he may perceive and penetrate into the deepest mysteries of the Universe. Those who are able to know the truth by direct perception do not need to be informed of it by the reading of books, the whole of the visible and invisible realm lies open before them, like a book in whose pages they may read the whole history of the world.   They know all the forms of life, because they are one with the source of life from which all forms were born, they need not study letters, because the *Word* itself is living in them.   They may be the instruments through whom eternal wisdom reveals itself to those who are entombed in matter; but in that case it is not the teacher revealing the truth, but the truth itself revealing itself through him.   These are the only *Illuminates* and *Theosophists* that have any real existence; not those who merely imagine to be what they not really are.

How pitiful must appear to the enlightened the war of opinions raging among those whom humanity believes to be the lights of knowledge and wisdom; how insignificantly small appear those lights before the sun of truth. What appears as a light to the ignorant, appears to the illuminated seer as a source of darkness and smoke, and the wisdom of the world becomes foolishness * before the eyes

---

* 1 Cor. iii. 19.

of the truth. The oyster in its shell may believe to be at the pinnacle of perfection, and that there is no higher existence than that which it enjoys in the ocean-bed ; the scientist, proud of the discoveries of his department of science, is frequently found to be swelled with vanity, knowing little how little he knows. Many of the representatives of modern science forget that the greatest inventions have been made—not by the professed guardians of science, but by men upon whom they looked with contempt, and that many useful inventions were introduced, not with the assistance, but in spite of the opposition of the learned. It may be disagreeable to call up unpleasant memories, but we cannot close our eyes to the fact that the inventors of railroads, steamships, and telegraphs have been ridiculed by professors of science, that men of science have laughed at the belief in the rotundity of the earth, that some of the legitimate keepers of the truth have often betrayed their trust, and that especially the followers of the medical profession, as a class, have often been prominent on account of their misunderstanding of the laws of nature, and of their opposition to truth, whenever it conflicted with their preconceived opinions.

Many useful discoveries have been made through the power of intuition ; assisted by a strong intellect, some seem to have been made by the aid of that intuition which comes from the devil, and their results are still a curse to mankind. For centuries the learned professions have been thriving on human suffering, and many of their followers, mistaking the low for the high, have dethroned the god of humanity and worshipped the fetish of Self in its place. The fear of an illusory devil external to man has served to swell the money-bags of Brahmins and priests, while the real internal devils, residing in the animal nature of man, were allowed to grow. For centuries many of the appointed servants of the Supreme have only served the golden calf, residing in their animal nature, feeding their followers with false hopes of immortality, and speculating on the selfish propensities of men to obtain material profits for their own selves. Those to whom humanity looks for protection against bodily ills, and who therefore—more than anybody else—should understand the real constitution of man, usually experiment with the

physical form to seek the cause of disease, being ignorant
of the fact that the form is the expression of life, the product
of the soul, and that external effects cannot be effectually
changed without changing the internal causes.   Many of
them refusing to believe in Soul, seek the cause of diseases,
in its external expression, where it does not exist.   Diseases
are the necessary results of disobedience to the laws of
nature, they are the consequences of "sins" that cannot
be forgiven, but must be atoned for by acting again in
accordance with natural laws.   In vain will the ignorant
ask the guardians of health for their assistance to cheat the
law of nature out of its dues.   Physicians may restore
health by restoring the supremacy of the law, but as long
as they know only an infinitesimal part of the law they can
only cure an infinitesimal part of the diseases afflicting
mankind ; they can often only suppress the manifestation
of one disease by calling another and more serious one into
existence.*   In vain will such investigators seek for the
cause for epidemic diseases in places where such causes
may be propagated, but where they are not created.   The
soul of the Earth in which such causes reside cannot be
seen with microscopes, it can only be recognized by a man
whose spiritual perceptions have been awakened by the
awakening into consciousness of his interior self.

A true conception of the nature of man will lead to the
comprehension of the fact that man, being as a microcosm
the true image, reflection and representative of the macrocosm of nature ; Nature has the same *organization* as
Man, although not the same external *form*.   Having the
same organs and functions, and being ruled by the same
laws, the organism of Nature is liable to experience
diseases, similar to those experienced by the organism of
man.   Nature has her dropsical swellings, her nervous
tremblings, her paralytic affections by which civilized
countries turn into deserts, her inflammatory affections, her
rheumatic contractions, spells of heat and cold, eruptions
and earthquakes.   If our physicians knew the nature of
man, they would also know the organization of Nature as
a whole, and understand more about the origin of epidemic
diseases, of which they now know merely the external
effects.

---

* See C. L. Hunt : "Vaccination."

What does modern medical science know of the constitution of man, whose life and safety is made to depend on that knowledge? It knows the form of the body, the arrangement of muscles, and bones, and organs, and it calls these constituent parts by names which it invented for the purpose of distinction. Having no supersensual perceptions it does not know the soul of man, but believes that his body is the essential man. If its eyes were open it would see that this visible body is only the material kernel of the " immaterial," but nevertheless substantial real man, whose soul-essence radiates far into space, and whose spirit is without limits. They would know that in the life-principle, in whose existence they do not believe, resides sensation, perception, consciousness, and all the causes that produce the growth of the form. Laboring under their fatal mistake they attempt to cure that which is not sick, while the real patient is unknown to them. Under such circumstances it is not surprising that the most enlightened physicians of our time have expressed the opinion that our present system of medicine is rather a curse than a blessing to mankind, and that our drugs and medicines do vastly more harm than good, because they are continually misapplied. This is an assertion which has often been made by their own most prominent leaders.

The ideal physician of the future is he who knows the true constitution of man, and who is not led by illusive external appearances, but has developed his interior powers of perception to enable him to examine into the hidden causes of all external effects. To him the acquisitions of material science are not the guides but only the assistants, his guide will be his knowledge and not his "belief," and his knowledge will endow him with *faith,* which is a power acting upon that part of man that cannot be reached by the administration of drugs.

If our medical students were to apply a part of the time which they employ for the study of certain external sciences which are practically useless to them for the development of their interior perception, they would become able to *see* certain processes within the organism of man, which are at present to them a mere matter of speculation, and which are not discoverable by any physical means.

But even the modern physician acts wiser than he knows. He may say that he does not believe in faith, and yet it is only faith that upholds him and by which he exists, because if men had no faith in him they would not employ him, and if his patients did not believe that he could benefit them they would not follow his directions. A physician without intuition, having no faith in himself, and in whom no one else has any faith, is perfectly useless as a physician, no matter how much he may have learned in schools.

There is nothing whatever that can be accomplished without the power of Faith, and there is no faith possible without knowledge. We can only accomplish that of which we are confident that we can accomplish it, and we can only be truly confident if we know by experience that we have the power to do it.

What does popular science know about Mind? According to the usual definition, Mind is "the intellectual power in man," and as by *man* she means a visible form, this definition makes of mind something confined within that visible form. But if this conception were true, there could be no transmission of thought to a distance. If no mind-substance did exist outside the visible form, there could be no transmission of thought from one such form to another. No sound can be heard in a space from which the air has been exhausted, and no thought can travel from one individual to another without a corresponding material existing between them to act as a conductor; but the possibility of thought-transference is now an almost universally admitted fact; its truth has been perceived long ago by children who make practical use of it in some of their games. Moreover, any one who doubts its possibility has it in his power to convince himself by either impressing his thoughts silently upon others, or—if he is of a receptive nature—by letting others impress their thought upon him. It must, therefore, be obvious even to the superficial observer, that popular science in regard to this fundamental doctrine has not yet arrived at the truth. Her logical deductions cannot be true as long as the premises from which she reasons are false, and her opinions in regard to the powers possessed by man cannot be perfect as long as she does not know the essential nature of Man.

How infinitely more grand and how much more reason-able is the conception of ancient science, according to whose doctrines everything that exists is an expression of the thoughts of the Universal Mind, pervading the infinity of space! This conception makes *Mind* a power in the realm of infinity, acting through living and intelligent instruments, and of *Man*, an intellectual power, an expression of the Universal Mind, able to receive, reflect, and modify the thoughts of the latter, like a diamond that becomes self-luminous through the influence of the Sun.

There is no reason why we should believe that an intelligent mind can exist only in a form which is visible and tangible to the external senses of man. There may be, for all we know, untold millions of intelligent or semi-intelligent beings in the universe, whose forms are constituted differently from ours, who live on another plane of existence than ours, and who are therefore invisible to our physical senses, but who nevertheless have a mind, and may be perceived by the superior power of perception of the awakened spirit. Nor is their existence a matter of mere speculation, for they may be perceived by those who have the power of interior perception whenever they enter the sphere of their mind.

All we know of external objects is the images which they produce in the sphere of our mind. Astral or spiritual beings produce no reflection upon the retina, but their presence may be felt when they enter the mental sphere of the observer, and they may be perceived with the eye of the soul.

The ideal scientist of the future having attained the power of spiritual perception, will recognize this truth. But when this time arrives scientific opinions will cease to be mere beliefs, and knowledge will take their place.

The common utilitarianism of our age is the result of a general misconception of the true nature of man, and of that which is really useful and worthy of his attention.

If we believe that the object of life is simply to render our material Self satisfied and to keep it in comfort, and that material comfort confers the highest state of possible happiness, we mistake the low for the high and an illusion for the truth. Our material mode of life is a consequence of the material constitution of our bodies. We are " worms of earth " because we cling with all our aspirations to earth. If we can enter upon a path of evolution, by which we become less material and more ethereal, a very different order of civilization would be established. Things which now appear indispensable and necessary would cease to be useful; if we could transfer our consciousness with the velocity of thought from one part of the globe to another, the present mode of communication and transportation would be no longer required. The deeper we sink into matter, the more material means for comfort will be needed; the essential and powerful god in man is not material—in the usual acceptation of this term—and independent of the restrictions laid upon matter.

What are the real necessities of life? The answer to this question depends entirely on what we imagine to be necessary. Railways, steamers, electric lights, &c., are now a necessity to us, and yet millions of people have lived long and happy knowing nothing about them. To one man a dozen of palaces may appear to be an indispensable necessity, to another a carriage, another a pipe, or a bottle of whisky. But all such necessities are only such as man himself has created. They make the state in which man now is agreeable to him, and tempt him to remain in that state and to desire for nothing higher. They may even hinder his development instead of advancing it. If we would rise into a higher state, in which we would no longer require such things, they would cease to be a necessity, and even become undesirable and useless; but it is the craving and the wasting of thought for the augmentation of the pleasures of the lower life which prevent man to enter the higher one.

To raise the evanescent man to a state of perfection enjoyed by the permanent ideal man is the great object of life; the *Arcanum*, that cannot be learned in books. It is the great secret, that may be understood by a child, but will for ever be incomprehensible to him who, living entirely in the realm of sensual perceptions, has no power to grasp it. The attainment of that which is the highest is the *Magnum opus*, the great work, of which the *Alchemists* said that thousands of years may be required to perform it, but that it may also be accomplished in a moment, even by a woman while engaged in spinning. They looked upon the human mind as being a great alembic, in which the contending forces of the emotions may be purified by the heat of holy aspirations and by a supreme love of truth. They gave instructions how the soul of mortal man may be sublinated and purified from earthly attractions, and its immortal parts be made living and free. The purified elements were made to ascend to the supreme source of law, and descended again *in showers of snowy whiteness,* visible to all, because they rendered every act of life holy and pure. They taught how the base metals—meaning the animal energies in man—could be transformed into the pure gold of true spirituality, and how by attaining spiritual life—allegorically represented under the *" Elixir of Life"* —souls could have their youth and innocence restored and be rendered immortal.

Their truths shared the fate of other truths ; they were misunderstood and rejected by the ignorant, who continually clamor for truth and reject it when it is offered, because, being blind, they are unable to see it ; their science is known only to those who are able to grasp it. Theology and Masonry have—each in its own manner —continued the teachings of the Alchemists, and fortunate is the Mason or the priest who understands that which he teaches. But of such true disciples there are only few. The systems in which the old truths have been embodied are still in existence, but the cold hands of Sensualism and Materialism have been laid upon the outward forms, and from the interior the spirit has fled. Doctors and priests see only the outward form, and few can see the hidden mystery that called these forms into existence. The key to the inner sanctuary has been lost by those that were entrusted with its keeping, and the true password has not been rediscovered by the followers of Hiram Abiff. The riddle of the Egyptian Sphinx still waits for a solution, and will be revealed to none unless he becomes strong enough to discover it himself.

But the truth still lives. It resides on the top of a " mountain " called *Faith into the eternal Law of Good.* It shines deep into the interior world of man, and sends its divine influence down into the valleys, and wherever the doors and windows are open to receive it, there will it dispel the darkness, rendering men and women conscious of their own godlike attributes and guiding them on the road to perfection, until, when all their struggles have ceased and the law has been restored, they will find permanent happiness in the realization of the highest universal ideal.

Y

# CHAPTER II.

THE REAL AND THE UNREAL.

" Allah !  Bi'-smi'-llah !—God is One."—*Koran.*

EVERYWHERE in the broad expanse of the universe we see
an almost infinite variety of forms, belonging to different
kingdoms and species, and exhibiting an endless variety of
appearances.  The substance of which those forms are
composed may, for aught we know, consist essentially of
the same primordial material, forming the basis of their
constitution, although the qualities of the various bodies
may differ from each other, and it is far more reasonable to
suppose that this one primordial eternal essence exists and
appears in the course of evolution in various forms, than to
believe that a number of different original substances have
come into existence either by being created out of nothing
or otherwise.  What this primordial essence—this immaterial substance*—may be we do not know, we only know
of its manifestation in forms which we call things.  Whatever may find expression in one form or another may be
called a thing, and a thing may change its substance and
yet the form remain the same, or its form may change and
the substance remain.  Water may be frozen into solid ice,
or be transformed by heat into invisible vapor ; and
vapor may be chemically decomposed into hydrogen and
oxygen ; yet, if the necessary conditions are given, the
energies which previously formed water will form water
again ; the forms and attributes change, but the elements
remain the same and may combine again in certain stipu·
lated proportions, regulated by the law of attraction.

---

* The *A'kasa* of the Brahmins or the *Iliaster* of Paracelsus, the
Universal *Proteus.*

As this hypothetical primordial substance or principle has no attributes which we can perceive with our senses, we cannot see it or feel it, and we therefore do not know the real substance of a thing; we only distinguish the peculiarities of the attributes of its form, and for the purpose of distinction and classification we give it a name. We may gradually deprive a thing of some of its attributes or substance and change its form, and yet it remains that thing as long as its character remains, and even after we destroy its form and dissolve its substance the character of the thing still remains as an idea in the subjective world, where we cannot destroy it, and we may clothe the old idea with new attributes and produce it under a new form on the objective plane. A thing exists as long as its character exists, only when it changes its character it ceases to be. A material thing is only the symbol or the representation of an idea; we may give it a name, but the thing itself remains forever hidden behind the veil. If we could on the physical plane separate a single substance from its attributes, and endow it with others at will, then one body could be transformed into another, as, for instance, base metals be transformed into gold; but unless we change the character of a thing, a mere change of its form will only affect its external appearance.

By way of illustration, let us look at a stick. It is made of wood, but this is not essential; it might be made of something else and still be a stick. We do not perceive the stick itself, we only see its attributes, its extension and color and density; we feel its weight, and we hear its sound if we strike it. Each of these attributes or all of them may be changed, and it may remain a stick for all that, as long as its character is not lost, because that which essentially constitutes it a stick is its character or an idea which has not necessarily a definite form. Let us endow that formless idea with new attributes that will change its character, and we shall have transformed our ideal stick into anything we choose to make of it.

We cannot change copper into gold on the physical plane, we cannot change a man into a physical child, but we may daily transform our desires, our aspirations and tastes by the omnipotent power of the will. In doing this we change our character, and make of man—even on the physical plane—a different being.

Nobody ever saw a real man, we only perceive the qualities which he possesses. Man cannot see himself. He speaks of *his* body, *his* soul, *his* spirit ; it is only the combination of the three which constitutes what we consider a *man*, the *Ego* in which his character rests is something for which we have no conception. As an idea and yet an individual unit he enters the world of matter, evolutes a new personality, obtains new experience and knowledge, passes through the pleasures and vicissitudes of life and through the valley of death, and enters again into that realm where in the course of ages his form will cease to exist, to appear again in a form upon the scene when the hour for his reappearance strikes. His form and personality change, his real *Ego* remains the same and yet not the same, because during life it acquires new attributes and changes its characteristics.*

We see that a plant ceases to grow when its roots are torn from the soil, and when they are replaced into the soil the growth may continue. Likewise the human *spirit*, man's higher self, takes root in the physical organism of man, and develops a soul through the latter, but when death tears out the roots, the soul rests and ceases to grow, until it finds again a physical organism to acquire new conditions for continued growth, and to improve its own real self.

What can this real *ego* be, which lives through death and changes during life, unless it is *The Will* itself, obtaining relative consciousness by coming in contact with matter? Is any man certain of his own existence? All the proof we have of our existence is in our consciousness, in the feeling of the *I am*, in which is the realization of our exist-

---

* A true appreciation of the essential nature of man will show that the repeated *reincarnation* of the human monad in successive personalities is a scientific necessity. How could it be possible for a man to develop into a state of perfection, if the time of his spiritual growth were restricted to the period of one short existence upon this globe ? If he could go on and develop without having a physical body, then why should it have been necessary for him to take a physical body at all ? It is unreasonable to suppose that the *spiritual* germ of a man begins its existence at the time of the birth of the physical body, or that the physical parents of the child could be the generators of the spiritual monad. If the spiritual monad existed before the body was born, and could develop without it, what would be the use of its entering any body at all ?

ence. Every other state of consciousness is subject to change. The consciousness of one moment differs from that of another, according to the changes which take place in the conditions which surround us, and according to the variety of our impressions. We are craving for change and death; to remain always the same would be torture. Old impressions die and are replaced with new ones, and we rejoice to see the old ones die, so that the new ones may step into their places. We do not make our impressions ourselves, but we receive them from the outside world. If it were possible that two or more persons could be born and educated under exactly the same conditions, having the same character and receiving always the same impressions, they would always have the same thoughts, the same feelings and desires, their consciousness would be identical, and they might be considered as forming collectively only one person. A person, having forgotten all the mental impressions he ever received, and receiving no new ones, might exist for ages, living in eternal imbecility, with no consciousness whatever except the consciousness of the *I Am,* and that consciousness could not cease to exist as long as there is in him that Will which enables him to *be.**

---

* This is the only possible condition in which a person, who has during his earthly life acquired no spiritual possessions, can possibly exist after death. A person whose whole attention is given to sensual pleasures, or to merely intellectual pursuits on the material plane, carries nothing with him into the subjective existence after the death of the body which can exist permanently. Nor could it be otherwise; for it is not *he* who dies; it is the false *egos* dying in him. A man who does not know his own true self cannot die, because he has not yet come to life; it is only nature, living and dying in him.

His sensations leave him at death, and the images caused in his mind by the recollection of the superficial knowledge which he has acquired during life will gradually fade away; the intellectual forces, which have been set into motion by his scientific pursuits, will be exhausted, and after that time the spirit of such a person, even if he has been during life the greatest scientist, speculator, and logician, will be nothing but an imbecile being, having merely the feeling that he exists, living in darkness, and being drawn irresistibly towards reincarnation; seeking to reimbody itself again under any circumstances whatever, to escape from nothingness into existence.

But he who acquires spiritual self-consciousness will be self-luminous and live in the eternal light. He brings a light with him into the darkness, and that light will not be distinguished, for it is eternal; while the light of this world is like darkness to him.

Under whatever form life may exist, it is only relative. A stone, a plant, an animal, a man or God, each has an existence of its own, and each one exists only for the others, as long as the others are conscious of his existence. Man looks upon the existences below him as incomplete, and the incomplete beings below him know little about him. Man knows little about any superior beings, and yet there may be such, looking upon him with pity as they would look upon an inferior animal that has not yet awakened to a realization of its real existence.

Those who are supposed to know, inform us that there is no being in the universe superior to the spiritual regenerated man; but that there are innumerable invisible beings who are either far superior or inferior to mortal man as we know him. In other words, the highest beings in the universe are such as have once been men; but the men and women of our present civilization may have to progress through millions of ages before they attain that state of perfection which such beings possess.

We are accustomed to look upon that which we perceive with our senses as real, and upon everything else as unreal, and yet our daily experience teaches us that our senses cannot be trusted if we wish to distinguish between the true and the false. We see the sun rise in the East, see him travel along the sky during the day and disappear again in the West; but every child now-a-days knows that this apparent movement is only an illusion, caused by the turning of the earth. At night we see the "fixed" stars above our heads, they look insignificant compared with the wide expanse of the earth and the ocean, and yet we believe that they are blazing suns, in comparison with which our mother Earth is only a speck of dust. Nothing seems to us more quiet and tranquil than the solid rocks under our feet, and yet the earth whereon we live whirls with tremendous velocity through space; the mountains seem to be everlasting, but continents sink beneath the waters of the ocean and rise again above its surface. Below our feet moves, with ebbs and tides, the swelling bosom of our apparently solid mother the earth, above our head seems to be nothing tangible, and yet we live on the very bottom of the airy ocean above us, and do not know the things that may perhaps live in its currents or upon its surface. A stream of light seems to descend from the sun to our planet, and yet darkness is said to exist between the atmosphere of the Earth and the sun, where no meteoric matter exists to cause a reflection; while again we are surrounded by an ocean of light of a higher order, which appears to us to be darkness, because the nerves of our bodies have not yet been sufficiently developed to react under the influence of the *Astral Light.* The image reflected in the mirror seems a reality to the unreasoning mind; the voice of an echo may be mistaken for the voice of a man; the elemental forces of nature may be loaded with the products of our own thoughts, and we may listen to their echo, believing it to be the voices of spirits of the departed. We often dream when awake, and while believing to be awake we may be asleep.

It is not scientific to say "we are asleep;" as long as we do not know who "*we*" are. We can only truly say that such and such functions of a physical or psychical organism, which we call our own, are asleep or inactive while others are active and awake. We may be fully awake relatively to one thing and asleep relatively to another. A *somnambule's* body may be in a state resembling death, while his higher consciousness is fully alive, and has even far superior powers of perception than it could employ if all the activity of his life-principle were engaged in performing the functions of his lower organism.

Solid matter looked at with the physical eye appears as a dense mass of unchangeable something, but examined with the eye of the intellect it appears as an aggregation of centers of energy easily penetrable to thought. A solid mass is therefore in reality a concentration of force, and what we behold in the form of matter of any kind is only the symbol of stored-up energy, a visible expression of the invisible force residing in matter. Seen with the eyes of the spirit, matter and force are known to be only *one*, the twofold activity of one eternal reality, the twofold manifestation of eternal power.

*Matter* is an external visible manifestation of force, having become latent; *Spirit* is an internal invisible active power. Both are the two different modes of manifestation of one primal cause.

If we turn from the consideration of form to that of space, and examine what relation extension and duration bear to the consciousness of forms, we find that their qualities change according to our standard of measurement and according to our mode of perception. To an animalculæ in a drop of water that drop may appear as an ocean, and to an insect living on a leaf that leaf may constitute a world. If during our sleep the whole of the visible world were to shrink to the size of a walnut or expand to a thousandfold its present dimensions, on awakening we should perceive no change, provided that change had equally affected everything, including ourselves. A child has no conception of its true relation to space, and may try to grasp the moon with its hands, and a person who has been born blind and is afterwards made to see, cannot judge of distances correctly. Our thoughts know of no intervening space when they travel from one part of the globe to another in an almost imperceptible space of time. Our conceptions of our relation to space are based upon experience and memory acquired in our present condition. If we were moving among entirely different conditions, our experiences, and consequently our conceptions, would be entirely different. Our idea of relative space is a mode of perception of distance, and there appear to be as many dimensions of space as there are modes of perception or consciousness. Space relatively to form can only have three dimensions, because all forms are composed of three dimensions—length, thickness and height. A consciousness existing in a mathematical point could have no conception of form, because such a point has no form. A consciousness existing in a line or in a plane without thickness could have no conception of form, because the former having only one, and the latter only two extensions, cannot exist as forms, but only as mathematical abstractions. Consciousness in the absolute sense is without form, but entering into relation to form, its relation to space will be threefold, because three is the number of form.

It is evidently an absurdity to talk about *forms existing in a fourth dimension of space;* because *three* is the number of form, and no form whatever, whether visible or invisible, can possibly exist without possessing the three factors, which are necessary to constitute it a form, namely, *length, breadth* and *thickness.* There may be innumerable invisible powers in space; but whenever any such power manifests itself in a form, it always belongs to three dimensions of space. *Absolute* Space like Matter and Motion is fundamentally *one*, and has no dimensions for any body. It only manifests dimensions, when it becomes *relative* to forms, and forms are necessarily *always* three dimensional.

Space in the absolute is independent of form, but forms cannot exist independent of space. We may imagine ourselves to be in the midst of a solid rock, and we will be there in space, although there will be no room in which we could move. Everyone knows that there exists a difference between good and evil, between love and hate, between knowledge and ignorance; but if two things or ideas differ from each other there is the idea of a distance of some kind between them, and distance means space, but a space that has in such cases no relation to form, and of which we can form no conception.

As our conception of space is only relative, so is our conception of time. It is not time itself, but its measurement, of which we are conscious, and time is nothing to us unless in connection with our association of ideas. The human mind can only receive a small number of impressions per second; if we were to receive only one impression per hour, our life would seem exceedingly short, and if we were able to receive, for instance, the impression of each single undulation of a yellow ray of light, whose vibrations number 509 billions per second, a single day in our life would appear to be an eternity without end.* To a prisoner in a dungeon, who has no occupation, time may seem extremely long, while for him who is actively engaged it passes quickly. During sleep we have no conception of time, but a sleepless night passed in suffering seems very long. During a few seconds of time we may, in a dream, pass through experiences which would require a number of years in the regular course of events, while in the unconscious state time has no existence for us.

In books on mystical subjects we find often accounts of a person having dreamed in a short moment of time, things which we should suppose that it would take hours to dream them; for instance the following: "A traveler arrived late at night at a station. He was very fatigued, and as the conductor opened the door of the car, he entered, and im-

---

* Carl du Prel: "*Die Planetenbewohner.*"

mediately fell asleep. He dreamed that he was at home, and living with his family; that he fell in love with a girl and married her; that he lived happy until he meddled with political affairs, and was arrested on a charge of having entered into a conspiracy against the government. He was tried, and condemned to be shot, and led out to be executed. Arrived at the place of execution, the command was given, and the soldiers fired at him, and he awoke at the noise caused by the shutting of the door of the car, which the conductor had shut behind him when our friend entered. It seems probable that the noise produced by shutting that door caused the whole dream."

In this state, when the experiences of the internal state mingles with the sensations of the external consciousness, the most erroneous impressions may be produced; because the intellect labors, logic and reflection exist; but reason does not act sufficiently powerful to discriminate between the true and the false.

But what is the difference between objective and subjective states of existence? Our bodies do not cease to live while we are asleep, but we have a different kind of perceptions in either state. The popular idea is that objective perceptions are real and subjective ones only the products of our imagination. But a little reflection will show that all perceptions, the objective as well as the subjective ones, are results of our "imagination." If we look at a tree, the tree does not come into our eye, but its picture appears in our mind; if we look at a form we perceive an impression made in our mind by the image of an object existing beyond the limits of our body; if we look at a subjective image or a thought, whether it be of our own creation or caused by the influence of another being, we perceive the impression which it produces on our mind. In either case the pictures exist in our mind, and we perceive nothing but the impressions made on the mind, and the only difference between the two is, that in the former case the impression is caused by something visible, and in the latter by something invisible to our physical sight, but the internal impressions may be as real as the external ones. If we close our eyes the latter vanish and the former appear more distinct. If our eyes are open, the former may become mixed with the latter, or be entirely superseded by them on account of their superior strength.

The fact is, that everything appears either objective or subjective according to the state of consciousness of the perceiver, and what may appear to him entirely subjective in one state may appear to him objectively in another. The highest truths have to him who can realize them an objective existence, the grossest material forms have no existence to him who cannot perceive them.

The basis upon which all exhibition of magical power rests is a knowledge of the relations that exist between object and subject. If we conceive in our mind of the picture of a thing we have seen before, an objective form of that thing comes into existence within our own mind, and is composed of the substance of our own mind. If by continual practice we gain sufficient power to hold on to that image and to prevent it from being driven away and dispersed by other thoughts, it will become comparatively dense, and be projected upon the mental sphere of others, so that the latter may actually believe to see objectively that which exists merely as an image within our own mind ; but he who cannot hold on to a thought and control it at will cannot produce its reflections upon the minds of others, and therefore such psychological experiments often fail, not on account of any absolute impossibility to perform them, but on account of the weakness of those who desire to experiment, but have not the power to control their own thoughts, and to render them solid enough for transmission.

Everything is either a reality or a delusion, according to the standpoint from which we view it. The words " real" and " unreal" are only relative terms, and what may seem real in one state of existence appears unreal in another. Money, luxury, fame, adulation, etc., appear very real to those who need them ; seen from the point of view of a god who has no use for them they appear to be only illusions. That which we realize is real to us, however unreal it may appear to another, and the appearance of reality changes as our consciousness changes. If my imagination is powerful enough to make me firmly believe in the presence of an angel, that angel will be there, alive and real, my own creation, no matter how invisible and unreal he may be to another. If your mind can create for you a paradise in a wilderness, that paradise will have *for you* an objective existence.

Everything that exists, exists in the universal Mind. If the individual mind becomes conscious of his relation to a thing, it begins to perceive it. No man can correctly conceive of a thing that does not exist, he cannot know anything with which he stands in no relation. To perceive, three facts are necessary : The perception, the perceiver, and the thing that is the object of perception. If they exist on entirely different planes, and cannot enter into relationship, no perception will be possible between them, and they will not know each other ; if they are one, there will be no perception, because the three being one, there can be no relation between them. If I wish to look at my face, and am not able to step out of myself, I must use a mirror to establish a relation between myself and the object of my perception. The mirror has no sensation, and I cannot see myself in the mirror, I can only see myself in my mind. The reflection of the mirror produces a reflection which is objective to my individual mind, and which comes to my subjective perception. Looked at from the standpoint of individual perception, I and the image produced in my mind, as well as the mirror, have each a separate existence ; but looked at from the standpoint of *The Absolute*, myself, the image and the mirror are only *One ;* the difference between us is merely one of appearance.

Reflection upon these facts will give us a key to an understanding of man's nature, and some of his mysteries. We cannot objectively see the light or the truth, as long as we are within the centre of the one or the other. Only when we enter beyond the centre of the light, can we see the source of the latter ; only when we fall into error, will we learn to appreciate the truth. As long as primordial man was one with the centre of universal power from which he emanated as a spiritual ray or entity in the beginning, he could not know the divine source from which he came. The will and imagination of the Universal Mind were his own will and imagination. Only when he began to "step out of himself" could he begin to imagine that he existed as a separate "Self ;" only when he began to act against the law, did he begin to realize that there was another law than his own. When man, as a spiritual entity, having attained perfection, enters again into the centre, his sense of self and separateness will be lost, but he will be in possession of knowledge. To see a thing, it must become objective. To know a thing, we must be separated from it. When we fully comprehend a thing, we become one with it, and know it by knowing ourselves.

This example is intended to illustrate the fundamental law of creation. The first great cause—so to say—stepping out of itself, becomes its own mirror, and thereby establishes a relation with itself. " God " sees His face reflected in eternal Nature ; the Universal Mind sees itself reflected in the individual mind of man. The Father comes to relative consciousness in the Son, but when He again retires into Himself the relation will cease ; the Father will then be again absolutely one with the Son. He will again become one with Himself, there will be no more relative consciousness, and " Brahm will go to sleep " until the night of creation has ceased. But God knows that he exists even after all his relation with external things has ceased, and does not need to look continually into a mirror to be reminded of that fact. Likewise the absolute consciousness of the great *I am* is independent of the objective existence of Nature, and He will still " sit on the great white throne after the earth and the heaven fled away from His face." *

If the world is a manifestation of the Universal Mind, everything that exists must exist in that mind ; there can be nothing beyond the Universal Mind, because it is necessarily infinite ; it can be only One, and there can be no beyond. We exist in that Mind, and all we perceive of external objects is the impressions which they produce upon our individual minds through the medium of the senses or by a superior mode of perception.

The superior powers of perceptions are those possessed by the *inner man*, and they become developed after the inner man awakens to self-consciousness. They correspond to the senses of the external man, such as seeing, hearing,

* St. John : Revelations xx. 2. If the old maxim is true that " it is above as it is below," it then follows that God never sleeps. Man's spirit is not unconscious when his physical body is asleep. On the contrary, it is more fully awake when centered in its own self-consciousness. Likewise the " sleep of Brahm " during *Pralaya* can only refer to his external creative activity, but not to his celestial existence in his own self-conscious light.

feeling, tasting, smelling, and other modes of perception, which are not yet developed in the physical man.

External sensual perceptions are necessary to see sensual things; the internal sensual perceptions are necessary to see internal things. Physical matter is as invisible to the spiritual sight as astral bodies are to the physical eyes; but as every object in nature has its astral counterpart within the physical form, it may see, hear, feel, taste, and smell with its astral senses those astral objects, and thereby know the attributes of the physical objects as well or still better than the physical man might have been able to do with his physical senses; but neither the physical nor the astral senses will be able to perceive, unless they are permeated by the light of the spirit which endows them with life.

If everything that exists is Mind, and if we ourselves are that Mind, all the forms of the subjective as well as the objective words can be nothing else but states of our Mind. Thought is the creative power in the universe. Thought-germs grow in the mind as the seeds of plants grow in the soil of the earth. The latter are quickened into life by the light of the sun, the former by the light of intelligence. At the beginning of a day of creation, Brahm, begins to create, his thoughts call worlds into existence. Things are materialized thoughts, or states of mind having been rendered objective. Few persons have the power to think spontaneously and independently, although all may believe to have that power; if they were able to manipulate thought they would be able to create. The majority of men only occupy themselves with the thoughts that come into their mind without their bidding; they are instruments or "mediums" through which the universal principle of mind thinks, but they are unable to originate a thought, much less to project it into objectivity through the power of the will. He who has gained the power to hold on to a thought may project it upon another, and the process will be facilitated if the "receiver" is in a passive state of sleep, hypnotism, or somnambulism. The expression "suggestion" is in such cases entirely inappropriate to describe what takes place; "Induction" would be more appropriate; for the passive person not merely acts upon the suggestion of his "magnetizer," but his will becomes a helpless instrument through which the thoughts of the former are induced to act upon the subjective or objective plane.

We usually look upon a thing as real if it is seen alike by several persons, while if only one person professes to see it, it being invisible to others, we may call it illusive; but all impressions produce a certain state of the mind, and a person must be in a condition—or state of mind—to enter into a relation with that state which the impression produces. All persons being in the same state of mind, and receiving the same impression, will perceive the same thing, but if their states differ, their perceptions will differ, although the impression coming to their consciousness will be the same. A horse or a lion may be seen alike by everyone who has his normal senses developed; because all men having normal human senses, may be in the same mental state, but if one is excited by fear, or has his attention otherwise absorbed, his mental state will change and his perception will differ from that of others. A drunkard in a state of *delirium tremens* may believe to see worms and snakes crawling over his body. His experience tells him that they have no external existence. Nevertheless they are horrible realities to him, and he seeks to rid himself of their presence. They really exist for him as the products of his own mental condition, but they do not exist for others who do not share that condition. But if others were to enter the same state they would see the same things, and he who sees them can make others see them, provided he is able to communicate to them his own consciousness—that is to say, his own mental state.

Our perceptions therefore differ—not only in proportion as the impressions coming from the objects of our perception differ— but also according to our capacity to receive such impressions, or according to our own mental states. If we could develop a new sense we would believe to be in a new world, and if our capacity to receive impressions were restricted to only one sense, we would only be able to conceive of that which could become manifest to us through that sense and the world which we could perceive would be very limited. Let us suppose the existence of a being whose mode of perception were entirely different from our own, and who could enter into only one state of consciousness; for instance, that of hate. Having all his consciousness concentrated into his guiding passion, he could become aware of nothing else but of hate. Such a "god of hate," incapable of entering into any other mental state, could perceive no other states but those corresponding with his own. To such a being the whole world would be dark and void, our oceans and mountains, our forests and rivers, would have no existence for him ; but wherever a man or an animal would burn with hate, there would be perhaps a lurid glow perceivable by him through the darkness, which would attract his attention and attract him, and on his approach that glow may burst into a flame in which the individual from whom it proceeded may be consumed. Any other mental state or passion may serve for a similar illustration. Hate attracts hate, and Love attracts love, and a person full of hate is as incapable to love as a being full of love is incapable to hate ; both are mental states, which, after a person has fully entered them, cannot be changed at will.

Man is that what he really wills. His whole being is nothing else but the ultimate product of a will acting in him ; not of his imaginary will, but of the real will, which is one and divine.

The *Bhagawad Gita* says : " Those that are born under an evil destiny " (having acquired evil tendencies by their conduct in former lives) " know not what it is to proceed in virtue or to recede from vice ; nor is purity, veracity, or the practice of morality to be found in them. They say the world is without beginning and without end, and without an Ishwar, that all things are conceived in the junction of the senses, and that attraction is the only cause." *

Those who believe that everything exists in consequence of the attraction of two principles, forget that there could be no attraction if there were not some cause that produces that attraction, and that the attraction would cease as soon as the cause that produced it would cease to exist. They are the deluded followers of a doctrine which they themselves cannot seriously believe. They agree that out of nothing nothing can come, and yet they believe that the power of attraction was caused by nothing, and that it continues to exist without a cause. They are the followers of the absurd *Two* which has no real existence, because the eternal *One* divided into two parts would not become two Ones but the two halves

---

* Bhagawad Gita, L. xvi.

of a divided One.   One is the number of Unity, and Two
is Division ; the One divided into two ceases to exist as a
One, and nothing new is thereby produced.   If the plan
for the construction of the world had been made according
to the ideas of the followers of Dualism, nothing could
have come into existence that did not already exist at a
time when nothing existed, because action and reaction, if
any existed, would have been of equal power, and there
could be no progressing of anything existing at present.
If *Ormuzd* (the principle of good) were of equal power
with *Ahriman* (the principle of evil) there would be an
end to all progression, and the state of the world from
all eternity would have been the same ; but behind Ormuzd
and Ahriman is the nameless and *invisible fire*, the *law of
evolution*, and Ormuzd continually conquers Ahriman by
the inherent power of good.   If the Parsi worships the fire,
he worships the invisible power of Good.   The visible fire
and the visible sun are the symbols which represent to
him the invisible power and spiritual sun, and it would be
difficult to find any symbols in nature more fit to represent
the infinite power of good and light, by which the dark
power of evil will be fully conquered in the end.

Whatever this power of good may be, it is beyond the
capacity of finite man to give it an appropriate name, or to
describe it, because it is beyond the comprehension of
mortal man.   It has been called " *God*," and as such it
has " many faces," because its aspect differs according to
the standpoint from which we behold it.   It is the *Supreme
cause*, from which everything comes into existence ; it must
be *absolute consciousness*, *wisdom* and *power*, *love*, *intelligence* and *life*, because these attributes exist in its manifestations, and could not have come into existence without
it.   It has been called *Space*, because everything exists in
space, but space itself is incomprehensible to us, although
we exist in it and are surrounded by it.   *Space* is a term
which has no meaning, unless it means extension, and extension is an attribute of *Matter*, but matter cannot exist
without *Motion*, and the motion of matter is caused by the
*Law*.   Space, Matter and Motion in the absolute are incomprehensible to us, because man being a relative being
can only comprehend that to which he stands in relation.
Being bound to a form he can only know that which exists
relatively to form.

*The Absolute*, independent of relations and conditions, is the original cause of all manifestations of power. An attempt to describe it would be equivalent with an attempt to describe something which has no attributes, or of whose attributes we can form no conception. When Gautama Buddha was asked to describe the supreme source of all beings, he remained silent, because those who have reached a state in which they can realize what it is, have no words to describe it,* and those who cannot realize it would not be able to comprehend the description. To describe the absolute we must invest it with comprehensible attributes, and it then ceases to be *The Absolute* and becomes *relative*. Therefore all theological discussions about the nature of "God" are useless, because "God" has no natural attributes, but *Nature* is His manifestation. If we use the word "God" in its legitimate meaning, as "*Good*," then to deny the existence of God is an absurdity, equivalent to denying one's own existence, because all existence can be nothing else but a manifestation of life, as "Good." To declare to possess an intellectual knowledge of God is equally absurd, because we cannot know anything of which we cannot conceive. He can only be spiritually known, but not scientifically described, and the fight between so-called *Deists* and *Atheists* is a mere quarrel about words which have no definite meaning. Every man is himself a manifestation of God, and as each man's character differs from that of every other, so each man's idea of God differs from that of the rest, and each one has a God (an ideal) of his own ; only when they all attain the same, the highest ideal, will they all have the same God.

To him who does not believe in the power of Good, the power of Good does not exist, and its existence cannot be demonstrated to him. To him who feels the presence of Good, Good exists, and to him its existence cannot be disputed away. The ignorant cannot be made to realize the existence of knowledge unless he becomes knowing ; those who know cannot have their knowledge reasoned away unless they forget what they know. The caricatures of gods set up by the various churches as representations of the only true God are merely attempts to describe that which cannot be described. As every man has a highest

---

* 2 Corinth, xii. 4.

ideal (a god) of his own, which is a symbol of his aspirations, so every church has its peculiar god, who is an outgrowth or a product of evolution of the ideal necessities of
that collective body called a church.   They are all true
gods *to them*, because they answer their needs, and as the
requirements of the church change, so change their gods ;
old gods are discarded and new ones put into their places.
The god of the Christian differs from that of the Jews, and
the Christian god of the nineteenth century is very different
from the one that lived at the time of Torquemada and
Peter Arbues, and was pleased with torture and *Autos-da-
Fé*.   As long as men are imperfect their gods will be imperfect ; as they become more perfect their gods will grow
in perfection, and when all men are equally perfect they
will all have the same perfect "God," the same highest
spiritual ideal and the same universal reality, recognized
alike by science and by religion ; because there can be
only one supreme ideal, one absolute Truth, whose realization is Wisdom, whose manifestation is power expressed
in Nature, and whose most perfect production is ideal
Man.

There are seven steps on the ladder, representing the
religious development of mankind : On the first stage man
resembles an animal, conscious only of his instincts and
bodily desires, without any conception of the divine element.   On the second he begins to have a presentiment
of the existence of something higher.   On the third he
begins to seek for that higher element, but his lower elements are still preponderating over the higher aspirations.
On the fourth his lower and higher desires are counter-
balancing each other.   At times he seeks for the higher,
at other times he is again attracted to the lower.   On the
fifth he anxiously seeks for the divine, but seeking it in
the external he cannot find it.   He then begins to seek for
it within himself.   On the sixth he finds the divine element
within himself and develops spiritual self-consciousness,
which on the seventh grows into self-knowledge.   Having
arrived at the sixth, his spiritual senses begin to become
alive and active, and he will then be able to recognize the
presence of other spiritual entities, existing on the same
plane.   His *will* then becomes free from every selfish
desire, his *thoughts* become obedient to his will, his *word*
becomes an act, and he may then rightfully be called an
*Adept*.

# CHAPTER III.

## FORM.

*"The Universe is a thought of God."—Paracelsus.*

ACCORDING to Plato the primordial essence is an emanation of the *Demiurgic Mind*, which contains from eternity the idea of the natural world within itself, and which idea *He* produces out of Himself by the power of His will.   This doctrine seems to be almost as old as the existence of reasoning man on this globe.   It contains essentially the same truth which has been taught by the ancient *Rishis*, and has been expressed—although, perhaps, in other terms —by the deepest thinkers of all ages, apparently from the first *planetary spirit*, that made his appearance on this earth, down to the modern philosophers who teach that the world is a product of ideation and will,* although the latter seem to forget that will and ideation cannot exist independently of something that wills and thinks, but are the functions of some unknown principle or Cause.

This *One* unknown cause comes into knowable existence when the unmanifested Absolute manifesting itself assumes a threefold aspect.   Upon this truth is based the doctrine of the *Trinity*, which we find represented in the most ancient religious systems of the East as well as in Christian symbolism, and without which even so-called "rational-istic science" becomes irrational ; because if the "mate-rialist" (correctly) states that there can be no matter without motion and no motion without matter, he must— to remain logical—add that the existence of matter and the activity of motion must have some cause.   He may not know that cause, but the cause nevertheless is there, even if we know nothing at all about it, except that it is.   The

---

* Schopenhauer : "Die Welt als Wille und Vorstellung."

trinity of rational science is therefore *Action*, *Reaction*, and *Causation*, or, in other words, *Matter*, *Motion*, and *Cause* (Potency).

The great Christian Mystic, *Jacob Boehme*, describes the Great First Cause as a trinity of will, thought, and action. His doctrine corresponds to that which is taught in the East, regarding the three emanations of Brahm, and of which that German shoemaker could at that time have hardly known anything, if he had not been an *Illuminate*. He says, in his book on " *The Three Principles*," that by the activity of the *Will-Fire* at the *Centre* the eternal consciousness of the latter was reflected in Space as in a mirror, and from this activity *Light* and *Life* were born. He then describes, how by the action radiating from the incomprehensible centre, radiating into the element of Matter, and the subsequent reaction from the periphery toward the centre, rotation, mixture of the essential substances and complexedness were caused, and how at last the *Ether*, the world of forms, came into existence, and grew into material density. Thus the will of the *Father* (Love) sent out the *Son* (Life), and through that action the power of the Father in the Son (Light), or the " *Holy Ghost* " became manifest, and its manifestation is the visible and invisible universe in one, with all its suns, stars, planets, their forms and inhabitants, with all the angels and demons, devas, elementals, men and animals, or in other words, with all the energies and powers and forms of the visible and invisible side of nature.

This trinity manifests itself on three different *planes* or *modes of action*, that have been termed *Matter*, *Soul*, and *Spirit*, or, according to the symbolism of ancient occult science, *Earth*, *Water*, and *Fire*. The *One* becomes manifest in the *Three*, but the Three is a whole and does not consist of three parts, of which one comes into succession after another, it springs into existence at once. *Reaction* cannot exist without *Action*, and both are due to a co-existing *Cause*. The *Father* does not become a Father before the arrival of the *Son*, and that which produces the Son is the power resting in the Father, his *Will* manifesting itself as the Spirit pervading all nature. There is no motion without matter or without cause ; no cause without an effect and without something upon which an effect is produced. There can be no extension and dur-

ation or "*Space*" without matter or motion, and no form
without space.   Absolute space is invisible, and we cannot
conceive of its form.   We cannot imagine it to be without
any limits, nor can we conceive of any limits to it with no
space beyond it ; relative space is limited and exists as a
form.   There can be no *empty* space, because "space "
means extension, and we cannot conceive of "nothing,"
nor can "nothing " have an extension.   Forms are—so to
say—space which has been rendered objective, crystalized
into some shape which may or may not be perceptible to
our senses, and no form can exist but in space.

These forms come into existence by the action of the
three elements, *Fire, Water* and *Earth,* neither one of
which exists without the other two ; because they are not
three different things *per se,* but only three aspects of the
eternal One.

*Spirit* or " Fire " is an immaterial, formless, and
universal element.   It is the matrix in which everything
was contained before it was thrown into objectivity by the
awakening of its Will.   It is the Will itself ; the source of
all power and the substance of which all is made.   " God
is a fire, to which none can approach except through the
Son."   The dark fire cannot be known to man except
through the light which emanates from it.   Life would never
be known, unless it becomes manifest, and to become
manifest, a form is required.   No magical process has ever
been accomplished without the magic fire, and to learn to
know the true nature of that fire is the great desideratum
of every occultist.

*Soul* or " Water " or " Light " is a semi-material element.
It is the organizing element of corporeal forms.   The soul
of microcosmic man corresponds to the soul of the macrocosm.   It is the playground of the elemental forces of nature,
existing in the astral plane.   It penetrates and surrounds
the planets as it surrounds and penetrates the bodies of
men and animals and all other bodies and forms, and all
material forms are—so to say—only " *materialized souls,*"
that will perish after the light has been extracted from
them.   The light is the redeemer from darkness on every
plane of existence.   It comes from the fire ; but it is not
itself the fire.   It is a principle in itself, and its attributes
are different from those of the fire.   It is itself the life of
everything.

*Matter* or "Earth" is an invisible material element pervading all space. Condensed by the organizing power of the soul, it clothes the forms of the latter and renders them visible on the physical plane. But not all forms are visible to the physical sense of sight, the material forms which we see are not the only forms in existence. The invisible world, hidden in the visible one, could be discovered by man if he were able to draw the veil from matter, because within the material form resides the invisible element of which the visible form is only the external expression.

From the interaction of the three primordial elements, Spirit, Soul and Matter, four compound principles become manifest, and these four added to the three former represent seven principles. This sevenfold division in the constitution of the Macrocosmos and Microcosmos was known to the ancient sages of the East as well as to Western Adepts, such as Paracelsus and others, and has recently been brought prominently to the notice of the public by the teachings of the Eastern Adepts.

As a matter of course, however, all such divisions are arbitrary, for man is an undivided whole, and we may divide his constitution in as many parts as we please for the purpose of facilitating this study. We may look upon him as a unity or in a dual aspect as a manifestation of Spirit acting in Matter, or as a trinity of Spirit, Body and Soul, or in his fourfold aspect as a representation of four states of consciousness; as a full accord of five harmonious powers, as a compound of four elements joined to the fifth, the quintessence of all things, as a revelation of six visible powers emanating from a seventh but invisible centre, etc. The sevenfold classification recommends itself on account of its simplicity, and because it can be easily seen to harmonize with the customary threefold classification.

Jacob Boehme teaches that of these seven principles or natural qualities, the first and the seventh are one, and refer to the Father; the second and sixth as one refer to the Son, and likewise the third and fifth to the Holy Spirit.

It has been stated as follows:

    1. A—The element of *Matter A'kâsa,* represented by "*Earth.*"

2. AB.—A combination of Matter and Soul, known
   as the *Astral Body*, a mixture of "Earth and
   Water."

3. B.—The *Soul*, known as the *Perisprit*, or the
   animal principle in man, represented by "Water."

4. ABC.—The *Essence of Life*, a combination of
   Matter, Soul, and Spirit, "Earth, Water, and
   Fire."

5. AC.—The *Mind*, a combination of Matter and
   Spirit, or "Earth and Fire" (the principle of
   Intellectuality).

6. BC.—The *Spiritual Soul*, a combination of Soul
   and pure Spirit, or "Water and Fire" (the
   principle of Spiritual Intelligence).

7. C.—Pure *Spirit* or "Fire," the incomprehensible
   First Great Cause.*

The division adopted by Paracelsus and in "Esoteric
Buddhism" is identical with the above, with the exception
that the *Jiva* or *Vitality* is counted as the second, and the
Astral body as the third principle; as follows :—1. The
physical body (Stoolasariram).   2. Vitality (Mumia).   3.
Astral Body (Sidereal body).   4. Animal Soul.   5. Intellectual Soul.   6. Spiritual Soul.   7. Spirit.

It is said that this division was also known to the
ancient Jews, and that the Hebrew Alphabet, consisting of
22 letters, was made with reference to it; because the
*three* in *seven* states produces *twelve* symbols, and 3 + 7
+ 12 = 22.

*Jacob Boehme* describes the action of these seven
principles in his own way.  He says :

"When the light was born at the *Centre*, the (spiritual)
Sun, and reacted upon the central fire, a terrible battle
ensued, causing an igneous eruption, and from the sun
proceeded a flash of storm and fire, an element, called
*Mars*.  Taken captive by the light, it assumed a place
and continues to agitate all nature.  The light, having
been enchained by Mars, proceeded further in the rigidity

---

* The Sanscrit terms for the seven principles are: 1, Pracriti ;
2, Lingasariram ; 3, Kamarupa ; 4, Jiva ; 5, Manas ; 6, Buddhi ;
7, Atma (Param-Atma, Brahmam, Parabrahm).—See "Five years of
Theosophy," p. 153.

of the element of matter (*Saturn*), and became corporeal in forms.

"Above the element called *Jupiter*, in the adstringent anguish of the whole body of this solar system, the *Sun* was not powerful enough to mitigate the horror, and there arose *Saturn*, the element, opposite to meekness, producing rigidity. The *Sun* is the heart of Nature, the Centre of Life ; *Saturn* represents corporeal nature or *Matter*. Without the action of the Life coming from the *Sun* upon *Matter*, there would be no production of forms. *Venus* is the daughter of the *Sun*. She rises out of the *water* of the universe, penetrates the hard element of matter and enkindles *Love*. *Mercury* (like the others, an invisible element) represents the principle of *sound*, or the *Word*, by whose activity the sleeping germs of everything are awakened to life. *Mercury* is continually impregnated by the substance of the *Sun*. In it is found the knowledge of that which existed before the light had penetrated into the solar centre. The *Moon* was produced directly from the *Sun* at the time of his becoming material. The *Moon* is the *spouse* of the *Sun*. She is the *Eve*, who was made out of a part of *Adam*, while the latter was asleep."

In this classification The *Sun* represents Wisdom, the *Moon*, Imagination, *Mercury*, the Mind substance, *Venus*, the Astral Body, *Mars*, the principle of Life, *Jupiter*, the element of Power, *Saturn*, primordial Matter ; but the significations of these planets differ according to the aspects we take of them.

All forms are the expression of either one or more of these elementary principles, and exist as long as their respective principles are active in them. They are not necessarily visible, because their visibility depends on their power to reflect light. Invisible gases may be solidified by pressure and cold, and rendered visible and tangible, and the most solid substances may be made invisible and intangible by the application of heat. The products of cosmic thought are not all sufficiently materialized to be visible to the physical eye, and in reality we see only a very small part of their sum. No one doubts that there is an immense amount of invisible matter in the universe, whether cometary or otherwise, and every improvement in the manufacture of optic instruments brings new realms of forms and life to our perception.

Each transformation of activity gives rise to changes of forms, and may bring new forms into existence. Solid ice may be transformed into invisible vapor, and condensed again into a tangible form. The more matter expands and the more its motion is made active, the more will it escape the perception of the physical senses, but its expansion does not necessarily render it less powerful to act. Steam is more powerful than water, and overheated to a certain degree it evolves electricity, and may become very destructive. The more the element of matter is condensed, the more inert does it appear; the more it expands, the farther will its sphere of activity reach.

All bodies have their invisible spheres. Their visible spheres are limited by the periphery of their visible forms; their invisible spheres extend farther into space. Their spheres cannot be always detected by physical instruments, but they nevertheless exist, and under certain conditions their existence can be proved to the senses. The sphere of an odoriferous body can be perceived by the organ of smell, the sphere of a magnet by the approach of iron, the sphere of a man or an animal by that most delicate of all instruments, the abnormally sensitive brain.

These spheres are the magnetic, coloric, odic, or luminous auras and emanations belonging to every object in space. Such an emanation may sometimes be seen as the *Aurora Borealis* in the polar regions of our planet, or as the photosphere of the sun during an eclipse. The " glory " around the head of a saint is no poetical fiction, no more than the sphere of light radiating from a precious stone. As each sun has its system of planets revolving around it, so each body is surrounded by smaller centres of energy evolving from the common centre, and partaking of the attributes of that centre. Copper, Carbon, and Arsenic, for instance, send out auras of red; Lead and Sulphur emit blue colors; Gold, Silver and Antimony, green; and Iron emits all the colors of the rainbow. Plants, animals, and men emit similar colors according to their characteristics; persons of a high and spiritual character have beautiful auras of white and blue, gold and green, in various tints; while low natures emit principally dark red emanations, which in brutal and vulgar or villainous persons darken almost to black, and the collective auras of bodies of men or plants or animals, of cities and countries, correspond to their predominant characteristics, so that a person whose sense of perception is sufficiently developed may see the state of the intellectual and moral development of a place or a country by observing the sphere of its emanations.

These spheres expand from the centre, and their periphery grows in proportion to the intensity of the energy acting within the centre. Who can measure the extent of the sphere of thought and the depth of the regions to which it may penetrate, who can determine the distance to which the power of Will and Love and spiritual Perception will act? We know the sphere of a rose by the odor that proceeds from the latter if we have the power to smell, we know the character of the mind of a man if we enter the sphere of his thoughts, provided that our inner senses are sufficiently developed to become conscious of the state of his mind.

The quality of psychic emanations depends on the state of activity of the centre from which they originate, for each thing and each being is tinctured with that particular principle which exists at the invisible centre, and from this centre receives the form of its own character or attributes. They are symbols of the states of the soul of each form, they indicate the state of the emotions. Each emotion corresponds to a certain color: Love corresponds to blue, Desire to red, Benevolence to green, and these colours may induce corresponding emotions in other souls, especially if the emotional element is guided by reason. Blue has a soothing effect, and may tranquilize a maniac or subdue a fever; Red excites to passion, a steer may be furious at the sight of a red cloth, and an unreasoning mob become infuriated at the sight of blood. This chemistry of the soul is not any more wonderful than the facts known in physical chemistry, and these processes take place according to the same law which causes Chloride of Silver to turn from white into black if exposed to blue or white light, while ruby red or yellow light leaves it unchanged.

The thoughts of the Universal Mind expressed in matter on any plane, comprise all the forms of the mineral, vegetable, and animal kingdoms on Earth, including the bodies and souls of all beings. Their physical forms are the expressions of three principles, and each material form contains within itself its ethereal counterpart, which may, under certain conditions, separate itself from the more material part, or be extracted therefrom by the hands of an Adept. These astral parts may be corporified and be rendered visible. Actually all bodies, even the most solid rocks, are nothing else but corporified astral appearances, whose innermost substance is the fire whose light is their life. Every individual being is a flame in creation whose light differs from others according to its own particular attributes.

Astral forms continue to exist for a while after the visible bodies to which they belong have had their fire extinguished. The astral corpses of the dead may be seen by the clairvoyant hovering over the graves, bearing the resemblance of the once living man. They may be artifically infused with life and with a borrowed consciousness, and made use of in the practices of *Necromancy* and *Black Magic*, or be attracted to " spiritual seances" to represent the spirits of the dead.

There are persons in whom this principle—either in consequence of constitutional peculiarities or in consequence of disease—is not very firmly united with the physical body, and may become separated from it for a short period.* Such persons are suitable " *mediums* " for so-called *spirit-materializations*, their ethereal counterparts may appear separated from their bodies and assume the visible form of some person either living or dead. It receives its new mask by the unconscious or conscious thoughts of the persons present, by the reflections thrown out from their memories and minds, or it may be made to represent other characters by influences invisible to the physical eye.

As the brain is the central organ for the circulation of nerve-fluid, and as the heart is the organ for the circulation of the blood, so the spleen is the organ from which the astral elements draw their vitality, and in certain diseases, where the action of the spleen is impeded, this " double " of a person may involuntarily separate itself from the body. It is nothing very unusual that a sick

---

* This intimate relation of the astral form and the physical body is often illustrated at so-called exposures of " spiritual mediums." If a materialized form is soiled by ink or soot, the coloring matter will afterwards be found on the corresponding part of the medium's body, because, when the astral form re-enters that body, it will leave the soiling matter on the corresponding parts of the latter.

person feels " as if he were not himself " or as if another
person was lying in the same bed with him, and that he
himself were that other.   Such cases of " Doppelgaengers,"
Wraiths, Apparitions, Ghosts, etc., caused by the separation of the Lingasariram from the physical form, can be
found in many works treating of mystic phenomena
occurring in nature.*

Usually these astral forms are without consciousness
and without any life of their own ; but they may be made
to be the seat of life and consciousness, by withdrawing
the life from the material form and concentrating it into
the astral body.   A person who has succeeded in doing
this may step out of his physical form and live independent
of the latter, and an Adept may even entirely remain outside his physical body and continue to live in his ethereal
and invisible form.†

The forms in the realm of Soul, in which the fourth
principle is the essential element, are still more ethereal and
more independent of a definite form.   This will not seem
incomprehensible, if we remember that they too are forms
of thought, and that a thought or an idea may take a
defined shape or may remain shapeless and undefined.   If
we, for instance, hear the word " animal," we conceive of
a living being of some shape or other, but give our conception no definite form ; but if the animal is described as
one with whose form we are acquainted, the picture of that
form will come to the consciousness of the mind.   Concentration of thought gives shape to ideas and condenses
the formless into forms.   Purely spiritual or abstract ideas,
such as love, faith, hope, charity, etc., have no shapes and
cannot be conceived as forms, they can at best be symbolized by forms which are made to guide our thoughts
towards the formless ideas whose attributes they are
intended to bring before our imagination.

---

* Adolphe D'Assier : " L'humanité posthume."

† The stories of fakirs who have been buried alive for months and
resurrected afterwards might here be used as illustration.   They are too
well known to need repetition in this place.   Moreover, phenomena,
however well attested they may be, can never stand in the place of
knowledge ; they furnish no explanation of the mysterious laws of
nature.   The occurrence of phenomena proves nothing but that they
occur.   Real knowledge is never attained by the observation of external
phenomena, it can only be attained by the knowledge of self.

Among the ancients it was customary to make such personifications of impersonal powers, and to describe their functions in symbols and allegories. The first Christians adopted that system. Modern religionism believes those allegories to represent dead persons and peoples, and knows nothing about the living principles which they represent.

As there are three elements represented in the three kingdoms of the physical plane, so there are three kingdoms of Elementals existing on the astral plane, corresponding to the elements of fire, water, and earth. Individual forms on that plane may often make their presence felt to men or animals, but under ordinary circumstances they cannot be seen. They may, however, be seen by the clairvoyant, and, under certain conditions, even assume visible and tangible shapes. Their bodies are of an elastic semi-material essence, ethereal enough so as not to be detected by the physical sight, and they may change their forms according to certain laws. Bulwer Lytton says: "Life is one all-pervading principle, and even the thing that seems to die and putrefy but engenders new life and changes to new forms of matter. Reasoning then by analogy—if not a leaf, if not a drop of water, but is no less than yonder star—a habitable and breathing world— common sense would suffice to teach that the circumfluent Infinite, which you call space—the boundless Impalpable which divides the earth from the moon and stars—is filled also with its correspondent and appropriate life."

And further on he says : " In the drop of water you see animalculæ vary ; how vast and terrible are some of these monster-mites as compared with others. Equally so with the inhabitants of the atmosphere. Some of surpassing wisdom, some of horrible malignity, some hostile as fiends to man, others gentle as messengers between Earth and Heaven." *

Our sceptical age is accustomed to admire in such descriptions the " fancy " of the writer, never suspecting that they were intended to convey a truth ; but there are many witnesses to testify—if it were necessary—that such invisible but substantial and variously shaped beings exist, and that they, by the educated will of man, can be made

---

* Bulwer Lytton : " Zanoni."

conscious, intelligent, visible, and even useful to man. This assertion is supported by the testimony found in the writings of Rosicrucians, Cabbalists, Alchemists, and Adepts, as well as in the ancient books of wisdom of the East and in the Bible of the Christians.

Such existences are, however, not necessarily personal beings. They may be impersonal forces, acquiring form, and life, and consciousness by their contact with man. The *Gnomes* and *Sylphes*, the *Undines* and *Salamanders*, do not entirely belong to the realm of fable, although they may be something very different of what the ignorant believe them to be. How insignificant and little appears individual man in the infinity of the universe! and yet there is only a comparatively insignificant part of the universe revealed to him by the senses. Could he see the worlds within worlds above, beneath, and everywhere, swarming with beings whose existence he does not suspect, while they, perhaps, know nothing of his existence, he would be overwhelmed with terror and seek for a god to protect him ; and yet there are none of these beings higher or as powerful as the spiritual man who has learned to know his powers, and in whom his own god has awakened to consciousness and strength.*

The beings of the *spiritual* plane are such as have once been men, their constitution is beyond the comprehension of those that are not their equals, and their ethereal forms in a state of perfection we cannot conceive. Having out-grown the necessity of residing in a form they enter the state of the formless, approaching evermore the Universal Mind, from which the power called *Man* emanated at the beginning. We may look upon a personal man as a single note in the great orchestra composing the world, and upon a *Dhyan Chohan†* as a full accord or a compound of notes in the symphony of the gods. There may be unhar-monious compositions of notes in music, and there are evil spiritualities as there is darkness in contradistinction to light, because a high grade of intelligence may be used for vile purposes ; but the good spirituality cannot be con-

---

* Paracelsus gives detailed descriptions of these beings.

† Son of Wisdom (Angel).

quered by evil, because it is protected by wisdom, which is essentially good, and of which evil is but the reverse.

There are good and evil spiritual beings, and either class may possess a great deal of knowledge and power; but only the good—that is to say, kind and benevolent powers, can be considered *wise*—because wisdom means a union of knowledge and love, from which the highest powers spring. To be wise, is to be good and beautiful and true. Evil spiritualities may be very strong, but they cannot overcome the good ones, because they lack wisdom, and wisdom is itself the divine will of God.

What is a spirit? Nothing else but a thought rendered alive by the will; a ray of light, receiving its impulse by the fire hidden therein. A thought without will is unsubstantial, like an image in a mirror; made active by the will, it assumes life, substance and form. We all are spirits as long as we have the will; but when the will leaves a man, his life goes with it, and his body, the shadow, fades away.

The realm of the Soul is the realm of the emotions. Emotions are not merely the results of physiological processes depending on causes coming from the physical plane, but they belong to a form of life on the astral plane, they often come and go without any apparent cause. The state of the weather, or circumstances over which we have no control, may cause certain emotions independently of our state of physical health. A person entering a room where every one is laughing is liable to participate in the common emotion without knowing the cause of the hilarity; a whole crowd may be swayed by the intense emotion of a speaker, although they may not fully understand what he says; one hysterical woman in a hospital ward may create an epidemic of hysteria among the other women, and a whole congregation may become excited by the harangue of an emotional exhorter, no matter whether his language is foolish or wise. A sudden accumulation of emotion or energy on the astral plane may kill a person as quickly as a sudden explosion of powder. We hear of persons who were "transfixed by terror" or "paralyzed by fear." In such cases the astral consciousness having become abnormally active at the expense of the consciousness on the physical plane, the activity of life on the physical plane may cease, and the affected person may faint, or perhaps die.

All forms come into existence according to certain laws. The solar microscope shows how, in a solution of salt, a centre of matter is formed, and how to that centre its kindred forces are attracted, crystalizing around it, and becoming solid and firm. Each kind of salt produces the peculiar crystals that belong to its class and no other, however often the process may be repeated. In the vegetable kingdom we see that the seed of one plant will attract to itself those forces which it requires to produce a plant resembling its parent; the seed of an apple-tree can produce nothing else but an apple-tree, and an acorn can grow into nothing else but an oak. The principal characteristics of an animal will be those that belong to its parents, and the external appearance of a man will correspond more or less to that of the race and family in which he was born.

As every mathematical point in space may develop into a living and conscious and visible being, after once a certain centre of energy (a germ) has been formed, so in the invisible realm of the soul astral forms may come into existence wherever the necessary conditions for their growth exist. In the same manner as an active motion on the physical plane may attract the universally diffused matter around a common centre, likewise an active emotion on the astral plane may crystalize around a thought into an invisible but nevertheless substantial entity, which may have an existence of long or short duration according to the intensity with which the forces composing it are concentrated upon its centre. As the forms on the physical plane correspond to the characters of the forces prevailing upon that plane, so the forms on the astral plane are expressions of the characteristics of the prevailing emotions on that plane. They may manifest themselves either in beautiful or in horrible shapes, because every form is only the symbol or the expression of the character which it represents.

The forms in the mineral kingdom are expressive of forces acting in straight and angular lines, those of the vegetable kingdom represent radiating and curved lines; the animal forms are expressions of forces acting on the astral plane, and the inhabitants of the astral plane may resemble visible animal or human forms. In those forms which belong exclusively to the astral plane the higher spiritual energies are not active. They may have a consciousness of their own and realize their existence, but under ordinary circumstances they have no more intelligence than animals, and cannot act intelligently and in accordance with reason. They follow their blind attraction, as iron is attracted to a magnet, and wherever they find an excessive amount of emotion evolved by a human being they are attracted thither as to a common centre, and their accumulation increases the activity of that centre and increases the size of its sphere. We therefore often see that if one emotion is not controlled in the beginning it may grow and become uncontrollable. Some people have died of grief and some others of joy.

But if these unintelligent forms are infused with the principle of intelligence proceeding from man, they become intelligent and act in accordance with the dictates of the master from which they receive their will and intelligence, and who may employ them for good or for evil. Every emotion that arises in man may combine with the astral forces of nature and create a being, which may be perceived by persons possessing abnormal faculties of perception as an active and living entity. Every sentiment which finds expression in word or action may call into existence a living entity on the astral plane. Some of these forms may be very enduring according to the intensity and duration of the thought that created them, while others are the creations of one moment and vanish in the next.

There are numerous cases on record in which some person or other having committed some crime is described as having been persecuted for years by some avenging demon, who would appear objectively and disappear again. Such demons may be, and perhaps can be nothing else but the products of the involuntary action of the imagination of their victims; but they are nevertheless real to the latter. They may be called into existence by memory and remorse, and their images, existing in the mind, may become objective by fear, because fear is a repulsive function; it instinctively repulses the object of which a man is afraid, and by repelling the image from the centre towards the periphery of the sphere of mind, that image may be rendered objective.

Instances are known in which persons have been driven to suicide, hoping thereby to escape these persecuting demons. Such demons are said to have in some cases taken even a tangible form. But whether tangible or intangible, the substance of which they are formed is merely a projection of substance of the person to whom they thus appear. They are, so to say, that person himself, and if the latter could injure or kill such a "ghost," he would merely thereby injure or kill his own body.*

An Adept in a letter to Mr. Sinnett says :

"Every thought of man upon being evolved passes into another world and becomes an active entity by associating itself—coalescing we might term it—with an Elemental—that is to say, with one of the semi-intelligent forces of the kingdoms. It survives as an active intelligence—a creature of the mind's begetting—for a longer or shorter period, proportionate with the original intensity of the cerebral action which generated it. Thus, a good thought is perpetuated as an active, beneficent power, an evil one as a maleficent demon. And so man is continually peopling his current in space with the offspring of his fancies, desires, impulses, and passions ; a current which reacts upon any sensitive or nervous organization, which comes in contact with it, in proportion to its dynamic intensity...... The Adept evolves these shapes consciously, other men throw them off unconsciously." *

---

* In the "Lives of the Saints," and in the history of witchcraft, we often find instances of the appearance of " doubles " in visible and even tangible forms. Such phenomena may take place in mediumistic persons, if by contrary emotions the Will becomes divided, acting in two different directions, and projecting thereby two forms; for it is the spiritual Will of man that creates subjective forms, consciously or unconsciously, and under certain conditions they may become objective and visible.

As an illustration of this law we may cite from the *Acta Sanctorum* an episode in the life of Saint Dominic. He was once called to the bedside of a sick person, who told him that Christ had appeared to him. The saint answered that this was impossible, and that the apparition had been produced by the devil, because only holy persons could have an apparition of Christ. As he said so, a doubt as to whether the apparition seen may not have been a true one after all entered his mind, and immediately a division of consciousness was produced, which caused the double of Dominic to appear at the other side of the patient's bed. The two Dominics were seen by the patient, and heard to dispute with each other, and while one Dominic asserted that the apparition had been the work of the devil, the other one maintained that it was the true Christ. The two Dominics were so exactly identical, that the

This testimony is corroborated by one coming from another source, and proving that to create subjective forms it is not necessary to give a distinct shape to our thoughts by the power of imagination, but that each state of feeling or sentiment may find expression in subjective forms, whether or not we may be conscious of their existence. A form is a state of mind, and a sentiment is a state of mind; a sentiment expressed will be represented by a corresponding form.

Mr. Whitworth, a clairvoyant, describes how in his youth, while seeing a German professor perform on an organ, he noticed a host of appearances moving about the keyboard —veritable Lilliputian sprites, fairies, and gnomes, astonishingly minute in size, yet as perfect in form and features as any of the larger people in the room. He described them as being divided into sexes and clothed in a most fantastic manner; in form, appearance and movement they were in perfect accord with the theme.

" In the quick measures, how madly they danced, waving their plumed hats and fans in very ecstasy, and darting to and fro in inconceivable rapidity, with feet beating time in rain-like patter of accord! Quick as a flash, when the music changed to the solemn cadence of a march for the dead, the airy things vanished, and in their place came black-robed gnomes, dressed like cowled monks, sour-faced Puritans, or mutes in the black garb of a funeral procession! Strangest of all, on every tiny face was expressed the sentiment of the music, so that I could instantly understand the thought and feeling that was intended to be conveyed. In a wild burst of sounding grief came a rush of mothers, tear-eyed and with dishevelled hair, beating their breasts and wailing pious lamentations over their dead loved ones. These would be followed by

patient did not know, which of them was the true saint, and which one his image, and he could not make up his mind what to believe; until at last the saint called upon God to assist him,—that is to say, he concentrated his will-power again within himself; his consciousness became again a unity, and the " double" disappeared from view.

Absurd as such stories may appear to our " enlightened age," their absurdity ceases when the occult laws of nature, and the fact of the possibilities of a *double consciousness* are understood.

* A. P. Sinnett: " The Occult World."

plumed knights with shield and spear, and host of fiery troops, mounted or foot, red-handed in the fiery strife of bloody battle, as the clang of martial music came leaping from the keyboard, and ever, as each change brought its new set of sprites, the old ones would vanish into the air as suddenly as they had come. Whenever a discord was struck, the tiny sprite that appeared was some mis-shapen creature, with limbs and dress awry, usually a humpbacked dwarf, whose voice was guttural and rasping, and his every movement ungainly and disagreeable."

He then describes how in his riper age he saw such fairy-like beings coming from the lips of persons talking, and which seemed in every action the very counterpart of the feeling conveyed in the uttered speech. If the words were inspired by good sentiments, these figures were transcen-dentally beautiful ; bad sentiments produced horrid-looking creatures ; hate was expressed by hissing snakes and dark, fiery devils ; treacherous words produced figures beautiful in front and disgusting and horrid behind; while love produced forms silvery, white, and full of beauty and harmony.

"On one never-to-be-forgotten occasion I was a pained witness to a scene of living faithfulness on one side and a double-faced, treacherous duplicity on the other. A fair young girl and her departing lover had met to exchange greetings ere he went on a distant journey. Each word of hers gave forth beautiful, radiant fairies ; but while the front half of each that was turned to the girl was equally fair to look upon, and smiled with all the radiant seeming of undying affection, the rear half of each was black and devilish, with fiery snakes and red-forked tongues pro-truding from their cruel lips, as gleams of wicked cunning danced in sneaking, sidelong glances from the corners of the half-closed eyes. These dark backgrounds of the little figures were horrible to look at, ever shifting, dodging, and seeming to shut up within themselves, as they sought to keep only bright and honest toward the trusting girl, and hold the black deception out of sight. And it was notice-able that while a halo of cloudless radiance surrounded the good outside seeming, a pall of thick vapor hung like a canopy of unbroken gloom above the other." *

---

* Religio-Philosophical Journal.

It would be absurd to suppose that these forms had any objective existence *outside* of the mind of the man who observed them. They were the creations of the involuntary action of his mind, and represented the various mental states which were produced in quick succession by the impressions his mind received; but they furnish a good illustration to the theory, that each form expresses a certain character, and that each mental state corresponds to a certain form, in which it may find its expression.

The above description coincides with what has been described by others, and proves that thoughts and sentiments are something substantial residing in the imagination of man, and which may affect his inner world for good or for evil, and that the necessity of controlling thoughts and desires is not a matter of little importance, but has a practical use. But those who reject such testimony and consider such forms as illusive may remember that not only such forms, but *all* forms, are only apparitions, and that they all represent invisible truths. Before the pure light of reason all illusions will disappear in the end and the truth appear—not hidden in forms, but in the sublime splendor of its purity—before the wondering gaze of spiritually-awakened Man.

But although subjective forms are manifestations of life they have no appropriate active will of their own. They are the creations of the thought of man acting upon the A'kâsa. They are only kept alive by the life-power that radiates into them from the life-centre in man. They are like shadows, vanishing when the fountain of light from which they drink is exhausted. When the psychical action of man, that gave them life, ceases to act, or acts in another direction, they will disappear sooner or later. However, as the corpse of a man does not dissolve immediately as soon as the principle of life has departed, but decays slowly or rapidly according to their molecular density and cohesion, likewise the astral forms created by the desires of man may require a considerable time for their dissolution according to the amount of will-fire made active in them. They continue to exist as long as man infuses life and consciousness into them by his thought and his will, and if they have once gained a certain amount of power, they may still cling to him, although he may not desire their companionship. They depend on him for their life, and the struggle for existence forces them to remain with the source from which they draw their vitality. If they depart from that fountain they die ; they are therefore forced to remain, and, like the phantom created by " Frankenstein," they persecute their creators with their unwelcome presence. To rid oneself of such a presence, he who is persecuted should direct the full power of his aspirations and thoughts into another and higher direction, and thereby starve them to death. In this way the spiritual principle of every man becomes his special *Redeemer*, who by the transformation of character saves him from the effects of his sin, and before whose pure light the illusions created by the lower attractions will melt like the snow under the influence of the sun.

Elemental forms being the servants of their creator—in fact, his own self—may be used by him for good or for evil purposes. Loves and hates may create subjective forms of beautiful or of horrid shapes, and, being infused with consciousness, obtain life, and may be sent on some errand for good or for evil. Through them the magician may blend his own life and consciousness with the person he desires to affect. A lock of hair, a piece of clothing, or some object that has been worn by the person he desires to affect, may form a connecting link between himself and the latter. The same object may be attained if that person is put into possession of an article belonging to the magician, because wherever a portion of anything with which the magician was connected exists, there will a part of his own elements exist, which will form a magnetic link between him and the person whom he wishes to affect. If he has developed his astral senses, distance will not prevent him to observe the person with which he is connected ; if he can project his astral form at a distance, his form may be present with his victim, although the latter may not be able to see it.

The astral image of a person may be projected consciously or unconsciously to a distance. If he intensely thinks of a certain place, his thought will be there, and consequently he will be there, for the thought of a man is the most important part of himself. Wherever a man's consciousness is, there is the man himself, no matter whether his physical body is there or not.

The history of spiritualism and somnambulism furnishes

abundant evidence that a person may be consciously and knowingly in one place, while his physical body lies dormant in another. Franciscus Xaver was thus seen in two different places at one and the same time. Likewise Apollonius of Tyana, and innumerable others mentioned in ancient and modern history.

The *Elemental* sent by a magician is an essential part of the magician himself, and if the victim is vulnerable by being mediumistic—with other words, by not having his own principles held together by the power of his reason and will, the latter may be injured by the former. But the former, too, if his astral form be materialized to a certain extent, even if not sufficiently to be visible to the eye, may be injured by physical force, and as the astral form re-enters the physical body, the latter will partake of the injuries inflicted upon the former.*

The magician, who by the power of his will has obtained control over the semi-intelligent forces of Nature, can make use of these forces for the purposes of good or evil. The helpless medium, through whom manifestations of occult power take place, can neither cause nor control such manifestations. He cannot control the elementals, but is controlled by them. The elements of his body serve as instruments through which these astral existences act, after the Medium has surrendered his will and given up the supreme command over his soul. He sits passively and waits for what these elementals may be pleased to do; he unconsciously furnishes them with his life and power to think, and his thoughts and the thoughts of those that are present may become reflected in these astral forms, or may enable them to manifest an intelligence of their own.

A medium for spirit-manifestations is merely an instrument for the manifestation of invisible forces over which he has no control, and the more mediumistic a person is, the less will he be liable to exercise a will of his own. The best of such mediums have been very unjustly blamed for "*cheating*," for a medium which would not "cheat" is as unthinkable as a mirror that would not reflect the objects before it. The thoughts of the persons visiting a Medium, and who are trying to find out his "impostures," are taken up by the Medium and reflected by him. It is therefore

---

* Des Mousseaux: "Mœurs des démons." Ennemoser: "Magie."

not the Medium's person that cheats, but his visitors cheating themselves through his instrumentality. A mirror that would not reflect *all* the objects that are brought before it, would be a very unnatural and deceptive thing ; a *Medium* who would only reflect such thoughts as he chose to reflect would be an impostor, for being able to exercise his own will he would not be in that passive condition which constitutes his mediumship.

The Adept in Magic is not the slave of these forces, but controls them by the power of his will. He may consciously infuse life and consciousness and intelligence into them and make them act as he pleases ; they obey his commands because they are a part of himself. The spiritualists do this unconsciously ; they frequently sing at their seances to produce harmony, and they know that the more the conditions are harmonious the better will be the manifestations. The reason for this is, that the more harmony ·exists in a circle, the less will there be any exercise of individual will, the less concentration of self, and the easier will it be for these influences to use the will and the vitality of the sitters.

These animal astral existences belong to the *kama rupa* form of existence, and their forms are therefore too ethereal to act directly upon gross matter. They, therefore, need the assistance of an intermediary principle, which is furnished by the second principle in man, the combination of soul and matter, called *Lingasariram*. This may be furnished by the astral elements of the living, or by the astral remnants of those whose bodies are dead.

The astral elements used by the Elementals in spiritual seances for the purpose of producing physical phenomena, are not only taken from the *medium*, but from all present, whose constitution is not strong, and who may therefore furnish such elements. In seances for *materializations*, they are also taken from the clothing of those present, and furnish material for the drapery of the " spirits," and it has been observed, that the clothing worn by people who frequently attend to such seances wears out sooner than usual.

To bring fresh-spilled blood into such " spiritual seances," would probably increase the strength of the " materializations " very much, and a knowledge of such facts has given rise to the abominable practices of *black*

4

*magic,* which are still going on in many parts of the world,
although secretly and unknown to the police. This
knowledge has also undoubtedly given rise to the sacrifice
of animals in the performance of religious ceremonies. A
certain executioner was unfortunately gifted with clairvoyance, and after having decapitated a person he could
see the "spirits" of dead people—sometimes even his
friends and relatives—pounce upon the fresh-spilled blood
of the criminal, and feed on its emanation and aura. He
became so disgusted that he had to resign his position.
It is also a fact that, at a time when the blood-drinking
mania in Europe was started by medical ignorance, many
people who practised it became insane, and others became
demoralized by it.

The astral remnant of man is without judgment and
reason, it goes wherever his instincts may attract it, or
wherever any unsatisfied craving may impel it to go. If
you wish to be haunted by the "ghost" of a man, attract
him by the power of love or hate which you felt for the
man. Leave some promise unfulfilled which you might
have fulfilled, and instinctively the astral form of the
deceased will be attracted to you to seek its fulfilment,
drawn to you by its own unsatisfied desire.

Such an astral form is not necessarily in any way consciously connected with the real *spirit* of that person, as
will be clear to those who have studied the doctrines of the
constitution of man. It may be merely that combination of
his lower principle, or his *astral corpse,* which made up the
*animal man.* But if the man was very brutish, having all
or nearly all his consciousness concentrated into his
animal elements, such a remnant may constitute all, or
nearly all, there ever existed of that person, except his
higher *reason,* which may have fled even before his death.
There are endless varieties of combinations of circumstances
existing on the astral as well as on the physical plane ; there
is no pattern by which all cases can be explained alike.
Their study belongs to the department of *Necromancy.*

It is not his fault if you do not perceive his presence and
hear his voice, it is because your astral senses are asleep
and unconscious ; you may feel his presence and it may
cause a feeling of depression in your mind; he speaks to you
but in a language that you have not yet learned to understand.
In those elementary remnants remains that which con-

stituted the lower nature of man, and if they are temporarily infused with life, they will manifest the lower characteristics of the deceased, such as have not been sufficiently refined to join his immortal part. If a music-box is set to play a certain melody and made to start, it will produce that same melody and no other, although it has no consciousness of its own. The remnant of emotional and intellectual powers in the astral remnant of man will, if this remnant is made to speak, become manifest in the same kind of language which the man during his life used to speak.

The fresh corpse of a person who has suddenly been killed, may be galvanized into a semblance of life by the application of a galvanic battery. Likewise the astral corpse of a person may be brought back into an artificial life by being infused with a part of the life-principle of the medium. If that corpse is one of a very intellectual person, it may talk very intellectually; and if it was that of a fool, it will talk like a fool. The intellectual action resembles mechanical motion in so far that if it is once set into action it will continue without any continual effort of the will, until it is exhausted or comes to a stop. We often see this in daily life. There are old and young people frequently seen who are in the habit of telling some favorite story, which they have already told many times, and which they repeat on every ocassion. It may be noticed, that when such an one begins to tell his story, it is of no use to tell him that one knows it already. He has to finish the story in spite of himself.

An orator or a preacher does not need to think and reason about each word he utters separately. When the stream of ideas once flows, it flows without any effort of the will. If ideas flow into the astral brain of a deceased person, infused with life by the medium, that brain will elaborate those ideas in the same way it was accustomed to do during life.

We also reason while we dream; we draw logical conclusions during our sleep; but reason is absent, and although, while we dream, our logic seems to be reasonable, nevertheless we often see that it was foolish when we awake and when our reason returns, or becomes active again.

The mental organism of man resembles a clockwork, which if it is once set into operation will continue to run until its force is exhausted ; but there is no clockwork which winds itself up without extraneous assistance, and there is no mental organism able to think without a power that causes it to begin the process of intellectuation.

In a departed soul the attraction of good and evil still continues to act, until the final separation of the higher and the lower takes place. It may follow the attraction of the higher principles in nature and be attracted to spirit, or it may again come into contact with matter through the instrumentality of mediumship, take again part in the whirling dance of life, although by vicarious organs ; follow once more the seduction of the senses, and lose entirely sight of the immortal self.

It is therefore not merely dangerous to a person to hold intercourse with the " spirits of the departed ; " but it is especially injurious to the latter,—as long as the final separation of their lower principles from the higher ones has not yet taken place. *Necromancy* is a vile art, and so has therefore always been abhorred. It may disturb the blissful dreams of the sleeping soul, which aspires to a higher state of existence. It is like roughly attacking a saint during his hours of meditation, and to force him to take an interest in affairs of the lower life, which can be of no use to him in his efforts to rise into a superior state. It is a step towards degradation ; and as every impulse has a tendency to repeat itself, the most terrible consequences may follow after what seemed to be at first merely some innocent amusement.

These astral remnants may be used by the black magician and by the elemental forces in nature for the purpose of evil. If they are unconscious, they will only serve as the instruments of the latter ; if they are conscious they may enter into an alliance and co-operate with them.

Such alliance, either consciously or unconsciously on the part of him who enters into such an *unspiritual* intercourse, may take place between an evil-disposed person and a very evil inhabitant of the astral plane, whose whole consciousness has been concentrated within his lower principles. We are convinced that many people who are in actual possession of powers to work *black magic* work evil unconsciously ; that is to say, that if they hate a person, they are often unconscious of the effects which their hate produces upon the latter, and of the mode in which it acts. The spiritual force created by their hate may enter the organism of the object of their hate and cause some bodily sickness, and the person from whom the evil power proceeds may be entirely ignorant of the fact that it was his own hate which produced the sickness. Such *black magicians* merely furnish the elements of evil, by which invisible powers act. The animal elements, existing in the soul of man, may, after having attained a certain degree of vitality, be projected by hate towards another person and enter his soul, even unknown to him, from whom they originate. But they are still a part of the life-principle of the person from whom they originated, and if they cannot take hold of the soul of him, against whom they are directed, they return again to the source from which they originated, and may kill him, from whom they emanated. It is therefore said, that if the will of the black magician is not strong enough to effect his evil purpose, the force will return and kill the magician.

This is undoubtedly true, and the grossest illustration of it is, if a person by a fit of rage or jealousy is induced to kill himself. It is the reaction following an unfulfilled desire, which induces the rash act ; the act is merely a result of his previous mental state.

The surest protection against all the practices of black magic, whether they are caused consciously or unconsciously, is to acquire strength of character,—in other words, *faith* in the divine principle within one's own soul.

As man becomes ennobled, the lower elements in his constitution are thrown off and replaced by higher ones, and in a similar manner a transformation may take place in the opposite way if he degrades himself by his thoughts and acts. Sensual man attracts from the A'kasa those elements that his sensuality requires, for gross pleasures can only be felt by gross matter. A man with brutal instincts growing and increasing may degrade himself into a brute in character, if not in external form. But as the form is only an expression of character, even that form may again approach an animal in resemblance.

The proof of this assertion is seen every day, for we meet every day in the streets brutish men, whose animal instincts are only too well expressed in their external forms. We meet with human snakes, hogs, wolves, and those upon whom alcohol has stampeds it seal, and it does not need the instructions given in books on physiognomy to enable almost anybody to read the character of certain persons more or less correctly expressed in their exterior forms.

In the physical plane the inertia of matter is greater than in the astral plane, and consequently its changes are slow. Astral matter is more active, and may change its form more rapidly. The astral body of a man whose character resembles an animal may therefore appear to the seer as an animal in its outward expression.*

The astral form of an evil person may appear in an animal shape if it is so filled with brutish instincts as to become identified in his imagination with the animal which is the expression of such instincts. It may even enter the form of an animal and obsess it, and it sometimes happens that it enters such forms for its own protection against immediate decomposition and death.

It would be useless to give anecdotes, illustrating instances, in which such things took place. The principal object of the reader should be to learn to know the essential constitutions of man, by observing the conditions of his own being and the law which regulates all forms of matter and functions. If he once understands the modes in which the law may act, it will be a matter of little importance to know in what particular cases it may have manifested itself in such modes. Accounts of phenomena can never supply the place of the understanding of the law.

Popular traditions speak of human beings having assumed the form of animals, roaming about and injuring men and cattle. Modern culture is prone to pronounce impossible everything that she cannot explain ; but the existence of such forms is theoretically not impossible, because a person may project his astral elements at a distance and make them appear in a material form, and that form is not necessarily human, because *man is what he thinks,* and his exterior shape may adapt itself to the true character by the power of his imagination.

---

* E. Swedenborg : "Heaven and Hell."

# CHAPTER IV.

## LIFE.

*" I never *was not*, nor shall I hereafter cease *to be.*"*
*Bhagwat Gita.*

THE universe of forms may be compared to a kaleidoscope in which the various forms of the original energy manifest themselves in an endless variety, appearing, disappearing, and re-appearing again. As in a kaleidoscope the pieces of variously-colored glass do not change their substance, but only change their positions, and, through the delusive reflections of mirrors at each turn of the instrument, are made to appear in new constellations and figures, so the *One Life* manifesting itself appears in an infinite number of forms and colors, acting as " matter " or " force," unconscious or conscious, blind or intelligent, voluntary or involuntary, from the atom, whose auras and others rush through a common vortex,* invisibly but nevertheless substantial, up to the blazing suns whose photospheres extend over millions of miles, and from the microscopic *Amoeba*, whose protoplasm manifests only the rudiments of instinct, up to perfect Man, whose intelligence conquers the gods.

Forms are isolated and materialized thoughts. If you can hold on to a thought and isolate it from others, you call into existence a form. If you can impart to that form your consciousness, you may make it conscious ; if you can invest it with the element of matter, you may make it visible and tangible ; but few persons are able to hold on to one single thought even for one single minute of time, because their minds are wavering and flickering ; few can transfer their consciousness, because they cannot

* Babbitt : " Principles of Light and Color."

voluntarily forget their own selves; few can control the element of earth, because it is their master, and they are attracted by it. The prototypes of all forms exist in the *Astral Light*, which is the Universal Soul in which resides the *Universal Mind;* the *A'kâsa or Universal Matter* being its more material substance. If a form comes into existence on the physical plane, its growth is simply a process by which something that already exists becomes visible and material, or, to speak more correctly, a lower state of vibration of the same element. This something is the idea or character of the form, and as each character is a unity, such a character will be distinctly expressed in all parts of the form. A human being—for instance—will not have the body of a man and the head of an animal, but its human character will be expressed in all its parts, and as the character constituting humanity is expressed in all human individuals, so is the character of an individual expressed in all its parts. This is a truth upon which the doctrines of Astrology, Phrenology, Chiromancy, Physiognomy, etc., are based, which—if rightly understood—are not only *possibly* true, but must be *necessarily* and *unavoidably* true, because Nature is a *Unity.* The nature of an animal, a plant, or a man, is a unity, and is therefore expressed in all the parts of each respective form. It can be scientifically demonstrated that each component part of an organism is a microcosm, in which are represented the principles composing that organism. We may by examining a part of a leaf know that it comes from a plant, and by looking at an animal substance see that it came from an animal, or by testing even the most minute part of a mineral or metal know that it belongs to the mineral kingdom. Likewise we may read a man's character in his hands or face or feet or in any other part of his body, if we have acquired the art how to read it correctly.

These things are known to physical science. But if the power of interior perception is once attained, a still greater world of wonders is opened before the astonished sight of the seer; he will then perceive that every part of an organism bears the correct impression of the form of the whole, and upon each particle is " photographed " by the *Astral Light* the picture of the body to which it belongs. The suns and planets in space as well as all terrestrial objects have their souls, else they could have no bodies; because their bodies are only the external expressions of the soul, and their character rests in their souls. Their souls act upon each other and are acted upon by all, and as the characters of these souls change, so change the physical forms. These astral influences, constituting the soul of the Universe, build up all forms, they modify the character and the growth of minerals, plants, and animals, they are the cause of endemic and epidemic diseases, they evolve in the course of ages variously-shaped animals, they predetermine to a certain extent the destiny of men,* and furnish the energies whose character impresses itself upon everything. Their *signatures* may be seen in the book of life belonging to every form, in the size and shape of features and limbs, in the lines of the hands, in the color of eyes and hair.† They are the forces by which the *Universal Mind* puts his mark upon everything, and those who are able to read may find the true history of every-thing written upon the leaves of its soul.‡ Likewise every *individual mind* prints his character upon every one of his thoughts, words, and acts, and upon the soul of everything which comes within his sphere.

Upon this law is based the science of *Psychometry.* By this science we may obtain a true history of past events. By psychometrically examining a stone taken from a house we may obtain correct information in regard to the former or present inhabitants of a house, or a fossil may give a true description of antediluvian scenery and of the mode of life of prehistoric animals or men. By the psychometrical examination of a letter we may obtain information about the person who wrote the letter and also of the place in

---

* This is to be taken in the same sense as heat and cold, rain and sunshine; miasmas and earthquakes may change the fortune and destiny of men who do not take due care to protect themselves against their effects; but as man by the power of his intellect has become able to guard himself against the inimical influence arising in the external plane; likewise by the exercise of his will and intelligence he may overcome the dangers threatening him from the astral plane.

† Debarolles: " Mystères de la main."

‡ Prof. W. Denton : "Soul of Things." J. R. Buchanan : "Manual of Psychometry.

which the letter was written. If this art were universally known and practised, criminals could be detected by examining psychometrically a piece of the wall, the floor, or the furniture of the room in which a murder or robbery was committed; it would make an end to convicting of innocent persons on circumstantial evidence, or to letting the guilty escape for want of proof; for the psychometer would, by the superior powers of his perception with the spiritual eye, see the murderer or robber or counterfeiter as plain as if he had seen them with his external eyes while the deed was committed.

Each form is the external expression of a certain character which it represents, and as such it has certain peculiar attributes, which distinguish it from other forms. A change of its character is followed by a gradual change of the form. An individual who becomes degraded in morals will, in the course of time, show his degradation in his external appearance; persons of a different appearance and different characters may, in the course of time, as their characters harmonize, resemble each other to a certain extent in appearance. Forms of life, belonging to the same class and species, resemble each other, and each nationality has certain characteristics expressed in the individuals belonging to it. A full-blooded Irishman will not easily be mistaken for a full-blooded Spaniard, although the two may be dressed alike, but if they both emigrate to America their children or grandchildren will in time lose the national characteristics which their ancestors possessed. Change of character changes the form; but a change of external form does not necessarily change the character. A man may lose a leg and become a cripple, and still his character may remain the same as before; a child may grow into a man, and still his character remain that of a child unless modified by education.

These facts are incontrovertible proofs that the character of a being is more essential than his external form; that the form is illusive, and that the reality is a principle which is independent of form. If the character of an individual were to depend on his inherited form, children born of the same parents and educated under the same circumstances would always manifest the same mental characteristic, but it is well known that the characters of such children often differ widely from each other, and they may possess characteristics which their parents do not possess.

If, as it frequently happens, children show the same or similar talents and intellectual capacities as their parents, such a fact is by no means a proof that the parents of the child's physical body are also the parents or producers of its intellectual germ; but it may be taken as an additional evidence of the truth of the doctrine of *reincarnation*, because the spiritual monad of the child would be naturally attracted, in its efforts to reincarnate, to the bodies of parents, whose mental and intellectual constitution would correspond nearest to its own talents and inclinations, developed during a previous earthly life.

Characters may exist independent of external conditions; the latter can only modify, but not create, the former. The best soil will not produce an oak tree unless an acorn is present, and a *Cholera Baccillus* will not produce cholera where the "predisposition" to that disease does not already exist. Forms may facilitate the development of character, but they do not create it, and persons that appear in every respect alike may be of a very different character.

How can we account for such moral and intellectual discrepancies in forms that are merely alike, as long as we shut our eyes to the truth, that that which is essential in a being, whether rational or irrational, is its character, and that its form is only the external expression of that internal and invisible character, which may survive after the form has ceased to exist, and after the dissolution of the form finds its expression again in another form! Forms die, but their character remains unchanged after their death, preserved in the *Astral Light*, like the thoughts of man stored up in his memory, after the events that called them into existence have passed away. A character does neither die nor change after it has left the form, but, after a time of rest in the subjective state, it will reimbody itself again in a new-born objective form, to grow and change its nature during the life of the form. Seen from this standpoint, "death" is life, because, during the time that death lasts, that which is essential in a form does not change; life is death, because only during life in the form the character is changed, and old tendencies and inclinations die and are replaced by others.

Each form is an incarnation of a certain character. Our passions and vices may die while we live; if they survive us they will be born again.

The character of an oak exists before the acorn begins to grow, but the growing germ attracts from earth and air such elements as it needs to produce an oak ; the character of a child exists as such before the physical form of the child is born into the world, and attracts from the spiritual atmosphere the elements to which its aspirations and tendencies are attracted.   Each seed will grow best in the soil that is best adapted to its constitution, each human monad existing in the subjective state will be attracted at the time of its incarnation to parents, whose qualities may furnish the best soil for its own tendencies and inclinations, and whose moral and mental attributes may correspond to its own.   The physical parents cannot be the progenitors of the spiritual germ of the child, that germ is the product of a previous spiritual evolution, through which it has passed in connection with former objective lives.   In the present existence of a being the character of the being that will be its successor is prepared.

Therefore, every man may be truly said to be his own father ; for he is the incarnated result of the personality which he evolved in his last life upon the planet, and the next personality which he will represent in his next visit upon this globe is evolved by him during his present life.

The development of a plant reaches its climax in the development of the seed ; the development of the animal body reaches its climax in the capacity to reproduce its form, but the intellectual and spiritual development of a man may go on long after he has acquired the power of reproduction, and it may not have reached its climax when the physical form is on the downward path, and ceases to live.   The condition of the physical body may undoubtedly furnish facilities for the development of character in the same sense as a good soil will furnish facilities for the growth of a tree ; but the best soil cannot transform a thistle into a rose-bush, and the son of a good and intellectual man may be a villain or a dunce.

As a primordial essence proceeds to manifest itself in forms, it descends from the universal condition to general, special, and finally individual states.   As it ascends again to the formless, the scale is reversed, and the individual units expand, to mingle again with the whole.   Life on the lowest planes manifests itself in an undifferentiated condition ; air has no strictly defined shape ; one drop of water in the ocean shares an existence common to all other drops; one piece of clay is essentially the same as another. In the vegetable and animal kingdom the universal principle of life manifests itself in individual form; still there is little difference between individual plants, trees, animals, and men belonging to the same species, and the peculiar attributes which distinguish one individual form from another cease to exist when the form disappears. That which essentially distinguishes one individual from another is independent of form, and exists after the form has ceased to live. Distinctions of form are perishable, but distinctions of character remain; those attributes which raise their possessors eminently above the common level begin at a state when external appearances cease to be of great consequence. Socrates was deformed and yet a great genius; the size of Napoleon's body was not at all in proportion with the greatness of his intellect. Honor and fame rise above the grave of the form, and the influence of great minds often grows stronger after the bodies that served them have turned to dust. Strong minds expand far beyond their physical form while they live. They do not die when the form disappears. Their characters continue to exist and may reappear upon the earth.

All characters may become reincarnated or reimbodied after they have left the form, but if an individual has no specific character of its own, the common character belonging to its species or class will be all that, after leaving the old body, can enter the new. If an individual has developed a specific character of its own, that distinguishes it from its fellows, that individual character will individually survive the dissolution of its form, because the law that applies to the whole, or to the class, will also apply to the part. A drop of water mixed in a body of water will become dispersed in the mass, it may be evaporated and condensed again, but it will never again be the same drop; but if a drop of some ethereal oil is mixed with the water, and the whole is evaporated in a retort, it will, after being condensed, form again the same individual drop in the mass. A high character may lose its individuality during life and sink to the common level, but if it has established a distinction from others, its individuality will survive the death of the form. To accomplish a change of character an individual form is required, to build up an individual form a character must exist.

If we wish to produce a form we must first decide upon its character. A sculptor who would aimlessly cut a stone, without making up his mind as to what form he desired to produce, would not accomplish anything great. The form is a temple of learning for the character, in which the latter gains experience by passing through the struggles of life. The harder the struggle the faster may the character of the individual become developed; an easy life may increase the size of the form, but will leave the character weak; a hard struggle may weaken the form, but will strengthen the spirit. Forms grow at the expense of other forms, the growth of character induces other characters to grow. Forms grow weak when they impart their own substance to others, characters grow stronger while they impart to others their strength. Individuals vampyrize each other as long as they require material forms, but a character that has once been formed finds the source of its strength within itself. In the lowest plane, where the physical life-impulse acts very slow, an isolated form may exist for a considerable time; a stone or a diamond may last for ages, because the consuming fire of life is not very active in them; but in forms in which life is very active, permanent isolation is not compatible with the existence of form. The higher we rise in the scale of life on the physical plane, the smaller grows the possibility of enduring isolation. An isolated scrub pine may live surrounded by snow and ice on an almost bare rock, where no highly-organized life can exist, and an animal life may live a comparatively isolated existence in a forest, where a man would soon starve to death. Life in forms requires other forms to feed upon, characters are self-existing, they require the contact with other characters only to try their own strength, and as they grow and use their power they increase their own fortitude.

The attributes which constitute character are formless; they may be expressed in a form, but after the form is dissolved they return to the formless again. Abstract ideas, such as "good, evil, wisdom, power, love, hope, faith and charity," etc., have no forms, but they may characterize a living being and render it good or bad, wise and powerful," etc. Still such qualities do exist, even if they are not manifest in forms ; forms cannot create their own attributes, but they are the expressions of principles which exist, and which may or may not become manifested in forms.

The " spirit," or *character*, is the originator of form, the astral forces of nature are the architects, and the physical plane of nature furnishes the material to render the form substantial, and to enable it to come into contact with the physical plane. Thought is the great power by which forms are called into existence. The thoughts of a person during life determine the tendencies of his soul while in the subjective state, and these tendencies attract other influences and bring him again into contact with form. An entity, attracted by the illusion of self, may fancy itself to be something distinct and isolated from the universal life, and look upon all other existences as being distinct from the whole. From this illusion arise innumerable other illusions. From the sense of self arises the love of self, the desire for the continuance of personality, giving rise to greed, avarice, envy, jealousy, fear, doubt and sorrow, pain and death, and to the whole range of emotions and sufferings, which frequently render life miserable, and afford no permanent happiness. If a person is miserable and can find no happiness in himself, the surest and quickest way for him to be contented is to forget his own personality, and to live in others, by blending his own consciousness with that of some others, or all. By feeling with others he will forget his own self, and for the time being cease to experience the sufferings produced by the illusion of self. A person who lives in a state of isolation on the emotional plane will care for nothing else but for his own personality. He concentrates all his energies into himself, and becomes more and more insignificant and spiritually small. Gradually he will sink to lower planes of thought, becoming—so to say—more and more heavy as his soul becomes dense ; and if once the downward impulse is given, and not arrested, he will sink lower and lower, until his personality, at the death of the form, disappears in the vortex and he ceases to exist as a man in human form, having already during life ceased to exist as a man in a human character. When his physical body is decayed and the " magnetic body " dispersed, the remnant of his soul elements may still continue to exist. Its movements will be guided by its controlling emotions, it will not go whither it chooses, for having no inteligence it can make no choice; but it will go whither it is attracted by its instincts, until its energies are exhausted and it ceases to exist as a form.

Thus the animal elements of a man who was during his life a great drunkard, may after his death be attracted to another living drunkard and be drawn to a grog-shop; those of a lewd person seek comfort in a brothel, those of an avaricious person stand guard over his buried treasures, etc., etc.; and all such remnants may have a certain amount of consciousness and memory left, and may be galvanized back temporarily into a living state by coming in contact with a medium. Thus endless varieties of *spooks, ghosts, vampires, incubi, succubi,* etc., may come into existence, and there are innumerable accounts given in books on magic, occultism and spiritualism, to illustrate such facts.

As on the physical plane, so on the astral plane, isolation produces starvation. An emotion to be kept alive must be fed by corresponding emotions, else it will devour its possessor. A person who loves another person or object intensely, and cannot gain the object of his desire, must transfer his love upon some other object, or he may perish in the attempt to suppress it. If the love is transferred to a higher ideal it will render man happy; if it is transferred to a lower one dissatisfaction may be the result. Stored-up anger will find some object upon which to spend its fury, else it may produce an explosion destructive to its possessor; tranquility follows a storm. The "black magician" who attempts to kill or injure another person by the intensity of his hatred, projected towards that person, may be killed or injured by the intensity of the force he has created, and which—if it is not sufficiently strong to effect his object—will react upon himself. Accumulated energy cannot be annihilated, it must be transferred to other forms, or be transformed into other modes of motion; it cannot remain forever inactive and yet continue to exist. It is useless to attempt to resist a passion which we cannot control. If its accumulating energy is not led into other channels it will grow until it becomes stronger than will and stronger than reason. To control it, it should be led into another and higher channel. Thus a love for something vulgar may be changed by turning it into a love for something high, and vice may be turned into virtue by changing its aim. Passion is blind, it goes where it is led to, and reason is a safer guide for it than the instinct. Love for a form disappears with the death of the form, or soon after; love of character remains even after the form in which that character was embodied ceased to exist.

The ancients said that *Nature suffers no vacuum.* We cannot destroy or annihilate a passion. If it is driven away another elemental influence will take its place. We should therefore not attempt to destroy the low without putting something in its place; but we should displace the low by the high; vice by virtue, and superstition by knowledge.

There are some persons who live in perfect isolation on the intellectual plane. They are such whose thoughts are entirely absorbed by intellectual labors, having no time or inclination to attend to the claims of their spirit. They are—so to say—living continually in the cupola of their temples, the head, while their hearts are made to starve and become petrified. They concentrate all their intellectual forces into their brains, and may become very learned in regard to the small details of life on this planet, but while they concentrate their attention upon the small, they often lose their capacity to enter into harmony with the whole. Seen from the standpoint of eternal truth, they are lunatics, living in the moonshine of their own imagination, dawdling away their life among the realm of illusions and perishing form and neglecting that which alone is lasting and permanent. They constitute to a great extent, the " materialists," " sceptics," and "rationalists " of our age. They throw away their birthright to immortality by arguing themselves into a belief in its impossibility, they may become criminals " for the sake of science," disregarding the laws of humanity; their astral corpses will continue to exist for a while after the death of their physical forms, until the intellectual power active therein is exhausted, but their spiritual aspirations having already deserted them during their life, there will be nothing left of them in the end to survive the dissolution of the soul.

All forms that nature produces are the products of universal life expressing itself in forms. They are manifestations of the *One* in *Three*, but as such they do not possess any life of their own. There still remains the un-manifested *One*, which must become active in the form if the form is to live. The Three rendered alive through the One, produces the Four, and *Four* is therefore the number of perfection. It represents the *square*, by means of which the Universe is constructed, and which finds its symbolic expression in the life-giving influences meeting from the four cardinal points, North, South, East and West.

Life is universally present in nature, it is contained in every particle of matter, and only when the last particle of life is departed from a form the form ceases to exist. It may remain for centuries inactive in a form, but when it begins to manifest itself, motion appears in the form, and the higher the form is developed the higher may be the activity of its life. Life in a stone does not appear to exist, and yet without life there would be no cohesion of its atoms. If the life-principle were extracted from a mineral its form would be annihilated. A seed taken from the tomb of an Egyptian mummy began to germinate and grow after it was planted in the earth, having kept its life-principle during a sleep of many centuries. If the activity of animal life could be correspondingly arrested, an animal or a man might prolong individual existence to an indefinite period. Stones may live from the beginning of a Manvantara unto its end; some forms reach a very old age, but if the life impulse is once given it is difficult—if not impossible—to arrest it.

Life may be transferred from one form upon another, and the power by which it may be transferred is the power of Love, because Love, Will and Life are essentially the same power, or different aspects of one, in the same sense as heat and light are modifications of motion. The power of hate may kill and the power of love has been known to call the apparently dead back to life. Love is a restoration of life and health, more powerful than all the drugs of the Pharmacopœia, and it is the *universal panacea* which the true physician applies.

Thus the sun is continually transferring his life, his will and his love to this globe without losing anything thereby. There is no actual loss; but merely a setting in motion of vibrations of life and light in the body of our planet by the central will-fire at the centre of our system, the sun. There are thousands of people sick, because the sun in them is grown cold ; they cannot make up their minds to be well ; they cannot form that firm resolution, which is neceesary to set the will at their own centre into motion, so that its vibrations would induce life and health in all parts of their system. Their disease is *Infidelity*. They are full of doubt, uncertain whether they ought to live or to die, and while we bemoan their miserable condition, they have neither the courage nor the will to be well, and instead of curing themselves, they hire a doctor to amuse them and to enable them to remain sick.

Every disease, without any exception, is in the first instance caused, directly or indirectly, by a weak or perverted will or a disordered imagination ; nor could it be otherwise, because man himself and the world wherein he lives is a product of will and imagination, and there is nothing else but these two factors to act upon. The more external the disease or the accident is, the more remote is it from these original causes ; but even an external accident is due to a disharmony existing between the will of subject and object, either consciously or unconsciously expressed. The origin of the majority of internal diseases can be traced to some emotion of the will or to some in-harmonious thought, to some irregular desire or some state of the mind, conceived either by the patient himself, or impressed upon him by another.

All things and all states are expressions of will and thought. People get sick, because they unconsciously will to be sick and this unconscious action of the will is induced by the imagination. If being sick were looked upon as a disgrace and punished by the law, there would be far less sick people in the world. The more the comforts for the sick are increased the more will there be people who need them. Many a man who hires a physician for his family thereby introduces the plague into his house. With the issuing of each diploma that creates a new doctor, a new herd of infection for the community is created, because the very sight of a doctor makes one think of disease and may cause disease, while there are thousands of sick persons that would be well to-day if they had never found it to be convenient to be sick.

What then is the use of our modern system of **quackery**

and dosing with medicine, be it legally or illegally done, if the cause of disease is not in the body, but in the will and the thought of the patient ? When will humanity arrive at an understanding of the eternal truth, that he who looks for redemption in external things is doomed to disappointment, while man's only true friend and redeemer is the God whom he carries within himself, nor can any man give to another the life, the truth or the Christ, but it is the life, the light and the truth itself giving itself to a man through the instrumentality of those that have been regenerated in the life and light of the spirit of truth. A physician or a preacher, having no faith in the power of good, and no self-consciousness of the presence of God within themselves, but are full of conceit in regard to their own learning and intellectual accomplishment, can cure neither the ills of the body nor those of the souls, they can only create illusions and act upon the imagination of the patient, but not infuse life into his will. They are not physicians, but clowns and reciters of stories which they themselves do not believe.

The true life-giving power rests in the source of all Good. "In him is life, and the life is the light of men."＊ Through its influence the elements composing lower forms of existence are gradually raised into higher states. It is everywhere present, and manifests itself wherever a form is capable to respond to its vibrations. It cannot be found by vivisection nor by chemical analysis, and modern scientific books say nothing about it ; yet it is an element in which and through which we all live, and if it were withdrawn from us for a single moment we would be immediately annihilated.

To be blind to the existence of the universal source of all good, is to be blind to the fact that is apparent everywhere, that grasses and trees, animals and men, live and grow. Without the power of life nothing living could come into existence. Truly the children speak a great truth when they say that "God made the grass grow;" but the learned, who cannot conceive of anything that transcends their sensual perception, cannot rise to the sublime conception of a universal, supreme, and therefore divine power. Our Materialistic philosophers desire to

＊ St. John i. 4

abolish their " God ; " and it is to be hoped that they will succeed, for the god of which *they* conceive is impotent. The supreme power of life in the universe is beyond conception, this they cannot abolish ; an attempt to destroy it would have to begin with their own annihilation.

Life is a manifestation of power, a function of the unimaginable *cause* of all existence. It must be a substantial principle, else it could not exist, because no activity can take place without substance. It has no forms, but is manifested in forms ; it continually advances from lower to higher forms, and as it advances the character of forms advances with it. The building of the " Temple of Solomon" goes on unceasingly. Invisibly act the elements of nature, the master builders of the universe. Life inhabits a form, and when the form is decayed it gathers the elements and builds itself a new house. A rock, exposed to the action of wind and rain, begins to decay on its surface, the elements gather again and appear in a new form. Minute plants and mosses grow on the surface, living and dying and being reborn, until the soil accumulates and higher forms come into existence. Centuries may pass away before this part of the work is completed ; but finally grasses will grow, and the life that was formally dormant in a rock now manifests itself in forms capable to enter the animal kingdom. A worm may eat a plant, and the life of the plant becomes active and conscious in a worm ; a bird may eat the worm, and the life that was chained to a form crawling in darkness and filth now partakes of the joys of an inhabitant of the air. At each step on the ladder of progression life acquires new names to manifest its activity, and the death of its previous form enables it to step into a higher one. The principle of life is not changed thereby, nor is the sun changed when he sends his rays upon the earth. A piece of black iron is rendered luminous, if exposed to heat, but remains iron for all that. Not the iron produces the light nor the form the life, but the former manifest themselves according to the qualites of the latter.

Forms are nothing but symbols of life, and the higher the life expresses itself the higher will be the form. An acorn is an insignificant thing compared with the oak, but it has a character, and through the magic action of life it may develop into an oak The germ of its individual life

is incarnated in the acorn, and forms the point of attraction for the universal principle of life. Its character is
already formed, and if it grows it can become nothing else
but an oak. Buried in the earth it may grow and develop
from a low into a higher state through the influence of the
highest, because the principle of life is contained in it.
But however great its potency for growth may be, still it
cannot germinate without the life-giving influence of the
universal fountain of life reaching it through the power of
the sun, and the sun could not make it grow unless the
principle of life were contained in the germ.

The rays of the sun penetrate from their airy regions to
the earth ; their light cannot enter the solid earth, which pro-
tects the tender seed or a plant from the fiery rays, whose
activity might destroy its inherent vitality. But the seed
is touched by the heat that radiates into the earth, and a
special mode of life manifests itself in the seed. This
life is not a new creation, but it is *The Absolute* becoming
manifest in a form. The seed begins to sprout, and the
germ struggles towards the source of the life-giving
influence, and strives towards the light. The roots have
no desire for light, they only crave for nutriment, which
they find in the dark caverns of matter. They penetrate
deeper into the earth, and may even absorb the activity of
the higher parts of the plant. But if the latter belongs to
a species whose character it is to grow towards the light,
its nobler portions will enter its sphere, and may ultimately bear flowers and fruits.

The soul of man being buried in matter, perceives
instinctively the life-giving influence of the supreme spiritual sun, while at the same time it is attracted by matter.
If man's whole attention is attracted to the claims of his
body, if all his aspirations and desires are directed to
satisfy the desire of his material form, he will himself remain
a thing of earth, incapable to become conscious of the
existence of Light. But if he strives for Light, and opens
his soul to its divine influence, he will enter its sphere and
become conscious of its existence. A time will arrive
when matter will lose its attractions for him, and as the
odor of the flower can exist after the flower and the roots
from which the latter drew its nutriment have ceased to live,
so will the character of that man, even after his physical
body has continued to exist, consciously survive, and

having followed the attraction of the immortal law, become himself one with the law, and be rendered immortal.

The true *Elixir of life* can only be found at the eternal fountain of life. It springs from the seventh principle, manifesting itself as spiritual power in the sixth and shedding its light down in the fifth, illuminating the mind. In the fifth it is manifest as the intellectual power in man, radiating down into the fourth and controlling by the power of Reason the turbulent elements of the latter. In the fourth it creates desires, calling forth life and instincts in the lower triad, and thereby enabling the forms to draw the elements which they need from the storehouse of nature. It forever calls men to life by the voice of truth, whose echo is the power of intuition crying in the wilderness of our hearts, baptizing the souls with the water of hope, and pointing out to them the true spirit which, coming to consciousness in their heart, may baptize them with fire and knowledge, and initiate them into the eternal life.

# CHAPTER V.

### HARMONY.

"Let no one enter here who is not well versed in mathematics and music."—*Pythagoras*,

"To listen to the music of the spheres" is a poetical expression, but it expresses a great truth; because the Universe is filled with harmony, and a soul who is in full harmony with the soul of the universe may listen to that music and undesrtand it. The world as well as man resemble musical instruments, in which every string should be in perfect order, so that no discordant notes may be sounded. We may look upon matter on the physical plane as a state of low vibration and upon spirit as the highest vibration of life, and between the two poles are the intermediary principles constituting the grand octave called *Man*.

A more *exact* study of the laws of harmony will undoubtedly give us a deeper insight into the laws which govern the functions of the principles of which Nature and man are composed. Woman is the image of Man, representing *Man's* beauty and will, while the male part of humanity is to represent reason and strength, but neither can continue to exist without the other, and neither a male nor a female being is perfect. Only that being is perfect in which the male and female elements are united.

That which saves the male portions of mankind from becoming brutes is the remnants of the female principle, still left in Adam when Eve was created out of "one of his ribs." That which constitutes the true woman is the eternal divine female principle, the eternal virgin, in her. That which brings woman near to the semi-animal male and which makes her discernible to him, is the male elements contained in her human organization. A man without any female elements in him would be a devil, a woman without any male elements would be an angel, but could not live upon a gross material planet such as the earth.

The *Moll* accord is the harmonious counterpart of the *Dur* accord ; but it has been proved that the existence of a family of *moll*-accords, existing independently of *dur*-accords, and running in parallel lines with the latter, is an impossibility. The most beautiful sound is not a single sound, but an accord of *three*. Such an accord is like a mental conception, which—for the purpose of realizing its existence as a unity—has to pass through three phases of consciousness ; viz : 1. that of being one with itself ; 2. that of being different from itself ; and 3. that of conceiving that these two states are only *one*.

Nature is the product of a cause, and everything in nature is ruled by the law of cause and effect. There can be no arbitrary ruler in the universe, and even if there were such a ruler, his decisions would be the effects of the action of his mind, and the actions of his mind would be determined by pre-existing causes, and he would therefore be subject to law. A being that is not subject to law is an unimaginable monster that cannot exist, because all beings come into existence through the law of cause and effect, and nothing can be without having come into existence ; only the eternal law itself, which is no-thing, self-existent, and absolute.

Here it might be objected, that the law could not exist, if there was not a cause of the law, in other words, a *law-giver ;* and such would be the case, if we had to deal with arbitrary laws ; but the *eternal* law of cause and effect requires no *law-giver ;* because it is eternal and therefore self-existent. Each *being* is subject to that law, because each is a product of it. The law of cause and effect calls all beings into existence ; but the law itself is not a *being*, and if man enters the state of *Nirvana*, he ceases to be subject to the law ; because as he is then *one* with the law, he *is* the law, and cannot be subject to any other law but himself, and has ceased to be a " being."

Man is a being and exists in the world, having come into existence according to the law of cause and effect. The form and quality of his body depend on the physical conditions under which he was born ; the state of his soul depends on the astral influences that concentrated their power upon him in consequence of his affinity; his character depends on the causes created during his previous existence, and these causes constitute his *Karma.* of which he himself is the creator. Man is himself a product of the law of cause and effect, and in all depart· ments of nature the effects produced are always in exact proportion to the causes that produced them. If we knew the causes well, we could easily calculate their effects. Each thought, each word, each act creates a cause, which acts directly on the plane to which it belongs, creating there new causes, which react again upon the other planes.* A thought is a mental state that may be expressed in a word, and the word may be made effective by an act. An act is the expression (the word) of a thought. Every form in nature has a threefold constitution, every symbol a three-fold meaning, every perfect act is a trinity. To perform an action three factors are necessary : the actor, the act, and the object acted on. To constitute a complete act three factors again are required : the motive, the will, and the performance. A motive or thought which finds no expression in an act will have no direct result on the physical plane, but it may cause great emotion in the sphere of mind, and these may again react on the physical plane. The best intention will produce no visible effect unless it is put into execution ; but intentions produce certain mental states, that may be productive of actions at some time in the future. The performance of an act will have an effect, no matter whether it was premeditated or not, but an act without a motive will not directly affect the planes of thought. Such an act is the result of insanity, and imposes no moral responsibility upon the performer, but it will, nevertheless, have its effects on the physical plane that may react upon the mind.

---

* *Paracelsus* explains how the morbid imagination of man may create states in the mental atmosphere which poison the imagination of nature, and how by a reaction of the Universal Soul upon the soul of man, epidemic diseases come into existence.

From the causes created on the physical, astral, and spiritual planes innumerable combinations of effects come into existence, creating new causes, that are again followed by effects, and every force that is put into action on either plane continues to act until it is exhausted by transformations into other modes of action, when its vibrations will be changed ; to others, and the previous effects will cease to exist.

It is highly interesting to study the actions of the law of cause and effect on the various planes of existence. By the threefold action of that law, as *thought*, *will*, and *performance*, on the physical, emotional, intellectual, and spiritual planes, a great many varieties ensue which give rise to endless modifications and varieties, and again produce innumerable secondary causes, which again produce effects. For instance, a good act performed on the physical plane with an evil thought, or an evil act performed with a good motive, or a good act with a good motive, or an evil act with an evil thought, produces certain effects upon one plane, while the motive affects another plane, and they both react upon higher planes, and there results are produced which react again upon the lower planes, and at last the actions of the law of *Karma* will become so complicated, that it is impossible to follow it into its details. Nor is it necessary that we should do so ; for we should not do good as a matter of speculation and for the purpose of acquiring good Karma ; but we should do good, because we love good on account of its goodness.

Man is not a being whose existence is separated from nature, but an integral part thereof. Heat and cold, sunshine and storms on the physical plane, affect his body, the elemental forces of nature act upon his soul, and the influence of the universal spirit radiates to his centre. Likewise man reacts upon the whole. By his physical labor he changes the face of the Earth, acting sometimes as a creator and at other times as a destroyer of forms ; his emotions produce currents in the soul of the world that give rise to new causes in the invisible realm, which again react upon the physical plane. His imagination may create thought-germs, that may in the course of time find expression in physical forms, his passions may give rise to epidemic diseases,[*] his collective and accumulative

---

[*] Paracelsus: " De Origine Morborum Invisibilium."

energies lead to convulsions in nature, and if harmony is restored in the universal Man, nature will be restored to harmony.

The discords in nature are produced by imperfect man. Having tasted of the tree of knowledge, he has learned to oppose his individual will to the order existing in nature, and he will continue to suffer the consequences of his sins until he recognizes the superiority of the All to that of the individual, and uniting his will with that of the whole, ends the conflict of separate interests, and thereby restores the unity and harmony of the whole.

Originally eternal nature was an harmonious whole, in which discords were created by a separation of interests among its constituents and an opposition of their individual wills to the will of the whole. In the beginning the universal will, radiating from the centre, became—so to say—reversed in the action of its surface rays, and thereby the sphere of illusions came into existence at the periphery sphere representing the visible world. But at the centre there still exists the immeasurable power of the uniform law, where light penetrates through the clouds that surround the spiritual sun. These clouds constitute the world of illusions, and the action of this law can be perceived in every form of activity in all departments of nature.

Plato wrote over the door of his academy: "Let no one enter here unless he is well versed in mathematics;" and Pythagoras demanded the additional knowledge of music. They meant to say that he who wishes to investigate the hidden mysteries of nature must be able to draw logical conclusions from his observations and attune his soul to the divine harmonies of the universe.

Nature is still a Unity, and every part of it stands in a certain definite relation to the whole; nothing is left to chance. Everything has its number, measure, and weight, and there is nothing in nature which is not ruled by mathematical laws. Suns and stars have their periodical revolutions. The molecules of bodies combine in certain proportions, known to chemistry, and in all events on the physical plane as well as in the realm of the emotions a certain regularity and periodicity has been observed. There are regular hours for the appearance of day and night, fixed intervals for spring and summer, autumn and winter, for ebbs and tides in the ocean and in the waters constituting the soul. The physiological and anatomical changes in animal forms occur at fixed periods, and even the events of life take place according to certain occult laws; because, although man's actions seem to be free, yet his actions are caused by his will, and his will is influenced by his mental states, which are again the effects of still deeper causes that find their origin in the supreme law.

The followers of Pythagoras knew every process in nature to be regulated by certain numbers, which are as follows:

| 3 | 9 | 15 | 45 |
| 4 | 16 | 34 | 136 |
| 5 | 25 | 65 | 325 |
| 6 | 36 | 111 | 666 |
| 7 | 49 | 175 | 1225 |
| 8 | 64 | 260 | 2080 |
| 9 | 81 | 369 | 3321 |

This table represents a succession of numbers, which are obtained by the construction of *Tetragrams* or *magic squares*, and it was believed that by the use of these numbers every effect could be calculated if the original number referring to the cause were known. If everything has a certain number of vibrations, and if these vibrations increase or diminish at a certain ratio and in regular periods, a knowledge of these numbers will enable us to predict a future event.

Every person has a certain number that expresses his character, and if we know that number, we may, by the use of the magic squares, calculate certain periodical changes in his mental and emotional states, which may induce him to make certain changes in his outward conditions, and in this way we may, perhaps, calculate approximately the time when some important changes may take place in his career. But as the numbers of men are known only to the enlightened, who do not require such calculations, these magic squares are at present of little practical value, and of none whatever for the purpose of "fortune-telling," or to satisfy idle curiosity in regard to future events.

This law of periodicity is, however, an universal law, and an attention to it may lead to some important discoveries. Its actions have long ago been known to exist in the vibrations producing light and sound, and it has recently been recognized in chemistry* by experiments tending to prove that all so-called simple elements are only various states of vibrations of one primordial element, manifesting itself in seven principal modes of action, each of which may be sub-divided into seven again. The difference which exists between so-called single substances appears, therefore, to be no difference of substance or matter, but only a difference of the function of matter or in the ratio of its atomic vibration.

The occultists of all ages have looked upon the Seven as being a sacred number. The religious books of the East speak of seven emanations of Parabrahm; and there is a sufficient number of passages in the *Apocalypse* and in other parts of the Bible to make it appear that the relation which this mysterious number bears to the construction of the universe has not escaped the attention of the Christian Fathers.

The ancient philosophers believed that there were seven planets in our solar system, and modern scientists base their claims of their superiority over the ancient astronomers upon the fact that they have discovered more planets and asteroids than were known in ancient times.

Eternal truths which are cognizable to the spiritual perception of the illuminated of to-day must be the same that were seen by seers thousands of years ago, because such truths do not change, neither can a true spiritual perception make any mistakes. It is, therefore, probable that if the exoteric doctrines of the ancients spoke of seven planets, the esoteric meaning was that there existed six planetary spheres, which, including the central sphere, produce seven. According to the prevailing opinion in regard to the nebular theory, our planetary system has been evolved from the original substance (fire-mist) that constituted the body of the sun, forming an immense sphere, extending beyond the orbit of Neptune. If we imagine in a sphere a centrifugal force radiating from the centre towards the periphery, and a centripetal force acting towards the centre, there will be a point between the centre and the periphery where the

---

* L. B. Hellenbach : "Die Magie der Zahlen."

two opposing forces meet. At that point their straight motions will either counteract each other and there will be a stand-still, or—what is more probable—the radial force will be broken and transformed into a revolving motion around a new centre formed at the place of contact. In such a case there would be not less than six bodies to enclose the seventh on all sides.

But as to the number of corporeal planetary bodies, visible on the sky, this is a matter belonging to the investigation of mundane astronomy. Occult science deals with principles; the ultimate outcome of the expressions of these principles in corporeal forms is a matter of secondary importance.

The number Seven represents the *scale of nature*, it is represented in all departments of nature, from the radiant sun, whose light is broken by a dewdrop into the seven colors of the rainbow, down to the snowflake crystalizing in six-pointed stars around the invisible centre. The law of seven has been found to rule in the development and growth of vegetable and animal organisms, in the constitution of the Universe, and in the constitution of Man. Seven is the rule by which the totality of existence is measured, but *Five* is the number of *Harmony*. If the fifth note in the musical scale is in accord with the first and the third, harmony will be the result. There are other accords which are harmonious, but the most perfect accord is caused by the harmony of the first, the third, and the fifth. The sounds may be harmonious, but to attain a perfect accord a third one is required. The same law rules in the constitution of Man. If his body (his first principle) is in accord with his instincts (the third), he may experience pleasant sensations, but full harmony and happiness is only attained when his fifth principle (his intelligence) fully assents in the union of the first and the third. Other parallels may be drawn between the musical scale and the scale of principles in man, and it will be found that both have their accords in *moll* and in *dur* that correspond to each other. Each man's life is a symphony, in which either harmonious or discordant tunes may prevail.

The power by which harmony is produced is the power of Love. Love produces harmony, hate causes discord. Love is the tendency of the disunited parts of one principle to unite again into one.  This tendency presupposes the power of mutual recognition, recognition is a manifestation of consciousness, consciousness is a manifestation of life.  Life, Love, Consciousness, Harmony, are essentially one, the opposite of which is discord and death. Why do some notes, if sounded together, produce harmony, if not on account of the similarity of the elements that compose them coming to the consciousness of our own mind?  Mutual recognition among friends causes joy, and joy means harmony, happiness, and content.

If two or more notes of exactly the same kind are sounded together, they produce neither harmony nor discord, they simply increase their own strength.  They are already one, and no relation exists between them; but if different notes are struck, each containing an element contained in the other, each sees its own counterpart represented in the mirror held by the other, and this recognition is joy.  If we listen to beautiful music the air seems filled with life.  If the principle of harmony exists within ourselves we may recognize it in the music, and it becomes alive in our soul.  A discordant being may listen to the most beautiful music and be left cold, because there is no harmony within his own soul.

If a principle becomes conscious of its own existence in another form, and recognizes its beauty in that form in its purity, and unalloyed by any adulteration, perfect harmony is the result.  If two or more things contain the same element, these elements are justly adapted to each other, and seek to unite, because they are constituted alike ; they vibrate together as one.  This tendency to unite creates *Love*, which manifests .itself on all planes of existence.  The planets are attracted to the sun and to each other, because they all contain the same elements, seeking to reunite, and the power of *gravitation* is nothing else but the power of love.  Man is attracted to woman and woman to man, because they perceive in each other the elements of their own highest ideal, and the more their common ideal becomes manifest in each, the more will they love each other and be fully contented.  Man and woman can only truly love each other if they are both either consciously or unconsciously attracted by the same ideal.  This ideal may be high or low, but the higher it is the more permanent will it be, and the greater will be their mutual happiness,

In each human being exist certain elements which are identical with those existing in all other human beings, and therefore *one* with the latter. Consequently, individual man only *appears to be* a separate being ; while in fact the whole of humanity is a unity and *one;* it is merely the outward expression of the *Universal Man*, which is manifest in many separate human forms. The dirtiest beggar in the street, the most vicious criminal, as well as the greatest king or queen in the world, is myself and yourself, for there is no distinction between one human being and another in the fundamental principle which constitutes a human being, and which is the *Universal Man*, the terrestrial *Adam* and the celestial *Christ.*

In other words : *Mankind* is only one, but it appears in many millions of various masks, and sometimes with very inhuman habits, because the mask which the forms wear hinders their free evolutions. This mask is the *personality* of each man, the instrument through which Adam acts, and which is full of imperfections. He, in whom the terrestrial Adam has become the celestial Adam, the Christ, sees in every man and woman not only his brother or sister, but his *own self.* A person who injures another, injures himself, for each man constitutes a power which acts upon humanity, and the good or evil he does will return to himself.

A man who attempts to fall in love with himself, or, with other words, to find in his person his own highest ideal, will never succeed in being contented and harmonious. A man who seeks to recognize himself as his own highest ideal becomes self-centred and vain. His love, instead of expanding to the periphery of his sphere, will act from its periphery to the centre, and he will become spiritually smaller every day. But the man or the woman who seeks the realization of their own ideal in the object of their love, will, if they find it, recognize it as their own self which they always possessed, although they were not aware of its possession until they found it in another form. He who possesses the truth recognizes it wherever he finds it in others, but he who does not possess it cannot recognize it. Our modern age often rejects the highest truths unless they bear the stamp of man-created authority : but the wise recognize the truth by its own light.

Light is darkness unless it is reflected by matter. Light

cannot illuminate itself, but it illuminates the darkness, and consequently the existence of light depends on the existence of matter. Love without an object cannot exist *relatively*. A person in love with himself loves nothing. Love, attached to nothing, exists in the *Absolute*. A love being attached to a high object is high, and if it is attached to a low object it is low, as life in a low form is low, and in a high form high; because love, and life, and harmony are the functions and attributes of one and the same principle in nature, they are only different aspects of one universal power. Where love exists there is life, and no life can endure without love, and the more the love expands over all, the more will the living spiritual power of man extend. The more love is concentrated upon a single object, the stronger will it be in that direction and infuse love and life in that object, and the more it is divided among different objects, the more will its power be dispersed.

Love, to be strong, must be pure and unalloyed with selfish considerations. If we love a thing on account of the use we can make of it, we do not in reality love that thing, but ourselves. Pure love has only the well-being of its object in view, it does not calculate profits, and is not afraid of disadvantages that may grow out of its love. The intellect calculates, but love follows the law of attraction.

Impure love is no love at all, it is merely attraction. It is weak, and does not enter into its object; it may cause a ruffle on the soul of another, but does not penetrate to the centre. Pure love penetrates and cannot be resisted, unless it is opposed by another love of equal strength, but streaming in another direction. The most potent love potion a person can give to another is to love that person without any selfish object in view. Such pure love will infuse itself into the soul of the beloved and call forth corresponding vibrations of love, because one mode of activity gives rise to similar modes, according to the universal law of induction.

This is undoubtedly true, provided that the love-germs in the soul of the beloved correspond in quality to those of the lover and are reached by the latter. The strongest sunshine cannot cause any plants to grow in a soil in which the seeds of the latter are too deeply imbedded to be reached by the heat of the sun, or too much obstructed by weeds to grow. Likewise the heart is the soil where psychic germs of all kinds are imbedded, ready to unfold, if accessible, to the magic power of love.

If you wish to progress on the road to perfection, take lessons in love. Learn to love the highest, and you will be attracted by it. Seek in every man those qualities which appear to be high, and cover his mistakes by charity and love. If you speak ill of another you speak ill of yourself, because he who prominently notices the faults of another must have the elements of those faults in himself. A vain person is repulsed by the vanity of another, a liar expects from others the truth, a thief does not wish to have his own property taken away. Virtues attract each other, producing harmony, but vices repulse each other, and discord is the result.

Each man is a mirror in which every other man may see his own image reflected, either as he is or as he may become in the future, for in every human soul exist the same elements, although in different states of development, and their development often depends on external conditions over which man has but little control.

An emotion suppressed and forced back on itself may become diseased and its direction perverted. A love which is neither transformed nor fulfilled, but harbored in the heart, creates phantoms and hallucinations just as stagnant water develops animal life. A love for a high ideal, which, instead of reaching up to the sphere of that ideal, seeks for it in lower spheres, will languish and starve or be attracted to lower ideals ; but, if love meets its corresponding love, harmony will be the result.

Love is the most necessary element for the continuance of life ; there is no life without love, and if man were to cease to love life he would cease to live. A love for a higher life will lead men to a higher condition, a love for a lower state will drag them down to a low. It often happens that if a person's love for a high ideal does not meet the object which it desires, it transfers its love upon something that is low. Old females without any offspring often transfer their parental affection upon some favorite cat or dog, and there are men who buy the semblance of love when no genuine love can be had.

Whenever a lower vibration is not entirely out of harmony with a higher one, the higher vibration may accelerate the

action of the lower one and bring it up to its own level, in
the same manner as a bar of iron, surrounded by an
insulated electric wire, may have electricity induced in it,
and through a long-continued and powerful action of the
higher vibrations upon the lower ones even the involuntary
actions of the body, such as the movements of the heart,
may become subject to individual will.   Two strings of a
musical instrument which sound not entirely out of harmony, may, by being sounded together for a certain length
of time, at last become harmonious ; a man living in more
refined society, which is not too far above his moral or
intellectual level, will become more refined, servants will
ape their masters, and animals take some of the lower
characteristics of those that attend to them, and friends
or married couples being continually in each other's company may finally resemble each other to a certain extent.

If the respective rates of the vibrations of two substances
are entirely out of harmony, they may repel each other,
and abnormal activity or excitement follows.   The animal
body, for instance, can be exposed without danger to a
comparatively high degree of heat, if the temperature is
gradually raised ; while an even lower degree of heat may
be very injurious if applied suddenly.   It is not for fancied
reasons that the occultist abstains from Alcohol and from
animal food.   The elements of such substances are in a high
state of activity, and by coming into contact with the
elements of the blood, they stimulate them and throw them
into an abnormal state of vibration, giving rise to emotions
on the astral plane, which may in their turn affect the
higher principles in man in an undesirable manner.   The
same is the case with other substances, whose odic emanations are red, while those emitting blue auras are of a
different character ; but even the highest elements draw
their nourishment indirectly from the lowest ones, and the
old saying that " a sound mind needs a sound body to
develop in " is not a mere fiction ; because, although a
sound brain (the instrument of the Mind) may exist in an
invalid body, still robust health is nevertheless useful and
desirable, and it is important, for the development of occult
powers, to select proper food and follow such laws of
Hygiene as the individual may require.

" What may be one man's food, will be another man's
poison ; " in the sphere of matter as well as in the sphere

of the emotions. Strong constitutions can bear strong food, weak minds will get frightened at unwelcome truths. Intemperance in food and drink is as bad as intemperance in emotion ; and self-restraint is equally necessary on both planes.

No man has ever become an Adept merely because he lived on vegetables ; a vegetable diet is, however, much preferable to meat-eating for various reasons. Apart from the self-evident fact that it is entirely untheosophical and opposed to the divine law of justice that he who strives after the attainment of a higher state of existence should destroy animal life, or cause others to destroy it for the purpose of gratifying his animal appetite, it will be plain to every one who investigates the laws of the higher life, that the loading of the human organism with animal substances will not facilitate its penetration by the light of the divine spirit.

Those who desire to become more spiritual and refined should avoid supplying their bodies with that which is gross ; those who desire to master their passions should not feed themselves with substances in which the elements of such passions reside ; those who wish to come into possession of more ethereal forms act unwisely if they supply the latter with substances which must necessarily render them more gross, and material and dense, and thus hinder the free movements of the spirit within. Instances may be known, where a person has attained a considerable degree of spiritual development in spite of living on the corpses of animals ; but such instances are very rare, and it may be said without hesitation that one of *the first steps to the acquisition of spiritual refinement is the abandonment of animal food.*

A great variety of different kinds of food produces disorders of the digestive organs and impurities of the blood ; a struggle for life ensues between the different auras, and excitement, fever, and disease is the result. The same law explains the origin of venereal and cutaneous diseases, and in the astral plane, a great variety of emotions, called into existence within a short space of time, may render a person insane.

Numerous cases of severe chronic diseases are known to have been cured by fasting—either voluntary or enforced. Man actually needs but little food. Gluttony is a habit, not a necessity.

Wherever two forces of an entirely opposite character
meet, disharmony will be the result, and as everybody has
his own peculiar emanations and auras and transmits them
to others, so everyone receives the magnetic auras of others
or of the locality by which he is surrounded, and these
emanations may be either wholesome or pestiferous; men
and women may either cure or poison each other by them,
and it may therefore be well to follow the advice which
Gautama Buddha gave to his disciples, and eat and sleep
alone.

Many people are very careful to have their food well
prepared, so that no unhealthy food enters the body;
while at the same time they are very careless as to what
emotions enter their mind; because they fail to realize
that purity of the emotions is as necessary as purity of the
body.

A strong force overcomes a weak force, and a stronger
emotion may render a weaker one inactive. If the strong
emotion is high, it elevates the lower, if the lower one is
the strongest, degradation is the result. Cautiousness
may keep combativeness in check or make man a coward;
but without cautiousness combativeness will fly off at a
tangent, and rashness and disaster may be the result.

The higher emotions evolute from the lower ones, and
by the control of reason vices grow into virtues. Intense
love of self may expand into love of wife and friends, or
widen still more into a love of country or a love of humanity. The more it expands the more it becomes refined.

Nothing in the universe can be annihilated, only the
form can be changed. An emotion cannot be killed, but
it can be educated up to a higher level.

Purely sexual instinct may be transformed into a pure
love of an elevated character by associating with a person
of the other sex, who is of a highly moral and intellectual
nature; brutal combativeness may be purified by leading
it into an intellectual channel, where the pen will take the
place of a cudgel: acquisitiveness may be elevated into a
craving for knowledge, and destructiveness into a desire
for the destruction of error.

It has been said that our vices are the ladder on which
we may climb up to heaven, and this is undoubtedly true,
because the only effective virtue which man can possess is
*energy*, and if we employ our energies for good instead of

evil, we turn our vice into virtue ; but he who possesses no energy is equally useless for good as he is for evil.

There can be nothing absolutely wrong in employing the natural instincts and emotions in a natural and legitimate manner ; the question is only whether such an employment will be useful for the purpose we have in view. If we have a sum of money at our disposal, we have a right to spend it for pleasure, or to buy something useful, or to throw it away.  In the same manner we may spend our physical forces, our vital energies, or our emotions, for the pursuit of useful pleasures or for the purpose of our higher evolution ; but as we cannot expend the same sum of money again after it is once spent, so the sum of energies expended for a low purpose will be lost for the higher object in view.  If a person has no higher object in view than to eat and drink, sleep and propagate his species, he may be thereby rendered perfectly happy, and if he follows the dictates of his nature, there can be nothing wrong ; but he who desires to assist the slow process of nature in developing himself into an immortal being, must take care not to waste his strength on lower attractions ; and in the course of time the energies which produced the lower emotions will develop into not less strong but higher emotions ; the whole of the lower activity will be transformed into a higher one.

Only that which is pure can be harmonious.

Singleness of purpose renders a motive pure, but a variety of purposes causes impurity.  If a person devotes himself to a certain mode of life, because all his desires are directed towards that end, his motive will be pure ; but if he has besides other objects in view, his motive will be impure, and may defeat his aim.

The word "*asceticism*" is continually misapplied.  A man who lives in a convent, or as an hermit in the wilderness, is not an "ascetic," if he has no desire for a life in the world ; for it is no act of self-denial to avoid that which we do not want.  "Asceticism" means *discipline,* and a person who is disgusted with the ways of the world undergoes a much more severe discipline, if he remains in the world, than if he runs away, and goes where he may enjoy his peace.  The real *ascetic* is therefore he who lives in the midst of the society whose manners displease him, and whose tastes are not his own, and who, in spite of all the temptations by which he may be surrounded, still maintains

his integrity of character. Strength only grows by resistance, and our enemies are therefore our friends, if we know
how to use them. A hermit living in the woods, where he
has no one to contradict and resist him, can gain no
strength. Such a life is only suitable for one who has
already gained full strength, and who wants to enjoy that
which he already possesses. Tranquillity is only suitable
for the Adept; the Neophite must go through the ordeal
of life.

Metals are purified by fire, and the emotions by suffering. The lower desires must starve to nourish the higher;
the animal passions must be crucified and die; but the
angel of Will removes the stone from the sepulchre, and
liberates the higher energies from the sphere of selfishness
and darkness ; and then the resurrected virtues will begin
to live and become active in a new world of enduring light
and harmony.

To obtain a clear view of the process of purification of
man, imagine yourself immersed in a mist of matter, surrounded by inimical influences from the emotions of the
astral plane that gradually lead to your dissolution.
Deep in yourself, in the cloudless centre of your soul, and
yet seemingly far above you, is your internal god, your
ethereal prototype, your real self, the immortal Adonai,
like a mirage, waiting to attract your more refined elements
towards himself. The more you concentrate your thoughts
and desires upon your lower self, and cling to the sphere
of desires, the more will the serene image grow dim and
shadowy; but if your aspirations and thoughts, made
effective by your Will and your acts, rise above the sphere
of self and cling to the pure ideal, then your higher energies
will flow towards it, making it grow more and more distinct and substantial, until your innermost self .and your
consciousness is united with it, and free from all earthly
attractions, looks down upon that which remains below,
and beholds in it only the shadow of its own immortal
reality. Desire results from attraction, attraction results
from the separation of two substances, analogous in their
essences and properties. We cannot desire a thing of
which we know nothing, and if we are attracted to a thing,
there must necessarily be in us a portion of it desirous to
reunite itself with the portion from which it is separated.
A human being possessed of a divine spark of the universal spirit knows intuitively the source from which it came

and with which it desires to become reunited, without needing any scientific demonstration to convince him intellectually of this truth.

To recognize the purity of the divine spark within is true adoration, to attempt to realize it is true meditation; to exert the will to bring one's self in perfect harmony with it, is aspiration or prayer. To express that prayer in acts, is to make it effective. True prayer is always efficacious on the plane whereon it is made to act. Prayer on the physical plane consists in physical works, on the astral plane it purifies the emotions through the action of the will; in the realm of the intellect study is prayer and leads to knowledge, and the highest spiritual aspirations lift man out of the turmoil of matter and bring him nearer to his own god.

There is not a single instance known in history in which true prayer has not been efficacious. If any man has not obtained that which he asked, it only proves that he did not know how to pray. True prayer means self-sacrifice; a giving up of the low upon the altar of the high. True prayer does not consist in words, but in actions, and the gods help him who helps himself; but he who expects that the gods should do for him that which he ought to accomplish himself, does not know how to pray, and will be disappointed. Prayer means a rising up in our thoughts and aspirations to our highest ideal, but if we do not ourselves rise up to it, we do not pray. If we expect our highest ideal to come down to us, we expect an absurdity and impossibility.

To attain the highest the spirit should be the master, the passions, the servants. A helpless cripple is the slave of his servant; a man who depends on ignorant servants to do work which he can do himself has, to a certain extent, to submit to their whims and imperfections, and if he changes his servants, that does not change his position. A person who has vulgar desires and tastes becomes the servant of these tastes; they dictate to him, and he has to exert himself to obtain the means to gratify their claims; but he who has no ignoble desires to serve, is independent and free and his own master. He has conquered matter, his strife with the astral elements ceases. For him discord can then no longer exist, and his purified elements will find their responsive vibrations in the eternal life of the universal spirit of Love.

# CHAPTER VI.

## ILLUSION.

*"Reason dissipates the illusions and visionary interpretations of things, in which the imagination runs riot."—Dr. Caird.*

THE first power that meets us at the threshold of soul's dominion is the power of imagination; it is the plastic and creative power of the mind. Man is conscious of being able to receive ideas and to put them into forms. He lives not entirely in the objective world, but possesses an interior world of his own. It is in his power to be the sole autocrat in that world, the master of its creations and lord over all it contains. He may govern there by the supreme power of his will, and if ideas intrude, which have no legitimate right to exist in it, it is in his power either to drive them away or suffer them to remain and to grow. His reason is the supreme ruler in that world, its ministers are the emotions. If man's reason, misled by the treacherous advice of the emotions, suffers evil ideas to grow, they may become powerful and dethrone reason, unless it employs the Will to suppress them.

This interior world, like the outer world, is a world of its own. It is sometimes dark, sometimes illuminated; its space and the things it contains are as real to its inhabitants as the physical world is real to the physical senses; its horizon may be either narrow or expanded, limited in some and without limits in others; it has its beautiful scenery and its dismal localities, its sunshine and storms, its forms of beauty and horrible shapes. It is the privilege of intellectual man to retire to that world whenever he chooses; physical enemies do not persecute him there; bodily pain cannot enter. The vexations of material life remain behind, but the emotions enter with him.

This interior realm of the soul is the *Temple of Man* wherein we should shut ourselves and lock the door against the intrusion of sensual impressions, if we desire to " pray." On the entrance of that temple are the *Dwellers of the Threshold*, our desires and passions, which are our own creations, and which must be conquered before we can enter. Within that temple exists a world, as big and as illimitable as the external unbounded universe, the forms of which we see with our physical eyes. This inner world is filled with the products of man's own creation ; some of them inactive, but others have become active and living entities, which may assume dominion and, by growing into power, dethrone the real king, *Reason*. In this inner realm each man is—or ought to be—the God whose spirit floats over the waters of the deep, and whose *fiat* calls into existence only that which is useful and good. The more this inner individual god will be in harmony with the God of the universe, the more will the two become one, and the greater will be the perfection of the inner world over the happiness of the individual. Only when man has found himself in that inner world, will he begin a life which must necessarily be immortal because it is free from change, and having become his own master, he can belong to nobody but himself—not to his lower— but to his *highest* self, which is one with the eternal *Christ* or the *Maha-atma* of the universe.

In that interior world is the battle-ground of the gods. There the gods of love and hate, the dæmons of lust and pride, and anger, the devils of malice, cruelty, and revenge, vanity, envy, and jealousy, may hold high carnival, they may stir up the emotions, and, unless subdued by Reason, they may grow strong enough to dethrone it.

Reason rests upon Truth. Wherever truth is disregarded illusions appear. If we lose sight of the highest, the lower will appear to be the highest, and an illusion will be created. *One* is the number of Truth, *Six* is the number of illusion, because the Six have no existence without the Seventh, they are the visible products of the one, manifesting itself as six around an invisible centre. Wherever they are six, there must be the seventh, although the presence of the latter may not be manifest. One is the number of life, and six the number of shadows from which life has departed.

Forms without life are illusive, and he who mistakes the form for the life or principle of which it is an expression is haunted by an illusion. Forms perish, but the principle that causes their existence remains. The object of forms is to represent principles, and as long as a form is known to be a true representation of a principle the principle gives it life ; but if a form is made to serve another principle than the one which called it into existence, degradation and death will be the final result.

The irrational forms produced by nature are perfect expressions of the principles they are intended to represent ; rational beings only are the dissemblers. Each animal is a true expression of the character represented by its form, only at the point where intellectuality begins deception commences. Each animal form is a symbol of the mental state which characterizes its soul, because it is not itself the arbitrary originator of its form, but rational man has it in his power to create, and if he prostitutes one principle in a form for another, the form will gradually adopt that shape which characterizes the prostituted principle, of which, in the course of time, it becomes a true expression.

Therefore we find that a man of noble appearance, by becoming a miser, gradually adopts the sneaking look and the stealthy gait of an animal going in search of its prey ; the lascivious may acquire the habits, and perhaps the appearance of a monkey or goat, the sly one the features of a fox, and the conceited the looks of a donkey.

If our bodies were formed of a more ethereal and plastic material than of muscles and bones, each change of our character would produce quickly a corresponding change of our form ; but gross matter is inert, and follows only slowly the impressions made upon the soul. For this reason the deduction of Phrenology, Physiognomy, etc., however much truth they may contain, cannot convey absolute truth. The material of which astral forms and souls are made are more plastic, and the soul of a villainous person may actually resemble a pool filled with vipers and scorpions, the true symbol of his moral characteristics, mirrored in his mind. A generation of saints would, in the course of time, produce a nation of Apollos and

Dianas, a generation of villains would grow into monsters and dwarfs. To keep the form in its original beauty the principle must be kept pure and without any adulteration.

One fundamental color of the solar spectrum, if unmixed, is as pure as another; one element, if free from another, is pure. Unmixed copper is as pure as unalloyed gold, and emotions are pure if free from extraneous mixing. Forms are pure if they represent their principles in their purity; a villain who shows himself what he is is pure and true, a saint who dissembles is impure and false. Fashions are the external expressions of the mental states of a country, and if men and women degenerate in their character their fashions will become absurd.

The want of power to discriminate between the true and the illusive, between the form and the principle, and the consequent error of apprehending the low for the high, is the cause of suffering. Man's material interests are frequently considered to be of supreme importance, and the interests of the highest elements in his constitution are forgotten. The power that should be expended to feed the high is eaten up by the low. Instead of the low serving the high, the high is made to serve the low, and instead of the form being used as an instrument of action for the principle, the principle is made to wait until the claims of the form are attended to; in other words, a low principle is substituted for a higher one.

Such a prostitution of principle in favor of form is found in all spheres of social life. We find it among the rich and the poor, the educated and the ignorant, in the forum, the press, and the pulpit, no less than in the halls of the merchant and in the daily transactions of life. The prostitution of principle is worse than the prostitution of the body, and he who uses his intellectual powers for selfish and villainous purposes is more to be pitied than she who carries on a trade with her bodily charms to gain the means by which she may keep that body alive. The prostitution of universal human rights for the benefit of a few individuals is the most dangerous form of prostitution on Earth.

The difference between vulgar prostitution of the body and the more refined prostitution of the intellectual faculties for the purpose of accomplishing selfish ends, is merely that in the first class merely the grossest parts of the human organization are misused, while in the other class the higher and more permanent parts are misused. The consequences of the latter kind must therefore be much more lasting than those of the former. There are few women in the world who have become degraded from an inclination to be so; in the great majority of cases they are the victims of circumstances which they had not the power to resist; but intellectual villains usually belong to the higher classes, where want and poverty are unknown.

To employ the intellectual powers for the mere purpose of "making money" is the beginning of intellectual prostitution. Blessed are they who are able to gain their bread by the honest work of their hands, for an employment which requires little intellectual attention will leave them free to employ their mental powers for the purpose of spiritual meditation and unfoldment; while those who spend all their mental energy upon the lower planes are selling their immortal birthright for a worthless mess of potage which may nourish the body while it starves the soul.

The greatest of all illusions is the illusion of "*Self*." Material man looks upon himself as something existing apart from every other existence. The shape of his form creates the illusion of being an independent substantial whole, and the changes in that form take place so slow and imperceptible, that the error is not perceived. Still, there is not a single element in his body, in the constitution of his soul, or in the mechanism of his intellect, that is not continually departing, and is replaced by others from the universal fountain of life. What belongs to him to-day belonged yesterday to another, and may belong to another to-morrow. In his physical form there is a continual change. In the bodies of organized beings tissues disappear slowly or quickly, according to the nature of their affinities, and new ones take their places, to be replaced in turn by others. The human body changes in size, shape, and density as age advances, presenting successively the symbols of the buoyant health of youth, the vigorous constitution of manhood, or the grace and beauty of womanhood, up to the attributes indicating old age, the forerunner of decay and cessation of activity in that individual form.

No less is the change in the soul. Sensation and desires change, consciousness changes, memories grow dim. No man has the same opinions he had when he was a child;

knowledge increases, intellect grows weak, and on the mental as well as on the physical plane the special activity ceases when the accumulated energy is exhausted by trans-formation into other modes of action or is transferred in other forms.

The lower material elements in the constitution of man change rapidly, the higher ones change slowly, but only the highest elements are enduring. Nothing can be said to belong essentially to man but the character of his sixth principle in its union with the seventh. He who cares a great deal for his lower principles, cares for things that are not his own, but which he has only borrowed from nature. While he enjoys their possession an illusion is created, making them appear to be an essential part of himself, and his imagination revels in their fancied possession. They are, however, not more an essential part of himself than the clothes which a man wears, a constituent part of the man. His only true self is his character, and he who loses the strength of his character loses all his possessions.

One of the kings of illusions is *Money*, the king of the world. Money represents the principle of equity, and it should be employed to enable every one to obtain the just equivalent for his labor. If we desire more money than we can rightfully claim, we wish for something that does not belong to us but to another, and we repulse the divine principle of truth. If we obtain labor without paying for it its proper equivalent, we deprive others of justice, and therefore deprive ourselves of the principle of truth, which is a more serious loss to ourselves than the loss of money to the defrauded.

Money as such is an illusion, only the principle of justice, which it represents, has a real existence. Never-theless we see the world lie at the feet of the form. The poor clamor for it, and the rich crave for more, and the general desire is to obtain the greatest amount of reward by giving the least possible equivalent. There are priests who save souls, and doctors who cure bodies for money ; law is sold to him who is able and willing to pay, fame and reputation and the semblance of love can be obtained for money, and the worth of a man is expressed in the sum of shillings or pounds which he may call his own. Starvation threatens the poor, and the consequence of superabundance the rich, and some of the rich take advantage of the distress of the poor to enrich themselves more.　Science exerts her powers to increase the amount of the material comforts of man.　It vanquishes the impediments presented by time and space, and turns night into day.　New engines are invented, and the work whose performance in former times required the use of a thousand arms, may now be accomplished by a child.　An immense amount of personal suffering and labor is thereby saved.　But as the means to satisfy the craving for comfort increase, a craving arises for more.　Things that formerly were considered luxuries now become indispensable needs.　Illusions create illusions, and desires give rise to desires.　The sight of the principle is lost, and the golden calf is put into its place.　Production is followed by over production, the supply exceeds the demand, the price of labor comes down to starvation rates, and on the rotten soil the mushrooms of monopoly grow.　The more the facilities increase to sustain the battle of life, the more increases its fury.　The noblest power of man, his intellect, whose destiny it is to form a solid basis for the highest spiritual aspirations of man, is forced to labor for the satisfaction of the animal instincts of man ; the body flourishes, and the spirit starves and becomes a beggar in the kingdom of truth.

From the love of self arises the love of possession.　It is the hydra-headed monster whose cravings can never be stilled.　Nearest to the illusion of self stands the illusion of *Love.*　True love is not an illusion, it is the power that unites the world and an attribute of the spirit ; but the illusion of love is not love, but only love's shadow.　True love seeks only for the happiness of the object it loves, but animal love cares for itself, and seeks only enjoyment.　True love exists, even if the form is dissolved ; false love dies, when the form to which it was attached decays.

Ideal woman is the crown of creation, and has a right to be loved by man.　A male being, who does not love the character of a woman, bears only the semblance of a man, and man is not a complete being unless he possesses woman's love.　A man who does not love beauty has no element of beauty in him.　But the man who only fancies woman's attractions, and not the woman herself, is repulsed by her.　If only his instincts attract him to her she sees his weakness and is repulsed by it.　She may be rendered vain enough by the possession of such charms as to enjoy the victory gained by them over a fool, but an intelligent woman looks upon such a victim as an object of pity and commiseration, and not as a source of strength.

Man loves beauty and woman loves strength. A man who is the slave of his desires is weak, and cannot command the respect of a woman he professes to love. If she sees him squirm under the lash of his animal instincts she will not be able to look upon him as her protector and god.

Man represents Reason, and woman represents Will. If the will is in harmony with reason it will be as *one*. If they act against each other illusions come into existence.

Another illusion is the craving for physical life, and well may he crave for it who has no character of his own, because, having lost his character, if he loses his life, he loses his all. Men and women cling to the illusion of life because they do not know what life is. They will submit to indignity, dishonor, and suffering rather than die. Life is a means to an end, and as such it is valuable; but why should life be so desirable as to sacrifice character for it? One life is only one temporary condition among a thousand similar ones through which the character of a man passes in its travels on the road to perfection, and whether he remains a longer or a shorter interval at one station, cannot be of any very serious importance to him. Man can make no better use of his life than to sacrifice it, if necessary, for the welfare of others; because this act will strengthen his own character, in which rests the source of his life, and the power by which he is enabled to reappear in a new form.

On the other hand, he who sneaks away from the battle of life for selfish purposes, or because he is afraid to continue its struggles, will not escape. He may wish to step out of life and destroy his body, but the law cannot be cheated. Life will remain with him until his natural days would have ended. He cannot destroy it, he can only deprive himself of the instrument through which he can act. He resembles a man who has to perform some work and throws away the instrument which would have enabled him to perform it. Vain will be his regrets.

But if, in the cases of sane suicides, the illusion called life continues after the death of the physical body, and consciousness remains with the astral form, then a serious question arises in regard to the disposal of the bodies of such unfortunate persons ; for wherever consciousness exists, there must be sensation, and as in such instances a magnetic connection is said to continue to exist between the astral man and his corpse, it appears not impossible that the *post mortem* communications of suicides are true, and that injuries inflicted upon the body may under certain conditions be felt very acutely by the disembodied man.

Another illusion is a great deal of what is called " science." True knowledge makes a man free, but false science renders him a slave to the opinions of others. Many men waste their lives to learn that which is foolish and neglect that which is true, mistaking that which is evanescent and perishing for the eternal. Nor is their desire for learning usually caused by a desire to learn the truth, else they would not reject the truth when they see it. In the majority of cases learning is not the aim but the means to the aim of the student, while his real objects are the attainment of wealth, position, and fame, or the gratification of curiosity. The true wealth of a nation or a man does not rest in intellectual acquirements, but in spiritual possessions, which alone will remain permanent.

There is nothing more productive of a tendency to the development of an extreme degree of selfishness than the development of a high degree of intellectuality, without any accompanying growth of spirituality. Whoever doubts this assertion let him observe the petty jealousies everywhere prevailing among the learned professions. Moreover, a high degree of intellectuality enables a person to take personal advantages over others who are less learned, and unless he possesses great moral powers he may not be able to resist the temptations that are put in his way. The greatest villains and criminals have been persons of great intellectual qualifications. A development of the intellect is necessary to understand spiritual truths after they are once perceived, but they cannot be perceived by the intellect without spirituality ; they can only be perceived by the power of the spirit. The development of spiritual powers of perception is, therefore, of supreme importance ; that of the intellect comes next. " Blessed is he whom the truth teaches, not by perishable emblems and words, but by its own inherent power ; not what it appears to be, but as *it is*." *

---

* Thomas de Kempis.

The love of power and fame are other illusions. True power is an attribute of the spirit. If I am obeyed because I am rich, it is not myself who commands obedience, but my riches. If I am called powerful because I enjoy authority, it is not myself who is powerful, but it is the authority vested in me. Riches and authority are halos thrown around men, which often vanish as quickly as they have been acquired. Fame is often enjoyed by him who does not deserve it, and the most honored man is he who has cause to respect himself on account of his acts.

Place of birth and condition of life are circumstances which are usually not matters of choice, and no one has a right to despise another on account of his nationality, religious belief, color of skin, or the act he may play on this planet. Conditions are illusions, caused by the consequences of other illusions; they do not belong to the essential character of man. Whether an actor plays the part of a king or a servant, the actor is, therefore, not despised, provided he plays his part well.

There are other illusions which come without being asked, and remain, although their stay is not wanted. They are the unwelcome visitors—*Fear*, *Doubt*, and *Remorse*, and they, like all other illusions, are caused by ignorance of the true nature of man and the extent of his powers. Men sometimes live in fear of a revengeful power which has no existence, and may die from fear of an evil that does not exist. They are often afraid of the effects of causes which they, nevertheless, continue to create; they may doubt whether they will succeed in cheating the law, not knowing that the real man is himself the law and cannot be cheated. Every acts creates a cause, and the cause is followed by an effect which reacts on him who created the cause, whether he may experience that effect in this life or in another. To escape the effect of the cause which has been created, he who created the cause must try to transform himself into another man. If his lower principles have led him into mistakes they will suffer, but if he succeeds in assimilating his nature with his higher principles, and thereby changes himself into a being of a different character, their suffering will not be of the greatest importance to him. Such is the only rational philosophy of the " forgiveness of sins," and priests could forgive sins if they were able to change the sinner into a saint. This can, however, only be done by the individual exertions of the "sinner," who may be instructed by one who is wise. To become sufficiently wise to instruct another about the laws or his nature it is of the utmost importance that the instructor should know these laws, and be acquainted with the true constitution of man.

Reason is the savior of man, ignorance is his death and unreason his suffering. Reason is the power of the mind to recognize the truth, and in the light of truth the shadows of doubt and fear and remorse cannot exist.

Illusions are dispersed by Reason through the power of Will. When the will is held in abeyance the imagination is rendered passive, and the mind takes in the reflections of pictures stored up in the Astral Light without choice or discrimination. When reason does not guide the imagination the mind creates disorderly fancies and hallucinations. The passive seer dreams while awake, and may mistake his dreams for realities, but his dreams may be his own creations, or they may be impressions caused by floating ideas taking possession of the unresisting mind, and, according to the source from which such impressions come, they may be either true or false. Various means have been adopted to suspend the discriminating power of will and render the imagination abnormally passive, and all such practices are injurious, in proportion as they are efficacious. The ancient Pythoness attempted to heighten her already abnormal receptivity by the inhalation of noxious vapors ; savage and semi-civilized people sometimes use poisons, or whirl in a dance until the action of reason is temporarily suspended ; others use opium, Indian hemp, and other narcotics, which not only suspend their will and render their mind a blank, but which also excite the brain, and induce morbid fancies and illusions.*

---

* The fumigations which were used at former times for the purpose of rendering reason inactive, and allowing the products of a passive imagination to appear in an objective state, were usually narcotic substances. Blood was only used for the purpose of furnishing substance to Elementals and Elementaries, by the aid of which they might render their bodies more dense and visible.

*Cornelius Agrippa* gives the following prescription : Make a powder of spermaceti, aloe wood, musk, saffron, and thyme, sprinkle it with the blood of a hoopop. If this powder is burnt upon the graves of the

Fortune-tellers and clairvoyants employ various means to fix their attention, to suspend thought and render their minds passive, and the images which they receive may be true or false; others stare at mirrors or crystals, water or ink,* but the Adept, while not forsaking the use of his reason, renders his imagination passive by maintaining, under all circumstances, a serene tranquillity of the mind. The surface of a lake whose water is in motion reflects only distorted reproductions of images projected upon it, and if the elements in the interior world are in a state of confusion, if emotion fights with emotion and the uproar of the passions troubles the mind, if the heaven of the soul is clouded by prejudices, darkened by ignorance, hallucinated by insane desires, the true images of things seen will be equally distorted. The divine principle in man remains in itself unaltered and undisturbed, like the image of a star

---

dead, the ethereal forms of the latter will approach, and may become visible.

*Eckartshousen* made successful experiments with the following prescription : Mix powdered frankincense and flour with an egg, add milk, honey, and rosewater, make a paste, and throw some of it upon burning coals.

Another prescription given by the same author consists of hemlock, saffron, aloes, opium, mandragora, henbane, poppy-flowers, and some other poisonous plants. After undergoing a certain preparation, which he describes, he attempted the experiment, and saw the ghost of the person which he desired to see; but he came very near poisoning himself. *Dr. Horst* repeated the experiment with the same result, and for years afterwards, whenever he looked upon a dark object, he saw the apparition again.

Chemistry has advanced since that time, and those who desire to make such experiments at the risk of their health, may now accomplish this in a more comfortable and easy manner by inhaling some of the stupefying gases known to chemical science.

* There are numerous prescriptions for the preparation of magic mirrors ; but the best magic mirror will be useless to him who is not able to see clairvoyantly ; while the natural clairvoyant may call that faculty into action by concentrating his mind on any particular spot, a glass of water, ink, a crystal, or anything else ; for it is not in the mirror where such things are seen, but in the mind ; the mirror merely serves to assist in the entering of that mental state which is necessary to produce clairvoyant sight. The best of all magic mirrors is the soul of man, and it should always be kept pure, and be protected against dust and dampness and rust, so that it may not become tarnished, and remain perfectly clear, and able to reflect the light of the divine spirit in its original purity.

reflected in water ; but unless its dwelling is rendered clear and transparent, it cannot send its rays through the surrounding walls. The more the emotions rage, the more will the mind become disturbed and the spirit be forced to retreat into its interior prison ; or if it loses entirely its hold over the mind, it may be driven away by the forces which it cannot control, burst the door of its dungeon, return to the source from whence it came, and leave man behind as a living corpse, a maniac, * in which the spiritual principle is entirely inactive.

If a person suffers his reason to give up the control over his imagination he surrenders one of the greatest prerogatives of man, and exposes himself to danger. In the normal condition reason guides the imagination to a certain extent ; in abnormal conditions the will of another may take its place, or it may roam without being guided, influenced only by previously-existing conditions. A person who dreams does not control the actions which he performs in his dream, although he may dream that he is exercising his will. The things seen in his dream are to him realities, and he does not doubt their substantiality, while external physical objects have no existence for him, and not even the possibility of their existence comes to his consciousness. He may see before him a ditch and dream that he wills to jump over it, but he does not actually exert his will, he only follows the impulses created during his waking condition. A person in a trance may be so much under the influence of a " magnetizer " as to have no active will of his own, and be only led by the imagination of the operator. The avenues of his external senses are closed, and he lives entirely in the subjective world, in which material objects can find no place, and in which such objects could by no means be introduced. Still what he sees is real to him, and if the operator creates a precipice in his imagination, perhaps represented by a chalk mark on the floor (to assist the imagination of the operator), the " subject " will, on approaching it, experience and manifest the same terror as he would in his normal state if a precipice were yawning under his feet ; and if the operator should have the cruelty to will the entranced to jump over its edge, the most serious consequences to the individual might follow. A

---

* See H. P. Blavatsky : " Isis Unveiled."

glass of water transformed into imaginary wine by the will of the " mesmerizer " may make the subject intoxicated, and if that water has been transformed into imaginary poison it may injure or kill the sensitive. A powerful " mesmerizer " ca⸗ form either a beautiful or a horrible picture in his mind, and by transferring it by his will upon the mental sphere of a sensitive, he may cause him—even if the latter is in his normal condition—either pleasure or suffering, while the mental images so created in the mind of the sensitive may again react upon others and be perceived by them.

If a person is *en rapport* with a magnetized subject, the image or even a thought existing in the mind of the former is immediately accepted as a reality by the latter.

Such states may be induced, not merely during the magnetic sleep, but also during the normal condition, and without any active desire on the part of a magnetizer. If the audience sheds tears during the performance of a tragedy, although they all know that it is merely a play, they are in a state of partial magnetization. Hundreds of similar occurrences take place every day, and there is sufficient material everywhere in every-day life for the student of psychology to investigate and explain, without seeking for cases of an abnormal character.

If a " Medium " submits the control over his imagination to another being he becomes his servant. This other being may be another person, or it may be an idea, an emotion, a passion, and the effect on the passive Medium will be proportionate to the intensity of the action manifested by them. It may be an elemental, an astral corpse, or a malicious influence, and the Medium may become an epileptic, a maniac, or a criminal. A person who surrenders the control over his imagination, indiscriminately, to every unknown power, is not less insane than he who would entrust his money and valuables to the first unknown stranger or vagabond that would ask him for it.

*Mediumship* is nothing else but a process of transfer of thought, and differs from an ordinary magnetic experiment only in so far as in the latter the operator is a visible person, while in the former the influence proceeds from an invisible source, and is the more dangerous because being invisible it is not known from whence it proceeds. If a magnetizer commands his subject to commit a mur-

der, the latter may commit it, even after he has awakened
from his sleep.   In such a case the operator is the murderer, and the subject merely the instrument.

How many murders and crimes are committed every
year through sensitive persons, who have been influenced
or "mesmerized" by visible persons or invisible thoughts
to commit them, and who had not sufficient will power to
resist, it is impossible to determine.   In such cases we
hang or punish the instrument, but the real culprit
escapes.   Such a "justice" is equivalent to punishing a
stick with which a murder has been committed, and to let
the man who used the stick go free.   Verily the coming
generations will have as much cause to laugh at the ignorance of their ancestors as we now laugh at the ignorance
of those who preceded us.

The state of the imagination is a great factor in the
observation and appreciation of things.   The savage may
see in the sculptured Minerva only a curious piece of
rock, and a beautiful painting may be to him only a piece
of cloth daubed over with colors.   The greedy miser, on
looking at the beauties of nature, thinks only of the
money-value they represent, while for the poet the forest
swarms with fairies and the water with sprites.   The artist
finds beautiful forms in the wandering clouds and in the
projecting rocks of the mountains, and to him whose mind
is poetic every symbol in nature becomes a poem and suggests to him new ideas ; but the coward wanders through
life with a scowl upon his face ; he sees in every corner
an enemy, and for him the world has nothing attractive
except his own little self.   The man who cannot be trusted
is ever mistrustful, the thief fears to be robbed, and the
backbiter is extremely sensitive to the gossip of others.

The cause of this is evidently that each man perceives
only those elements which exist in his own mind, and if
any foreign element enters, it is immediately tinctured
and colored by the former.   The world is a mirror wherein every man may see his own face.   To him whose soul
is beautiful, the world will look beautiful ; to him whose
soul is deformed, everything will seem to be evil.

The impressions made on the mind by the effects of the
imagination may be powerful and lasting upon the person.
They may change or distort the features, they may render
the hair white in a single hour ; they may mark, kill, dis-

figure, or break the bones of the unborn child, and make the effects of injuries received by one person visible upon the body of another with whom that person is in sympathy. They may act more powerfully than drugs ; they cause and cure diseases, induce visions and hallucinations, and may produce stigmata in so-called saints. Imagination performs its miracles, either consciously or unconsciously, in all departments of nature. By altering the surroundings of animals at such times their color can be changed at will. The tiger's stripes are said to correspond with the long jungle grass, and the leopard's spots resemble the speckled light falling through the leaves.* The forces of nature, influenced by the imagination of man, act on the imagination of nature, and create tendencies on the astral plane, which, in the course of evolution, find expression through material forms. In this way man's vices or virtues become objective realities, and as man's mind becomes purified, the earth becomes more beautiful and refined, while his vices find their expression in poisonous reptiles and noxious plants.

The soul of the world has its animal elementary existences, corresponding to those existing in the animal soul of man. Either are the products of thought-evolution. The Elementals in the soul of man are the products of the action of the thought in the individual mind of man ; the elemental forms in the soul of the world are the products of the collective thoughts of all beings. Animal elementary powers are attracted to the germs of animals, and grow into objective visible animal form, and modify the characters and also the outward appearance of the animals of our globe. We therefore see that as the imagination of the Universal Mind changes during the course of ages, old forms disappear and new ones come into existence. Perhaps if there were no snakes in human forms, the snakes of the animal kingdom would cease to exist.

But the impressions made on the mind do not end with the life of the individual on the physical plane. A cause which produces a sudden terror, or otherwise acts strongly on the imagination, may produce an impression that not only lasts through life but beyond it. A person, for instance, who during his life has strongly believed in the

---

* Sir John Lubbock: "Proceedings of the British Association."

existence of eternal damnation and hell-fire, may, at his
entrance into the subjective state after death, actually
behold all the terrors of hell which his imagination during
life has conjured up.   There may have been no premature
burial, the physical body may have been actually dead ;
but the terrified soul, seeing before it all the horrors of its
own vivid imagination, rushes back again into the deserted
body and clings to it in despair, seeking protection.
Personal consciousness returns, and it finds itself alive in
the grave, where it may pass a second time through the
pangs of death, or, by sending out its astral form in search
of sustenance from the living, it may become a vampire,
and prolong for a while its horrible existence.* Such
misfortunes are by no means rare, and the best remedy
for it is knowledge or the cremation of the body soon after
death.

In the state after death the imagination neither creates
new and original forms nor is it capable of receiving new
impressions ; but it—so to say—lives on the sum of the
impressions accumulated during life, which may evolute
innumerable variations of mental estates, symbolized in
their corresponding subjective forms, and lasting a longer
or shorter period until their forces are exhausted.   These
mental states may be called illusive in the same sense as
the forms and events of the physical life may be called
illusive, and life in "heaven" or "hell" may be called a
dream, in the same sense as life on the earth is called a
dream.   The dream of life only differs from the dream
after death, that, during the former, we are able to make
use of our will to guide and control our imagination and
acts, while during the latter that guidance is wanting, and
we earn that which we have sown, whether it is pleasant or
not.   No effort, whether for good or for evil, is ever lost.
Those who have reached out in their imagination towards
a high ideal on earth will find it in heaven ; those whose
desires have dragged them down will sink to the level of
their desires.

It is said that the most material and sensual thoughts
create  forms in the subjective condition which will appear
to him who created them, after he enters that sphere, even

---

\*Maximilian Perty : " Die mystischen Erscheinungen in der Natur."

more gross, dense and material, than the material forms of the terrestrial world; nor does this seem incomprehensible, if we remember that everything is composed of thought-substance, and that the terms "density," "materiality," etc., are merely relative terms. What appear to us dense and material now, may appear ethereal or vaporous, if we are in another state, and things which are invisible to us now may appear grossly material then. A due consideration of the relations existing between consciousness and what we call "matter" will make it appear that there may be worlds more dense and material to its inhabitants than our physical world is to us; for it is the light of the spirit that enlivens matter, and the more matter is attracted by sensuality and concentrated by selfishness, the less penetrable to the spirit will it become, and the more dense and hard will it grow, although it may for all that not be perceptible to our physical senses; the latter being adapted merely to our present state of existence.

We should enter the higher life now, instead of waiting for it to come to us in the hereafter. The term "heaven" means a state of spiritual consciousness and enjoyment of spiritual truths; but how can he who has evolved no such consciousness and no spiritual power of perception enjoy the perception of things which he has not the power to perceive? A man without that faculty entering heaven would be like a man blind and deaf and without the power to feel. Man can only enjoy that which he is able to realize, that which he cannot perceive does not exist for him.

The surest way to be happy is to rise above all selfish considerations. People crave for amusement and pastimes; but to forget one's time is to forget one's self, and by forgetting themselves they are rendered glad. People are rendered temporarily happy by illusions, because while they enjoy an illusion, they forget their own personal selves. The charm of music consists in the temporary absorption it causes to the personality in the harmony of sound. If we witness a theatrical performance and enter into the sprit of the play, we forget our personal sorrows and live—so to say—in the personality of the actor. The actor who understands how to absorb our attention, absorbs our personal consciousness and becomes inspired by our own enthusiasm ; an actor from whom the sympathy of the audience is withheld, will find it difficult to play his part well. An orator who is in full accord with his audience becomes inspired with the sentiments of his audience ; it is his audience that gives expressions of his feelings through him ; while he speaks he may forget the part he has intended to speak and give expression to that which his audience feels. Without being aware of it, we actually live and feel and think within each other.

If we enter a cathedral or a temple, whose architecture inspires sublimity and solemnity, expanding the soul; where the language of music speaks to the heart, drawing it away from the attachment to the earth; if the beauty and odor of flowers lull the senses into a forgetfulness of self, such illusions may render us temporarily happy to an extent proportionate to the degree in which they succeed in destroying our consciousness of personality and self, and as such they are immeasurably better than other illusions that appeal to the lower personal self; but if we seek for the truth in the outward expression of a form, instead of looking for it in the principle which the ferm is to represent, we will be led into darkness instead of being led into light. For this reason the belief in external gods strengthens the illusions of self; they induce men to become cowards, to ask for favors which they do not deserve, in preference to other men that deserve them ; they help to establish the autocracy of priests, and to put the false priest upon a throne from which the true god has been excluded. Such misconceptions destroy the dignity of mankind, and a religious system based upon such practices degrades men instead of elevating their character. He who has grown to live above the illusion of form and recognizes the existence of the true god in his heart, needs no illusions to guide his attention. He carries the temple of the eternal God in his own soul, and worships it without ceremonies and rites, by perpetual adoration.

# CHAPTER VII.

## CONSCIOUSNESS.

*" I am that I am."—Bible.*

EVERYTHING in the universe is a manifestation of mind;
for the universe itself is an expression of eternal wisdom.
Everything therefore is mind; possessing consciousness in
the absolute, and being capable of manifesting relative consciousness. *Consciousness in the Absolute* means unconsciousness in relation to things. *Absolute self-consciousness*
means the full realization of one's own existence, a godlike
state of self-existence, independent of any external object; a
state of eternal life within one's own light. *Self-consciousness* means the realization of one's own existence independent of other things; while *relative consciousness* means
the realization of one's own existence with reference to
the objects of one's perception. *Unconsciousness in the
absolute* is non-existence, a term without meaning; while
*relative unconsciousness* means ignorance in regard to that
of which one does not know that it exists. Consciousness
means knowledge and life; unconsciousness is ignorance
and death. An imperfect knowledge is a state of imperfect
consciousness in relation to the object of knowledge; the
highest possible state of consciousness is the full realization
of the truth. Consciousness means existence. Non-con-
sciousness is non-existence,—nothing. Self-consciousness

is self-existent, independent of any object. Relative exist-ence is the consciousness of the relation between subject and object.

A thing has no existence relatively to ourselves before we become conscious of its existence. A person who does not realize his own existence is unconscious, and for the time being, to all practical purposes, as far as he him-self is concerned, dead. A state of existence is incompre-hensible unless it is experienced and realized, and it begins to be from the moment that it is realized. If a person were the legal possessor of millions of money and did not know it, he would have no means to dispose of it or enjoy it. A man may be present at the delivery of the most eloquent speech, and, unless he hears what is said, that speech will have no existence for him. Every man is endowed with reason and conscience, but if he never listens to its voice, the relation between him and his conscience will cease to exist, and it will die for him in proportion as he loses the power to hear it. Symbols have a meaning to him who understands their meaning, but for the ignorant nothing but the forms which he sees and feels exist; their meaning has no existence for him.

A man may be alive and conscious in relation to one thing, and dead and unconscious relatively to another. One set of his faculties may be active and conscious, while another set may be unconscious and its activity suspended. A person who listens attentively to music may be conscious of nothing but sound; one who is wrapt in the admiration of form is only conscious of seeing; another, who suffers from pain, may be conscious of nothing but the relation that exists between him and the sensation of pain. A man absorbed in thought may believe himself alone in the midst of a crowd. He may be threatened by destruction and be unconscious of the danger. He may have the strength of a lion, and it will avail him nothing unless he becomes conscious of it; he cannot be immortal unless he becomes conscious of immortal life. The more a person learns to realize the true state of his existence, the more will he become conscious of his existence. If he does not realize his true position, illusions will be the result. If he fully knows himself and his surroundings, he will be con-scious of his own powers, he will know how to exercise them and become strong.

To become conscious of the existence of a thing is to perceive it. To perceive it means to enter into relation with it, and to feel the existence of that relation. Life itself is a manifestation of consciousness; motion is a manifestation of life. A thing without consciousness of any kind is unthinkable and could not exist. Even the most immovable mountains are states of mind, corporified eternal thoughts, and as such they are expressions of consciousness. They feel the power of gravitation, and speak through the mouth of the echo. The body of our mother earth, although devoid of self-consciousness and intellectual reasoning, is nevertheless conscious of the presence of the sun, turning with incredible velocity around its axis; each of its parts strives to receive the full influence of his light, and after receiving his blessing gives way to another part to be blessed likewise. Stars and planets, worlds and molecules, are attracted toward each other, all by the action of eternal love, which could produce no reaction on absolute unconsciousness if such a thing could exist.

Absolute self-consciousness belongs only to God. He alone is self-existent and independent of any outside conditions. He is self-sufficient, and needs nothing to excite consciousness or knowledge in Him. Man's self-consciousness, in so far as the realization of a divine presence has not awakened within him, is as much an illusion on his imaginary self-existence, because it is then not his true real "I," but *nature* that has become self-conscious in him; producing that ever-changing and impermanent sense of the *ego*, which appears from hour to hour and from day to day chameleon-like under different attributes. This artificially produced *ego* is a mere nothing, and one proof of it is that the great majority of people continually require some stimulus to enable them to know that they exist. If they are alone and without "pastime" they are miserable. If they are only in company with themselves, they are then in company with nothing. Without an amusement of some kind they would become insane or die.

But he, in whom the divine consciousness of his true inner self has awakened, will require no external stimulus to let him know that he lives. He may be shut up in a prison or in a tomb, he carries his own light with him; he cares little for the company of men, if he is in company with his God

Man is an organism, in which either God or nature, or the antithesis of God, the devil, may become self-conscious. If only nature is self-conscious in him, he has then no real life or consciousness of his own. It is absurd of him to speak of dying, because he has never yet come to life. If God has become self-conscious in him, he will be one with God, whose temple he is, If the self-consciousness of the devil resides in his house, then is he a personal devil for all practical purposes and intents.

From the moment that man becomes relatively conscious of the existence of a spiritual power within his soul, he enters into relationship to that power, he attains spiritual consciousness; but it may still be a long time until that power becomes fully alive and self-conscious in him.

The vulgar have only the consciousness of the animal within themselves. It is the hog in one that is given to gluttony; the goat in another that is given to lewdness; the tiger in one that kills; the snake in another that stings by the power of calumny; the fox in another from which he receives his cunning. They are houses which the master has never inhabited, or which he has deserted, and which are filled with animals. It is the animals that are living and acting in them, the persons themselves have no life.

As everything that exists is of a threefold nature, so there are three modes of perception: the physical perception, the perception of the soul, and the spiritual perception. The former reaches the surface of things, the second the soul, and the third reaches into their innermost centres. To see is to think with the organ of sight. A thought sent to the surface of the object of perception will see only the surface; a thought becoming conscious in the centre will see that which exists at the centre.

Everything that exists, exists within the Universal Mind, and nothing can exist beyond it, because the Universal Mind includes all, and there is no " beyond." Perception is a faculty by which mind learns to know what is going on within itself. Man can know nothing but what exists within his own mind. Even the most ardent lover has never seen his beloved one, he merely sees the image which the form of the latter produces in his or her mind.

If we pass through the streets of a city the images of men and women pass review in our mind while their bodies meet our own; but for the images which they produce within our consciousness, we would know nothing about their existence. The images produced in the mind come to the consciousness whose seat is the brain; if man's consciousness were centered in some other part of his body, he would become conscious in that part of the sensations which he receives. He might, for instance, see with his stomach or hear with his fingers, as has been actually the case in some somnambulic states.

From the relations existing between object and subject, physical senses came into existence. There could be no perception without resistance. If our bodies were perfectly transparent to light we could not perceive the light, because light cannot illuminate itself. The *Astral Light* penetrates our bodies, but we are not able to see it with our physical eyes, because the physical body offers no resistance to it; but when the physical body begins to sleep, and life retires from the outer into the inner man, the astral man may become conscious of the existence of that higher light, and see it like beautiful stars, or sheets of light, resembling the electric light falling through a crystal globe.

At the time when we fall asleep, consciousness gradually leaves its seat in the brain and merges into the consciousness of the "*inner man.*" It may then begin to realize another state of existence; and if a part of the consciousness still remain with the brain, the perception of the inner consciousness may come to the cognizance of the lower personal self. We may, therefore, in that half-conscious state, between sleeping and waking, when our consciousness is—so to say—oscillating between two states of existence, receive important revelations from the higher state and retain them in the memory of the external self. The more our consciousness merges in that higher state, the better will we realize the higher existence, but the impressions upon our personal self will become dim and perhaps not be remembered; but as long as the greatest part of our consciousness is active within the material brain, the perceptions of the higher state will only be dim and mixed up with memories and sensations of the lower state of existence; the images will be confused.

When the turmoil of external life ceases and the external senses come to rest, then is the time for the inner senses to become more active, and then the neophyte may enjoy

6

communion with his master, the divine Adonai. Then
may he receive lessons from the world of the spirit, and
problems that were too difficult for him to be solved while
his external senses were fully alive may now become clear
to him in his " sleep," and even be remembered when he
" awakens " again to external life.

The tranquillity of the outer senses facilitates the action
of the inner senses. It is said of Socrates, that he once
stood for eighteen hours immovable and absorbed in
thought; but in the fully illuminated seer, the external and
internal consciousness are as one. Jacob Boehme was in
a state of divine illumination for three weeks, and followed
during that time his occupation as a shoemaker.

Life, sensation, perception and consciousness may be
withdrawn from the physical body and become active in
the astral body of man. The astral man may then become
conscious of his own existence independent of the physical
body, and develop his faculties of sense. He may then see
sights which have no existence for the physical eye, he
may hear sounds that the physical ear cannot hear, he may
feel, taste, and smell things whose existence the physical
senses cannot realize, and which consequently have no
existence to them.

What an astonishing sight would meet the eyes of a
mortal, if the veil that mercifully hides the astral world
from his sight were to be suddenly removed! He would
see the space which he inhabits occupied by a different
world full of inhabitants, of whose existence he knew
nothing. What before appeared to him dense and solid
would now seem to be shadowy, and what seemed to him
like air space he would find peopled with life.

All houses are " haunted," but not all persons are equally
able to see the ghosts that haunt them, because to perceive
things on the astral plane requires the development of a
sense adapted to such perceptions. Thoughts are " ghosts,"
and only those that can see thoughts can see " ghosts,"
unless the latter are sufficiently materialized to refract the
light and to become visible to the eye.

Nor is it necessary that the person whose " ghost "
haunts a house should have died. There are many living
persons whose spirits haunt the houses which they formerly
inhabited. Each thought, expressed with a certain intensity
of will; each curse and each blessing that comes from the

heart, gives birth to a spirit that may haunt a place and even produce external and visible effects under certain conditions.

We may feel the presence of an astral form without being able to see it, and be just as certain of its presence as if we did behold it with our eyes; for the sense of feeling is not less reliable than the sense of sight. The presence of a holy, high, and exalted idea that enters the mind fills it with a feeling of happiness, with an exhilarating influence whose vibrations may be perceived long after that thought has gone.

Each human being may be looked upon as an unlimited sphere of consciousness with a visible centre. Each resembles a living *nebula*, of which only the solid kernel is visible. Visible man is not all there is of man; but surrounded by an invisible mental atmosphere, comparable to the pulp surrounding the seed in a fruit; but this light, or atmosphere, or pulp, is the mind of man, an organized ocean of spiritual substance, wherein all things exist. If man were conscious of his own greatness, he would know that within himself exists the sun and the moon and the starry sky and every object in space, because his true self is God and God is without limits.

To see a thing is identical with feeling it with the mind. The mind of man extends through space; it is therefore not merely the images of things we see but the things themselves that exist within the periphery of our mind, however distant from the centre of our consciousness they may be; and if we were able to shift that centre from one place to another within the sphere of the mind, we might in a moment of time approach to the object of our perception.

If you throw a handful of sand into a quiet lake, does not every grain form a centre of motion upon the surface, from whence proceed concentric waves in all directions? Can you tell where the realm of one such motion is limited, and do they not all move in the same lake? Likewise each individual being constitutes a centre of consciousness in the sea of eternity, whose ripples of thought extend into the depths of the infinite mind.

As it is, the centre of consciousness of normally constituted man is located in the brain, and, if the mind feels an object, the impressions have to travel all the way to the brain. If we look at a distant star our mind is actually there and in contact with it, and if we could transfer our consciousness to that place of contact, we would be ourselves upon that star and perceive the objects thereon as if we were standing personally upon its surface.

If we were not able to *feel* with the mind, we would not be able to become conscious of the character of the things we see and whose qualities are invisible to us; but the individual spheres of beings enter and pervade each other and exchange their sensations like the circular rings produced if a handful of pebbles is thrown into a lake.

Perception is *passive imagination,* because if we perceive an object, the relation which it bears to us comes to our consciousness without any active exertion on our part. But there is an *active perception* or *imagination* by which we may enter into a relation with a distant object in space by a transfer of consciousness. By this power we may act upon a distant object if we succeed in forming a true image of it in our own consciousness. By concentrating our consciousness upon such an object we become conscious in that place of the sphere of mind where that object exists. Instead of perceiving an already existing relation we establish consciously a relation between such an object and ourselves. If I can form in my mind a true image of an absent person, and cling to it with my will, I am then identified in my mind with that person, and am actually with him or her. My real " I " is everywhere, and wherever I locate my consciousness, there am I consciously myself, all except the physical form. How could I be nearer to a friend than to be in perfect harmony with his soul, and identified with him in his own consciousness?

Consciousness is existence, and there are as many states of consciousness as there are states of existence. Every living being has a consciousness of its own, the result of its sensations, and the state of its consciousness changes every moment of time, as fast as the impressions which it receives change; because its consciousness is the perception of the relation it bears to things, and as this relation changes, consciousness changes its character.

If our whole attention is taken up by animal pleasure, we exist in an animal state of consciousness; if we are aware of the presence of spiritual principles, such as hope, faith, charity, justice, truth, etc., in their highest aspects, we live in our spiritual consciousness, and between the two extremes there are a great variety of gradations. Consciousness itself does not change, it only moves up and down on the scale of existence.

There is only one kind of consciousness which never changes its form, because its relation to things never changes, it being in relation with nothing except with itself. It is the divine consciousness of existence *per se*, the realization of the *I am*. It cannot change, because existence *per se* never changes; its change would involve non-existence or the annihilation of all.

When the Absolute One Life becomes relative in a form the degree of its manifestation depends on the state of the activity of life expressed in the organization of its form. In a low organized form there may be sensation, but there is no intelligence. An oyster has sensation and consciousness, but no intelligence and no power of discrimination. A man may have a great deal of intellect and no consciousness of the existence of spirituality, sublimity, justice, beauty, or truth. If these divine principles have become fully alive and self-conscious in him ; then, and only then, is he in possession of *Divine Wisdom.*

The lowest existences follow implicitly the laws of nature or of *Universal Wisdom;* they have no wisdom of their own. The highest spiritual beings follow their own wisdom ; but their wisdom is identical with the universal law. The difference between the lowest beings and the highest ones is, therefore, that the lowest ones perform the will of God unconsciously and unknowingly ; while the highest ones do the same thing knowingly and consciously. It is only the intermediary beings between the lowest and highest who imagine that they are their own law-givers, and may do what they please.

The muscular system exercises its habitual movements in the act of walking, eating, etc., without being especially guided by a superintending intellect, like a clockwork that, after being once set in motion, continues to run ; and a man who is in the habit of doing that which is right and just, will act in accordance with the law of justice instinctively, and without any consideration or doubt.

Each state or existence has its own mode of perception, sensation, instinct, consciousness and memory, and the activity of one may overpower and suppress that of the other. A person being only conscious of the sensations created by some physical act, is at that time unconscious of spiritual attractions. One who is under the influence of chloroform may lose all his external sensation of pain, and yet be conscious of his surroundings. One in a state of trance may be fully awake on a higher plane of existence, and entirely unconscious of what happens on the physical plane. The muscular system may be semi-conscious and overpower the intellect, or the conscious and intelligent brain may control the muscular system.

A person may climb up to the most dizzy heights of a tower or a mountain peak, and if there is a rail or a staircase to afford him even an imaginary protection, he will not be very liable to become overpowered by the sense of danger. His intellect may be aware of danger, but reason teaches the unreasoning animal man, filling the muscular system with the sensation of security, and he will not be very liable to fall. But if you remove the protection, the sensation of danger presenting itself before the mind impresses the unreasoning animal instincts with the overpowering illusion of fear, and danger may become imminent. The body becomes conscious of the attraction of the chasm, the intellect too weak to guide the will to resist the tendency of the excited body to follow that attraction, and the person may fall.

The unintelligent muscular system is conscious of nothing else but the attraction of Earth. In it the element of Earth predominates, and unless it is upheld by the intellect and will, it seeks to act according to the impulse created in it by that attraction. The astral body *per se* is unintelligent, and unless infused with the intelligence coming from the higher principles, it follows the attractions of the astral plane. These attractions are the emotions created by desires. As the physical body, if unguided by reason, may fall and perish by the fall, so the astral body, following the attractions of love and hate, may refuse to obey the intelligent principle of man, and seek its own destruction. The animal consciousness of man is that unreasoning brute instinct which impels him to seek for the gratification of his natural desires.

Correctly speaking, there is no such thing as animal reason, animal intellect, animal consciousness, etc. Consciousness, reason, intelligence, etc., in the absolute, have no qualifications; they are universal principles, that is to say, functions of the *Universal One Life*, manifesting themselves on various planes in mineral, vegetable, animal, human, astral and transcendental forms.

The condition of a person whose consciousness is no more illuminated by reason, is seen in cases of emotional mania, and sometimes in cases of actual obsession. In such cases the person will act entirely according to the impulses acting upon his lower consciousness, and when he recovers his reason, be entirely unconscious of his actions during that state. Such states manifest themselves in only one person, or they may simultaneously affect several persons, and even whole countries, becoming epidemic by the law of induction, as has been experienced in some wholesale " obsessions " occurring during the Middle Ages.* They are often observed in cases of hysteria, may be witnessed at religious meetings, during theatrical performances, during the attack upon an enemy, or at any other occasion, where the passions of the multitude are excited, inducing them to acts of folly or bravery, and enabling people to perform acts which they would be neither willing nor able to perform if they were guided only by the calculations of their intellect.

Merely imaginary self-consciousness exist; when thought and will are divided. We then live in our imagination; but the will is dormant and inactive. Only when will and thought become united and act as one then will true self-consciousness become manifest. The self-conscious will, receiving its light from thought, is a god or a devil according to its *tincture*. In its full development it is a power beyond the comprehension of normal man. It enables its possessor to blend his own consciousness with that of any other person, to enter into communication with any other person in any part of the world, although that other person may not become aware of his presence, unless he has developed his own power of spiritual perception to a certain extent. If we steadily concentrate our thought upon a person or a place, the highest thought-energies, residing in the fifth principle of man, will actually visit that place, because thought is not bound by the laws of gross matter regarding time and space, and we are able to think of a far-off place as quick as of one that is near.

---

* " Histoire des diables de Loudin."

Our thoughts go to the desired locality, for that locality, however far it may be, is still within the sphere of mind. If we have been there before, or if there is something to attract us, it will not be difficult to find it. But under ordinary circumstances our consciousness remains with the body. We may even realize our presence at the place which we visit, but on returning to our normal state we cannot remember it, because the semi-material principles of our soul, in which resides memory, have not been there to collect impressions and transfer them to the physical brain. But if our will has become one with our thought so as to accompany the latter, then our consciousness may go with them, being projected there by the power of the will, and illuminated by thought. We shall then visit the chosen place consciously and know what we are doing, and our astral elements may carry our memory back and impress them upon our physical brain. The reason why such things sometimes take place at the time of death, and the conscious appearance of the dying person occurs at a distant place, to visit a friend, is because at the time of dying the will becomes again free and unites with the thought of the person, thus forming a veritable spirit, a union of will and thought.

It sometimes happens that the "double" of a sleeping person is attracted to a distant place; acting, however, like an automaton, without intelligence. This simply shows that the will of the person was not set free. His thought was there, but not his conscious will; nor could the will leave the sleeping body of a person that has not become sufficiently spiritual, because the *will is the life*, and if it were to leave the form the body would die.

There are a great number of cases on record where, in consequence of a sudden and intense emotion, for instance, the desire to see a certain person, the will has become prominently active, and projecting itself from the physical body has rendered the thought of the person conscious and visible at a distance. In cases of home-sickness we find some approach to an instance of this. The person separated from home and friends, having an intense yearning to see his native place again, projects his thoughts and his unconscious will to that place. He lives—so to say—spiritually in that place, while his physical body vegetates in another. The life-elements pass more and more to these astral elements at the expense of the life-elements necessary to supply the wants of the physical body. There seem to be nothing particularly important the matter with the patient, he has a little fever, becomes weaker, and finally dies—that is to say, he goes where he desires to go, although his gradual going is imperceptible and unrecognizable to physical senses.

Sometimes in cases of sickness a similar process takes place. When, from whatever cause, the union between the physical form and the astral body becomes weakened, the astral form may separate itself for a while or permanently from the physical form and follow a stronger attraction, and in such cases it may be seen by persons gifted with *second sight.*

The symptoms of such a beginning of separation may often be observed in cases of severe sickness, when the patient has the sensation as if another person were lying in the same bed with him, and as if that person were in some way connected with him, and he would have to take care of the latter. As recovery takes place, the principles whose cohesion has been loosened become reunited, and that sensation disappears.

A higher state of consciousness than that of the normal state is often observed in cases of trance and somnambulism ; a lower state than the normal one is witnessed in cases of drunkenness or intoxication of some kind.

A case is cited in Dr. Hammond's book on insanity, in which a servant, while in a state of intoxication, carried a package with which he had been entrusted to the wrong house. Having become sober, he could not remember the place, and the package was supposed to be lost ; but after he got drunk again he remembered the place, he went there and recovered the package. This goes to show that when he was drunk he was another person than when he was sober; man's individuality continually changes according to the conditions in which he exists, and as his consciousness changes he becomes another individual, although he still retains the same outward form. Instead of getting drunk a man may become full of the wine of the spirit. In that case he may, while in that state, write down very high and exalted ideas, which he may not fully remember after his return to his normal state, and perhaps he may then not even understand his own writings.

If a person is in the hypnotic state, subject to the will "magnetizer," it is the consciousness of the latter which takes possession of the former, and uses his mental organism as if it were his own. If a hypnotizer causes his subject to commit a crime, it is he who commits it through the instrumentality of the hypnotized; if a medium lies, it is the lying thoughts of him who consults the medium that are echoed back through the latter, nor could he be a genuine medium if he did not reflect lies as well as the truth.

All men are mirrors, in which the world is reflected; all men are mirrors reflecting each other's thoughts and acting them out. Experience shows, that there is not a day in the year that not some hypnotizer consciously or unconsciously commits a crime through another person; and while the real culprit goes scot free, the weak-minded instrument is punished. Thousands of marriages are the outcome of "hypnotization." Man exists as an individual only as long as he is in possession of divine reason, and this reason is not an attribute of the human form, but a function of the divine Spirit which illuminates it.

In the state of trance the consciousness is entirely concentrated on the higher planes, and the mind may even forget the existence of the physical body. In the state of intoxication the person may only be conscious of his animal existence and entirely unconscious of his higher self. A somnambule in the lucid condition looks upon her body as a being distinct from her own self, who is, to a certain extent, under her care. She speaks of that being in the third person, prescribes sometimes for it as a physician prescribes for his patient, and often shows tastes, inclinations and opinions entirely opposed to those which she possesses in her normal condition. Somnambules often give promises which they fulfil when they return to their normal condition, although, when they awake, they do not remember of ever having made any promise at all.

If man's consciousness changes from one state to another, his tastes and inclinations change accordingly. While his thoughts revel in animal pleasures, the realm of the spirit will be closed to him, nor will he desire to enter it; if he has once attained the power to perceive the things of the spirit, animal pleasures and the knowledge of which terrestrial science is proud will appear absolutely worthless to him. Persons while in a trance may love another person intensely, because they are then capable to perceive his interior qualities, and they may detest him when they are in their normal condition, because they then merely behold his external attributes.*

This higher self, which often seems to care so little for the earthly troubles that vex and perplex the lower self, is the real man, who continues to live when the body of the person with which he is connected during life no longer exists. It is the individual which, through a long chain of reincarnations, has become connected with many personalities, extracting from each the elements which are worthy to be preserved, and assimilating them with his own. Only few persons mentioned in history have succeeded in uniting their personality with their own divine and impersonal Atma. Such that have succeeded are the truly enlightened, and require no more incarnations.

The highest state of spiritual consciousness is the full and complete realization of divine truth. Even while physical consciousness is active the consciousness of the higher principles may be so exalted as to render the body little conscious of pain. History speaks of men and women whose souls rejoiced while their earthly tabernacles were undergoing the tortures of the rack, or were devoured by flames at the stake.

Man leads essentially two lives, one while he is fully awake, another while he is fully asleep. Each has its own perceptions, consciousness and experiences, but the experiences of that state, called "deep sleep," are not remembered when we are fully "awake." At the border-land between sleep and waking, where the impressions of each state meet and mingle, is the realm of confused dreams, which are usually remembered, and seldom contain any truth.

This state is, however, favorable to receive impressions from the higher self, or to see the pictures existing in the astral light. In the former case the higher self may use symbolical forms and allegorical images to convey ideas to the lower self, and to give it admonitions, forebodings, and warnings in regard to future events; in the latter case faces and forms of persons that previously occupied the

---

* H. Zschokke : "Verklaerungen" (Transfigurations).

room of the sleeper may be seen, or his mind may wandﬔ to scenes to which he is unconsciously attracted.

There are, however, various kinds of dreams, and it would be wrong to deny that some of them may not be useful. The higher self may make use of the impressibility of the lower self during the time of half-conscious slumber to impress it with useful visions and warn it of danger, and to teach it lessons which the lower self would not be able to understand while his physical senses are fully active and the voice of intuition drowned in the noise of the struggle produced by the contending emotions. Many a difficult problem has been solved during sleep, and the terrestrial world is not always without any reflex of the light from above. The mind of the sleeper during the sleep of the body may come into contact with other minds, and pass through experiences which he does not remember when he awakes. Man, in his waking condition, often has experiences which he afterwards does not remember, but which he, nevertheless, enjoyed at the time when they occurred, and which at that time were real to him.*

---

* Man has not only a double consciousness, but he leads two lives which are separate and yet one. Each of these lives has its own experiences, and if while in one state we do not remember the experiences of the other state, this does not disprove the truth of our assertion. A man may live and undergo certain experiences in a certain place, while his body is asleep, or unconscious, or half-conscious in another place ; and if the physical body returns to its normal state, it may or may not remember what happened to him while he was in the other state. But there are some exceptional cases, in which the consciousness of both states may become blended, and then the person may remember where he had been and what he had been doing while in that other case. One of such extraordinary cases is mentioned in *A. P. Sinnett's* "Incidents in the Life of Madame Blavatsky." Speaking of her sickness in *Tiflis*. Madame Blavatsky says, that she had the sensation as if she were two different persons, one being the Madame Blavatsky whose body was lying sick in bed, the other person an entirely different and superior being. "When I was in my lower state," she says, "I knew who that other person was and what she (or he) had been doing; but when I was that other being myself, I did not know nor care who was that Madame Blavatsky." It is therefore very well possible that Madame Blavatsky's "transcendental *Ego*," with all its consciousness, faculties, and powers of perception, in fact, her *real self*, was consciously and really undergoing certain mysterious experiences in Tibet, while the physical instrument, which we call "Madame Blavatsky," was sick at Tiflis ; but such an explanation will be incomprehensible to those persons who imagine the physical body of a person to be the whole of

A mixture of the various states of sensations and perceptions produces the normal consciousness of man. Man feels in himself at least two sets of attractions that come to his consciousness, the " earthly " and the " fiery " elements. One set drags him down to earth and makes him cling with a firm grasp to material necessities and enjoyments, the other set, lifting him up into the region of the unknown, makes him forget the allurements of matter, and by bringing him nearer to the realm of abstract ideas of the good, the true, and the beautiful, gives him satisfaction and happiness. The greatest poets and philosophers have recognized this fact of double consciousness, or the two poles of one, and between those two poles ebbs and floods the normal consciousness of the average human being.

Goethe expresses this in his " Faust" in about the following terms :—

> " Two souls, alas ! are conscious in my breast,
> Each from the other tries to separate.
> One clings to earth, attracted by desire,
> The other rises upward," etc.

One attraction arises from Spirit, another from matter. By the power of Reason Man is enabled to choose which way he will follow, and by the power of his Will he is enabled to follow his choice. He may concentrate his consciousness entirely on the lower plane, and sinking into sensuality, become entirely unconscious of the existence of higher aspirations, or he may live entirely in the higher planes of thought and feeling, grow to realize fully the beauties, realities, and truths of the spirit, and become dead to the attractions of matter. A self-centered and narrow-

---

his person, and his physical form to be his own *real self.* Only when the relations existing between the higher and lower self will be fully understood by our would-be philosophers will their eyes become opened to a realization of the truth that man's phenomenal terrestrial self is nothing else but a temporary illusion, a bundle of ever-changing powers and principles held together by the power of the divine Spirit, and endowed by the latter with the faculty to perceive, to think, to will and to remember ; a fleeting cloud of living matter, illuminated for the time being by the light of the spirit, a mere instrument through which impersonal forces act ; while the real self of man exists in another region of thought, and is known only to those who are passing through the process of spiritual regeneration.

minded man may have his consciousness narrowed down
to a small sphere ; a great and liberal mind may expand it
without any limits, until the whole of space will appear to
him to be filled with his own consciousness, and his power
of perception will enable him to penetrate all the mysteries
in Nature.   Few may be able to reach such a state, and
few will be able to comprehend its possibility ; but there
have been men who, on the threshold of Nirwana, were
able to concentrate the powers of their minds in centres
beyond the attraction of earth, and while their physical
bodies continued to live on this planet, the divine self,
leaving its human form, could consciously roam through
the interplanetary spaces and see the wonders of the
material and spiritual worlds.   This is the highest form of
Adeptship attainable on earth, and to him who accomplishes
it the mysteries of the Universe will be like an open
book.

Every man and woman, however, can feel within their
souls the presence of the divine Spirit, even if they cannot
yet see its light.   This is the beginning of that true spiritual consciousness, to which we should cling at all times and
which finds its expression in the adoration of the highest
good.   Still such states are yet far from spiritual self-
consciousness, which is a full realization of individual
existence within the spiritual realm, and as such is known
only to few.   Even the most devout worshipper, as long
as the divine Spirit has not awakened within his soul, will
merely feel the beauties of the spiritual realm in the same
sense as a blind man may enjoy the warm rays of the
sunshine without being able to see the light ; only when
the process of spiritual regeneration has fairly begun will
he be able to see the sun of glory within his own soul, and
the illusive self-consciousness of his former state which
caused him to believe that he was a permanent being, will
be transformed into that real self-conscious state in which
he becomes self-luminous in the light of the Truth, a state
in which man actually knows that he exists as an eternal,
self-existent and immortal power in God.

# CHAPTER VIII.

### DEATH.

*" Omne bonum a Deo, imperfectum a Diabalo."—Paracelsus.*

CONSCIOUSNESS is knowledge and life ; unconsciousness is ignorance and death.   If we are conscious of the existence of a thing, a relation exists between ourselves and that thing.   If we are unconscious of its existence, neither we nor that object ceases to exist, but there is no relation between us.   As soon as we begin to realize that relation, the character of the object  perceived in the sphere of our mind becomes a part of our  mental constitution, and we begin to *live* in relation to it.   We then possess it in our consciousness.   If we lose its possession, we may regain it by the power of  recollection and  memory.   To know an object is to live  relatively  to it,  to forget it is to die in relation to it.

Unconsciousness, ignorance and death are, therefore, synonymous terms, and every one is dead in proportion as he is ignorant.   If he is ignorant of a fact, he is dead relatively to it, although  he may be  fully alive in  many other respects.   We cannot be conscious of everything at once, and, therefore,  as our impressions  and  thoughts change, our consciousness and  relation to certain things change, and we continually die relatively to some things and begin to live relatively to others.   Relative death and unconsciousness occurs every moment, and we are not aware of its occurrence.   We meet hundreds of corpses in the streets, which are entirely dead and unconscious in regard to certain things of which we are conscious, and relatively to which we are alive ; and we may be dead in regard to many things to which others are alive and conscious. Only simultaneously occurring omniscience in regard to everything that exists would be absolute life without any admixture of death.

Each principle in man has a certain sphere of consciousness, and its perceptions can only extend to the limits of that sphere. Each is dead to such modes of activity as are in no relation with it. Minerals are unconscious of the action of intelligence, but not of the attraction of Earth; spirit is dead to earthly attraction, but not to spiritual principles. If we can change the mode of activity in a form, we call into existence a new state of consciousness, because we establish new relations of a different order; the old activity then dies and a new one begins to live.

If the energy which we are now using for the purpose of digesting food, for performing intellectual labor and for enjoying sensual pleasures, were used for the purpose of developing spirituality, we would be in a comparatively short time rewarded for our labor by becoming superior beings, of a state so far above our present condition, that we can at present not even conceive of it.

In the constitution of average man life is especially active in the animal body, and he clings to the life of that body as if it were the only possible mode of existence. He knows of no other mode of life, and is afraid to die. A person whose centre of life and consciousness is in his astral body will be conscious of another existence, and his physical body will be only so far of value to him, as by its instrumentality he may act on the physical plane. Physical death is a continuation of the activity of life in higher principles. If we, by some occult process, could concentrate all our life into our higher principles before our body ceases to live, we might step in advance of death and live independent of our physical body.

Such a transfer of life and consciousness is not beyond possibility. It has been accomplished by some, and will be accomplished by others. The material elements of the physical body are continually subject to elimination and renewal. By restricting the renewal of these elements within the limits of the utmost necessity, and at the same time withdrawing our consciousness from the exterior and concentrating it upon the interior plane, we may, in course of time, change the compound parts of the physical body into more ethereal ones, until its physical molecules become entirely replaced by finer elements belonging to the astral plane, when its organization will require no more food from the physical plane, and become invisible to the physical eye.* It would, however, be absurd to suppose that immortality could be obtained by means of gymnastic exercises and semi-starvation and without an awakening of the inner life. If the divine life awakens in man, the grossly animal elements in his constitution will die and disappear without any external aid.

No one would be willing to look upon such a change as *death*, and yet it would be nothing else but a mode of dying slow as far as the physical body is concerned, while at the same time it is a resurrection of the real man into a superior form of existence. Death—whether slow or quick—is nothing but a process of purification, by which the imperfect is eliminated and rendered unconscious. Nothing perishes but that which is not able to live. Principles cannot die, only their forms disappear.

Only that which is perfect can remain without being changed. Truth, wisdom, justice, beauty, goodness, etc., cannot be changed ; it is merely the forms in which they become manifest that can be destroyed. If all the wise men in the world were to die in one moment, the principle of Wisdom would nevertheless exist, and manifest itself in due time in other receptive forms ; if Love were to leave the hearts of all human beings, it would thereby not be annihilated, it would merely cease to exist relatively to men, and men would cease to live while love would continue *to be*. Eternal principles are self-existent, and therefore independent of forms, and not subject to change ; but forms are changeable, and cannot continue without the presence of the principles whose instruments for manifestation they represent.

The human body is an instrument for the manifestation of life, the soul is an instrument for the manifestation of spirit. If the life leaves the body, the latter begins to disintegrate ; if the spirit leaves the soul, the latter begins to dissolve. A person in whom the spiritual principle has become entirely inactive is spiritually dead, although his body may be full of life and his soul full of animal desires,

---

* *The Theosophist:* "Elixir of Life."

Such spiritless living corpses are often seen in fashionable society as well as in the crowds where the vulgar assemble. A person in whom the principle of reason has become inactive is intellectually dead, although his body may be full of animal life ; lunatics are dead people, in whom only the non-intellectual or semi-intellectual principles continue to live. If the soul leaves the body, the latter dies but the soul lives. If the soul dies, God continues to be.

The soul, like the body, is a compound organism, composed of various elements. Some of these elements may be fit to receive the Light of the spirit, others are not fit to do so. If, therefore, a person, during his earthly life has not purified his soul sufficiently so as to enter the spiritual state immediately after the death of the physical body, a separation of the pure and impure elements from the still impure remains must take place in the state after death. When the final separation is accomplished, the spiritual elements enter the spiritual state (which, in fact, they have never left) ; and the lower elements, which may or may not possess a certain remnant of consciousness of their own, remain in the lower plane, where they gradually disintegrate.

If the organization of the physical body becomes impaired to such an extent that the principle of life cannot employ it any longer to serve as an instrument for its activity, it ceases to act. Death may begin at the head, the heart, or the lungs, but life lingers longest in the head, and it may still be active there to a certain extent after the body, to all exterior appearances, has become unconscious and ceased to live. The power of thought may continue for a time to work in its habitual manner, although sensation has ceased to exist in the nerves. This activity may even grow in intensity as the principles become disunited ; and if the thought of the dying is instensely directed upon an absent friend, it may impress itself upon the consciousness of that friend, and perhaps cause him to see the apparition of the dying. At last vitality leaves the brain, and the higher principles depart, carrying with them their proper activity, life and consciousness, leaving behind an empty form, a mask, an illusion. There need not necessarily be any loss of consciousness in regard to the persons and things by which we may be surrounded :

the only consciousness which necessarily ceases is that which refers to his personality, of physical sensation, pain, weight, heat and cold, hunger and thirst, which may have affected the physical form. As his life departs from the brain, another state of consciousness may come into existence, because he enters in relation to a different order of things. " The principle, carrying memory, emerges from the brain, and every event of the life which is ebbing away is reviewed by the mind. Picture after picture presents itself with living vividness before his consciousness and he lives in a few minutes his whole life again. Persons in a state of drowning have experienced that state and regained their life. That impression which has been the strongest, survives all the rest ; the other impressions disappear to reappear again in the dévachanic state. No man dies unconscious, whatever external appearances may seem to indicate to the contrary ; even a madman will have a moment, at the time of his death, when his intellect will be restored. Those who are present at such solemn moments should take care not to disturb, by outbursts of grief or otherwise, that process by which the soul beholds the effects of the past and lays the plan for its future existence."*

The process of the parting of the *perisprit* from the physical remains is described by a clairvoyant as follows : —" At first I saw a beautiful light of a pale blue color, in which appeared a small egg-shaped substance about three feet above the head. It was not stationary, but wavered to and fro like a balloon in the air. Gradually it elongated to the length of the body, the whole enveloped in a mist or smoke. I perceived a face corresponding in features to that which was so soon to be soulless, only brighter, more smooth, more beautiful, yet unfinished, with the same want of expression that we observe in a new-born infant. With every breath from the dying body the ethereal form was added to and became more perfect. Presently the feet became defined, not side by side, as the dying man had placed himself, but one hanging below the other, and one knee bent, as new-born infants would be in an accidental position. The body appeared to be enshrouded in a cloudlike mist. A countless host of other presences

---

* Extracted from the letter of an Adept.

seemed to be near. When the whole was complete, all slowly passed out of sight." *

This ethereal body is the soul-body or *perisprit* of the person that died. It is not the spirit itself, but it may still be made luminous by the spirit, as it was during life. It may still contain the good and evil tendencies which it acquired during life. If man's spirit rises above the attractions of his lower self, his lower self would be unconscious and desintegrate ; but if he clings to his animal nature with a great intensity of desire, a centre of consciousness will become established therein, and its sense of personality may continue to exist for a while in his animal soul even after the physical body is dead.

The time during which an astral corpse may remain in this state before it is entirely dissolved depends on the density and strength of its elements. It may differ from a few hours or days to a great many years. Man is made up of a great many living elements or principles, of which each one exists in its own individual state while they all receive their life from the spirit. When the spirit withdraws they become separate, while each one may retain for a while its own particular life and consciousness in the same sense as a wheel which is once set into motion will continue to run until after the force is exhausted, even if the original motive power is withdrawn.

The astral remnant of a man is, therefore, not the man, but a part of his psychic organism, which may or may not be conscious that it exists, and which may or may not be connected with the spiritual monad whose instrument it was during life.

This Kama loca state is the " land of the shadows," the *Hades* of the ancient Greeks, and the " purgatory " of the Roman Catholic Church. Its inhabitants may or may not possess consciousness and intelligence, but the astral souls of average honest men and women possess no intelligence of their own ; they can, however, be made to act intelligently by the power of the *Elementals*. Paracelsus says :—" Men and women die every day, whose souls during their lives have been subject to the influence and guidance of Elementals. How much easier will it be for such Elementals to influence the sidereal bodies of such

---

* A. J. Davis describes a similar scene.

persons and to make them act as they please, after their
souls have lost the protection which their physical bodies
afforded ! They may use these soul-bodies to move physical objects from place to place, to carry such objects
from distant countries, and to perform other feats of a
similar kind that may appear miraculous to the unin-
itiated."

The state of consciousness of the animal soul after the
physical form has become unconscious and lifeless may,
therefore, differ widely in different persons, according to
the conditions that have been established during its connection with the body. The soul of an average person in
Kama loca with only moderate selfish desires is not conscious and intelligent enough to know that its physical
body has died, and that it is itself undergoing the process
of disintegration ; but the soul of a person whose whole
consciousness was intensely centred in self may be conscious and intelligent enough to remember its past life and
to feel its impending fate. Seeking to prolong its existence
it may cling for protection to the organism of some living
being, and thereby cause an obsession. Not only weak-
minded human beings but also animals may be subject to
such an obsession.

To a body without sensation or consciousness it can
make no difference under what conditions it may continue
to exist or perish, because it cannot realize its existence ;
but to a soul in which the spark of divine intelligence
has kindled consciousness and sensation, its surrounding
conditions will be of importance, because it can realize
them more or less fully according to the degree of its consciousness. Such surroundings, in the state after death,
each man creates for himself during life by his thoughts,
his words, and his acts. Man is creating all his life the
condition wherein he will live in the hereafter.

Thought is material and solid to those that live on the
plane of thought. Even on the physical plane every form
that exists is materialized thought, grown or made into a
form; the world of the souls is a world in which thought itself
appears material and solid to those who exist in that world.
Man is a centre from which continually thought is evolved,
and crystallizes into forms in that world. His thoughts
are things that have life and form and tenacity ; real
entities, solid and more enduring than the forms of the

physical plane. Good thoughts are light and rise above us, but evil thoughts are heavy and sink. The world below us to which they sink is the sphere of the grossest, most diseased, and sensual thoughts evolved by evil-disposed and ignorant men. It is a world still more material and solid to its inhabitants than ours is to us; it is the habitation of man-created personal deities, devils, and monstrosities invented by the morbid imagination of man.

They are only the products of thought, but, nevertheless, they are real and substantial to those who live among them and realize their existence. The myths of hell and purgatory are based on ill-understood facts. " Hells " exist, but man is himself their creator. Brutal man creates monsters by the working of his diseased imagination during life ; disembodied man will be attracted to his creations. There are few persons who are not subject to evil thoughts ; such thoughts are the reflex of the lurid light from the region of evil, but they cannot take form unless we give them form by dwelling on them and feeding them with the substance taken from our own mind. Love is the life of the good, malice the life of the evil. An evil thought, evolved unconsciously, is an illusion without life ; an evil thought, brought into existence with malice, becomes malicious and living. If it is embodied in an act, a new devil will be born into the world. The horrors of hell exist only for those who have been conscious, voluntary, and malicious colaborers in peopling it with the products of their fancy ; the beauties of heaven are only realized by him who has created a heaven within himself during his life.

Pain is only caused if a being exists under abnormal conditions. Devils do not suffer in hell, because they are there in their own natural element ; they would suffer if they had to enter in heaven. They belong to the darkness and suffer in the presence of light. A man suffers if his head is kept under water ; a fish suffers if he is taken out of the water. A cruel and vicious person may enjoy sights which will horrify others; but if he still has some good elements within his organization, they will suffer until they have become separated from evil. If there are spiritual powers for good, there must be spiritual powers for evil ; for Evil is merely perverted Good. If man is a temple of God, he may likewise be a residence for the Devil. If man has a spirit, that spirit can enter into relations with either of the two states ; but for a spiritless man, an animal, neither God nor the Devil has any use ; nor can the highest Dhyan Chahan of evil exert any power over a man unless that man has already a devil in him.

We can only be conscious of the existence of things, if a relation exists between ourselves and the things. A person who has created nothing during life that could have established a relationship with his immortal self will have nothing immortal with which to enter into relationship with after death. If his whole attention is taken up by his physical wants, the sphere of his consciousness during life will be confined to those material wants. When he leaves his material habitation material wants will no longer exist for him, and his consciousness of them ceases. Having created nothing in his soul that can enter into relation with spirit, his soul will neither lose that which it never possessed nor gain that which it never desired, but remain a blank. If we hire a priest or a professor to do our thinking for us, we create no spiritual aspirations or living thoughts for ourselves. If we are contented to believe the opinions of others, we have no knowledge of our own. The artificial knowledge which has thus been created by the reflection of the thought of others on the mirror of the individual mind has no power of penetration. Those minds which have been fed on illusions will have no substance after the illusions have passed away. The only knowledge which can remain with the spirit is that which it knows itself.

Every cause is followed by an effect. Illusions that have been created in the mind are forces that must become exhausted before they can die. They will continue to act in the subjective state and produce other illusions by the law of harmony that governs the association of ideas, and all illusions will end in the sphere to which they belong. Selfish desires will end in the sphere of self, unselfish aspirations and thoughts will bring their own rewards if they were good, and their own punishment if they were evil. Life is a continual death or exchange of conditions under which we exist. Our desires for things change as the conditions under which we exist assume a different character. Before we are born our state of life depends on the state of the mother's womb ; but having been born into the world, we care nothing more for the placenta and membranes that furnished us with nutriment and life during our fœtal existence. Being infants, our interests are centred upon the breasts of the mother, but these breasts are forgotten after we need them no more. Things which absorbed the whole of our consciousness during our youth are discarded as we grow older. If we throw off the physical body, the desire for that which was attractive to it and important for its existence is thrown off with it, or perishes soon afterwards.

But if the soul again approaches the material plane, and through the influences of mediumship again enters into relationship with it, the old consciousness and the old desires, that had gone to sleep, reawaken, and its physical sensations return. If the influence of the medium is withdrawn, it relapses in its state of stupor or unconsciousness.

There are innumerable varieties of conditions and possibilities in the world of spirit and on the astral plane, as there are upon the physical plane. If the mind begins to investigate these things separately, and without understanding the fundamental laws of nature upon which such phenomena are based, it may as well despair of ever being able to form a correct conception of them. If a botanist were to examine separately each one of the thousands of leaves of a large tree, for the purpose of finding out the true nature of the latter, he would never arrive at an end ; but if he once knows the tree as a whole, the color and shape of the individual leaves will be easily known. Likewise, if we once arrive at a correct conception of the spiritual nature of man, it will be easy to follow the various ramifications of the one universal law.

There is no death for that which is perfect, but the imperfect must perish sooner or later. So-called death is simply a process of elimination of that which is useless. In this sense we all are continually dying every day, and even wishing to die, because every reasonable person desires to get rid of his imperfections and their consequences and the sufferings which they cause. No one is afraid to lose that which he does not want, and if he clings to that which is useless, it is because he is unconscious and ignorant of that which is useful. In such a case he is already partly dead to that which is good, and must come to life and learn to realize that which is useful, by dying to that which is usefulness. This is the so-called *mystic death,* by which the enlightened come to life, which involves the unconsciousness of worthless and earthly desires and passions, and establishes a consciousness of that which is immortal and true. The reason why men and women are sometimes afraid to die is because they mistake the low for the high, and prefer material illusions to spiritual truths. There is no death for the perfect, and he who is imperfect must throw away his imperfectness, so that that which is perfect in him may become conscious and live. This mystic death is recommended by the wise as being the supreme remedy against real death. This mystic death is identical with a spiritual regeneration.*

Hermes Trismegistus says: " Happy is he whose vices die before him;" and the great teacher Thomas de Kempis writes: " Learn to die now to the world" (to the attractions of matter), " so that you may begin to live with Christ"

A person whose vices have died during his earthly life does not need to die again during his life as a soul. His sidereal body will dissolve like a silver cloud, being unconscious of any desires for that which is low, and his spirit will be fully conscious of that which is beautiful, harmonious, and true ; but he, whose conscience is centred in the passions that have raged in his soul during life, can realize nothing higher than that which was the highest to him during his life, and cannot gain any other consciousness by the process of death. Physical death is no gain, it cannot give us that which we do not already possess. Unconsciousness cannot confer consciousness, ignorance cannot give knowledge. By the *mystic death* we arrive at life and consciousness, knowledge and happiness, because the awaking of the higher elements to life implies the death of that which is useless and low. " Neither circumcision nor uncircumcision availeth, but a new creature." †

There are *Esprits soufrants*, our suffering souls. They are the " revenants " or " restants," the astral bodies of victims of premature death, whose physical forms have perished before their spirits became ripe enough to separate from the soul. They remain within the attraction of the Earth until the time arrives that should have been the

* John iii. 3.

† Gala. vi. 15.

termination of their physical lives according to the law of their Karma. They are under normal conditions, not fully conscious of the conditions in which they exist; but they may be temporarily stimulated into life by the influence of mediumship. Then will their half-forgotten desires and memories return and cause them to suffer. To rouse such existences from their stupor into a realization of pain for the purpose of gratifying idle curiosity is cruel, and may be very injurious to such souls, as it may reawaken their thirst for life and for the gratification of earthly desires.

The soul of the sane suicide, however, or that of a malicious person, may be fully conscious and realize the situation in which it is placed. Such existences may wander about earth, clinging to material life, and vainly trying to escape the dissolution by which they are threatened. Partly bereft of reason, and following their animal instincts, they may become *Incubi* and *Succubi*, *Vampires* stealing life from the living to prolong their own existence, regardless of the fate of their victims. The soul-bodies of the dead may be either unconsciously or consciously attracted to mediums for the purpose of communicating with the living. By using the astral emanations of the medium they may become materialized, and be rendered visible and tangible, and appear like the deceased person himself. But if a deceased person was in possession of high aspirations and virtues, his soul-corpse will not actually be the actual entity which it represents, although it may act in every respect as the person whose mask it wears. If we blow into a trumpet it will give the sound of a trumpet and no other. The soul-corpse of a good person, if infused artificially with life, will produce the thoughts it used to produce during life; but there will be no more of the identity of that person in the corpse than there is the identity of a friend in the wire of a telephone, if we recognize his voice and manner of expression through such a wire.

The revelations made by such "spirits" are only the echoes of their former thoughts, or of thoughts impressed upon them by the living, as a mirror reflects the faces of those that stand before it. They do not give us a true description of the spirit's condition in the world of souls, because he is himself ignorant of that condition. At the time when Plato was living, such souls returned, giving descriptions of Hades and of the deities that were believed to exist in that place. At the present day the souls of Roman Catholics will return and ask for masses to be relieved from purgatory, while the Protestants refuse to be benefited by the ceremonies of the Catholic Church. The souls of dead Hindus ask sometimes for the performance of sacrifices to their gods, and every " spirit " appears to be domineered by those ideas in which he believed during his life. The discrepancy in their reports prove that their tales are usually only the products of the imagination of the irrational soul.

If man has a " spirit," that spirit must be immortal. Having become conscious in man, it cannot become unconscious again, because it is self-existent and independent of all conditions but those which it creates itself. The self-consciouness of the *I Am* is indestructible, because it exists in the absolute eternal *One*. The more the lower elements cling to that principle in which absolute consciousness rests, the more will they partake of its state and be rendered conscious and immortal. The object of man's life is to become conscious that *He is*—not an illusive personal form—but an impersonal, immortal reality. The object of his existence is to render the unconscious spirit conscious and the mortal soul immortal; the object of death is to release that which is conscious from that which is unconscious, and to free the immortal from the bonds of ignorance and of matter.

The tree of life grows and produces a seed, and this seed may have to be planted again, to grow into a tree and produce another seed, and this process may have to be repeated over and over again, until at last the spiritual consciousness slumbering in the seed awakens to immortal life. Again and again may the soul be forced by the law of evolution to incarnate into flesh. Unconscious of any relation to personalities, it will be attracted to such conditions as may be best suited for its further development, as its Karma decides. It will be attracted to overshadow a man whose moral and intellectual tendencies and qualities correspond to its own, careless whether it enters the world as a new-born babe through the door of the hut of a beggar, or through the palace of a king. It does not care for personal conditions, because it is unconscious of its own state.

Thus a man that reigned as a king in a former incarnation may be reborn as a beggar, if his character was that of a beggar, and a liberal beggar may create as his future successor a king or a being of noble birth. Both act without freedom of choice at the time of their visit to the Earth, following unconsciously their Karma. But the Adept whose spiritual consciousness is awake, will be his own master. He has grown above the sense of personality, and thereby gained immortal consciousness during his earthly life. He has thrown away his lower self, and death cannot rob him of that which he no longer possesses and to which he attaches no value. Being conscious of his existence and of the conditions under which he exists, he may follow his own choice in the selection of a body, if he chooses to reincarnate, either for the benefit of humanity or for his own progression. Having entirely overcome the attractions of Earth, he is truly free. He is dead and unconscious to all earthly temptations, but conscious of the highest happiness attainable by man. The delusion of the senses can fashion for him no other tabernacle to imprison his soul, and before him lies open the road to eternal rest in Nirvana.

If a person has once attained a certain amount of spiritual knowledge, he will—if it is necessary for him to reincarnate again—not need to follow the blind law of attraction; but he will be able to choose the body and the conditions most suitable to him. He may then reincarnate himself in the body of a child, or in the body of a grown person, whose soul has been separated by disease or accident from the body, and the latter may thus be brought to life again, if no vital organ is too seriously injured to carry on the functions of life again. Cases are known in which a certain person apparently died, and finally came to life again, when from that time he appeared to be an entirely different man; so, for instance, he may have died as a ruffian and after his recovery become suddenly like a saint, so that such a sudden change appeared inexplicable on any other theory than that an entirely different character had taken possession of his body. Such people may, after their recovery takes place, speak a language they never learned; talk familiarly of things they never saw; call people by their names, of which they never heard; know all about places, where their physical bodies never have been, etc., etc. If phenomena could prove anything, such occurrences might go to prove the theory of the reincarnation of living adepts.

To die—in the real meaning of the term—is to become unconscious in relation to certain things. If we become unconscious of a lower state, and thereby become conscious of a higher existence, such a change cannot properly be called death. If we become unconscious of a higher condition, and thereby enter a lower one, such a change is followed by degradation, and therefore degradation is the only possible death, because death in the absolute does not exist. Degradation takes place if a human faculty is employed for a lower purpose than that for which it was by nature intended. Degradation of the most vulgar, the lowest material type takes place, if the organs of the physical body are used for villainous purposes, and disease, atrophy and death are the common result. A higher and still more detrimental and lasting degradation takes · place, if the intellectual faculties are habitually used for selfish and degrading purposes. In such cases the intellect, that ought to serve as a basis for spiritual aspirations, becomes merged with matter, his spiritual consciousness ceases to exist,—in other words, his consciousness is entirely bound down to the plane of personality and selfishness, and becomes inactive in the region of impersonality and life. The lowest and most enduring degradation takes place if man, having reached a state in which his personality has, to a certain extent, been absorbed by his impersonal *I*, degrades his spiritual self by employing the powers which such an amalgamation confers for villainous purposes of a low character. Such are the practices of *black magic*. A person who for want of any better understanding employs his intellectual faculties for his own selfish purposes, regardless of the principle of justice, is not necessarily a villain, but simply ignorant of his own interests. Such persons cannot die spiritually, because they have not yet come spiritually to life. The murderer may commit a murder to save himself from being discovered of some crime, and not for the purpose of robbing another person of life. A thief may steal a purse for the purpose of enriching himself, and not for the purpose of rendering another man poor. Such acts are the result of ignorance, and ignorance has no permanent life ; persons usually act evil for selfish purposes and not for the pure love of evil. Such acts are the result of personal feelings, and personal feelings cease to exist when the personality to which they belong ceases to exist. Such a personal existence ceases when his life on the physical plane or in Kama loca ceases to act. The higher, immortal and impersonal *I* of the man is neither a gainer nor loser on such an occasion, it remains the same as it was before the compound of forces representing the late personality was born.

The real villain, however, is he who performs evil for the love of evil without personal considerations. A person who is no more influenced by his sense of personality, and has thereby gained spiritual life and powers, is a magician. Those who employ such powers for the purposes of evil have been called *black magicians* or *Brothers of the Shadow*, in the same sense as those who employ their spiritual powers for good purposes have been called *Brothers of Light*. The white magician is a spiritual power for good ; the real black magician is a living power of evil attached to a personality that performs evil instinctively and for the love of evil itself. This power of evil may kill the man or the animal that never offended it, and by whose death it has nothing to gain, destroys for the love of destruction, causes suffering without expecting any benefit for itself, robs to throw away the spoils, revels in torture and death. Such a person calls to life an impersonal evil power, which is a part of himself, and which continues to exist after his personality ceases to exist on the physical plane. Many incarnations may be needed before such a power will come into existence and become strong, but when it once lives it will perish as slow as it grew. "Angels," as well as "devils," are born into the world, and children with villainous propensities and malicious characters are not very rare. They may be the product of such forces as in former incarnations have developed a tendency for evil, without becoming fixed in evil by developing any spiritual consciousness in the direction of evil.

Every power which may be employed for a good purpose, may also be used for an evil purpose. If we can by magnetism decrease the rapidity of the pulse of a fever-patient, we may also decrease it to such an extent, that the subject ceases to live. If we can force a person by our will to perform a good act, we may also force him to commit a crime.

It appears to be unnecessary to enter into details in regard to the practices of Black Magic and Sorcery. It is more noble and useful to study how we can benefit mankind, than to satisfy our curiosity in regard to the powers for evil. To show to what aberrations of mind a craving for the power of working black magic may lead, it may be mentioned that the would-be black magician, *Giles de Rays, maréchal* of France, and better known as "Blue Beard," who was executed for his crimes at Nantes, killed and tortured to death during a few years not less than one hundred and sixty women and children for the purpose of practising Necromancy and Black Magic.

The white magician delights in doing good, the servant of the black art revels in cruelty and crime. The former co-operates with the Divine Spirit of Wisdom, the latter co-operates with the animal and semi-intellectual forces of nature ; the former will be exalted in God and united with Him ; the latter will ultimately be absorbed by the devils with which he has associated and which he called to his aid.

To raise our consciousness into the spiritual plane is to live ; to let it sink to a lower level is to die. The natural order of the universe is that the high should elevate the low ; but if the high is made to serve the low, the high will be degraded. Everywhere in the workshop of nature the high acts upon the low by the power of the highest. The highest itself cannot be degraded. Truth itself cannot be turned into falsehood, it can only be rejected and denied. Reason itself cannot be rendered foolish, it can only be refused obedience. The universal and impersonal cannot itself become limited, it can only come into contact with such personalities as are able to approach it. The highest does not suffer by breaking its connection with the low, the low alone suffers and dies.

The impersonal and real is everywhere, and manifests itself in the consciousness of man. Man's consciousness rotates between the two poles of good and evil, of spirit and matter ; the attraction from below may be equal to the attraction from above. The omnipresent influence of the great spiritual Sun renders him strong to overcome the attraction of matter, and assists him to come victorious out of the struggle with evil. Man is not entirely free as long as he is not in possession of perfect knowledge, which means, of a perfect consciousness of the truth ; but he is free to allow himself to be attracted by a love for the truth or to repulse it. His spiritual aspirations may be in co-operation with nature or act against it. He may become united with the principle of truth, or he may sever his connection with it and sell his inherited rights to immortality, like the biblical Esau, for a comparatively worthless mess of pottage. The Centaur in his nature, whose lower principles are animal, while the upper parts are possessed of intellect, may carry away his spiritual aspirations and lull them into unconsciousness by the music of its illusions.

Bodies may be comparatively long-lived, and some souls, compared with others, may be very enduring ; but there is nothing permanent but the consciousness of love and the consciousness of hate. Love is light, and hate is darkness, and in the end love will conquer hate because darkness cannot destroy light, and wherever light penetrates into darkness, there will love conquer, and hate and darkness will disappear.

# CHAPTER IX.

## TRANSFORMATIONS.

*" Be ye transformed by the renewing of your mind."—Rom. xii. 2.*

THE Universe is a manifestation of thought, and thought is an action of Mind. The mind whose thought can bring an universe into existence must be an Universal Mind, embracing in its totality all the individual minds that ever existed, and containing the germs of everything that will ever come into existence.

Mind is a motion of will. Without the will acting either consciously or instinctively (mechanically) within the mind, there would be no production of thought; nor could the will produce any orderly thought on the mind if there were no Wisdom, and it will therefore be safer to say: The Universe is a product of thought, will and wisdom; nor could either of these three ever produce anything, if they were seeking to act independently of each other; they must necessarily be one, and that *one*, representing itself in three different aspects, as *Creative Thought, Universal Will* and *Divine Wisdom*, is commonly called *God*. It will therefore be best to say: *The Universe is a manifestation of God*.

I am well aware that the use of such an expression always gives rise to innumerable misunderstandings in the minds of theists, atheists and pantheists; because each of these classes has its own conception of " God;" forgetting

that the finite mind cannot conceive of the infinite, and
that the universal God is beyond the understanding of anything less than its own divine self.

A man's life does not reside outside, but within his own
body, and likewise God does not live outside of His own
creation; but His power acts inside of Nature.  God is
everything in Nature, and also in that which is not produced by nature, and therefore supernatural and eternal,
such as Justice and Truth.  Nevertheless Nature is not
God; everything is not divine; but everything is a state
of being wherein, under certain conditions, the power of
God can become manifest.  Likewise a stone or a tree is
not nature; but in each stone and in every tree certain
qualities of natural laws are revealed.

If God is all and one, then there can be only one
original power and one original substance; and power and
substance themselves can only be two modes of manifestation of the eternal One.  There can be neither "matter"
nor "motion" *per se;* these two terms signify merely two
aspects of that which is beyond our conception.  If our
minds were independent of the conceptions of time and
space, we might perceive how it was that the One ever came
to manifest itself as a Three and to create a world; but as we
are ourselves His creatures, we cannot encompass our
Creator, we cannot penetrate with our curiosity into the
sanctuary of the mystery of mysteries; we can merely rise
up in our thought to the throne of the Eternal, and seek to
*feel* the power of God within our own heart, and then we
will know more about Him than if we study the whole
library of the Vatican, or learn by heart the *Encyclopædia
theologica.*

Jacob Boehme, a man who was capable to open his
eyes and to see the truth, and who was therefore not
under the necessity of depending on mere belief in what
he might have imagined to be true in consequence of drawing logical inferences from external observations, says:
"The eternal foundation, the will of God, became desirous
of conceiving of something, and as there was nothing but
its own self, this universal consciousness conceived of its
own self; 'it looked within itself,' or, to express it in other
words, 'God beholds Himself in the mirror of His own
eternal Wisdom.'"

Human language is not well adapted to the discussion

of eternal truths which are beyond finite comprehension, and which can never be understood unless we call to our aid that very light of whose existence we desire to obtain proof. Therefore, the external reasoner and doubter, he who relies solely on his own intellectual reasoning, will never arrive at eternal truth, because he rejects the light of the spirit, and extinguishes—not the light—but his own capacity of understanding.

If there is only one God in the universe; there can be only one power. This power is called the *Will*, and it is fundamentally the same, whether it manifests itself in the spiritual plane, as divine love, wisdom, life, light, justice and truth ; on astral plane, as attraction, repulsion, emotion, passion, desire ; in the physical plane, as motion, light, heat, magnetism, electricity, cohesion, chemical affinity or any-thing else. All these powers and forces and energies are and can be nothing else but manifestations of Will acting on the higher planes with and on the lower ones without self-consciousness. God never changes, and the Will never changes. Nothing ever changes except the mode of the manifestation. All these assertions require no other proof but one's own observation. If you doubt them, look within yourself, and ask yourself whether or not they are true.

If there is only one God in the Universe, there can be only one Substance. This substance can fundamentally likewise be nothing else but the Will, but for the sake of distinction we may call it the *Mind*, because it is by means of a mental imagery that the Will creates thoughts within itself. We might also call it " Imagination " or " Ideation '; but whatever words we may use, there is each and every one of them liable to be misunderstood, because words are merely symbols, and to the understanding of any symbol a key is necessary. This key is the understanding itself, which can be given by no man because it is a self-existent principle that is not of man's making, but will come to him by its own grace, if he makes himself ready for its reception.

This one Substance is fundamentally the same in all departments of nature. It constitutes the body of God, and therefore of the highest angels. It forms the vehicle of Spirit and Light and Thought ; it is everything ; from the Astral Light that pervades the world, down to the most grossly material objects. The highest mountains no less than the most minute atoms are corporified Mind ;

thoughts rendered solid and material by the inactivity of their inherent Will. If the will of God were to begin to move within the foundations of the earth, the world which we now occupy would be dissolved in the twinkling of an eye.

All is one, and the one is in eternal rest. Nevertheless we find no absolute rest anywhere; but wherever we look we find a continual change of form and activity, a transformation of the images existing in the infinite mind. If the mode of activity of the will is changed within a form, the form changes its attributes; but form itself is nothing. It is merely an external appearance. There is consequently no change of anything except of the appearance and mode of manifestation of that which eternally *is*.

Forms are shapes of the Will, tinctured by the Imagination, or, we may also say, they are shapes of mind, whose qualities are determined by the action of the will residing in them. They are all certain states of Mind and Will, and as such they are enduring or not according to the quality and intensity of the vibrations of the divine light that causes them to exist as an appearance on the screen of creation. They are all manifestations of their own inner spiritual light, rendered objective and corporeal. If the will and thought constituting a form are divine, the form will be perfect; if the will is impure, or the thought inharmonious, there will be disharmony in the form which is their external expression.

The perfection and duration of a form depends on the quality of the character expressed therein. A thought which is a perfect expression of the truth is everlasting and beautiful; it will require no circumstantial evidence to prove that it is true; its truth will be self-evident to every one who is capable to perceive it. Every one who possesses truth himself is an authorized expert in knowing the truth, while the sceptic and liar cannot see the truth, however learned he may otherwise be.

A thought once formed exists as an image in the mirror of eternity. To remember a thought, is to look for it in the Astral Light and to behold it there. The Astral Light is the book of nature, where every thought becomes engraved and every event recorded. The stars on the sky exist and every one may see them. Likewise ideas exist like stars on the inner sky of the Universal Mind, shedding their rays into the minds of men, and he who is able to open his eyes sufficiently can behold them there. No one can monopolize an idea, they are accessible to all who can grasp them, and they are sometimes grasped simultaneously by receptive minds. No one can create a body out of nothing, no one can create an idea ; all that men can do is to take the already existing materials and to put them into new shapes. A man who thus evolves a new and grand idea kindles a new star in the heavens, whose light may be seen by every one.

Not only do the thoughts of men impress themselves into the Astral Light, but the Universal Mind takes cognizance of everything that exists, and every event that takes place on the physical plane is recorded in the memory of nature. Every stone, every plant, every animal as well as every man, has a sphere in which is recorded every event of its existence. Each is like a light of which we can see only the grossly material wick ; but neither the flame nor its luminous sphere of living light. In the Astral Light of each is stored up every event of its past history and of the history of its surroundings ; so that every thing—no matter how insignificant it may be—can give an account of its daily life, from the beginning of its existence as a form up to the present, to him who is able to read. A piece cf *lava* from Pompeii may give to the *Psychometer* a true description of the volcanic eruption that devastated that town and buried it under its ashes, where it remained hidden for nearly two thousand years ; a floating timber carried by the Gulf Stream to the far North may give to the inhabitants of the North a true picture of tropical life ; and a piece of bone of a *Mastodon* may teach the vegetable and animal life of antediluvian periods.*

The pictures impressed in the Astral Light react upon the mental spheres of individual minds and may create in them emotional disturbances, even if these pictures do not come to the full consciousness of their minds. Deeds committed with a great concentration of thought call living pictures in the Astral Light into existence, that may cause impressible persons to commit similar acts.

If the true nature of the constitution of man were properly understood, *capital punishment* would soon be aban-

---

* Prof. Wm. Denton : "Soul of Things."

doned as perfectly useless, unjust and contrary to the law of nature. That which commits a murder or any other crime is a conscious and invisible power, which cannot be killed, and which does not improve in character by being separated from its external form. The body is innocent, it is merely an instrument in the hands of the invisible culprit, the *inner man.* The face of even a criminal bears an expression of peace when the soul has departed. By severing the bonds between this intellectual and vicious power and the physical form, we do not change its tendency to act evil; but while during the life of the body the action of that power was restricted to only one form, having been liberated, it may now incite numerous other weak-minded people to perform the same crime for which the body was executed. Thus by *capital punishment* evil is not abolished, but its sphere of action increased. As far as the theory of influencing other would-be criminals with fear, by making an example of one, thus to prevent others from committing crimes, is concerned; it is well known that criminals do not look upon any punishment as being something which they have deserved for their deeds, but as being a consequence of having been so careless as to allow themselves to be caught, and they usually make up their minds, that if they were permitted to escape, they would be more careful—not to be caught again.

The destruction of a form is entirely useless for the purpose of annihilating the principle which it represents, because the form is not the character, nor can the destruction of the form in any way improve or ameliorate that character. He who steals away the life of any being, whether legally or illegally, merely destroys the conditions under which a Spark of the Divinity was striving to unfold its light and to obtain consciousness, and he thereby commits a crime against God; while the punishment of the culprit exists nowhere except in his imagination, because if he is not afraid to die, death will be no punishment to him. All that killing can possibly accomplish is to produce a change of external effects, creating thereby internal causes which are far more injurious even if they are less evident. We are against killing for the sake of convenience; but on the other hand we would not subscribe to that sentimental policy that never wards off a blow and submits to be killed. He who permits himself to be killed by another, is committing murder through him. From a misunderstanding of the relations existing between a principle and the form in which it finds its expression result the most ludicrous effects; not the least of which are the vagaries of those who attempt to improve the condition of the world by doctoring the external effects of internal causes, whereby invariably worse evils come into existence. If we wish to prevent the growth of an evil tree, it is of little use to lop off the leaves and the twigs, or even to hide the tree behind a screen. The living force in the roots and in the trunk will act with renewed strength, producing new branches and leaves, which the screen cannot cover from sight.

All forms are nothing but symbols by which internal principles find their expression; to successfully change a form it must be endowed with a new principle. We may melt iron a thousand times, we cannot transform it into gold, nor could we transform a sinner into a saint if we were to baptize him with all the water that runs into the sea, but we only make a piece of iron magnetic by endowing it with magnetism, and a villain may become honest if the light of the true understanding enters his heart.

Each being in nature represents a mental state in a certain condition of vibration. Each represents a melody in the great symphony of the music of the spheres; and as one sound of an instrument may cause a similar vibration in a corresponding instrument, likewise the principle expressed in one form may call a similar principle in another form into action.

If mankind as a whole were so far awakened from their slumber as to be able to recognize the existence of eternal principles, instead of merely beholding the perishing form, then would the *golden era* begin and the paradise be again established upon the earth. Then would they cease to run after illusions and shadows, or to put their faith into worthless objects. Then would they behold the Holy Spirit in everything and the Redeemer within themselves. Then would the world be transformed by the magic power of love, and the darkness of ignorance be changed into the light of knowledge by the influence of the rays of divine wisdom.

But what else can an eternal principle be, except a state of living will tinctured by divine thought? Even the highest spiritual beings and planetary spirits can be nothing else but self-conscious thoughts of God, vehicles for the divine will

and instruments for its manifestation; all being obedient
to divine law, order and harmony, without which they
could not be divine or eternal.

God does not need the world to enable him to be what
He is, but Nature requires God to enable her to exist.
The principle of life requires no form, but forms need the
principle of life to enable it to live. Likewise eternal love
and justice and truth are self-existent, self-sufficient and
independent of any object or form; but they cannot
manifest themselves without appropriate forms, and the
forms that require them to enable them to love, to be just
and true. In other words: God is independent of His
creation; but creation is dependent on Him.*

Thus the sun could exist without our earth, but the earth
not without the sun; a man can be without truth; but
eternal truth nevertheless remains what it is, even if there
were no one to recognize it.

Thus we see that nothing will ever change or be transformed, except by the influence of another principle. A
natural product grows by the influence of natural principles,
and that which is divine in man by the influence of the
Divine; while that which is devilish in man will grow by
the aid of the Devil.

All things are made of will and thought, and therefore
thought and will can act even upon corporeal substances.
Anything a person touches receives a part of his own spirit.

A lock of hair, a piece of clothing, the handwriting of a
person or any article he may have touched, handled, or
worn, may indicate to an intuitive individual that person's
state of health, his physical, emotional, intellectual, and
moral attributes and qualifications. The picture of a
murderer may be impressed on the retina of his victim,
and in some instances be reproduced by means of photo-
graphy; but it is surely impressed on all the surroundings
of the place where the deed occurred, and can there be
detected by the psychometer, who may thus come *en rapport* with the criminal, and even follow the events of his
life after he has left that locality, and hunt him down just
as the bloodhound traces the steps of a fugitive slave.†

---

* See Jacob Boehme, " Aurora " 23.

† Emma Hardinge Britten : " Ghost Land." The case cited in this
book, in which a clairvoyant followed the tracks of a murderer through
several towns and caught him at last, is quoted in several German
publications of the last century.

This tendency of the Astral Light to inhere in material bodies gives amulets their power and invests keepsakes and relics with certain occult properties. A ring, a lock of hair, or a letter from a friend, may not only conjure up that friend's *cture in a person's memory, but bring him *en rapport* w..h a peculiar mental state of which that person was or is a representation. Why do people put so much value upon the keepsakes received from a friend that they often dawdle away their time in playing with them? Is it that their memory is so weak as to require such a stimulus; or is there something of that friend about them which the soul feels and perceives, but which cannot be recognized externally? If you wish to forget a person, or free yourself from his magnetic attraction, part from everything that reminds you of him. Articles belonging to a person may bring us in sympathy with that person, although the fact may not come to our consciousness, and this circumstance is sometimes used for purposes of black magic.

The existence of a power, by which a disease may be transferred upon a healthy person, even in " non-contagious " cases, by means of some article belonging to the sick person, is generally believed in by the people in eastern countries. It must, however, be remembered that in making such experiments the success depends on the amount of faith which the magician can employ. Without faith, nothing can be accomplished, but "faith" means " will without any doubt," such as is attained by experience.

As every form is the representation of a certain mental state, every substance has its sympathies and its antipathies ; the loadstone attracts iron, and iron attracts the oxygen of the air; hygroscopic bodies attract water; some substances change their colors under certain colored rays, others remain unaffected, etc.

The ancients attributed certain virtues to certain precious stones, and imagined that the Garnet was conducive to joy, the Chalcedony to courage, the Topaz promoting chastity, the Amethyst assisting reason, and the Sapphire intuition. A spiritual force to be effective requires a sensitive object to act upon. But every spiritual or any other force can only come to the cognizance of him who is receptive for it. If a person cannot feel the occult influences of nature, it does not necessarily follow that they do not exist, and that there may not be others who may be able to perceive them because their impressional capacities are greater.

Only the ignorant man believes that he knows everything. What is really known is only like a grain of sand on the shore of the ocean in comparison to what is still unknown. Physiologists know that certain plants and chemicals have certain powers, and to a certain extent they explain their secondary effects. They know that Digitalis decreases the quickness of the pulse by paralyzing the heart; that Belladonna dilates the pupil by paralyzing the muscular fibres of the Iris; that Opium in small doses produces sleep by causing anæmia of the brain, while large doses produce coma by causing congestion; but why these substances have such effects, or why a chemical compound of Nitrogen, Oxygen, Carbon, and Hidrogen may be exceedingly poisonous in one chemical combination, while the same substances if combined in a different stœchiometrical proportion may be used as food, neither chemistry nor physiology can tell us at present. If we, however, look upon all forms as symbols of mental states, it will not be more difficult to imagine why strychnine is poisonous, than why hate can kill, or fear paralyze the heart.

If all things are made of imagination and will, then surely drugs are the same, and by giving drug a to a patient, we merely induce a corresponding activity in his will, and act upon the imagination of his nature. The fact that the patient is not himself conscious of it, does not change the matter. There are many processes going on in his system of which he has no knowledge. We, therefore, see that even the most rabid anti-mind curer and drug-doctor acts after all himself upon the mind of the patient.

The power to receive, transform and evolve thoughts is the power of Imagination. If an idea enters into the mind, the mind seeks to clothe it into a form, and this power may be exercised independently of any active application of the will.

Imagination is, therefore, an active power, and it forms the basis of all artistic and magical operations. Art and magic are closely related together; both give objective form to subjective ideas. The artist exercises this power when he mentally projects the picture formed in his mind

upon the canvas and chains it there by the use of his pencil
or brush ; the sculptor shapes the picture of a form on his
mind and embodies it in the marble. He then employs
mechanical force to free the ideal from all irregularities,
and resurrects it from the tomb, out of which it may rise
as a materialization of thought. The magician forms an
image on his mind and makes it perceptible to others by
projecting it into their mental spheres.

By this law many of the feats performed by Indian
fakirs may be explained. They may cause tigers and
elephants or anything else appear before a multitude, by
merely forming the images of such things in the sphere of
their mind, and as that sphere extends through space, they
may locate these images wherever they chose. What the
spectators see on such occasions is nothing else but the
thoughts of the conjuror, rendered objective and visible by
his will.

In the case of an artist mechanical labor executes the
work, and the artist will finish his work the sooner the
more he works to that end. In the case of a magician,
concentration of thought executes his work, and he will
succeed the better the more his thought is concentrated
upon the work he desires to perform ; but the greatest
amount of labor will not enable a person who is not an
artist to produce a real work of art, and the greatest concentration of thought will not enable a person whose will
is not free to perform a true magical feat.

As long as the world exists no man has ever changed an
opinion or an idea, except by the influx of another idea ;
nor has any Alchemist ever changed any inferior metal
into gold except by the influence of that principle which
constitutes gold ; nor has evil ever been transformed into
good, except through the action of the superior power of
good.

The processes of nature are alchemical processes and
not merely chemical ones ; because, without the principle
of life acting upon the chemical substances of the earth, no
growth would result. If the force of attraction and repulsion were entirely equal, everything would be at a standstill.
If growth and decay would go hand in hand, nothing
could grow, because a cell would begin to decay as soon as
it would begin to form. The chemist may take earth, and
water, and air, and separate them into their constituent

elements, and recombine them again, and at the end of his
work he will be with his work where he began.    But the
Alchemy of nature takes water, and earth, and air, and
infuses into them the fire of life, forming them into trees
and producing flowers and fruits.    Nature could not give
her life-imparting influence to her children if she did not
possess it; the chemist who has no life-principle at his
command cannot perform the wonders of Alchemy.

*Johannes Tritheim* says: " The *Spiritus Mundi* resembles a breath, appearing at first like a fog and afterwards
condensing like water.    This ' water' (A'kâsa) was in the
beginning pervaded by the principle of life, and light was
awakened in it by the *fiat* of the eternal spirit.    This *spirit
of light*, called the soul of the world (the Astral Light), is
a spiritual substance, which can be made visible and tangible by art; it is a substance, but, being invisible, we call
it spirit.    This ' soul' or *corpus* is hidden in the centre of
everything, and can be extracted by means of the spiritual
fire in man, which is identical with the universal spiritual
fire (the Astral Light), constituting the essence of nature
and containing the images and figures of the Universal
Mind."

" This Light (Astral Light) resides in the Water (A'kâsa)
and is hidden as a *Seed* in all things.    Everything that
originated from the *spirit of light* is sustained by it, and
therefore this spirit is omnipresent; the whole of nature
would perish and disappear if it were removed from it ; it
is *the principium* of all things."

There were true Alchemists during the Middle Ages who
knew how to extract that *Seed* from the soul-essence of the
world, and there are some who have the power to perform
that process to-day.    " It is an eternal truth, that without
our secret magical fire nothing can be accomplished in our
art.    The ignorant will not believe in our art because they
do not possess that fire ; and without that fire all their
labor is useless.    Without that fire spirits cannot be bound,
much less can they be acted upon with material fire." *

The most important alchemical work is the generation
of *man;* it requires not only the chemical combination of
physical substances, but involves a chemistry of the soul
and an influence of the spirit, and all must harmoniously

---

* J. Tritheim : " Miraculosa," Chap. xiv.

act together, if a human being and not a human monster and mental *homunculus* is to be the result. If the rules of Alchemy were better understood and adhered to, scrofula, cancers, syphilis, tuberculosis, and other inherited diseases would disappear, and a strong and healthy generation of men and women would be the result.

The true alchemical laboratory is the body of man, the *alembic* is the soul, the magic fire the will, having become free. Ignorance is like lead, but by the addition of mercury, representing knowledge, it becomes transformed into the pure gold of wisdom. Nothing will ever be accomplished without a mortification of the earthly residua, and it is for that purpose necessary to practise a continual sublimation of thought by sending the aspirations of the soul up to the highest good, and to coagulate the wisdom received, so that it may be incorporated into the soul and even the body become luminous in the light of the spirit.*

All this can be accomplished only in proportion as the will becomes free and ceases to be the slave of that compound of elementals and animals which constitutes the illusive *ego* of man. Not only should the will be free of all lower desires, but free likewise from the dominion of the imagination. The will is the sun, the imagination the moon. The moon must obey the sun, not the sun to the moon. Thought must become obedient to the will and the

---

* To answer the question whether or not any one ever succeeded in making gold grow in this manner, we will say that there is a German book in existence entitled, "Collection of historical accounts regarding some remarkable occurrences in the life of some still living Adepts." It was printed in 1780; and among many most interesting anecdotes about successful attempts of making gold grow, there are copies of the legal documents and decisions of the court at Leipzig in regard to a case where, during the absence of the *Count of Erbach*, in the year 1715, an Adept visited the countess in the castle of *Tankerstein*, and out of gratitude for an important service which had been rendered to him by the countess, he transformed all the silver she had into gold. When the count returned, who, as it seems, kept his own property separate from that of his wife, he claimed that gold for himself, appealing to a certain statute of the law, according to which treasures discovered upon or below the surface of a certain piece of land belong to the proprietor of that territory ; but the court decided that as the material (the silver) out of which the gold had been made belonged legally to the countess, consequently this gold could not be classified as a hidden treasure, and did not come within the reach of that statute. The count thereupon lost his case, and his wife was permitted to keep the gold.

**will** must be in harmony with wisdom, while wisdom is acquired in no other way but by obedience to the law.

He who obeys the laws of nature and acts as her servant, becomes the master of nature and renders her obedient to him. He who obeys the divine laws of God and is a true servant of God, will be in possession of divine power, and God will fulfil his desires.

The will becomes free tnrough knowledge. Not by means of what is usually called "knowledge," and which consists in opinions formed by intellectual speculation and drawing inferences, but by means of the knowledge of the soul; such as is the result of the soul's own perception and experience.

Only when the will has become free, will it be able to act at a distance and to perform the wonders of Magic and Alchemy, which are regarded as miracles by the ignorant and denied by the foolish, because no man can be found who is able to perform them; they all being the slaves of worldly desires.

The will of God is free and identical with the law. It is not influenced by any selfish desire nor by exhortations and prayers. It never deprives any creature, however low it may be in the scale of evolution, of any of its rights, or gives them to another; it is deaf to persuasions, unaffected by bombast and bragging, and can neither be bribed with money nor be deluded with shows.

If the actions of the Universal Mind were not subject to the eternal law of cause and effect, but guided by the arbitrary whims and notions of some invisible power or god contained therein, the most extraordinary results were liable to follow, and the age of actual miracles would begin. The earth would perhaps stand still for a day or a year and begin to revolve again the next; sometimes it might turn fast and at other times slow, and there is no end to the absurdities which might take place; especially if this imaginary power could be induced to follow the advices of its worshippers.

To the superficial observer the processes of nature seem to be the results of chance. The sun shines and the rain falls upon the land of the pious as well as upon that of the wicked; storms and fires rage, careless whether they destroy the life and property of the learned or that of the ignorant, because they are the necessary results of the law of cause and effect. The interest of individuals cannot control the welfare of the whole. While the welfare of the human body seems to be, to a certain extent, under the control of the will of the individual, the processes of nature, as a whole, appear to be unguided by the reason of the Universal Mind.

Man's reason can prevent an outburst of his emotions; but where is the personal god to control the emotions of the soul of the world? God does not prevent the growth of warts, or cancers, or tumors, God being the law cannot act in contradiction with Himself. His blessings are accompanied by curses. Man's foot crushes the insect, because man's perception and intelligence does not pervade his feet; God does not prevent the growth of a stone in the bladder, because the high cannot manifest itself in the low, wisdom cannot be active in an unconscious form; the means must be adapted to the end. The music that can be made with a harp cannot be made with a stick. The intelligence of the Universal Mind can only manifest itself through instruments adapted for intellectual manifestation.

Wisdom is not a product of the organization of man. It is eternal and universal. It finds its expression in the fundamental laws upon which the universe with all its forms is constructed. It is expressed in the shape of a leaf, in the body of an animal, in the organism of man. Its action can be found everywhere in nature, as long as the beings in nature live according to nature. There are no diseases in nature which have not been originally created by powers which acted contrary to the laws of nature and became therefore unnatural. Outward appearances seem to contradict this assertion; because we find animals affected with diseases, and epidemic diseases are even of frequent occurrence in the vegetable kingdom. But a deeper investigation into the occult laws of nature may show that all the forms of nature, minerals, vegetables, and animals, are merely states or expressions of the states of the Universal Mind—in other words—products of the imagination of Nature; and as the imagination of Nature is acted on, influenced and modified by the imagination of man, a morbid imagination of man is followed by a morbid state of the Universal Mind, and morbid results follow again on the physical plane. This law explains why periods of great moral depravity, sensuality, superstition, and materialism may be followed by plagues, epidemics, famine, wars, etc., and it would be worth the while to collect statistics to show that such has invariably been the case.

The elementary forces of nature are blind and obey the law that controls them. If hailstones were wise, they would not indiscriminately destroy the crops ; if the sun were a vehicle for intellectual labor, he might perhaps be persuaded sometimes to change the directions of his rays. Stones have no intelligence, because they have no organization through which intelligence can act, but if an intelligent power sets them into motion, they obey the law by which their movement is guided. As the organisms rise in the scale of evolution and development, their consciousness becomes more manifest. Consciousness becomes manifest as instinct in the animal creation. It teaches the bird to fly, the fish to swim, the ants to build their houses, the swallows to make their nests. Acting through the nerve centres and the spinal cord it induces the actions of the heart and lungs and other organic and involuntary actions of the body.

The brain is the most highly developed instrument for the manifestation of mind. It performs the intellectual labor of the organism, acting as a centre of attraction for the collection of ideas, as a workshop for their transformation, and as a focus from which they are reflected again into the Astral Light. But with the power of performing intellectual labor the highest manifestation of God in man is not yet obtained. If we wish to know the wisdom and majesty of God, we must prepare ourselves to become fit receptacles for His love.

To accomplish this, we need not seek to acquire anything by our own power. All selfish efforts are useless for that purpose. All we need is to throw away the obstacles in our possession that hinder us from seeing the light of the truth, and which consist of our own selfish thoughts and desires. If man accomplishes this herculean task, then will the door to the mystery be open before him ; his mind will become illuminated with wisdom, and in his own soul he will behold the glory of his Creator.

# CHAPTER X.*

### CREATION.

*"And God said: Let us make Man."—Bible.*

THE most important question that was ever asked, and is still asked with anxiety and often with fear, is the same that was propounded thousands of years ago by the Egyptian Sphinx, who killed him that attempted to solve the riddle and did not succeed: What is man? Ages have passed away since the question was first asked, nations have slain each other in cruel religious warfare, making vain efforts to impose upon each other such solution of the great problem as they believed they had found, but from the tombs of the past only re-echoes the same question— What is Man? And yet the answer seems simple. *Common sense,* if divested of religious or scientific prejudices, tells us that man, like every other form in the universe, is a collective centre of energy, a solitary ray of the universally present Divine Light which is the common source of everything that exists; he is a true child of the great Spiritual *Sun.* As the rays of our sun only become

---

* The term *Creation* is frequently misunderstood. Neither the *Bible* nor any other reasonable book says that anything had ever been created out of nothing. Such a superstition belongs entirely to modern materialistic Science, which believes that life and consciousness could grow out of dead and unconscious things. The word "Creation" means the production of *forms*; *form* in the absolute is not a thing, it is nothing but an illusion, and, therefore, if a form is produced, nothing but an illusion has been created.

visibly active in contact with dust, so the divine ray is absorbed and reflected by matter. It mingles for a while with matter, and draws up towards the sun such elements as are sufficiently refined to escape the attraction of Earth.

The sun-ray plays with the waves of the ocean : the heat created by the contact of water with light from above extracts from below the refined material, and the vapors rise to the sky, where, like the ghosts of the seas, they wander in clouds of manifold shapes traveling freely through the air, playing with the winds, until the time arrives when the energies which keep them suspended become exhausted and they once more descend to earth. In a similar manner the divine ray of the spiritual sun mingles with matter while dwelling on Earth, absorbing and assimilating whatever he chooses or what corresponds to his needs. As the butterfly flits from flower to flower, tasting the sweets of each, so the human monad passes from life to life, from planet to planet, gathering experience, knowledge. and strength, but when the day of life is over, night follows, and with it follows sleep bringing dreams of vivid reality. The grossest elements remain to mingle again with earth, the more refined elements—the *astral elements* —which are still within the attraction of the planet float about, driven hither and thither by their inherent tendencies, until the energy which holds them together is exhausted, and they dissolve again in the plane to which they belong ; but the highest spiritual energies of man, held together by love freed from the attraction of Earth, ascend to their source like a white-robed spirit, bringing with it the products of its experience beyond the limits of matter. Man's love and aspiration do not belong to Earth. They create energies which are active beyond the confines of the grave and the funeral-pyre ; their activity may last for ages, until it becomes exhausted, and the purified ray, endowed with the tendencies impressed upon it by its last visit to the planet, again seeks association with matter, builds again its prison-house of animated clay, and appears an old actor in a new part upon the ever-changing stage of life.

Some of the greatest philosophers have arrived at a recognition of this truth by speculation and logical reasoning, while others whose minds were illuminated by wisdom, have perceived it as a self-evident fact by the power of intuition.

To build the new house the impressions gathered by its previous visits furnish the material. The slothful rich man of the past may become the beggar of the future, and the industrious worker in the present life may develop tendencies which will lay the foundation of greatness in the next. Suffering in one life may produce patience and fortitude that will be useful in another; hardships will produce endurance; self-denial will strengthen the will; tastes engendered in one life may be our guides in another ; and accumulated energies will become active whenever circumstances require it during an existence on the material plane either in one life or another, according to the eternal law of cause and effect.

A child may burn its fingers by touching the flame, and the adult may not remember all the circumstances under which the accident occurred ; still the fact that fire will burn and must not be touched will remain impressed upon the mind. In the same manner the experiences gained in one life may not be remembered in their details in the next, but the impressions which they produce will remain. Again and again man passes through the wheel of transformation, changing his lower energies into higher ones, until he has attained knowledge by experience, and he becomes—what he is destined to be—a god.

There is a certain stage in the spiritual evolution of man, when he will become self-conscious in the spirit. He will then remember the events of his previous life; but to remember them in his present state of imperfection would be merely a hindrance in his progress. It has been said, that by not remembering the errors of our past lives and their evil consequences, man is liable to commit his previous errors again ; but we ought not to do good merely as a matter of speculation and to avoid evil consequences resulting therefrom, but from an inherent desire to do good, regardless of what the resulting consequences may be.

Man, like the majority of organized beings, is an atom in the immensity of the universe ; he cannot be divided and still remain a man ; but unlike other and lower organized beings, whose realization of existence is confined to the physical or astral plane, that which constitutes him a Man and distinguishes him from an animal is an integral and conscious part of the highest spiritual energy of the universe, which is everywhere present; and his spiritual consciousness is, therefore, not limited to a certain locality in the physical world.

Who made Man?—Man makes himself during every day of his life. He is his own creator. The clay—the material body—that clings to the ray of the manifested *Absolute*, is taken from Earth; the energies, called the *soul*, are the products of the astral plane; the highest energies, called the *spirit*, belong to "heaven." Animal man, like the lower orders of nature, is a product of the blind law of necessity, and may even be produced artificially.* As such, his mother is Nature, the ever immaculate virgin, who presents time-born man to his father, the infinite spiritual principle, to be transformed into a god. The physical attributes of the child and its mental qualifications are the result of inheritance or previously existing conditions. Like the tree that can send its roots into the neighboring soil and gather the nutriment by which it is surrounded, but cannot roam about in search of food at distant places, so physical man has only a limited choice in the selection of such means of development as he may require; he grows, because he cannot resist the law of necessity, and the impulses given by nature. But as reason begins to enlighten him, the work of creation begins. The intelligence within says to the will: "Let us make man." She urges the will, and the will sullenly leaves its favorite occupation of serving the passions and begins to mould animal man in accordance with the divine image held up before him by wisdom.

*Let us make Man* means: Let us make a divine man out of an animal man; let us surround the divine ray within us with the purest of essences gathered from the lower planes; let us throw off everything which is sensual and grossly material, and which hinders our progress; let us transform the emotions into virtues in which the spiritual ray may clothe itself when it reascends to its throne.

Let us make man! It depends entirely on our efforts what kind of a man we shall make. To make an average man or even a superior one in the common acceptation of the term is not a very difficult matter. Follow the rules

---

* See *Paracelsus.* "Homunculi."

of health and the laws of diet, provide above all for yourself and never give anything away, unless by doing so you
are sure to get more in return. You will then make a
respectable animal, a "self-made" man, prominent, independent and rich—one who lives and dies on the plane
of selfishness, an object of envy for many; respected
perhaps by many, but not by himself.

But such is the influence of the higher nature in man,
that even on that plane an apparent unselfishness will often
bring material reward, and while the inexorable miser is
despised by all, he who occasionally confers little favors
makes friends, and may get his favors returned with
interest.

There is another class of self-made men; those who
appear prominently on the intellectual plane. They stand
before the world as the world's benefactors, as philosophers, teachers, statesmen, inventors, or artists. They
have what is called *genius*, and instead of being mere imi-
tators, they possess originality. They benefit themselves
by benefiting the world. Intellectual researches that
benefit no one are unproductive; they resemble physical
exercise with dumb-bells, by which muscular strength may
be gained, but no labor accomplished. An intellectual pursuit may be followed for merely selfish purposes; but unless
there is a love for the object of that study, little progress
will be made, and instead of a sage, a bookworm will be
the result. The majority of the learned live in their own
darkness, seeking only for the fruits that others have
gathered; but true genius is a magician who creates a
world for himself and for others, and his light expands as
he grows in perfection.

Intellectual labor alone cannot be the true object of life;
infinite truth cannot be grasped by the material brain. He
who attempts to arrive at the truth merely by the intellectual
labors, without consulting the heart, will find it a difficult
work. The heart is the seat of Wisdom, the brain the seat
of the reasoning intellect, and receives its life from the
heart. The heart and the head should work together in
harmony, to kill the dragon of ignorance, dwelling upon
the threshold of the temple.

In the allegorical books of the *Alchemist* the *Sun* represents Love; he is the "*heart*" of our solar system; the
*Moon* represents the Intellect or the "brain;" *Earth*

represents the physical *Body*.  If the male *Sun* cohabits with the female *Moon* in the *water of Truth*, they will produce a son whose name is *Wisdom*.  The intellect is the material man whose bride is Intuition, the divine woman ; no man or woman is perfect as long as the celestial marriage has not taken place through the power of Love.*

Man is not merely an intellectual workshop ; but a temple wherein resides the spirit of God.  The materials of which Man is constructed are the seven principles that flow into him from the store-house of universal nature, the builder is the will, reason the superintendent, and wisdom the supreme architect.  The building goes on without noise, and no sound of the hammer is heard, because the materials are already prepared by nature ; they only require to be put into their proper places.  The highest is the Spirit, and Spirit alone is immortal.  Such of the lower elements as may harmonize with it amalgamate with the spirit, and are rendered immortal.  Pure spirit can only find its corresponding vibrations in the highest spiritual elements, such as are furnished by the higher principles, and consist of the purest thoughts, aspirations, and memories produced by the fifth, in which resides the intellectual power of man.  Pure intelligence is Spirituality, but intellectual power laboring only in the lower planes of thought can bring to light no spiritual treasures, unless it is penetrated by the light of Wisdom, which enables it to distinguish the pure metal from the material dross.  A very intellectual and learned person may be very unhappy and unharmonious, if his tendencies are towards evil, and his mind incapable to be illuminated by the light of truth.  Wisdom is the perfect recognition of the truth ; it resides in the spiritual principle of man, and sends its light down into his fifth principle, where it may be seen by the power of intuition, shining through the clouds of matter like the sunlight penetrating a fog.

The fifth principle receives its stimulus from the fourth, the rational nature of man.  We cannot build a house without solid material, and we may just as well attempt to run a steam-engine without fuel or water as to make a genius out of a being without any emotions or intellect. The stronger the emotions are, the more enduring will

* "The Perfect Way, or the Finding of Christ."

be the spiritual temple, if they can be made to fit into the walls and pillars. A person without any emotions is without virtues, he is without energy, a shadow, neither cold nor warm, and necessarily useless. The passionate man is nearer to the spirit, if he can guide his passions in the right direction towards the source of all good, than the man who has nothing to guide and nothing to conquer.

To produce a perfect building, or a perfect man, the proportions must be harmonious. Wisdom guides the work and love furnishes the cement. An emotion is either a virtue or a vice according to the manner in which it is applied. Misapplied virtues become vices, and well-directed vices are virtues. A man who acts according to the dictates of prudence alone is a coward; one who indiscriminately exercises his generosity is a spendthrift; courage without caution is rashness; veneration without knowledge produces superstition; charity without judgment makes a beggar, and even one-sided justice, if too stern and unbending and untempered by mercy, produces a miserly, cruel, and despicable tyrant.

The irrational soul, impelled only by its desires and un-guided by wisdom, resembles a drunken man who has lost his physical balance; it totters from side to side, falls from one extreme into another, and cannot guide its steps. Only an equilibrium of forces can produce harmony, beauty and perfection. The irrational soul, swayed by uncontrollable emotions, forms an unfit habitation for the divine ray, that loves peace and tranquillity.

The control of the emotions is the difficult struggle, that is allegorically represented by the twelve labors of Hercules, which the oracle of Zeus commanded him to perform. Every man who desires to progress is his own Hercules and works for the benefit of the king (his Atma), whose orders he receives through the divine oracle of his own intuition. He is constantly engaged in battle, because the lower principles fight for their lives and will neither be conquered. They are the products of matter and they cling to their source.

Whence do the emotions come?

The cosmologies of the ancients express under various allegories the same fundamental truth; that " in the beginning" the *Great First Cause* evolved out of itself, by the power of its own will, certain powers, whose action and reaction brought the elementary forces that constituted the world into existence. These elementary forces are the Devas of the East, the Elohims of the Bible, the Afrites of the Persians, the Titans of the Romans, the Eggregores of the book of Enoch. They are the active agents of the cosmos, beneficial or detrimental according to the conditions under which they act, intelligent or unintelligent according to the nature of the instrument through which they act. They are not self-conscious rational entities, but may manifest themselves through self-conscious organisms endowed with reason ; they are not individuals, but may become individualized by finding expression in individual forms. Love and hate, envy and benevolence, lust and greed are not persons, but their shadows may become personified in human or animal forms. An extremely malicious person is the embodiment of malice, and if he sees the demon in an objective form, he beholds the reflection of his own soul in the mirror of his mind. Ideas exist everywhere, but we cannot perceive a thought unless it first enters the sphere of our soul. The spirit that enters our soul obtains his life from ourselves, and if we do not expel it from our soul he may grow strong by vampirizing our life. Like a parasite growing on a tree and feeding on its substance, it may fasten its feelers around the tree of our life, and grow strong while our own spirit grows weak. A thought, once taking root in the soul, will grow, unless it is expelled by force, until it will become expressed in an act, when obtaining a life of its own by that act, it will leave its place to a successor. Those elementary forces of nature are everywhere, and always ready to enter the soul if its doors are not defended. To call up a wicked spirit we need not go in search of him, we need only allow him to come. To call up a devil means to give way to an evil thought, to vanquish him means to resist successfully a temptation to evil.

The elementary powers of nature are innumerable, and their classification gave rise to the pantheons of the Greeks and to the mythologies of the East. The greatest power is *Zeus*, the father of the gods, or the source from which all other powers take their origin. Minerva, the goddess of wisdom, springs from his head, her origin is the noblest of all, but Venus, the daughter of the Sun, arising from the ocean of the universal Soul, conquers all by her beauty.

She holds together the worlds in space by the power of her attraction, binds souls to souls, chains the good to good, and binds the evil to evil. She is the mother of the minor gods that combat each other, because love of self, love of possession, love of fame, love of power, etc., are all only children of the universal power of love. They fight among themselves like children, because action gives rise to reaction, love is opposed by hate, hope by fear, faith by doubt, etc. To control them the god of *Power* (Mars) must be united with the goddess of Love—in other words, the passions must be held in obedience by the Will.

Each power exists and is held in its elementary matrix or vehicle, the A'kâsa, the *Universal Proteus*, the generator of form, which finds its outward expression in Matter. They are all brought into life by desire for existence. This ever-turning wheel of desire is the eternal circle of evolution and involution, or the *snake*, "whose head shall be crushed by the heel of the woman," meaning Wisdom, the eternal virgin, whose "daughters" are *faith*, *hope* and *charity*.

The snake of evil cannot enter the soul, if the latter is defended by wisdom. If an evil thought enters the soul and we do not immediately reject it, we harbor a devil in our heart, whose claims we take into consideration, we give him a promise and induce him to remain, and like an unwelcome creditor he will continually argue his claims until they are fulfilled.

The lower triads of principles in the constitution of man receive their nutriment from the inferior kingdoms of nature. If the body is overfed or stimulated by drink, the emotional element will become excessively active and the intellect will become weak. Too stimulating food or drink is injurious for higher development, because life will in such cases withdraw its activity from the higher principles and be made to work in the lower principles of man. Large quantities of otherwise healthy food will be injurious for the same reason. The principle of life which transforms the lower energies into higher ones is the same principle which causes the digestion of food. If it is squandered in the lower organs, the higher organs will suffer. Some men are habituated to meat-eating, and they require it; others are used to alcohol, and if they would suddenly discontinue its use they will suffer; but meat and alcohol are, under normal conditions, unnecessary for the human system, and often they act positively injurious.

A pure person requires pure food, but to the impure impurities become at first a luxury, and afterwards a necessity. "God said: Behold, I have given you every herb, bearing seed, which is upon the face of all the earth, and every tree, in which is the fruit of a tree yielding seed, to you it shall be for meat." *

The principal argument of the lovers of animal food is that it "gives bodily strength, and is necessary for those who have to perform manual labor." This argument is based upon an erroneous opinion, because animal food does not give as much strength as a vegetable diet; † it only stimulates the organism, and induces it to use up the strength which it already possesses in a short period of time instead of saving it up for the future. The consequences of an exclusive animal diet are gluttony, extreme sensuality, combativeness, cruelty; and stupidity, indolence, physical and psychical apathy, are the necessary consequences of over-stimulation.

Darwin says that "the hardest-working people he ever met are the persons that work in the mines of Chili, and that they are living on an exclusively vegetable diet." The country people in Ireland live almost without meat-eating, and yet they are strong and enduring. The common Russian eats very little meat and enjoys good health. The strongest people that can perhaps be found anywhere are the country people in the South of Bavaria, and they eat meat only on exceptional occasions and holy-days. Horses, bulls, elephants are the strongest animals, and live on vegetable food, while the prominent traits of character of the flesh-eating animals are cowardice, irritability and cunning. A bear kept at the Anatomical Museum at Giessen showed a quiet, gentle nature as long as he was fed on bread, but a few days' feeding on meat made him, not stronger, but vicious and dangerous.

Each animal form is an expression of that animal's character, and he who takes it up in his system receives a

---

* Genesis i. 29.

† According to the calculations made by Prof. J. v. Liebig, the same amount of albuminous substances for which, if in the form of animal food, is paid 100d., can be bought in the shape of peas for 9d., and in that of wheat for 4d.

part of that character in his own constitution. If men were to live on the meats of tigers and cats, wolves and hyenas and birds of prey, the effect would soon be seen in a state of greater demoralization.

Let those who desire to know the truth in regard to meat eating seek the answers to their questions not with the intellect of the head, but through the voice of wisdom speaking in the interior of their heart, and they will not be mistaken.*

Another question arises in regard to the eating of flesh ; it is the question whether or not man has a right to kill animals for his food. To the professed Christians who claim to believe in the Bible there seems to be no cause for any doubt, because the command is plain : " *Thou shalt not kill.*" And yet this command is disregarded daily by millions of professed " Christians," who base their illusory right to kill animals upon a misunderstood verse of their Bible. If it is said that God permitted man to " have dominion over the fish of the sea, and over the fowls of the air, and over the cattle, and over every living thing that moveth upon the earth," † we should know that by the terms "fish," and "fowl," and "cattle," etc., are meant the elementary forces in him, which find their objective representations in the animal kingdom, and that it is nowhere said that man is permitted to take away a life which he is not able to give. Man's prerogative is to appease suffering, not to cause it ; not to interrupt the work of evolution, but to assist it. Christianity and Murder are incompatible terms.

Meat is stimulating, and stimulating food creates a desire for stimulating drink. The best cure for the desire for alcoholic drink is to avoid the eating of meat. It is doubtful whether there is any passion in the world more devilish and more detrimental to the true interests of humanity and of individual happiness than the love of Alcohol. As meat-eating endows man with illusory strength, that soon fades away, leaving its possessor weaker than he was before ; likewise stimulating drinks lull him into an illusory happiness, which soon disappears, and is followed by lasting and real misery, causing suffering to himself and to others. It causes a long list of diseases

---

* See Dr. A. Kingsford ; The Perfect Way in Diet."
† Genesis i. 26.

of the internal organs, and leads to premature death ; it is the cause of by far the great majority of all crimes committed in civilized countries. To those who look upon man as a rational being, it seems incomprehensible why civilized nations will suffer an evil in their midst that fills their jails, hospitals, lunatic asylums, and graveyards, and why men will "put an enemy in their mouths" that destroys their health, their reason, and their life ; but those who look deeper see that the dawn of reason has only begun, and that the spiritual faculties of the majority of men still sleep in the icy embrace of ignorance and illusion. Reforms are necessary, but they cannot be inaugurated by force. *

The body politic resembles the individual body. It is of no use to destroy the means to gratify a desire as long as the desire itself is suffered to exist. The evils that affect mankind are the outcome of their desires for such evils. Means to gratify evil desires will exist as long as they are patronized, and if they are abolished other means will be found. Weeds are not destroyed by cutting their leaves, if the roots are allowed to remain.

To eat and drink and sleep for the purpose of living, and not to live for the purpose of eating, drinking, and sleeping is a maxim which is often heard, but which is not frequently carried out. A great deal of nutriment daily taken by men serves no other purpose than to comply with habit, and to gratify an artificially created desire. The more a man is gross and material, the greater is the quantity of food he desires ; and the more food he takes, the more gross and material will he become. Noble and refined natures require little nutriment ; ethereal beings and "Spiritual" entities require no material food.

The means should always be adapted to the end in view. If the end is low and vulgar, low and vulgar means will be needed ; if it is noble and high, equally high and noble means are required. A prizefighter, whose main object is to develop muscle, will require a different training from that of one who desires to develop the faculty to perceive spiritual truths. Conditions that may be suitable for the development of one person may be impraticable for another. One man may develop faster through poverty,

---

* See Dr. A. Kingsford : " The Alcoholic Controversy.

another through wealth ; one man may need as his initial psychic stimulus the gentle and exalting influences of married life, while another one's aspirations may rise higher if independent of earthly ties. Each man who exercises his will for the purpose of his higher development is, to the extent he exercises it, a practical occultist. Every one grows necessarily in one direction or in another ; none remain stationary. Those who desire to outstrip others in growth must act.

One of the Tibetan *Mahatmas* says in a letter :

"Man is made up of ideas, and ideas guide his life. The world of subjectivity is the only reality to him even on this physical plane. To the occultist it grows more real as it goes further and further from illusory earthly objectivity, and its ultimate reality is *Parabrahm*. Hence an aspirant for occult knowledge should begin to concentrate all his desires on the highest ideal, that of absolute self-sacrifice, philanthropy, divine kindness, as of all the highest virtues obtainable on this Earth, and work up to it incessantly. The more strenuous his efforts to rise up to that ideal, the oftener is his will-power exercised and the stronger it becomes. When it is thus strengthened, it sets up a tendency, in the gross shell of *Stula-sharira*, to do such acts as are compatible with the highest ideal he has to work up to, and his acts intensify his will-power doubly, owing to the operation of the well-known law of action and reaction. Hence in occultism great stress is laid on practical results.

Now the question is : What are these practical results, and how are they to be produced? It is a well-known fact derived from observation and experience that progress is the law of nature. The acceptance of this truth suggests the idea that humanity is in its lower stages of development, and is progressing towards the state of perfection. It will approach the final goal when it develops new sensibilities and a clear relation with nature. From this it is obvious that a final state of perception will be arrived at when the energy that animates man co-operates with the *One Life* operating in the *Cosmos* in achieving this mighty object; and knowledge is the most powerful means to that end.

Thus it will be clear that the ultimate object of nature is to make man perfect through the union of the human

spirit with the *One Life.* Having this final goal before
our mind, an intellectual brotherhood should be formed by
uniting *all* together, and this is the only stepping-stone
towards the final goal. To produce this practical result,
*union*, we must hold up the highest ideal, which forms the
*real man*, and induce others to look up to it. To lead
our neighbors and fellow-creatures to this right path, the
best means should be pursued with self-sacrificing habits.
When our energy as a collective whole is thus expended,
in working up to the highest ideal, it becomes potent, and
the grandest results are produced on the spiritual plane.
As this is the most important work in which every occultist should be engaged, an aspirant for higher knowledge
should spare no efforts to bring about this end. With the
progressive tide of evolution of the body as a whole, the
mental and the spiritual faculties of humanity expand. To
help this tide on, a knowledge of philosophical truths
should be spread. *This is what is expected from an
aspirant for occult knowledge, and what he should do.*"
The will is developed through action and strengthened
by faith. The movements of the body, such as walking,
are only successfully performed by a person because he
has a full and unwavering faith in his power to perform
them. Fear and Doubt paralyze the will and produce impotency ; but hope and faith produce marvelous results.
The lawyer or physician who has no faith in his own ability
will make blunders, and if his clients or patients share his
doubts, his usefulness will be seriously impaired ; whereas
even the ignorant fanatic or quack may succeed, if he has
faith in himself.

Bulwer Lytton says : " The victims of the ghostly one
are those that would aspire and can only fear." Fear and
Doubt are the hell-born daughters of ignorance that drag
man down to perdition ; while Faith is the white-robed
angel that lends him her wings and endows him with
power. "Samsayatma Vinasyati " (the doubter perishes),
said Krishna to Arjuna, his favorite disciple.

Even blind faith without knowledge may be more useful than imperfect knowledge without faith, and consequently without action. Strong faith, even if resting upon
an erroneous conception, may act powerfully in producing
results ; faith produces an exalted state of the imagination,
which strengthens the will, banishes pain, cures disease,
leads to heroism, and transforms hell into heaven.

The only way to develop will-power is to act. Each act creates a new impulse, which, added to the already existing energy, increases its strength. Good acts increase the power for good ; evil acts, the power for evil ; but those whose actions are neither good nor evil acquire no power for either. A person who acts only from impulse manifests no will, and if he obeys his lower impulses he passively develops into a criminal or a maniac. The most horrible crimes are often committed without any proportionate provocation, because the perpetrators had not the power to resist the impulses that prompted them to such acts. Such persons are not wicked ; they are weak and almost irresponsible beings ; they are the servants of the impulses that control them, and they can be made the helpless instruments and victims of those who know how to call forth their emotions : they are like the soldiers of two opposing armies, who are not necessarily personal enemies ; but are made to hate and kill each other by appeals to their passions. The oftener such persons give way to impulses, the more is their power of resistance diminished, and their own impotency is their ruin. It is of little use to be merely passively good, if abstinence from wrong-doing may be so called. A person who does neither good nor evil accomplishes nothing. A stone, an animal, an imbecile, may be considered good, because they do no active evil ; a person may live a hundred years, and at the end of his life he may not have been more useful than a stone.*

There is nothing in nature which has not a threefold aspect and a threefold activity. The *Will-power* forms no exception to this rule. In its lowest aspect the Will is that power which induces the voluntary and involuntary functions of the physical organism ; its centre of activity is the spinal cord. In its higher aspect it is the power which induces psychic activity ; it is diffused through the blood which comes from the heart and returns to it, and its actions are governed, or can be governed, by intellect acting in the brain by means of the impulses, influences, and auras radiating from there. In its highest aspect the *Will* is a living and conscious power having its centre in

* " He who is neither hot nor cold, but lukewarm, will be spued out by nature."—*Bibl.*

the heart; but this kind of Will is known only to those who are illuminated by divine *Wisdom*.

The will, to become powerful, must be free, which means that it must be obedient to universal law, to become free of the bonds of self. If we desire an object, we do not necessarily attract that object, but the object attracts us. Eliphas Levi says: "The will accomplishes everything which it does not desire;" and the truth of this paradox is seen in everyday life. Those who crave for fame or riches or love are frequently disappointed; the rich miser is poorer than the beggar in the street, and happiness is a shadow that flies before him who seeks it in material pleasures. The surest way to become rich is by being contented with what we have; the safest way to obtain power is to sacrifice ourselves for others; and if we desire love, we must distribute the love we possess to others, and then the love of others will descend upon us like the rain descends upon the earth.

The development of the Will is a process of growth, and the only true way to develop the Will is by being obedient to the universal Law. Then will we become masters of our Will, and our Will will become a serviceable instrument in our hands; but as long as the Will is governed by personal desire, it is not *we* who control our will, but it is our desire. As long as we do the will of the lower animal I, we cannot be gods; only when we perform the will of the Divinity, within ourselves, we will become free of the bondage of the animal elements, and be our own masters.

Man in his youth longs for the material pleasures of earth, for the gratification of his physical body. As he advances, he throws away the playthings of his childhood and reaches out for something higher. He enters perhaps into merely intellectual pursuits, and after years of labor he may find that he has been wasting his time by running after a shadow. Perhaps love steps in and he may think himself the most fortunate of mortals, only to find out, sooner or later, that ideals can only be found in the ideal world. He may become convinced of the emptiness of the shadows he has been pursuing, and, like the winged butterfly emerging from the chrysalis, he stretches out his feelers into the realm of infinite spirit, and is astonished to find a radiant sun where he only expected to find darkness and death. Some arrive at this light sooner; others arrive later, and many are lured away by some illusive light and perish, and, like insects that mistake the flame of a candle for the light of the sun, scorch their wings in its fire.

Life is a continual battle between error and truth; between man's spiritual aspirations and the demands of his animal instincts. There are two gigantic obstacles in the way of progress: his misconception of God and his misconception of Man. As long as man believes in a whimsical reasoning God who distributes favors to some and punishes others at pleasure, a God that can be reasoned with, persuaded and pacified by ignorant man, he will keep himself within the narrow confines of his ignorance, and his mind cannot sufficiently expand. To think of some place of personal enjoyment or heaven, does not assist man's progression. If such a person desists from doing a wicked act, or denies himself a material pleasure, he does not do so from any innate love of good; but either because he expects a reward from God for his "sacrifice," or because his fear of God makes him a coward. We must do good, not on account of any personal consideration, but because to do good is best. To be good is to be wise; the fool expects undeserved rewards; the wise expects nothing but justice. The wise knows that by benefiting the world he benefits himself, and that by injuring others he becomes his own executioner.

What are the powers of Man, by which he may benefit the world? Man as a created being has no powers belonging to him. Even the substance of which his organization is made up, does not belong but is only lent to him by Nature, and he must soon return it to her. He cannot make any use of it, except through that universal power, which is active within his organization, which is called the *Will*, and which itself is a function of the universal principle, the *Spirit*.

Man is merely a manifestation of this universal principle in an individual form, and all the spiritual powers he seems to possess belong to the Spirit. Like all other forms in nature he receives life, light and energy from the universal fountain of Life, and enjoys their possession for a short span of time; he has no powers whatever which he may properly call his own.

**8**

Thus the sunshine and rain, the air and earth, does not belong to a plant. They are universal elements belonging to nature. They come and help to build up a plant, they assist in the growth of the rosebush as well as the thistle; their business is to develop the seed, and when their work is done, the organism in which they were active returns again to its mother, the Earth. There is then nothing which properly belongs to the plant but the seed, for it alone can continue to exist without the parental organism after having attained maturity, and in it is contained the character of the species to which it belongs.

Life, sensation and consciousness are not the property of man; he does not produce them. They are functions of the universal Spirit and belong to that universal power, which has been called God. This Spirit, the *One Life*, furnishes the principles which go to build up the organism called *Man*, the forms of the good as well as those of the wicked. They help to develop the germ of Intelligence in man, and when their work is done, those elements return again to the universal fountain of Life. The germ of Divinity is all there is of the real man, and all that is able to continue to exist as an individual, and it is not a man, but a Spirit, one and identical with the Universal Spirit, and one of His children. How many persons exist in whom this divine germ reaches maturity during their earthly life? How many die before it becomes mature? How many do not even know that such a germ exists? Who can answer these questions?

To this Universal Principle belong the functions which we call Will and Life and Light; its foundation is Love, a Fire to which nothing that can perish will ever approach. To this Universal Principle belong all the fundamental powers which produced the universe and man, and only when man has become one and identical with that Spirit can he claim to have any powers of his own.

But the Will of this Universal Spirit is identical with the *Law*, and man who acts against the Law acts against the Will of the Spirit, and as the Spirit is man's only real Self, he who acts against that Law destroys himself.

The first and most important object of man's existence is, therefore, that he should learn the law, so that he may obey it and thereby become one with the law and God. A man who knows the Law knows himself, and a man who knows his divine Self knows God.

The only power which man may rightfully claim his own is his *Knowledge;* it belongs to him because he has acquired it by the help of the powers lent to him by nature and the Spirit which is active therein. Not the "knowledge" of the illusions of life, for such knowledge is illusive, and will end with those illusions; not mere intellectual learning, for that intellect will be exhausted in time; but the spiritual knowledge of the heart, which means the power to grasp the truth by feeling and understanding, to feel it intuitively, and to see that which we feel by the light of the spiritual intelligence of the mind.

What has been said about the Will is equally applicable to the Imagination. If man lets his own thoughts rest, and rises up to the sphere of the highest ideal, his mind becomes a mirror wherein the thoughts of God will be reflected, and in which he may see the past, the present and future; but if he begins to speculate within the realm of illusions, he will see the truth distorted and behold his own hallucinations.

The knowledge of God and the knowledge of Man are ultimately identical, and he who knows himself knows God. If we understand the nature of the divine attributes within us, we will know the Law. It will then not be difficult to unite our Will with the supreme Will or the cosmos; and we shall be no longer subject to the influences of the astral plane, but be their masters. Then will the Titans be conquered by the gods; the serpent will have its head crushed by Divine Wisdom (Sophia); the "devil" will be conquered, and instead of being ruled by demons, we shall become rulers and gods.

It is sometimes said that it does not make any difference what a man believes so long as he acts rightly; but a person cannot be certain to act rightly, unless he knows what is right, and we, therefore, see the most horrible acts of injustice committed in the name of justice, errors proclaimed as truths, and forms mistaken for principles. The belief of the majority is not always the correct belief, and the voice of reason is often drowned in the clamor of a superstition based upon an erroneous theological doctrine. An erroneous belief is detrimental to progress in proportion as it is universal; such belief rests on illusion; knowledge is based on truth. The greatest of all religious teachers therefore recommended *Right Belief* as being the first step on the *Noble Eightfold Path.**

Perhaps it will be useful to keep in mind the following rules :

1. Do not believe that there is anything higher in the universe than the immortal principle of good obtaining self-consciousness in man, and that man is exactly what he makes himself—not what he pretends to be—and nothing else. The true religion is the recognition of truth ; idols are playthings for children.

2. Learn that the All is one and that everything is thyself; man is a component and integral part of universal humanity, and that what affects one acts and reacts on all.

3. Realize that man is an embodiment of ideas, and his physical body an instrument which enables him to come into contact with matter and control it; and that this instrument should not be used for unworthy purposes. It should neither be worshipped nor neglected.

4. Let nothing that affects your physical body, its comfort, or the circumstances in which you are placed, disturb the equilibrium of your mind. Crave for nothing on the material plane, live above it without losing control over it.

5. Never expect any favors from anybody, but be always ready to assist others to the extent of your ability, and according to the requirements of justice. Never fear anything but to offend the moral law and you will not suffer. Never hope for any reward and you will not be disappointed. Never ask for love, sympathy, or gratitude from anybody, but be always ready to bestow them on others. Such things come only when they are not desired.

6. Learn to distinguish and to discriminate between the

---

* The eight stages on the *noble eightfold Path* to find the truth are, according to the doctrine of Gautama Buddha, the following :

1. Right Belief.
2. Right Thought.
3. Right Speech.
4. Right Doctrine.
5. Right Means of Livelihood.
6. Right Endeavor.
7. Right Memory.
8. Right Meditation.

The man who keeps these *angas* in mind and follows them will be free from sorrow, and may become safe from future rebirths with their consequent miseries.

true and the false, and act up to your highest ideal of virtue.

7. Learn to appreciate everything (yourself included) at its true value in all the various planes. A person who attempts to look down upon one who is his superior is a fool, and a person who looks up to one who is inferior is mentally blind. It is not sufficient to *know of* the worth of a thing, its worth must be realized, else it resembles a treasure hidden in the vaults of a miser.

Louis Claude de Saint Martin (the Unknown Philosopher) says:

"This is what should pass in a man who is restored to his divine proportions through the process of regeneration:

"Not a desire, but in obedience to the law.

"Not an idea, which is not a sacred communication with Good.

"Not a word, which is not a sovereign decree.

"Not an act, which is not a development and extension of the vivifying rule of the word.

"Instead of this, our desires are false, because they come from ourselves.

"Our thoughts are vague and corrupt, because they form adulterous alliances.

"Our words are without efficacy, because we allow them to be blunted every day by the heterogeneous substances to which we continually apply them.

"Our acts are insignificant and barren, because they can but be the results of our words."

Such and similar instructions are nothing new; they have been pronounced in various forms by the philosophers of all ages, and have been collected in books, and men have read them without getting any better for it, because they could not intellectually see the necessity for following such advice. These doctrines have been taught by the ancient Rishis and Munis, by Buddha and Christ, Confucius, Zoroaster and Mahomed, Plato, Luther and Shakespeare, and every reformer. They have been preached in sermons, and are written in poems and prose, in works of philosophy, literature, fiction, and art. They have been heard by all, understood by some, and practiced by a few. To learn them is easy, to realize them is difficult, to adopt them in practical life is divine. The highest spiritual truths cannot be intellectually grasped, the reasoning powers of half-animal man cannot hold them until they become accustomed to them ; average man can only look up to those ideals which are perceptible to his spiritual vision in moments of aspiration, and only gradually can he grow up into that plane when, becoming less animal and more intuitive, he will be able to realize the fact that moral growth is not necessary to please a god whose favor must be obtained, but that man himself becomes a god by that growth, and that he can stimulate it only by making his energies act on a higher plane. The highest energies are latent in the lower ones ; they are the attributes of the spiritual soul, which in the majority of men is still in a state of infancy, but which in future generations will be more universally developed, when humanity as a whole, having progressed higher, will look back upon our present era as the age of ignorance and misery, while they themselves will enjoy the fruits of the higher evolution of Man.

# CHAPTER XI.

### LIGHT.

*"Let there be Light."—Bible.*

FORM, personality and sensuality are the death of spirit; the dissolution of form, loss of personality and unconsciousness of sensuous perceptions, render spirit free and restore it to life. The elementary forces of nature, bound to forms, become the prisoners of the forms. Being entombed in matter they lose their liberty of action and move only in obedience to external impulses; the more they cling to form, the more dense, compact, heavy and dull will they become, and the less will be self-acting and free. Sunlight and heat are comparatively free; their elements travel from planet to planet, until they are absorbed by earthly forms. Crystallized into matter they sleep in trees and forests and fields of coal, until they are liberated by the slow decomposition of form, or forcibly set free by the god of fire. The waves of ocean and lake play joyfully with the shore. Full of mirth they throw their spray upon the lazy rocks. The laughing waters of the wandering brook glide restlessly through forest and field, dancing and whirling and playing with the flowers that grow by the side of their road. They rush without fear over precipices, falling in cascades over the mountain sides, uniting, dividing, and uniting again, mingling with rivers and resting at last for a while in the sea. But when winter arrives and King Frost puts his icy hand upon their faces, they crystallize into individual forms, they are then robbed of their freedom, and like the damsels and knights of the enchanted castle, they are doomed to sleep until the warm breath of youthful Spring breaks the spell of the sorcerer and kisses them back into life.

The fundamental laws of Nature are the same in all her departments, and man forms no exception to the general rule. He is a centre around which some of the intelligent as well as some of the unintelligent forces have crystallized into a form. Bound by the laws of the Karma which that centre created, they are doomed to dwell in a form, and to partake of the accidents to which forms are exposed; imprisoned in a personality, they partake of the sufferings which the tendencies of that personality have called into existence. They may be exposed to desires whose thirst increases in proportion as they are furnished with drink, to passions whose fire burns hotter in proportion as their demand for fuel is granted; they are tempted to run after shadows that ever fly, to grasp at hopes that ever beckon and vanish as soon as they are approached, to sorrows that enter the house although the doors may be closed against them, to fears whose forms have no substance, to illusions that disappear only with the life of the form. Like Prometheus bound to a rock, the impersonal spirit is chained to a personality, until the consciousness of his herculean power awakes in him, and bursting his chains he becomes again free.

Not all the elements that go to make up a complete man are enclosed in his material form. The far greater part of them is beyond the limits of his physical body; the latter is merely a centre in which those invisible elements meet. The elements that exist beyond stand in intimate relation with those that are within, although the elements within the form may not seem to be conscious of the existence of those beyond. Still they act and react upon each other.

The character of man is far more important than his physical form. Thought can create a form, but no form can produce a thought; and yet the substance of thought is invisible as long as it has not clothed itself in a form. Air exists within and beyond the physical body; it is invisible, and yet it is an important element of the body, a man who could not breathe would be very incomplete. The ocean of mind in which man exists is as necessary to his soul-life as the air is to his body, he cannot breathe if deprived of air ; he cannot think if deprived of mind. The outer acts upon the inner, the inner upon the outer, the above upon the below, and the little upon the great. A man who could live independent of his surroundings would be self-existent, he would be a god.

The spirit is not confined by the form, it only over-shadows the form ; the form does not contain the spirit, it is only its outward expression ; it is the instrument upon which the spirit plays, and which reacts upon its touch, while the spirit responds to its vibrations. An ancient proverb says : " Everything that exists upon the Earth has its ethereal counterpart above the Earth, and there is nothing, however insignificant it may appear in the world, which is not depending on something higher ; so that, if the lower part acts, its preceding higher part reacts upon it." *

The greatest philosophers in ancient times taught that the νομς that alone recognized noumena, always remained outside the physical body of man ; that it overshadowed his head, and that only the ignorant believed it existed within themselves. Modern philosophers have arrived at similar conclusions. Fichte writes : " The real spirit which comes to itself in human consciousness is to be regarded as an impersonal pneuma—universal reason—and the good of man's whole development therefore can be no other than to substitute the universal for the individual consciousness."

The greatest of all teachers, Gautama Buddha, says : " The permanent never mingles with the impermanent, although the two are one. Only when all outward appear-ances are gone, is that one principle of life left, which exists independently of all external phenomena. It is the fire that burns within the external light when the fuel is expended and the flame is extinguished, for that fire is neither in the flame nor in the fuel, nor yet inside either of the two, but above, beneath, and everywhere."

This real and permanent Self is an impersonal principle. Hermes Trismegistus says : " His father is the Sun, his mother the stars, and his body the generations of men." It is not attracted into the physical body of man, but the soul of man may unite itself with that principle. It is the

---
* Sohar Wajecae.

real Ego of every person, and the person who succeeds to merge his personality into that Ego is thereby rendered immortal. It is the true and living Christ of the real Christians, not the dead " Jesus " but the living Saviour who remains with His followers unto the end of the world; and every one who unites his own self with that Christ—no matter what his creed or confession may be—will become as true and veritable a Christ as ever lived upon the Earth. It is the λογος of the ancients, the Adam Kadmon of the Hebrews, the Osiris of the Egyptians, the Iswar of the Hindus, the way, the light, and the truth, the divine Self of every man and the Redeemer for all.

The whole of a man is not enclosed within the small circle that circumscribes his terrestrial life. He who has found the *Master* within himself knows the true insignificance of his own personal self. The life of the latter is made up of a comparatively small number of years passed among the illusions of the terrestrial plane ; the life of the former is made up of the essence of a great many of such lives, he has retained of them only that which is useful and grand while the worthless parts have been rejected. He who has once realized the presence of his God laughs at the idea of having ever imagined himself to be something more than a bundle of semi-conscious elements from which the Higher Self may draw nutriment if it finds anything therein compatible with its own nature. What is all the power and glory of earthly kings compared with the divine Man, the King in the realm of the soul? What is all the science of this earth but nonsense, if compared with the self-knowledge of the regenerated man? Well may he who has welcomed the *Lord* in his soul be willing to renounce money, power and fame, terrestrial loves and all the illusions of life, if it can be called " renunciation " to refuse to touch things upon which one looks with indifference, if not with contempt. How can he who has never seen the image of the true Saviour in his heart love Him, and how can he who has once beheld it cease to love and adore Him with his whole mind and with all the faculties of the soul? Such things are too sacred to be divulged by the spirit of God to him who is not worthy to receive God in his soul ; they will not be understood by those who cannot yet rise above limitation ; let those who know the things of which we have attempted to write rejoice and worship in silence.

He who has succeeded in merging the elements constituting his soul with that divine and ethereal higher self will
feel its power in his own heart.   This principle baptizes
his soul with fire, and he who receives this baptism of fire
is ordained a priest and a king.   He who is full of its
influence is the true " vicegerent of God," because the
supreme power of the universe acts through its instrumentality.   This principle fills his person with a peace "which
passeth understanding," attracts the hearts of men to him,
and sheds blessings upon every one who approaches his
presence.   It forgives the sins of men, by transforming
them into other men who have not sinned and need not to
be forgiven ; it does not require to hear confession to give
advice, because it can read the innermost thoughts of every
man, and its admonishing voice is heard in the heart that
has learned to understand its language.   The development
of the power to perceive it confirms men's faith by enabling
them to recognize that to be true which they heretofore
only believed to be so, and being taught by the truth itself,
they can make no mistake ; it communicates with man—
not by being absorbed by man, but by absorbing the soul
of man into itself ; it brings the dying to life, because,
being immortal, he who is united with it partakes of its
own immortality ; the marriages it celebrates can never be
dissolved, because in this principle all humanity is bound
together to one indissoluble whole ; to separate from it
would be death to the part that separates itself from the
whole.   The sphere in which this principle still lives is the
sphere of eternal life ; it is the only true and infallible
"church," and its power cannot be taken away.   This
church is truly "catholic," that is to say, universal ; nothing can live without its jurisdiction, because nothing can
continue to exist without the authority of life.   Still it has
no particular name, requires no fee for initiation, no ceremonies or rites.   Heathens and infidels may enter it without changing their creed ; opinions cease to exist where
the truth is revealed.

But this true principle of Christ is not the Christ of
popular Christianity ; it has long ago been driven away
from the modern Christian temples, and an illusion has
remained in its place.   The money-changers and tradesmen
have again taken possession of the temple of mind, sacri-
ficing the life-blood of the poor at the altars of wooden

gods, closing their eyes to the truth and worshipping tinsel, squandering the wealth of nations for the glorification of self. The true " Son of Man " is still scoffed at by His nominal followers, traduced by His pretended friends, crucified by men who do not recognize in Him the only source of their life. Killed by men in their own hearts, ignorantly and foolishly, because they do not know what they are doing, and that their own life-substance departs at the time when He departs from their life.

Modern civilization adores the religion of selfishness, and rejects the gospel of love ; she debases her own dignity by crouching at the feet of idols, where she should stand up in her own dignity and purity as the queen of the whole creation. Humanity is still dreaming and has not yet fully awakened to life. She searches for a god in her imagination, and cannot realize that he can only be found in the truth. Men and women clamor for the coming of a god, and yet this god is ever ready to come to them as soon as he is admitted into the heart, by submitting to him their will.

This unknown god is attainable to all. He is ever ready to be born in every heart where the conditions for his birth are prepared. He always begins to come to life in a " manger " between the elemental and animal forces in man. He can only be born in a lowly place, because pride and superstition are his enemies, and in a heart filled with vanity he would soon suffocate. The news of his birth sends a thrill of pleasure through the physical body, and the morning stars sing together for joy, heralding the dawn of the day for the resurrection of the spirit. The three magicians from the East, *Love, Wisdom and Power*, appear at the manger and offer their gifts to the new-born babe. If *Herodes*, the king of pride and ambition, does not succeed in driving it out of the country, it begins to grow, and as it grows its divinity becomes manifest. It argues with the intellectual powers in the temple of the mind, and silences them by its superior knowledge. It penetrates into mysteries, which intellectuality, born of sensual perceptions, cannot explain. Grey-headed material science, sophistry hoary with age, old logic based upon misconceptions of fundamental truths, give way, and are forced to acknowledge the wisdom of the half-grown god.

Living in the wilderness of material desires, it is vainly

tempted by the devil of selfishness. It cannot be misled by personal considerations, because being impersonal it has no personal claims. The "devil" can give to it nothing that it does not already possess, because being the highest it rules over all that is low.

This principle is the first emanation of The Absolute. It is the "only-begotten" son of its father, and it is as old as the father, because the manifested Absolute could only become a "father" at the time when the "son" was born.* It is the living *Word*, and every man is a *Christ*, in whom the "Son of God" becomes manifest. It is the divine self of every man, his own original ethereal counterpart without any infirmities, because the latter only belong to the form. It is not a personality, but it may become individualized in man and yet remain in its essence impersonal, a living principle, ubiquitous, incorruptible and immortal. This is the great mystery before which the intellect, reasoning from particulars to universals, stands hopelessly still, but which the soul, whose inner spiritual perceptions are alive, beholds with astonishment and wonder. The spirit is formless and cognizes the formless; the intellect is connected with form, and can only behold the formless in the light of the spirit. The intellect deals with the finite, and can only grasp the infinite, if illuminated by that very principle whose existence is doubted before the illumination took place.

As long as the wavering intellect doubts the existence of spirit, it cannot become conscious of its existence, because only the steady light of unclouded reason can penetrate into the depths where the spirit resides. Mere "belief" is a confession of ignorance; true faith is based upon conviction. But we cannot be convinced of the existence of something we do not know and of which we are unconscious, except by becoming conscious of its existence. Consciousness, knowledge and realization of the existence of something can only begin at the moment when that something begins to become conscious within ourselves. We may search for the god within us, but we cannot artificially bring him to life. We can prepare the conditions under which he may awake to consciousness within ourselves, by divesting the mind from all emotional and

---

* Bible: St. John i. 1; Hebrews i. 3.

intellectual predilections and prejudices, and when the divine principle has awakened within us, then has arrived the moment of "grace." Such a grace is not a favor conferred by a partial, whimsical, and personal god, it is the effect of a strong desire, which has the power to grant its own prayers, and if that desire does not exist, it is useless to "pray." As well may an acorn enclosed in a stone beg to be developed into an oak as a man whose heart is filled with desires for the low ask to become conscious of the high. To put implicit belief in the statement of bonze or priest is weakness, to enable ourselves to recognize the truth is strength, to arrive at conviction through knowledge confers the only true faith.

Tennyson speaks of the *beginning* of true faith when he says—

> " We have but faith, we cannot know,
> A beam in darkness, let it grow."

We cannot intellectually know ; but when the beam has grown, it constitutes *spiritual knowledge*, which is identical with the *living faith*.

When the divine and impersonal principle begins to become conscious in the personal man, it acts upon him from the five points of attraction, represented by the five-pointed star, and in Christian symbology by the *cross*. The body begins to feel new sensations, the pulse begins to throb with more vigor, the animal forces stirred up in their " hells " by the arrival of " Christ " become more active, pains may be experienced in the head, the palms of the hands, and the soles of the feet, and in other parts of his body, and the candidate for immortality—whether he be a Christian, a Turk, a Brahmin, a Jew, or an Infidel—may thus physically experience the process represented in the martyrdom of Christ.* The interblending of the immortal with the mortal will necessarily cause suffering to the latter until the lower elements are entirely subjected and rendered unconscious.

There is no salvation except through suffering ; pains accompany man's entrance into the world, pains accom-

---

* The above remark does not refer to *stigmata*, which are a result of a state of exalted imagination, while the pains referred to are the result of the penetrating power of the spirit, infusing a new life into the physical form.

pany his spiritual regeneration.  The low must die so that
the high may live, and as the low is gifted with consciousness and sensation, it suffers acutely during its transformation.  Only he who has tasted the bitterness of evil can
fully realize the sweetness of good, only he who has suffered
the heat of the day can fully appreciate the cool of the
evening breeze.  He who has lived for ages in darkness
will know the true value of light when he enters its realm ;
he who has been buried in illusions will rejoice when he
rises up into real knowledge.

What is true in regard to individual man is equally true
in regard to humanity as a whole.  Christ, the divine principle in the kingdom of Spirit, impelled by the infinite love
that radiates from the centre of the All, eternally descends
into the hearts of mankind, to partake of their suffering and
to show them the way to perfection.  Compared with the
" ram " of the intellect whose power resides in his horns,
He is the " lamb " of wisdom, having no will of His own,
but doing the will of the Father.  He takes upon His
shoulders the sins of the world, for He Himself is without
sin.  He can gain no personal benefit by His descent into
matter; being perfect Himself, He needs no further perfection; it is the sins of men and women that induce Him to
shed His love and light and life into humanity.  Being one
with humanity, He suffers with all mankind, He suffers with
them on account of their sins ; and as men and women
become conscious of His divine presence, they become
aware not merely of their own individual evils, but of the
sufferings of humanity as a whole ; they begin to suffer
with and for each other, they recognize in the Christ principle the universal link that binds them all together into
one harmonious whole by the power of infinite Love.

Realizing their true nature as sons of the eternal God,
they die to all that is animal and low, and the more they
die to the latter the more will they become alive in the
spirit, wherein exists the only true, real, and immortal life.
The motto of the ancient Rosicrucian fraternity was : *In
Deo nascimur, in Jesu morimur, reviviscimus per Spiritum
Sanctum;* that is to say, their souls, like those of all other
men, were born from the universal fountain of all Good ;
they died to their semi-animal natures by entering into the
spiritual body—" the spiritual church "—of Christ, and
becoming one with the Christ spirit, they gained eternal

life by being penetrated, illuminated, and glorified by its
divine light.   Their "church" had nothing whatever to do
with any external church organization ; the temple wherein
their spirits met and held holy communion of thought, was
the universal temple of the *Holy Ghost*, representing Love,
Wisdom and Sanctity, and they symbolized it by a circle,
representing the sphere of thought, wherein *Mercury*
(Intelligence) and *Venus* (Love) were joined together.

   This conjunction of the principle of Love and Intelligence
within the soul of man constitutes the true " Rosicrucian "
and Adept.   It is not to be obtained by any external ceremonies and rites ; but by the entire sacrifice of the self-will
of semi-animal man to the eternal will of God ; whereby the
lower self is rendered inactive and helpless, as if it were
nailed upon a cross ; while the divine self of man becomes
revealed in its own light.
   Of these real Rosicrucians no "history" can be written ;
because they have nothing to do with external things ; but
live in eternity.

---

   ° Of late the most grotesque and fabulous stories about the " Rosicrucians " have been put into circulation, and some enterprising publishers
have brought out books about their "ceremonies" and "rites." All
such speculations are based upon the mistaken idea that the Rosicrucians
were a certain sect or organization going by that name, and being bound
together by some creed or belief, and using external ceremonies and signs.
There is no doubt that some such " secret societies " existed, calling
themselves " Rosicrucians," and some such are still in existence.   They
have, however, nothing in common with the true Rosicrucian principle ;

These ideas are not new, they have not come into existence with the advent of Modern Christianity; they are eternal truths, as old as the world, and they have been represented in various fables and allegories among the nations of this globe. In the "Old Testament" we find the doctrine of salvation represented in the story of Noah's ark. Noah represents the spiritual man, and the ark the spiritual church. Only those elements of the psychic organism of man which enter the spiritual realm are saved, while those who remain in a lower state are doomed to destruction. Upon the waters of thought floats the ship containing many compartments; the *window* of knowledge is open to enable the divine Man to look out upon the watery waste. The intellectual *raven* is sent out to discover dry land, but it can find no place to rest, and returns to the ark; the *dove* of spiritual intelligence alone can find solid ground in the realm of the spirit; she returns with the emblem of peace, the doubts recede, and the ark is turned into a temple resting upon the top of the mountain of knowledge.

Blessed is he whose ark during his terrestrial life is guided upon this *Ar-ar-at* of Faith; it will enable him patiently and with indifference to bear the ills of terrestrial life until the soul is released from her bonds, and returns to her home in the eternal kingdom, having become separated from all the attractions of matter.

After this separation, *Isis*, the goddess of nature, the mother of his body, an ever-immaculate virgin, Mary,† will take care of her son. The life-principle which was active

---

no more than the Christ spirit has anything to do with the organization of some so-called "Christian" sect. He in whom the Christ lives is a real Christian, not he who merely professes a belief in Him with his mouth. Likewise he who lives in the light that shines from the centre of the Cross is a Rosicrucian, and not he who merely belongs to a sect by that name. A true Christian can only be known by his acts, and likewise there is no need for the true Rosicrucian to use passwords and signs for the purpose of making himself known. The only sign by which the brothers recognize each other is the light of the Truth.

† Maja (Illusion).

in him during his earthly existence will be laid in a new
sepulchre, "wherein was man never yet laid," it will be
transferred and embodied in new vegetable or animal
forms.*  Entering again into the wheel of transformation
and evolution, it may help to produce grain, and assist in
the growth of the grape ; hidden in bread and wine, it may
again enter the human form ; but the soul, having partaken
of the immortal life of the spirit, will have become self-
existent in God, and suffer no further migrations.  He who
partakes of material food enters into communion with
the life-principle of nature, while he who assimilates his
nature with the spiritual principle, becomes one with the
spirit that constitutes his higher self, communicates with
the real Christ.

In the ancient mysteries the ceremony called the trans-
figuration and communion was performed in a similar
manner as it is now taking place in the Christian churches.
The initiator presented bread and wine to the candidates
before the final revelation was made.  This ceremony
represents the descent of the spirit into matter, by which
the soul is at once nourished with the " bread of life," and
stimulated into a higher kind of spiritual activity by the
"wine of divine love," and its efficacy will be proportionate to the receptivity of the mind of the candidate.

The great Christian mystic, Jacob Boehme, says : " What
we eat or drink affects merely the physical body, but does
not affect the spirit.  That which the ceremony symbolizes
exteriorly must take place interiorly, else the ceremony
will be of no use.  Those who wish to commune with the
spirit must rise up to it in their thoughts ; the high will
not come down to mingle with that which is low."

Thus it seems that the original Christian allegory was
intended to describe an occult process, which must have
been known long before the establishment of the external
Christian church.  It is based upon an universal law of
nature, and as such it must have existed as long as
humanity existed.  The Indian *Yogi*, who, by the practice
of Yog,† unites his lower self with his higher self; the
Brahmin, who by meditation and study merges his *Atma*
with the universal *Parabrahm ;* the Buddhist who attempts

---

* A. P. Sinnett : " Esoteric Buddhism," chap. ii.

† " To bind."

to annihilate his lower self that his formless self may be absorbed in Nirvana, all follow the same process ; but the ignorant, whether they may call themselves Brahmins, Buddhists, Christians, or anything else, and who look upon the allegorical representations of natural and "supernatural" forces described in pictures, and books, as being the images of existing personal deities, are idolators.

How much more grand and sublime is practical Christianity than the mere theoretical christianism of our times ! Jesus of Nazareth, whether he ever existed or not, represents the ideal man whose example we ought to follow. Without being a true follower of the ideal Christ, a belief in a person can be of no value. How superior is knowledge to mere opinion and belief, how infinitely greater the living spirit of Christ to a mere belief in the historical person whose memory is worshipped by those who cling to external symbols and cannot rise up to a realization of spiritual facts ! Why do men close their eyes and grope in darkness while they are surrounded by light, why do they cling to death when the door of immortal life is open before them ?

Those who cling to external symbols without knowing the meaning of the latter, cling to illusion. To convert an ignorant person by substituting one form of illusion for another is useless, and the money and labor expended for such " conversions " is wasted. Ignorance exchanged for ignorance remains ignorance still ; a change of opinion cannot establish conviction, and a pretence to knowledge does not make a man wise.

If a man knows the truth, it matters little by what name he may call it, or under what form he may attempt to express that which cannot be made into form. The Buddhist, who looks upon the image of Buddha as a figurative representation of a living principle, and who, in memory of a once living person in whom that principle found its fullest expression, and whose example he wishes to follow, offers flowers and fruits at his shrine, is as near the truth as the Christian who sees in the picture of Jesus of Nazareth the representation of his highest ideal.

There had been a great deal of time and labor spent to prove or disprove that the founder of Christianity was a person living in Palestine at the beginning of the Christian era. To know whether or not such a person by the

name of *Jesus*, or perhaps *Jehoshua*, ever existed, and
whether he existed at the time indicated by theologians,
may be a matter of great historical interest, but it cannot
be of supreme importance for the salvation of Man;
because persons are only forms, and as such they are limited
and parts of the whole, and the whole cannot be subor-
dinate to the part. If the Man described as Jesus in the
New Testament lived, he was undoubtedly an Adept, and
as such he was a true "Son of God," because every one in
whom the spirit of God awakens to consciousness is a
*Son of God* * and an incarnation of the *Word*. For all we
know, he may have been the most perfect incarnation of
the spirit of truth that ever existed, but the truth existed
before the person was born, and it is not the belief in the
person that can save mankind from evil, but the recognition of the truth, of which the outward form can be nothing else but the external expression. Those who believe
in the still living eternal spirit of Christ, whether they
believe in His person or not, are the true worshippers, but
those who do not follow His words, but believe in His
person, worship only a form without life—an illusion.

The doctrines of the Jesus of the Gospel grow in sublimity in proportion as their secret meaning is understood;
the tales of the Bible in regard to His deeds and the miracles
which He performed, and which to the superficial observer
appear incredible and absurd, represent eternal truths and
psychological processes which are not merely things of the
past, but which occur even now within the realm of the
soul of man, and in proportion as man ceases to be a
"Christian," and comes nearer to Christ, veil after veil
drops from his eyes, and a new life awakens in him, and a
new and infinite vista of thought rises up before his
astonished eyes.

The theory of the redemption of man does not date from
the time when the historical Christ is supposed to have
been born. The history of Christ finds its prototype in
the history of Krishma. The Greeks taught the redemption
of the soul under the allegory of Amor and Psyche. *Psyche*
(the human soul) enjoys the embraces of her divine lover
*Amor* (the sixth principle) every night. She feels his
divine presence and hears the voice of intuition in her

* Revelations xx. 7.

heart, but she is not permitted to see the source from which that voice proceeds. At a time when the God is sleeping (when the voice of her intuition is silent) her curiosity awakes and she wishes to see the god. She lights the lamp of the intellect and proceeds to examine critically the source of her happiness ; but at that moment the god disappears, because the clouds and illusions created by her lower intellectual powers hide the higher spiritual truths from view. Despairingly she wanders through the lower regions of her emotions and through the sphere of sensual perceptions. She cannot find her god by the power of reasoning from the material plane. Ready to die, she is saved by the power of her love for her redeemer ; that attracts her to him. She follows that attraction and becomes united with him, no more unconsciously but conscious and knowing his attributes, which are now her own.

Modern Christianity has not destroyed the Olympian gods. They were allegorical representations of truths, and truths cannot be killed. The laws of nature are the same to-day as they were at the time of Tiberius ; Christianism has only changed with symbols and called old things by new names, and the dead heathen gods have been resurrected in the form of Roman Catholic saints.

Modern writers have represented the same old truths in other forms, in prose and in verse. Goethe—for instance —represents it beautifully in his " Faust." Dr. Faust, the man of great intellect and celebrated for his learning, in spite of all his scientific accomplishments, is unable to find the truth.

> " The unknown is the useful thing to know
> That which we know is useless for our purpose."

Despairing at the impotency and insufficiency of intellectual research, he enters into a pact with the principle of evil. By its assistance he attains wealth, love and power, he enjoys all that the senses are capable to enjoy, still feeling intuitively that selfish enjoyment cannot confer true happiness. Neither the splendor of the imperial court, nor the beauty of Helen of Troy, who returns from the land of shadows at his request, nor the orgies of the *Blocksberg,* where all human passions are let loose without restraint, can satisfy his craving for more. Lord of the Earth, he sees only a single hut which is not yet his own, and he takes even that, regardless of the fate of its inhabitants. Still he is not satisfied until, after having recovered a part of land from the ocean by his labors, he contemplates the happiness which others may enjoy by reaping the benefit of his work. This is the first unselfish thought that takes root in his mind. It fills him with extreme happiness, and in the contemplation of the happiness of others his personality dies and his higher self becomes glorified and immortal.

Truth knows that it *is*, but it cannot intellectually and critically examine itself unless it steps out of itself, and, stepping out of itself, it ceases to be one. The eye cannot see itself without the aid of a mirror ; good becomes only known to us after we have experienced evil ; to become wise we must first become foolish and eat the forbidden fruit. An impersonal power not having been embodied in a form, would know that it exists, but would know nothing more. To learn the conditions of existence it becomes embodied in form and acquires knowledge ; having gained that knowledge, form is no longer required.

The desire for personal existence imprisons the spirit of man into a mortal form ; he who during his life on Earth conquers all desire for personal existence becomes free. The divine Buddha, resting under the Boddhi-tree of wisdom, and having his mind fixed on the chain of causation, said : " Ignorance is the source of all evil. From ignorance spring the *Sankharas* (tendencies) of threefold nature-productions of body, of speech and thought (during the previous life) ; from the Sankharas springs (relative) consciousness, from consciousness spring name and form, from this the six regions (the six senses) ; from this springs desire, from desire attachment, from attachment existence, birth, old age, death, grief, lamentation, suffering, dejection and despair. By the destruction of ignorance the Sankharas are destroyed, and their consciousness, name and form, the six regions, contact, sensation, desire, attachment, existence, and its consequent evils. From ignorance spring all evils, from knowledge come cessation of this mass of misery. The truly enlightened one stands, dispelling the hosts of illusions like the sun that illuminates the sky."

The power which diffuses the sense of personality is the same which caused the existence of man; it is the power of love, and the more the love of a person expands over all others the more will the consciousness of personality be diffused. We esteem a person according to the degree in which he prefers common interests to the interests of his own personality. We admire generosity, and unselfishness, and benevolence, and yet such qualities are absurd and useless, if we believe that the highest object of man's existence is his own personal happiness on the physical plane; because the highest happiness in that plane consists in the greatest amount of possessions pertaining to that plane. To give is to experience a personal loss. But if the man strives for impersonal power, to give away personal possessions will be his gain, because the less he is attracted to personal possessions the more he will expand his personality. To give with the view of expecting some benefit in return is useless for such a purpose, because a person having such an object in view simply gives up one personal possession for another. He is a tradesman that clings to his goods, and is only willing to part with something good provided he can get something better in exchange.

Neither the white nor the black magician has any such personal considerations. The inveterate villain does not obey his selfish emotions, but controls them and creates emotions in others which they cannot resist, and in this way he makes others accomplish his purpose. He hates whom he chooses to hate, and his will, if directed against the person he hates, is freighted with evil. His touch may bring disease, and his evil eye may be poison to persons who, having very little will-power of their own, are unwilling to resist its influence. The emotions which he calls forth attract to themselves corresponding elements; he enters into co-operation with the evil forces of the astral plane, whom he either commands or propitiates, or he makes a compact with them by gratifying their evil desires and invoking their aid. Instead of expanding his powers he concentrates them into a focus. His will is rather forcible than powerful, and is sometimes rendered so by certain practices, such as the careless endurance of physical pain, and by such ceremonies as may assist his imagination. The energies which he accumulates in his astral body may continue to exist long after the death of his physical body, until they are exhausted by suffering and disintegrated in the astral plane. He opposes his individual will to the cosmic will, and the result is isolation and death.

The white magician strengthens and expands his will-power by bringing it into harmony with the universal will. Not to counteract, but to assist the process of evolution, is his object, and as the progress of the evolution in nature is towards unity, the first manifestation of his will is a universal love for humanity, and each act by which he expresses this love strengthens his will. To unite one's will with the universal will does not mean a merely passive contemplation and perception of spiritual truths, but an active penetration into the process of evolution, and a real co-operation with the beneficent powers, the master-builders of the sidereal universe.

Such a union is not produced by an inactive acquiescence with the decrees of an inexorable fate, and patient indifference to whatever may happen; much less by a submission of one's will to the dictates of another person who claims to be furnished with divine authority, but by a strong determination to accomplish whatever is in our power for the good of humanity, and by expressing that determination through action.

A man may surrender his will to the will of another man, if he believes the latter to be more wise than himself, and by doing so he may become strong in mastering his own self; but he should never surrender his reason and never act contrary to the dictates of his conscience. The convent discipline of the Middle Ages may have been conducive to strengthen the will-power of those that were subjected to it, but it was destructive to reason, and instead of gods imbeciles were created.

According to the unselfishness and the spiritual power of a person his individual influence may extend over a family, a village, a town, a country, or over the whole Earth. Every one desires influence, and seeks to obtain power by obtaining wealth and position. But the influence gained by such possessions is not individual power. A fool may be a pope, a king, or a millionary, and people may bow in obedience before him on account of his position and wealth. They may despise his person and adore his possessions, which he himself adores, and to which his person is as subject as the lowest one of his slaves. Such a person is not a commander; it is his wealth that commands him and the others. His wealth in such a case is the reality, and he himself an illusion. When his wealth is squandered his own personality disappears, and those who used to crouch at his feet may spurn him away from their table. The spiritual power of a person is independent of such artificial aids; a virtuous person is esteemed in proportion as his qualities become known, and the spiritually strong exerts a powerful influence over all his surroundings.

To this class belong all those who have risen above the crowd by the power of their own will and intelligence, and not in consequence of merely external circumstances, such as are conveyed by birth, money or favoritism. It is the internal qualities of a man, and not merely his external possessions, that are constituting his virtue.

Opposed to love is hate. Hate is love reversed; it is the opposite pole of the same power that in its manifestation for good is called love, and in its manifestation for evil is named hate. Hate, like love, is an impersonal power, and the being whose consciousness of personality is merged into hate becomes himself an impersonal power for evil and as such he may cause evil. His impersonal self may be, to a certain extent, as powerful for evil as the impersonal self of him who employs his faculties for good, but at the end, when the tension between the two poles will have reached its natural limits, the law of justice will prevail with the good.

The reason why love must prevail over hate is because love being associated with wisdom is stronger than hate. Love unites and attracts all; it even converts hate into love by the power of truth. Hate disunites and repulses. Love is related to wisdom, and hate is based on ignorance. Both are enduring and independent of form, but only that which is good and wise is immortal. Wisdom is therefore the true redeemer of good, and at the same time the destroyer of evil. Love, acting from the centre to the periphery destroys the consciousness of personality and elevates the soul over the attraction of the Earth, expanding the limits of its activity as it increases in power. Tending downwards from the periphery to the centre it produces

form, personality, selfishness, unconsciousness and death.
Awakening again in the form it expands and grows again,
and attracting the most refined and spiritual elements of
the form within itself it saves them from the tomb of matter and resurrects them from the form.

Man may be compared with a planet revolving around
its own centre ; above the orbit in which he turns is light,
below it darkness, but his own personality is crystallized
in the centre. The light above and the darkness below
attract him, and both are filled with life and strong
power ; only in the centre is the material form, held together by the cohesion of selfish attractions, rendered
unconscious and immovable by its density, chilled by its
remoteness from the spiritual sun. The farther he travels
from that centre, the more will he approach the light or
the shadow, and having reached a certain point at which
the attraction of his personal self ceases, he will either
rise up to the source of light or sink into the shadow,
according to his tendencies which lead him to permanent
good or to permanent evil. A change from darkness to
light, from evil to good, is only possible as long as man, in
his revolutions around the centre of his own self, has not
transcended the orbit where the attraction of self ceases,
and where the attraction of light and shadows counteract
each other. Having transcended that orbit, no return is
possible, he has then committed the *unpardonable sin*
which only the impersonal man can commit ; because personal man, being bound to a form, and under the influence
of love for self, is not free to act as he pleases. As long
as he clings to self he acts ignorantly and under the pressure of selfish considerations. Mistaking the low for the
high, he clings to the low and perishes with it. Only he
who has attained the knowledge of self will be able to
choose free, because he will know the nature of that which
he chooses ; the blind have no freedom of choice. Only at
the end, when all will have attained knowledge and freedom,
will be the final resurrection of humanity, as a whole, the
parting of light and shadow, and the restoration of good.
Then will be the day of Judgment referred to in the Revelation of St. John, when after the ending of the seventh
round of the life-wave around the planetary chain, the
" bottomless pit " will be opened and the good and evil
will part. But no personal judge may be there, nor any
persons that could be judged, but only the power of good

and evil, of which former personalities constitute an integral part, and the power of the law.*

The *unpardonable sin* is to knowingly and willfully reject spiritual truth. In a certain sense all sins are "unpardonable," because they all cause effects which have to become exhausted before they can cease; but if a person *knowingly* and *willfully*, without any selfish considerations, rejects the truth, it proves that he has a determinate preference for evil, that he loves evil better than good, and that he is therefore amalgamated with evil. He who is ignorant is not responsible for his acts, but he who knows the truth and rejects it will suffer its loss. Only the good will survive, and he who chooses evil will perish in evil. It is therefore dangerous for men to acquire occult knowledge, before they have become sufficiently wise to select only that which is good.

Man passes through several resurrections. His life-principle resurrects in the plants growing on his grave and in the worms feeding upon his body, his astral soul resurrects from the body, his true self from the elementary forces connected with the activity of his soul. Besides these resurrections there are continually resurrections taking place within the soul of man; there is the resurrection from selfishness to a true realization of truth, the resurrection from ignorance to knowledge, and his liberation from the attraction of evil. Good and evil will finally resurrect from the form, the good a blessing and the evil a curse; but the ignorant that know neither good nor evil will have no resurrection, because they have no spiritual life. They will remain chained to the form and sleep crystallized in space and "live not again until the thousand years† are finished,"‡ when they may again begin their labor of developments at the commencement of a world.

But *He that is* will still "sit upon the great white throne" after the earth and the heaven have fled away from His face,§ and the powers of good, the sons of wisdom, "over which the second death has no power," will be with Him §§ as priests and kings, when, after the Pralaya is ended, He stretches forth His hands and commands again : *Let there be Light.*

---

* St. John : Revelations xx. 1.
† The Pralaya.      ‡ St. John : Revelations xx. 5.
§ Revelations xx. 2.      §§ Ibid., xx. 6.

# CHAPTER XII.

## CONCLUSION.

*" He to whom time is like eternity, and eternity like time, is free."—*
*Jacob Boehme.*

To picture the eternal and incomprehensible in forms, and to describe the unimaginable in words, is a task whose difficulty has been experienced by all who ever attempted it. The formless cannot be described in forms, it can only be represented by allegories which can only be understood by those whose minds are open to the illumination of truth. The misunderstanding of allegorical expressions in the sacred books has led to religious wars, to the torturing, burning and killing of thousands of innocent victims ; it has caused the living wives of dead Hindus to be burned with the corpses of their husbands, it has caused ignorant men and women to throw themselves before the wheels of the car of the *Juggernath*, it causes the endless quarrels between some 200 Christian sects, and while the truth unites all humanity into one harmonious whole, the misunderstanding of it produces innumerable discords and diseases.

The Bible says : "The secret things belong unto the Lord ;" and the Bhagwat Gita repeats the same truth in the following words : "Those whose minds are attracted to my invisible nature have a great labor to encounter, because an invisible path is difficult to be found by corporeal beings." The greatest poets of the world have had occasion to regret the poverty of human language, which rendered it impossible to express the language of their hearts in words ; and those whose minds have been fully opened to the knowledge of spiritual truths, the wisest of all men, such as Buddha, have left no written records of their doctrines ; perhaps their conceptions were too grand to be expressed in words, and can be understood only by those who feel as they felt, and whose hearts are open to the sunlight of divine illumination.

Let us attempt to put the impressions intuitively received, regarding the Divine Source of all Being, into language, although we well know that language is inadequate to describe it, and an attempt to put that which cannot be grasped by the intellect into words, will give rise to misconceptions in those who are unable to think with their hearts.

Far, in the unfathomable abyss of space, far beyond the reach of the imagination of man, unapproachable even by the highest and purest angel or thought, self-existent, eternal, resplendent in its own glory is the *Shining One*, whose palpitating Centre is invisible Fire, whose rays are Light and Life, pervading the Universe to its utmost limits, penetrating every form and causing it to live and to grow. Their harmonious vibrations are undulating through space, filling all animate and inanimate beings with the substance of Love. Meeting primordial matter in space, they form it into revolving globes, and chain them together by Love, manifesting itself as attraction and guiding them on in their restless revolutions. Penetrating into the hearts of animals and men, they create sensation and relative consciousness, cause the form to feel, to perceive and to know its surroundings, call into life the emotions of love and its reaction hate with all their attending virtues and vices. Penetrating deep into the hearts of men, they kindle there the divine fire in whose light man may see the image of the Shining One, and know it to be himself.

But it is beyond the power of man to describe in language that which cannot be described, to combine words, so that the reader may form an intellectual conception of something for which no intellectual conception exists; for in the presence of the highest, the unthinkable ideal, intellectual labor ceases, and spiritual adoration begins. Intellectual labor is a function which man shares with the animals; but the divine prerogative of spiritual man and his highest destiny is to live in eternal perception and adoration of the highest Good, of which the intellect cannot conceive, and for which we can find no name.

In this eternal universal principle is the source of all Power. In it alone is *magic power* contained, even to the extent of creating new worlds and to call a new universe of forms into existence. It is the only *Philosopher's Stone* and the only *Elixir of Life* or *Universal Panacea*, and can be had everywhere and at any time without expense, by every one who knows how to seek for it. It can attain self-consciousness and self-knowledge only in the organism of man, because the lower animals are not yet far enough advanced to be used as its vehicles and instrument; but the man in whom it has awakened to life shares its attributes and obtains magic power; for he is a living temple of God. The man in whom God has not awakened is, as long as he remains in that condition, merely an intellectual animal, and having no Spirit active within his heart, he can possess no spiritual or *magical* powers. Some modern "Philosophers," who say that *man* has no magical powers, are right from their own point of view; for the "man" known to external science is merely an intellectual animal, having no spiritual and therefore no magical power; the real man only begins to exist when he is reborn in the Spirit. True philosophers have recognized this fact. Schopenhauer says: "In consequence of the action of 'grace,' the entire being of man becomes remodelled, so that he desires no longer anything of that for which he was craving heretofore, and becomes so to say a new man."*

Everything in nature has a threefold nature, and likewise the allegories of the sacred books of the East as well as those of the West have a threefold meaning—an exoteric, an esoteric, and a secret signification. The vulgar- the learned as well as the unlearned—can see only the exoteric side, which, in the majority of cases, is so absurd, that its very absurdity should serve as a warning to people endowed with common sense not to accept these fables in their literal meaning; there is, however, nothing too absurd to attract the attention of the ignorant, and we see them, therefore, split into three classes, namely—first, into those who implicitly believe their literal meaning; secondly, into those who reject them on account of their supposed absurdity, never suspecting a deeper meaning; and, thirdly, into those who are irritated at their absurdity, and valiantly fight the man of straw which they have themselves set up in their minds.

Those who are willing to learn can be instructed, but they that believe that they already know, refuse to be

---

\* "Welt als Wille und Vorstellung." I., 625.

taught. For this reason the legitimate guardians of the truth, the teachers of science and religion, like those who have no intellectual power, are often the last ones to recognize the truth. Those who are not able to think cannot be taught, and those who live entirely within the region of intellectual speculation reject the light of their own intuition. The *esoteric* meaning of symbols may be understood by those whose intellect is open to intuition, and may be explained to all who do not reject the truth ; but the *secret* meaning of the sacred symbols cannot be explained in words, it can be understood only by those who have entered the practical way.

*How can we enter the path ?*—Only in practical experience is life. Petrified speculative science, mouldy speculative philosophy, and dried-up speculative theology groan in the embrace of death. Humanity awakes from her slumber and asks them for the bread of wisdom, but receives only a stone. She turns to science, but science is silent, wraps herself up in her vanity and turns away ; she turns to philosophy, and old philosophy answers, but her talk is an incomprehensible jargon, and confuses matters still more. She turns to theology, but theology threatens the obnoxious questioner with hell, and bids her to remain ignorant. But the people, on the whole, are no longer satisfied with such answers; they are no longer contented with the assertion that the truth is known to a few, and that they themselves must remain ignorant, they want to enjoy it too.

If we wish to enter the path to infinite life, the first requirement is

# TO KNOW.

Knowledge is the perception and understanding of truth. We can only know that which we perceive. *All* knowledge arrived at by logic, however exact, is only *negative* knowledge, but not positive ; for truth is spiritual and can be recognized only by spirit. By intellectual reasoning and mathematics we can find out what a thing is *not ;* but never what it actually *is.* We say that one and two added together make three ; meaning that they can make nothing else but three ; but what the three actually is, still remains a mystery. We say that if we chemically combine Sulphur and Carbon, the result can be nothing else but a compound of Sulphur and Carbon ; but for all that we do not know what that combination is, as long as we have not perceived its attributes.   There are two principal modes of perception, namely, seeing and feeling.   Each of these modes, if unaccompanied by the other, is unreliable ; only if we simultaneously see and feel a thing do we know that it exist.

Thousands of years have passed away since mankind first saw the sun and stars, and modern telescopes have brought them nearer to us.   Nevertheless our knowledge of these cosmic bodies, and the conditions of life existing upon them, consists merely of speculation and opinions, which may be overthrown at any time, when our means for observation are supplanted by better ones.   We give names to the substances discovered by the spectroscope, but we will not know the true nature of the stars as long as we are not able to partake of their consciousness and feel the qualities of the life and characters embodied in their forms.

For thousands of years mankind has intuitively felt the presence of the Unknown.   Those who felt the presence of the universal Spirit, know that it exists.   Generations after generations have disappeared from earth after spending their lives in vain efforts to know not God whose power they felt but whom they could not see with their eyes, and even our greatest theologians seem to be very far from a true knowledge of God.   Only when the mind of the regenerated man has become illuminated by divine wisdom will he be able to know the true God, for he will see His image within his own soul.

If we are able to see and feel the external attributes of a thing, we may begin to understand what these qualities are, but we will, for all that, still be ignorant of its interior qualities and its true character.  To know the latter it will be necessary to enter into its spirit, and this can only be done by the spirit of man, not by his external senses.  The spiritual principle in man, if once awakened to self-consciousness, has attributes and functions far superior to those of the external man ; it has the power to perceive, to see and to feel the internal qualities of things which are imperceptible to the external senses ; it can identify itself with the object of its observation and partake of its consciousness, it becomes for the time being as one with that object and shares its feelings, it sees that object objectionally and partakes of its subjective sensations.

Thus does a lover partake of the joys and sorrows of the object he loves, and feel as if he were one with it in spirit although separated from it in the form ; for love is the power by which such a divine state is attained, it penetrates all things, and coming from the centre of all it goes to the centre.

What is it that prevents us to love and to know all things but our own prejudices and predilections ? We do not see things as they are but as we imagine them to be. He who desires to know all things should not look upon them with his own eyes, but with the eyes of God ; he should not think the thoughts suggested by external appearances, but he should *let the Divine Spirit do its thinking within his mind.*

To obtain true knowledge we must render ourselves able to receive it ; we must free our minds from all the intellectual rubbish that has accumulated there through the perverted methods of education of modern civilization. The more false doctrines we have learned the more difficult will be the labor to make room for the truth, and it may take years to unlearn that which we have learned at the expense of a great deal of labor, money, and time. The Bible says that "we must become like little children before we can enter the kingdom of truth." The principal thing to know is to *know ourselves;* if we know ourselves, we will know that we are to be the kings of the universe. The essential *Man* is a *Son of God*, he is something far greater, far more sublime and far more powerful than the insignificant animal described as a man in our scientific works on anthropology.

Well may *Man* who knows his true nature be proud of his nobility and power ; well may the *man* known to external science be ashamed of his weakness. Well may the former consider himself superior to the gods, and the latter, a worm of the earth, crawl into a corner and ask for the protection of a real man who is a god. The true Man is a divine being, whose power extends as far as his thoughts can reach ; the irrational man is a compound of semi-animal forces, subject to their caprices and whims, with a spark of divine fire in him to enable him to control

**9**

them, but which spark, in the great majority of cases, is
left to smoulder and vanish.   The former is immortal, the
latter lives a few years among the illusions of life.   The
former knows that he lives for ever in the All, the latter
expects to die, or perhaps to obtain a lease on his personal
existence by the favor of some personal god who may
permit him to carry his iniquities into a sphere, in which
only the pure can exist.*

There are three kinds of knowledge, the useful, the
useless, and the harmful.   The most useful knowledge is
the one which relates to the essential nature of man, to his
destiny, and to his possibilities.   There is no higher
knowledge than the practical knowledge of *religion ;* that
is to say, the knowledge of all that *relates* to the spiritual,
emotional, and physical nature of man.   He who has this
knowledge is necessarily the true physician for the soul as
well as for the body, and he heals by the power of his
spirit.   An attempt to separate religion from science and
the practice of morality from the practice of medicine
leads to illusions of the most dangerous kind.

The useless knowledge is the knowledge of, or rather
the adherence to, illusions and falsehoods ; it is no real
knowledge, although it embraces a great deal of what is
considered of great importance in civilized countries that
men should know.

The harmful knowledge consists in scientific attain-
ments without any corresponding perception of the moral
aspect of truth.   It is only partial knowledge, because it
recognizes only a part of the truth.   A high intellectual
development without any corresponding growth of morality
is a curse to mankind.   Knowledge to be good must be
illuminated by Wisdom ; knowledge without wisdom is
dangerous to possess.   Misunderstanding and misapplication of truths are the source of suffering.

The attainment of power is often not accompanied with
any proper understanding how to apply that power wisely.
The invention of the fulminates of mercury, of gunpowder
and nitro-glycerine, has caused much suffering to a large
part of humanity.   Not that the substances applied, or
the forces which are liberated, are intrinsically evil, but

---

* Revelations xxi. 27.

their misapplication leads to evil results. If all men were intelligent enough to understand the laws which govern them, and wise enough to employ them for good purposes only, no evil results would follow.

If we proceed a step further and imagine intellectual but wicked and selfish people possessed not only of the power to employ explosives, poisonous drugs, and medicines to injure others, but able to send their own invisible poisonous will to a distance, to leave at will the prison-house of the physical body and go in their *astral forms* to kill or injure others, the most disastrous results would follow. Such forbidden knowledge has been and is sometimes possessed by people with criminal tendencies, a fact which is universally known in the East, and upon the possibility and actuality of such, facts have been established on many occasions, and among others by many of the witch trials of the Middle Ages. Modern scientists may now laugh at these facts, but the doctors of law, of medicine, and of theology of their times, were as sure of their knowledge then as their modern representatives are of their own opinions to-day, and the former had as many intellectual capacities as the latter. The only difference is that the former knew these facts, but gave a wrong explanation ; the latter refuse to examine them, and give no explanation at all.

Man is continually surrounded by unseen influences, and the *astral plane* is swarming with entities and forces, which are acting upon him for good or for evil, according to his good or evil inclinations. At the present state of evolution man has a physical body, which is admirably adapted to modify the influence from the astral plane, and to shelter him against the "*monsters of the deep.*"

If the physical body is in good health, it acts as an armor, and, moreover, man has the power, by a judicious exercise of his will, to so concentrate the *odic* aura by which he is surrounded, as to render his armor impenetrable ; but if by bad health, by a careless expenditure of vitality, or by the practice of mediumship, he disperses through space the odic emanations belonging to his sphere, his physical armor will become weakened and unable to protect him ; he becomes the victim of elementaries and elemental forces, his mental faculties will lose their balance, and sooner or later he will, like the symbolical *Adam and Eve, know that he is naked,* and exposed to influences which he cannot repel. Such is the result for which those ignorantly crave who wish to obtain knowledge without corresponding morality. To supply the ignorant or weak with powers of destruction would be like providing children with gunpowder and matches for play.

Only an intelligent and well-balanced mind can discriminate properly and dive into the hidden mysteries of Nature. "Only the pure in heart can see God." He who has reached that stage need not search for an *Adept* to instruct him; the higher intelligences will be attracted to him, and become his instructor, in the same manner as he may be attracted by the beauty of an animal or of a flower.

A harp does not invent sound but obeys the hand of a master, and the more perfect the instrument, the sweeter may be the music. A diamond does not originate light, but reflects it, and the purer the diamond the purer will be its lustre. Man does not invent original thought, will, and intelligence. He is a mirror in which the thought of God and the imagery of nature is reflected, an instrument through which the eternal will or the animal will expresses itself; a pearl filled with a drop of water from the universal ocean of intelligence.

"If you eat from the tree of true knowledge you will surely die." Your personality will be swallowed up by a realization of the fact that personal isolation is only an illusion, and that you are one with the all. But as your personality dies, a greater truth opens before you, and you become not only God-like, but God.

He who ascends to the top of a high mountain need not inquire for somebody to bring him pure air. Pure air surrounds him there on all sides. The realm of wisdom is not limited, and he whose mind is receptive will not suffer from want of divine influx to feed his aspiration.

The school in which the occultist graduates has many classes, each class representing a life. The days of vacation may arrive before the lesson is learned, and what has been learned may be forgotten during the time of vacation; but still the impression remains, and a thing once learned is easily learned again. This accounts for the different talents with which men are endowed, and for their propensities for good or for evil. No effort is lost, every cause creates a corresponding effect, no favors are granted, no injustice takes place.    Blind to bribes and deaf to appeals is the law of justice, dealing out to every one according to his merits or demerits ; but he who has no selfish desire for reward, and no cowardly fear of punishment, but who dares to act rightly because he cannot do wrong, identifies himself with the law, and in the equilibrium of the law will he find his *Power.*

The second requirement is

## TO WILL.

If we do not want to receive the.truth we will not obtain it, because it rests in the spirit, and the spirit is a power that exercises the universal law of attraction ; it attracts the mind that corresponds to its vibrations, and is repulsed by discords.

Men believe that they love the truth, but there are few that desire it.    They love only welcome truths ; those that are unwelcome are usually rejected.    Opinions which flatter the vanity and are in harmony with accustomed modes of thought are accepted ; strange truths are often regarded with astonishment and driven away from the door.    Men are often afraid of that which they do not know, and, not knowing the truth, they are afraid to receive it.    They ask new truths for their passports, and if they do not bear the stamp of some fashionable authority they are looked upon as illegitimate children, and are not permitted to grow.

*How shall we learn to love the truth ?*    By being obedient to the law.    *How can we become convinced of its goodness ?*    By doing our duty.    Irrational man asks for external proofs, but true man    requires no other certificate for the truth but its own appearance.    There can be no difference between speculative and practical *knowledge;* an opinion based upon mere speculation is no knowledge. Knowledge can only be attained by speculation, if the speculation is accompanied by experience.    Those who want to know the truth must practise it ; those who cannot practise it will not know it ; speculations without practice can only lead to doubtful opinions.

Man can have no actual desire for a thing which he does neither feel nor see, and which he therefore not knows. How can we love a thing of which we know not whether it is good or evil, whether it will benefit or injure us, if we approach it.  Many followers of the church profess to love God, and have not the remotest c. ception of what God is.  Many profess to love Christ, and despise and reject Him if they meet Him in man.  Such a "love of God and Christ" is a pretence and an illusion, it exists only in the brain and not in the heart.  We can only love that of which we know that it is good, because we feel it to be so : and where else could we feel the presence of God except within our own heart ?  To learn to desire God means therefore to enter a mental state in which we can feel the presence of the Divine principle within our own heart ; to learn to know God means to learn to know our own Divine Self.

To enter a state in which universal truth may come to our direct perception, no intellectual labor but spiritual development is required.  We must become master of our own thoughts and desires, and be able to sink our thoughts into the invisible centre of All.

We do not have far to go in search of that *Centre*, it exists within the heart of each human being ; for the soul of each human being is an exact image of the soul of the universe, and as the great Spiritual Sun exists in the centre of the Universe, likewise the image of that sun exists within the heart of each human being.  If we only permit this divine light to shine within our own soul, we will know the truth, for the truth is only one, and the one existing within our own heart is identical with the one existing within the centre of the universe.

If we desire to see the pure light of the terrestrial sun, the atmosphere must not be obscured by clouds and fogs ; if we desire to see the eternal light of the spiritual Sun existing within the heart, the realm of the soul must not be clouded by material desires.  We must by the power of our will dispel the fogs and mists created by the vapors coming from the material plane.  We must become our own masters in our own house.  To do this requires effort and perseverance, and the average investigator, finding it easier to accept ready-made creeds, than to educate his spiritual faculties, usually remains satisfied with his own superstitions, or argues himself into a belief that spiritual causes cannot be known.

Men do not seriously desire the truth, because they cannot estimate what they do not know and they do not know it because they cannot reach what they do not seriously desire. Mere curiosity, or a wish to learn to know the truth at our leisure without neglecting the claims of the elementary kingdom composing our soul, cannot attract the spirit. Man is chained to the kingdom of the Elementals with a thousand chains. The inhabitants of his soul appear before him in their most seductive forms. If they are driven away they change their masks and renew their petitions in some other form. But the chains by which man is bound are forged by his own desire. His vices do not cling to him against his will. He clings to them, and they will desert him as soon as he rises up in the strength and dignity of his manhood and shakes them off. There is a method, by which we may, without any active effort, obtain that which we desire, and this is that *we should desire nothing except what the divine spirit desires within our own heart.*

The third requirement is, therefore,

# TO DARE.

We must dare to act and throw off our desires, instead of waiting patiently until they desert us. We must dare to tear ourselves loose from accustomed habits, irrational thoughts, and selfish considerations, and from everything that is an impediment to our recognition of the truth. We must dare to conquer ourselves and to conquer the world ; dare to face the ridicule of the ignorant, the vilifications of bigots, the haughtiness of the vain, the contempt of the learned, and the envy of the small ; dare to proclaim the truth if it is useful to do so, and dare to be silent if taunted by the fool.* We must dare to face poverty, suffering, and isolation, and dare to act under all circumstances according to our highest conception of truth.

All this might be easily accomplished, if the will of man were free ; if man were his own master and not bound with the chains of the soul ; but man is a relative being, and as such his will can only be free to a certain extent ; it can only enjoy a relative liberty as long as it is a slave to desire. Man may perform certain acts and leave others

* Prov. xxvi. 4.

undone if he chooses ; but his internal desire determines his choice, and man acts in obedience to it. A man who is free of external desires has the power to will that which his nature does not desire, and not to will that to which the desires of that nature attract him.

To make the will free, action is required, and each action strengthens the will, and each unselfish deed increases its power. *In unity is power.* To render our will powerful we may unite it with the will of others, and if the desires of the others are different from ours, our will thereby becomes free from our own desires. *In action is strength.* If we oppose our will to the will of others, by acting against the desires of others, we increase its strength, but we become thereby isolated from others.

There is only *one* universal power of will, because divinity is a whole. It may act in the direction for good and in the direction for evil ; but its action for good is the strongest, because it emanates from the eternal source of all good. This will-power being the collective sum of all will-power in the universe, is the power that moves the worlds. It is necessarily immeasurably stronger than any individual will-power can possibly be, because the whole is larger than the part, and the infinite greater than the finite. He who unites his own will with the universal will becomes powerful ; he who exercises his will by opposing it may become strong, but while the former attains eternal life with the whole, the latter causes his own destruction, as he will finally be crushed by the opposing force, which is immeasurably stronger than he. *Dare to obey the Law, and you will become your own Master, and the Lord over all.*

Philosophical courage is a quality for which men are respected everywhere. The Red Indian prides himself at his indifference to physical pain, the Fakir undergoes tortures to strengthen his will-power, the civilized soldier is eager to prove his contempt for danger, and to measure his strength with the strength of the enemy. But there are deeds to perform that require a courage of a superior kind. It requires only momentary outbursts of power or temporary efforts of will to perform a daring deed on the physical plane, and after it is accomplished it is followed by satisfaction and rest ; but in the realm of the soul there is no rest for those who have not succeeded in eradicating that which is evil. A continual and unremitted strain is needed to keep the emotions subjected, and this strain is rendered still more fatiguing by the circumstance that it depends entirely on your own will whether or not we will endure it, and that if we relax the bridle and allow our emotions to run free and disorderly, sensual gratification is the result. It requires a courage of the highest order to act under all circumstances in obedience to the law. Long may the battle last, but each victory strengthens the will ; each act of submission renders it more powerful, until at last the combat is ended, and over the battlefield where the remnants of the slain desires are exposed to the decomposing action of the elements hovers the spiritual eagle, rising towards the sun and enjoying the serene tranquility of the ethereal realm. *The only true way to obtain courage is to rise above fear.*

Metals are purified by fire and the spirit is purified by suffering. Only when the molten mass has cooled can we judge of the progress of the purification ; only when a victory over the emotions is gained, and peace follows after the struggle, can the spirit rest to contemplate and realize the beauty of eternal truth. In vain will men attempt to listen to the voice of truth during the clash of contending desires and opinions, only in the silence that follows the storm can the voice of truth be heard.*

The fourth requirement to the recognition of the truth is therefore

## TO BE SILENT.

This means that we must not allow any desire to speak in our heart, but only the voice of the truth ; because the truth is a jealous goddess and suffers no rivals. He who selects wisdom for the bride of his soul must woo her with his whole heart and dismiss the concubines from the bridal chamber of his soul. He must clothe her in the purity of his affection and ornament her with the gold of his love, for wisdom is modest, she does not adorn herself but waits until she is adorned by her lover. She cannot be bought with money nor with promises, her love is only gained by acts of devotion. Science is only the handmaid of wisdom,

---

*" Light on the Path," by M. C.

and he who makes love to the servant will be rejected by the mistress; but he who sacrifices his whole being to wisdom will be united with her.

The Bhagwat Gita, says: "He who thinketh constantly of me, his mind undiverted by any other object, will find me. I will at all times be easily found by a constant devotion to me."

The Christian Mystic, Jacob Boehme, an illuminated seer, expressed the same truth, in the form of a dialogue between the master and his disciple, as follows:

The disciple said to the master: "How can I succeed in arriving at that supersensual life, in which I may see and hear the Supreme?"

The master answered: "If you can only for a moment enter in thought into the formless, where no creature resides, you will hear the voice of the Supreme."

The disciple said: "Is this far or near?"

The master answered: "It is in yourself, and if you can command only for one hour the silence of your desires, you will hear the inexpressible words of the Supreme. If your own will and self are silent in you, the perception of the eternal will be manifest through you; God will hear, and see, and talk through you; your own hearing, desiring and seeing prevents you to see and hear the Supreme."*

These directions are identical with those prescribed by the practice of *Raja-Yog*, by which the holy men of the East unite their minds with the formless and infinite. Religious services are calculated to elevate the mind into the region of the formless, and, in fact, all religious systems can have no other legitimate object than to teach methods how to attain such states. Churches are not worthy the name of church, which means a *spiritual union*, unless they serve as schools in which the science of uniting one-self with the eternal fountain of life is practically taught. But it is easier to allow one's mind to revel among the multifarious forms and attractions of the material plane, and to listen to the Syren song of the Elementals inhabiting the soul, than to enter the apparently dark caves of the formless, where at first no sound is heard in the eternal stillness of night but the echo of our voice, but where alone true power resides. It is easier to let our minds be con-

---

* Jacob Boehme: "Theosophical Writings," book vi,

trolled by thoughts that come and go without our bidding
than to hold fast to a thought and command it to remain,
and to close the doors of the soul to all thoughts that have
not the seal of truth impressed upon their forms ; and this
is the reason why the majority of men and women prefer
the illusions of finite life to the eternal realities of the
iufinite—why they prefer sufferings to happiness, and
ignorance to a knowledge of truth.

To be silent means to let no other language be heard
within the heart but the language of God, to *listen to the
voice of Divine Wisdom speaking within the heart ;* but
this state will be arrived at only after the storm of the
passions, the battle of desires, and the conflict of the
intellectual forces is over.

He who has learned to know, to will, to dare, and to be
silent, is upon the true path that leads to immortal life, and
will know how to practise *interior meditation* or *yog ;* but
by those who move merely in the sensual plane, or whose
minds are concentrated upon external things of the physical
or intellectual plane, even the meaning of these words will
not be understood.

Various instructions are given in the books of the East
in regard to the practice of this interior meditation, but
they all teach the same thing, namely, a concentration of
man's higher consciousness to a single point within his own
centre.

In the *Oupnekhata* the following directions are
given :—

" Breathe deep and slow, and concentrate your unwavering attention into the midst of your body, into the region
of the heart. The lamp in your body will then be protected against wind and motion, and your whole body will
become illuminated. You must withdraw all your senses
within yourself like a turtle, which withdraws its members
within the shell. Enter your own heart and guard it, and
Brahma will enter it like a fire or a stroke of lightning. In
the midst of a big fire in your heart will be a small flame,
and in the centre of it will be *Atma.*"

*Herocarcas,* an abbot of a convent upon the mount
*Athos,* gives to his monks the following directions to
acquire the power of true clairvoyance : " Sit alone in your
room, after having the door locked against intrusion, concentrate your mind upon the region of the navel and try to

see with that. Try to find the seat of your heart (sink your consciousness into your heart), where the centre of power resides. At first you will find nothing but darkness; but if you continue for days and nights without fatigue, you will see light, and experience inexpressible things. When the spirit once recognizes his own centre in the heart, he will know what he never knew before, and there will be nothing hidden before his sight, whether in heaven nor upon the earth."

Let us compare with these statements one received from an unlearned person, who possesses the power to see interior truths. He says : "Sink your thoughts downward into the centre of your being, and you will find there a germ which, if continually nourished by pure and holy thoughts, will grow into a power that will extend and ramify through all parts of your body. Your hands and feet and your interior organs will *become alive;* a *sun* will appear within your heart and illuminate your whole being. In this light you will see the the present, the past, and the future, and by its aid you will attain the true knowledge of self."  *

Man is himself a thought, pervading the ocean of Mind. If his soul is in perfect accord with the truth, the truth will unite itself with his soul. A talented musician will not need a scientific calculation of the vibrations of sound to know whether a melody which he hears is melodious or not; a person who is one with the truth will recognize himself in everything that is true.

What is sound? If everything is fundamentally will, sound can be nothing else but a manifestation of will. Will may act either relatively, unconsciously, or consciously, or even in a self-conscious state. Sound manifests the same attributes. The noise made by the knock of a hammer carries with itself no emotions or intelligence ; it can awaken them only by means of association of ideas. But a piece of music or a song carries with it the qualities with which it has been endowed by the musician or the singer. Music is a language that speaks to the heart without any previous agreement as to what sounds are meant to signify certain words, as is done by telegraphing.

Music produces in every receptive soul the sentiments

---

* J. Kerning, " Key."

that its melodies are intended to represent; and the more the music is a true representation of these sentiments, the more will this be the case. Likewise there is sound carrying intelligence. The words spoken by a person awaken corresponding thoughts in the mind of an intelligent person, and they will be impressive in proportion as they are true. If he who tells a lie does not at least for the time being imagine it to be true, his words will act at best upon the imagination, but not upon the will. A good actor knows that he must imagine himself to be the person whose part he plays, if he wants to produce the desired effect. Intelligent speech carries with it the power to induce intelligent thoughts in an intelligent being, as the sunshine carries with it life to the seeds in the soil. There is a still higher form of sound; it is not known to everybody. It is the self-conscious divine word, that speaks within the heart of the awakened.

The spirit is like a breath. To the eloquent speaker, being inspired by the truth of what he says, words will come without consideration; they form themselves in his soul and not in his brain. In him who is conscious of speaking the truth, it is not so much the man that speaks, as rather the truth speaking through him, and he may inspire his hearers with his own sentiments, even if they do not understand his language, because the will emanating from him is endowed with his own emotional attributes.

Every sound is vitalized, if it comes from a living source; but it can have no higher vitality than the source from which it originates. A sound produced by the striking of a fiddle bow upon a tuning fork can manifest no higher consciousness than that of the tuning fork, no matter how it is treated mechanically. A merely mechanical noise cannot produce living effects, no more than a piece of dead wood cause a tree to grow in the soil. It cannot be the carrier of life, unless it comes from a living being.

The attempts that have been made to " vitalize " sound by merely mechanical means, and to cause it to act with life and intelligence, have failed on account of a misunderstanding of that fundamental law of nature, according to which forms do not produce principles, but are merely vehicles or instruments for their manifestation. If I want to vitalize anything, I can only vitalize it with my own vitality, having no other vitality at my command, nor can I cause the universal principle of life to vitalize anything according to my will, unless I have obtained command over it by becoming divine. Everybody is continually " vitalizing " himself and the words which he speaks ; but only a self-conscious divine spirit could spiritualize inanimate things.

The word of God, being God itself, can vitalize sound. It is the creative Power in the universe. He in whom the divinity has not become self-conscious cannot command that power. There is, therefore, no danger that the world would be exploded, if " the Adepts were to let the secret out as to how the trick is done." Such a revelation would be as useless to mankind as to tell a beggar how he could invest his money, if he had any to invest.

The will of a person may " vitalize " apparently inanimate objects, as is often done at spiritistic seances ; but in that case it is accomplished by its action upon living invisible beings, and without any conscious action of the medium. Therefore, the wonders of the mechanical application of living sound, if any such have ever been performed, can be due only to mediumship.

To act consciously and intelligently upon the elemental powers of nature requires the possession of an intelligent and self-conscious power, the magic power of the (spiritual) will of an Adept. Merely mechanical combinations can produce nothing but merely mechanical results.

Natural forces are subject to natural law, and, therefore, intellectual man, acting in accordance with natural law, can make them subservient to his purposes, by establishing the conditions under which they will act ; but the divine Word of God is above nature, and above any conditions that man can establish. Man can govern it in no other

---

* It is an absolute impossibility to transform matter into motion or sound, or sound into life or spirit ; because the seven forms of eternal nature are eternal and unchangeable. All that can be changed is their mode of action. Darkness cannot be changed into light, although it may be penetrated by it : neither does a red-hot iron change into light, although light becomes manifest therein by means of the heat. " Each of the original forms of eternal nature retains forever its own centre." (" *Jacob Boehme.*" " Threefold Life.")

It is true that each of the seven principles contains potentially the other six, and that the higher may be awakened or " liberated " in the lower ; but this can only be done by the action of the higher inducing the corresponding latent higher principle to become active within the lower. Merely mechanical motion cannot call life or consciousness into action in a form, without the action of a living and conscious power to act upon the life and consciousness latent therein.

way, than by becoming one with divine Law ; but then he ceases to be a man, and becomes a God, governing his own self and all the laws of his nature.

Every form in nature is a symbol of an idea and represents a sign or a letter. A succession of such symbols forms a language, and the totality of all forms in nature is the language of nature. He who is a true child of nature, that means to say, he whose will is pure and whose mind free of error, will understand the language of nature and know the character of everything. His mind will be like a clear mirror, wherein the attributes of natural things are reflected and enter the field of his consciousness.

Such a language means a radiation of the essence of things into the centre of the human mind, and a radiation from that centre into the universal ocean of mind. Man in a state of purity, being an image and an external expression of the highest principle, is able to reflect and reproduce the highest truth in its original purity, and man's expressions ought, therefore, to be a perfect reproduction or echo of the impressions which he receives ; but average man being immersed in matter, as a result of a combination of principles on a lower scale of evolution, receives the pure original rays only in a state of refraction, and can therefore reproduce them only in an imperfect condition. He has wandered away from the sun of truth, and beholding it from a distance it appears to him only as a small star, that may perhaps vanish from sight. Everything in Nature has its name, and he who has the power to call a thing by its proper name can make it subservient to his will. But the proper name of a thing is not the arbitrary name given to it by man, but the expression of the totality of its powers and attributes, because the powers and attributes of each being are intimately connected with its means of expression, and between both exists the most exact proportion in regard to measure, time and condition.

There is only one genuine and interior language for man, the symbols of which are natural and must be intelligible to all, and this language is a direct communication of thought. This interior language is the parent of the exterior one, and being caused by the radiation of the first cause which is unity, and with whom all men are one, it follows that if the original irradiation of the supreme ray were existing in all men in its original purity, all men would understand the same interior language, and also the same exterior one, because the latter is the external expression of the former. In fact this original language still exists, but few understand it, and none can learn it except by the process of interior evolution. The interior language, breathes—so to say—spirit ; while the exterior one is only a succession of sounds.

Each word in that interior language is the character of the thing itself, a sign and symbol which men cultivate unknowingly ; each is the centre of each being, and whoever reaches that centre is in possession of the word and the sign. . These symbols are the essential characteristics which distinguish one individual or group of individuals from others ; by these symbols are harmonious souls attracted, and by them one artist recognizes another artist in beholding his works without seeing his person.

Men have ever been desiring an universal language. Such an universal language cannot be arbitrarily constructed, or, if so constructed, would be more difficult to learn than any other. True . language must express the harmony of the soul with the nature of things, and as long as there is distinction of character and disharmony there can be no universal, harmonious language.

But if there is an universal language of nature, there is also a universal language of God, and this divine language is the *Word of God* that speaks within the heart of the awakened. It is the voice of the Truth itself that speaks the Word, and if you cannot hear that voice, you are not called to teach, because it would then not be the truth speaking through your mouth, but the devil of your own conceited self. He who lives in the spirit of this world and in his sins, cannot truly teach any one. He who does not live in the spirit, can have no spiritual life and cannot impart it to others. He may repeat like a parrot what he has heard, or tell what he has read in books. He may say what he fancies to be true, but he is not an instrument for the manifestation of truth.

The only true teacher is *the Truth, the Word, the Christ.* He says : "I am the light of the world, and he who follows *Me* will have life eternal." He does not say : "Go to this parson or that professor and get from him a description of what he thinks how the light is supposed to look," but He advises us to follow Him and find the true understanding ourselves. Only when all the book-makers on theosophical subjects will be in possession of the living truth and of self knowledge in regard to what they are writing about, will we have a true divine science; only when all the ministers of the church will become ministers and servants of God, so that God may speak through them, will we have the true religion taught.

There is a threefold expression of the divine principle; a physical, and intellectual, and a divine word. The first is the language of nature, the second the language of art, the third one is power. Each thought is represented by a certain allegorical sign; each being is a characteristic symbol and living exterior image of its interior state. Each body is the symbol of an invisible and corresponding power, and Man, in whom the highest powers are contained, is the most noble symbol of nature, the first and most beautiful letter in the alphabet of earth. For every thought there is an outward expression, and if we have a thought which we cannot express by symbols, it does not follow that such symbols do not exist, but that we are unacquainted with them. A word or a language is the expression of thought, and to be perfect it must give perfect expression to the thought it is intended to convey. By giving a false expression to thought the power of language is lost. In our present state of civilization words are often used more for the purpose of concealing than revealing thought. Lying is therefore disgraceful, and involves a loss of power and subsequent degradation. To give pure and perfect expression to thought is White Magic; to act upon the imagination so as to create false impressions is witchcraft, deception and falsehood. Such witchcraft is practised every day and almost in every station of life, from the priest in the pulpit who wheedles his audience into a belief that he or his church possesses the keys of heaven, down to the merchant who cheats with his goods, and to the old maid who secures a husband by the means of artificial teeth and false hair; down to the physician who makes a living by exciting a morbid imagination in his patients and persuading them that they are "really sick." Such practices are publicly denounced and silently followed; they will lead to a universal disappearance of faith and trust, they will necessarily lead to active evil and bring destruction upon the nation that allows them to grow; because, as the power of good increases by practice, in the same manner increases the power of evil.

Man's mission is to do good; that means to do that

which is most useful for his development. By doing good,
sensual matter is eliminated ; his material constitution will
become more and more refined, and his interior illuminated
by the light of wisdom, until even his physical body may
assume the attributes of the astral form, and man himself
be a living soul. Therein alone lies the secret of eternal
beauty and youth, the true Elixir of Life. By doing evil
he attracts to himself the unintelligent and material principles of Nature, the elements of evil ; his higher principles
become more and more material and heavy until, dragged
into the mire of matter by his own weight, he is unable
to rise to the light, he becomes metaphysically petrified,
and his power of intuition lost.

Man's actions are his writings. By putting his thoughts
into action, he expresses them and records them in the
book of life. He writes them all over his body and upon
his face ; they will appear in the lustre of his eyes and in
the grace of his movements. An angelic soul cannot fail
to impress its beauty upon the form.

Evil acts are followed by a degradation of character,
producing an increased corporification of sensual elements
and an incrustation of the soul. Selfish desires bleach the
hair before their time, bend the back, wrinkle the face,
and are the cause of endless ills ; for all of which there is
no other remedy but goodness of will.

Good actions dissolve existing incrustations produced
by evil deeds, and re-establish the soul in its former condition. Repentance, unless followed by action, is useless.
It is like the inflammation caused by a thorn in the flesh ;
it causes pain by gathering to its assistance the vital forces
of the body ; but unless the thorn is removed by the
active intervention of the individual, an abscess and putre-
faction will be the result. Man's acts are his creations,
they give form to his thoughts. The motive endows them
with character, the will furnishes them with life.

An intention is useless as long as it is not put into action.
A sign, a letter, or a word is useles unless it conveys a meaning which is realized by him who employs it ; a symbol
represents an idea, but no symbol can be efficacious unless
it is intellectually applied. The most potent magical signs
are useless to him who cannot realize what they mean,
while to him who is well versed in occult science, a single
point, a line, or any geometrical figure, may convey a vast
meaning.

Let us in conclusion attempt to explain exoterically and esoterically a few of the most important magical signs. We may succeed to a certain extent in giving these explanations in words ; but their secret spiritual meaning cannot be expressed in language ; language can merely attempt to guide the reader into a region of thought in which he may be able to perceive the secret meaning with the eyes of the spirit :

*The Pentagram or the Five-pointed Star.*

In its *external* appearance it is merely a geometrical figure, found everywhere as a trade mark or ornament. Superstitious and credulous people once believed, that if it were drawn upon the doors of their houses it would protect them against the intrusions of the sorcerer and the witch.

In its *esoteric* signification the four lower triangles represent the four elementary forces of nature, and as the lines of each triangle are intimately connected or identical with those forming the other lines, the sum of these lines forming only one broken line without any interruption, likewise the four lower elements are intimately connected and identical with the fifth element, the quintessence of all things, situated at the top of the figure ; representing the head, the seat of intelligence in man.

The spiritual knowledge of the Five-pointed Star is identical with its practical application. Let us beware that the figure is always well drawn, leaving no open space, through which the enemy can enter and disturb the harmony existing in the Pentagon in the centre. Let us keep the figure always upright, with the topmost triangle pointing to heaven, for it is the seat of reason and Wisdom, and if the figure is reversed ignorance and evil will be the result. Let the lines be straight, so that all the triangles will be harmonious and of equal size, so that the symbol will grow without any abnormal development of one principle at the cost of another. Then the lower triangles will send their quintessence to the top, the seat of intelligence, and the top will supply the lower triangles with power and stimulate them to grow. Then when the time of probation and development is over, the triangles will be absorbed by the Pentagon in the centre and form into a square within the invisible circle connecting the apices of the triangles, and our destiny will be fulfilled. There is no higher duty for man to perform, than to keep the Five-pointed Spiritual Star intact; it will be his protection during life and his salvation in the hereafter.

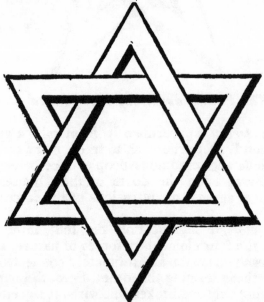

*The Double Triangle or Six-pointed Star.*

This is one of the most important magical signs, and spiritually applied it invests man with power. Its *exoteric* meaning is merely two triangles joined together, so that they partially cover each other, while the apex of one points upwards and the apex of the other downward. It is sometimes surrounded by a circle or by a snake biting its tail, and sometimes with a *tau* in the middle.

Its *esoteric* meaning is very extensive. It represents among other things the descent of spirit into matter, and the ascension of matter to spirit, which is continually taking place within the circle of eternity, represented by the snake, the symbol of wisdom. Six points are seen in the star, but the seventh cannot be seen; nevertheless the seventh point must exist, although it has not become manifest; because without a centre there could be no six-pointed star, nor any other figure existing.

But who can describe in words the secret or spiritual signification of the six-pointed star and its invisible centre? Who can intellectually grasp and describe the beauties and truths which it represents? Only he who can practically apply this sign will grasp its full meaning. Knowing that sign practically means to realize the nature of "God" and the laws of eternal nature, it means to know the process of evolution and involution going on within the microcosm of man and corresponding to those of the macrocosm of nature. It means to possess the power to enter within one's own interior soul and to behold the majesty of God in His light. It means to forget one's own self and the world of illusions and to be absorbed in the depths of eternity, where thought ceases and only adoration exists. To him who cannot realize within his heart the divine mysteries of nature, the blinding light shining from the centre of the figure has no existence; but the enlightened sees in that invisible centre the great Spiritual Sun, the heart of the Cosmos, from which Love and Light and Life are radiating for ever. He sees the seven primordial rays of that light shining into invisible matter and forming visible worlds upon which men and animals live and die, and are happy or discontented according to their conditions. He sees how by the breath of that invisible centre suns and stars, planets and satellites are evolved, and how, if the day of creation of forms is over, it reabsorbs them into its bosom. Verily the six-pointed star is a most potent magical sign, and it requires the wisdom of God to understand it, the omnipotent power of the *One Life* to apply it to its fullest extent.

In its external signification the Christian *Cross* is a symbol of torture and death.   The sight of a Cross calls up in the mind of the pious the memory of a historical event said to have taken place in Palestine some two thousand years ago, when a noble, good and just man was executed as a criminal upon a cross.   If the element of hate is predominating in the soul organization of the Christian beholding the Cross, its sight may call into action very "unchristian" feelings about the wickedness of the Jews.

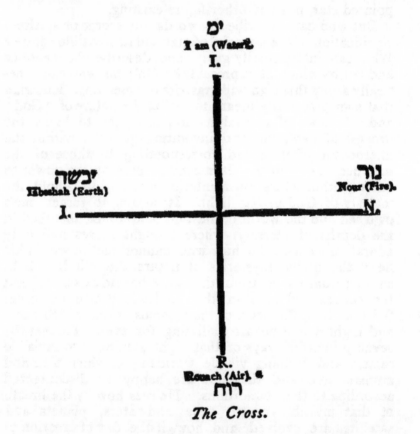

*The Cross.*

The internal impression caused by the sight of the

---

* Compare *J. R. Skinner*, " Key to Hebrew-Egyptian Mystery."

Cross will differ according to the standpoint from which we behold it.

The *esoteric* meaning of the Cross is very ancient, and the Cross has existed as a secret symbol probably thousands of years ago before the Christian *era*. The philosophical *Cross* represents, among other things, the principle of matter and that of spirit intersecting each other, forming the quaternary which, when it is inscribed in the square, forms the basis of knowledge for the Occultist. The horizontal line represents the animal principle, for the heads of animals are bowed to the earth. Man is the only being upon the globe who stands erect; the divine principle within him keeps him upright, and, therefore, the perpendicular line is the symbol of his divinity. The cross represents Man, who has acted against the law, and thereby transformed himself into an instrument for his own torture. From the beginning of his existence, as a ray of the divine spiritual Sun, he represented a perpendicular line, cutting in the direction of the Universal Will of the source from which he emanated in the beginning. As the distance from that source increased, and as the ray entered into matter, it deviated from the originally straight line and became broken, creating thereby a division in its own essence and making two parts out of the original Unity, thus establishing in matter a separate will, acting not in accordance with univeral Law, but even in opposition to it. If man follows again the dictates of the Law, he will then be taken from the Cross and resume his former position. "To take up one's Cross," means to sacrifice one's own desires to the rule of divine Law. By doing so the evil and animal desires remain crucified and die, but the divine element will be resurrected and enter the Light.

Who can know the practical spiritual signification of the *Cross* except he who has been nailed thereon and suffered the pangs of crucifixion of thought and desire and of the mystic death? The external Christian sees only the wooden Cross, but he whose spiritual perception is open sees the living Cross in its glory. Sublimely stands that Cross upon the mountain of the living Faith ; magnificent is its aspect. Far into space shines the light radiating from its centre and illuminating the darkness with its beneficent rays, which give life to all who behold it. Rise, oh man, up to your

divine dignity, so that you may see the true Cross, the true
Light.   Not the dead wooden Cross, the emblem of ignorance and suffering, nor the glittering cross made of brass,
the emblem of vanity, sectarianism and superstition ; but
the Living Golden Cross, the emblem of Wisdom which
each true *Brother of the Golden and Rosy Cross* carries
deeply buried within his own heart.   This cross is the
full-grown Tree of Life and of Knowledge, bearing the fruits
of salvation and immortality, the dispenser of Life, the protector against evil.   He who knows practically the true
mystery of the Cross is acquainted with the highest wisdom;
he who is adorned with the true Cross is safe from all
danger.   Infinite power of the Cross !   In thee is Wisdom
revealed.   Buried deep, deep in the realm of Matter is thy
foot, teaching us *Patience ;* high, high into heaven reaches
thy crown, teaching us *Faith.*   Lifted by *Hope* and ex-
tended by *Charity* are thy arms, Light and Sunshine
surround thee.   Link upon link the chain of creation
encircles the Cross ; worlds within worlds, forms within
forms, illusions upon illusions surround it like clouds and
nebulous mists ; but in the *Centre* is the Reality in which
is hidden the jewel of priceless value, the *Truth.*   Let the
dew of heaven which comes from the true Cross descend
into your hearts and penetrate into your soul and body, so
that it may crystallize into form.   Then will the darkness
within your mind disappear, the veil of matter will be rent,
and before your spiritual vision will stand revealed the
angel of truth.
    The present material age is ever ready to reject without
examination the symbols of the past whose meaning it
cannot realize because it knows them not.   Engaged in
the pursuit of material pleasure, it loses sight of its true
interest, and exchanges spiritual wealth for worthless
bawbles.   Losing sight of his destiny, man runs after a
shadow, while others embitter their lives for the purpose of
propitiating an angry God, and to buy from him happiness
in a life of which they know nothing.   Ruled by fear,
many bow before the Moloch of superstition and ignorance,
while others wilfully shut their eyes to the light of divine
reason and madly rush into the arms of a dead and cold
material science to perish in her stony embrace ; but the
wise, whose far-seeing perception reaches beyond the narrow
circle of his material surroundings, and beyond the short

span of time which embraces his life on earth, knows that it is in his own power to control his future destiny. He raises the magic wand of his will and quiets the tempest raging in the astral plane. The emotions which were rushing to his destruction obey him and execute his orders, and he walks safely upon the waters under whose calm surface is hidden the abyss of death, while above his head shines the bright constellation formed of Truth, Knowledge and Power, whose centre is Wisdom and whose germs can be found in the spiritual self-consciousness of every human being.

**THE END.**

# Index

CPSIA information can be obtained
at www.ICGtesting.com
Printed in the USA
BVHW080009040419

544581BV00001B/90/P

9 781603 862691